## Praise for T

"I finished this book with a heart full of joy, gratitude, and infield dirt. *The Prospects* is the kind of perfect sports romance that happens when a genuine love of the game meets stubborn human goodness. Tenacious, sexy, effervescent, doggedly hopeful, and endlessly charming, with characters to root hard for and an irresistible voice—I completely adored it."

—CASEY MCQUISTON, author of *Red, White & Royal Blue*

"The queer romcom I've been waiting for! Gene is the short king of my dreams and Luis is the secret cinnamon roll I want to wrap in a warm hug! *The Prospects* is a love letter to baseball, the Pacific Northwest, and trans joy. I adored every second of it!"

—ALISON COCHRUN, author of *The Charm Offensive*

"A gorgeously written tale of queer joy and trans possibility, a heart-stealing romance and a loving tribute to the art of baseball—particularly the beauty, struggle, and camaraderie of the minor leagues. But what I love most of all about this book is how much it is a story about hope, how deeply comforted and at home I felt in both its honesty and its optimism. This is my favorite book—of this and any year."

—ANITA KELLY, author of *Love & Other Disasters*

"KT Hoffman has written a thrillingly swoony and big-hearted love story between two baseball players whom you can't help but root for, even as they root against each other. Gene's love for baseball is infectious, despite the scrutiny he faces as the first openly trans player in professional baseball. In this way, *The Prospects* is a beautifully resonant appeal to a future where gay and trans people are celebrated, and even expected, in sports. Reading *The Prospects*, my heart beat fast, my feelings soared, and then I got tickets to a minor league game."

—SABRINA IMBLER, author of *How Far the Light Reaches*

"Funny, tender, and hot, this book made me feel like I could dream bigger for myself. KT Hoffman's debut is, pardon the sports analogy, a home run. If you liked *Ted Lasso*, you will love *The Prospects*."

—JOHN PAUL BRAMMER, author of *¡Hola Papi!*

"Everything I love about baseball is everything I love about KT Hoffman's brilliant debut: endlessly hopeful, stomach-swoopingly dramatic, and so singular and special, you know you're watching history being made. Gene and Luis felt so real to me that I'm in that dugout, I'm turning that play at second base, I'm in their homes and meeting their families, and their bright future spools on and on in front of my eyes. I fell in love with them as they fell in love with each other, and that experience felt like such a gift. *The Prospects* is the book I will reread every time I want to go back to a world where I feel safe, and loved, and where big-hearted underdogs can rule the world. I can't even express how much I adore this beautiful, joyful book."

—ALICIA THOMPSON, author of *With Love, from Cold World*

"This book is optimism and grit, dedication and unbridled joy. I fell in love with baseball, Gene and Luis, and the earnest beauty of KT Hoffman's writing. . . . An absolute delight."

—RACHEL LYNN SOLOMON, author of *The Ex Talk*

# The Prospects

# The Prospects

A NOVEL

KT HOFFMAN

THE DIAL PRESS
NEW YORK

Published in the United States by The Dial Press, an imprint of Random House, a division of Penguin Random House LLC, New York.



LIBRARY OF CONGRESS CATALOGING-IN-PUBLICATION DATA
Names: Hoffman, KT, author.
Title: The prospects : a novel / KT Hoffman.
Description: First edition. | New York : The Dial Press, [2024]
Identifiers: LCCN 2023020036 (print) | LCCN 2023020037 (ebook) |
ISBN 9780593596869 (trade paperback ; acid-free paper) |
ISBN 9780593596876 (ebook)
Subjects: LCGFT: Transgender fiction. | Gay fiction. | Sports fiction. | Novels.
Classification: LCC PS3608.O47825 P76 2024 (print) |
LCC PS3608.O47825 (ebook) | DDC 813/.6–dc23/eng/20230503
LC record available at https://lccn.loc.gov/2023020036
LC ebook record available at https://lccn.loc.gov/2023020037

Printed in the United States of America on acid-free paper

randomhousebooks.com

2 4 6 8 9 7 5 3 1

First Edition

*Book design by Jo Anne Metsch*

*For Glenn Burke, Lou Sullivan, & anyone else who had to be the first. Thank you for the worlds of dreaming & hoping & wanting you made possible.*

## Author's Note

This book is an optimistic one, in which the characters search for and cling to hope in all its many forms. It is also about a gay transgender man existing in the very cisgender, heterosexual space of men's professional baseball. There are, accordingly, brief instances of verbal and systemic transphobia and homophobia, as well as references to the misogyny trans men often continue to face after we come out.

Please also know that, just as trans people use many different words to describe our bodies, for reasons as varied as the people those words describe, Gene chooses his because they are comfortable to him. They may not be the words every trans man would choose, but they are his.

Finally, this book contains brief depictions of panic attacks.

“The dream lives!”

—DAVE SIMS, announcing the return of playoff baseball to the Pacific Northwest

PART ONE

# Triple-A Beaverton

# 1

## APRIL

**Current record: 0–0**

Gene Ionescu has always loved every detail of baseball, but none quite so much as its near-complete indifference to the body. In few other sports can a five-foot, two-inch sprinter appear on the same roster as a six-foot, five-inch pitcher. Size—muscle, height, maybe a few extra inches of reach or long running legs—helps. But baseball also rewards the patient, the crafty, and, perhaps most of all, the optimistic.

It's that hope, more than anything else, that makes Gene a good baseball player. He plays baseball because he is an optimist; he is an optimist because he has to be.

On April first, four days before a new season starts, in the most optimistic moment of the most optimistic sport, when every last thing feels possible, Gene sits on the floor of his apartment, wrestling with an Allen wrench.

Vince finds him like that, hunched over and cursing. "You've had five months of offseason to do this. Why the sudden burst of productivity?"

"Well, I *meant* to do it in November, but my brain finally decided to recognize a deadline today, and I'm trying to make the most of it," Gene says. He gestures to the bookshelf he's been working on for the last hour. "Except I can't figure out why this screw doesn't fit. What if I just throw the whole thing away and embrace minimalism?"

Vince drops onto Gene's couch, picks up the IKEA instruction manual, and sets his feet on the dented, partially unpacked cardboard box Gene uses as an ottoman. A moment later, he jangles the bag of hardware in Gene's direction. "Because you're using the wrong screws. You need the short ones, and a Phillips-head," he says.

Probably not the kind of assistance IKEA envisioned when its cartoon directions told Gene not to assemble heavy furniture alone, but it works.

Last spring, when he was assigned to start the season with the Beaverton Beavers—the Triple-A minor league team for the Portland Lumberjacks—an unfamiliar number texted him less than an hour after the rosters were announced.

*This is Vince Altman. I play for Beaverton. Would love to have you over for coffee, get to know you!*

"Love" had actually been a heart emoji, but what endeared Vince to Gene from the start, what surprised and impressed him, was the introduction. As if any self-respecting baseball player could fail to recognize the name of Portland's former golden boy.

A day later, *the* Vince Altman told Gene over coffee in his kitchen that he had a husband—with whom he lived and about whom the entire team, and very nearly no one else, knew. He became the first, and thus far only, queer man currently in baseball to welcome Gene to their small, often lonely club.

A season and a small lifetime later, Gene rents the one-bedroom, gable-roofed attic of Vince's house in the hills of Southwest Portland. If someone had told Gene when he signed his contract that former Cy Young–winning pitcher Vince Altman would become his best friend, that he would let Gene stay in his house for free—that he was gay-married, no less—Gene would never have believed them.

But, Cy Young Award and all, the guy can be a pain in the ass.

"So. You excited to play your boyfriend next week?" Vince asks.

Gene pushes the bookshelf off his lap and flops, perhaps a little more dramatically than the situation calls for, onto his back. "You can't be mean to me on my birthday."

"Like fuck I can't."

Gene already has to see Luis Estrada twenty-four times a season, which is twenty-four more times than he'd prefer. He doesn't get why they have to talk about him, too. Because Luis Estrada is not Gene's boyfriend, not even close. He's the thorn in Gene's side, the popcorn kernel stuck between his teeth, the crack in his ass—and still somehow the blandest man alive.

Every time Beaverton plays his team, Luis makes some absurd catch, always when Gene is at the plate. Luis never even reacts to it. Just tosses the ball back to the pitcher like nothing happened. Plus, Luis won last year's minor league Gold Glove over Gene, then didn't even bother showing up to the ceremony, and Gene has always been a rather impressive grudge-holder.

But before those twenty-four games, before the Gold Glove and the absurd catches and barely justified grudges, Luis and Gene shared a baseball diamond for one strange, sublime season of college ball. It was the abrupt end to their time as teammates that then begot the sharp-jointed discomfort that makes itself known between them now, every time their schedules collide.

Of course, Vince ignores all those details in favor of latching onto one offhand, year-old comment about Luis's perfect hair that he can't even prove Gene made.

(Gene stands by said comment. But still.)

"I would rather," Gene starts; Vince groans, and Gene talks right over it, "wear the Beavers' mascot costume to my ex-boyfriend's wedding—"

"—than spend even one minute with Luis Estrada," Vince finishes. He considers, then admits, "That was a pretty good one."

It's becoming something of a series. Other entries have included: *I would rather clip your dogs' toenails during an earthquake, I would rather ask the clubby to make the post-game spread vegetarian-friendly*, and *I would rather get stuck next to the bathroom on the roadie bus all the way to Albuquerque.*

The point is, he'd rather open the season against basically any other team, any other opposing shortstop. But such is life, and such is Gene's luck. They'll play Luis twenty-four times, and Gene will avoid him as much as possible. It's not like Luis Estrada has ever sought out friendly small talk anyway.

"All the more motivation to open the season with a win," Gene says. "So, what did you get me for my birthday?"

"Oh, was that today?" Vince says, feigning surprise. "Shit, I didn't get you anything."

"Perfect! Then you can finish this shelf for me while I go raid your fridge."

"You should stay up here," Vince says, nonchalant only in the most practiced sense of the word.

Gene narrows his eyes. "What's happening downstairs?"

"Nothing," Vince lies.

As if on cue, another set of footsteps comes up the stairs separating Gene's apartment from the rest of the house. Jack—taller than his already-tall husband, a certified bear, and handsome in the most comforting of ways—pops his head into Gene's apartment.

He signs, "Hello, Gene," the same as he does every time they see each other. Jack has a hearing aid on each side, but he doesn't always wear them, and prefers signing regardless. To sign Gene's name, he forms each of his hands into the letter G and swipes them in two arcs at the corners of his mouth. A G and a smile, a sign name he gave Gene early after meeting him.

"Hey, Jack," Gene signs back—the letter J, his pinky tracing the shape of the letter in the air in a curl around his chin, an alteration of the sign for "beard," like the auburn one Jack has. "What's happening downstairs?"

Gene says the second part out loud as he signs it, careful to face Jack when he does. Jack knows Gene well enough to lipread okay when Gene speaks, but he's explained that it's harder than signing. So Gene practices his signing with Vince sometimes, on the bus and in their hotel room. Gene is still nowhere near fluent—it's easier to understand Jack's hands than to form the right words with his own—but he's amazed how much easier it comes to him now than it did a year ago.

Jack raises his eyebrows. "Did you tell him?" he signs at Vince, his hands lovingly accusatory.

"I said nothing," Vince answers.

"We're done setting up," Jack signs, with a hand wave and a shoulder shrug that, in concert, sort of imply *Oh well, what're you going to do, my husband can't keep a secret to save his life*.

"We?" Gene asks.

Jack raises his eyebrows. Aloud, he says, "Did he really not tell you about the party?"

"You guys threw me a *party*?"

Vince throws up his hands. "I told you I didn't tell him!" It comes out half-laugh, half-exasperation. "A*nd* you gave me the hard job. You know I can't keep a secret."

"But you also can't make cake," Jack counters.

Gene drags himself up off the ground. "There's cake?"

He always means to make himself one, but his birthday gets consumed by anticipation of and preparation for baseball season's onset every year—all the things he spent the offseason delaying—and he never ends up with enough time. He can't remember the last birthday he even managed a box mix.

"Don't get too excited," Vince says. "It's just cheesecake."

He might wink at Jack when he says this, but Gene can't be entirely sure. Vince ushers Gene down the hall, toward the stairwell. The wide-planked, age-smoothed hardwoods groan underfoot, the rhythm familiar and comfortable.

The Altman house is almost as historic as they come in Portland, which is to say, it's from the early 1900s. It's still newer than anywhere Gene lived back in Brooklyn. When the season ended and he could have gone back to spend the fall in New York with his dad and the rest of their family, he instead stayed here to settle further into his life in this city, this house.

Gene likes Oregon's stubborn green, the offseason spent on damp hiking trails; he likes the slick outdoor stairs that lead up to his apartment door and the chipped-paint porch outside it. He likes the runs he takes around the neighborhood, the topographical map of sidewalk cracks he has memorized. Contrary to the popular opinion of his teammates—most of whom go home to other states or other countries after the season's last out is made—Gene likes the unrelenting rainy season most of all. The sounds it makes against his warped windows, the patterns the water leaves in his arm hair, the puddles that consume the streets for weeks at a time, and the games it delays.

During baseball season, each day plays out to the soundtrack of Gene's preset alarm reminders to do all the basic things—wake up, make his bed, eat something before he has his morning coffee. But he doesn't need an alarm to remember to leave the windows open, whenever he can and sometimes even when he shouldn't, or to walk the quarter-mile to the grocery store for the goat cheese he forgot when he went there last. He does not need a reminder to make dinner with the Altmans—Vince's help mostly coming in the shape of taste-testing—every Tuesday and Friday, or to take his meandering run on Sunday mornings, the one that trails him along the Willamette River waterfront.

In the last year, his life has developed dozens of the kinds of oddities you only collect in a place you've made your home.

When he thunders down the Altmans' stairs—his stairs, too—two at a time and into the kitchen, it really does feel like that. Like home, strange and perfect. Eight or so of their teammates circle around the kitchen island, the last thing he sees before he is engulfed in the triple embrace of The Kyles. He hasn't seen Kyle Clark, Kyle Nguyen, and Kyle Rivera since last season, but the team's sturdy, steady outfielders are as sturdy and steady as they've always been, their chests broad under their matching XL, XL, and XL T-shirts.

"Happy birthday, Nes," they say, a chorus of three separate accents—Queens, Atlanta, and Caracas, respectively.

"Thanks, guys," Gene tries to say, before Kyle Nguyen hefts him over a shoulder and carries him into the adjoining dining room to a clamor of indiscriminate shouts from their team. From Kyle's shoulder, Gene gives their manager an upside-down wave as she falls into step with her players.

"Hey, Baker," he says.

"Nes. How are the drills going?"

"Good, I think," Gene says. He's bulked up a little since last September. By his standards, at least, the months of effort translating mostly to a bit of extra arm muscle and shoulders more defined than he has ever seen on himself. Still, nothing Gene does will ever make him look like the other guys on the team. He has found a comfortable niche as the teammate small enough to lift into the air, fireman-style, after a good, solid win.

In his grandest fantasies, Gene gets to just settle in and enjoy that niche this season—none of the constant change and scrutiny that have defined his career so far. He's made his way up to the highest level of the minor leagues with respectable speed, yes, but as the first trans man to get his name sewn out in patches across the back of a professional baseball jersey, Gene has no expectations of breaking into the majors. The career that he *has*—even if it pays like shit, runs him ragged, isn't the career of anyone's dreams—is still a fucking miracle for a guy like Gene.

"You gonna hit us some homers this year?" Baker teases, like she can hear him overthinking it.

Gene has never hit a home run as a professional baseball player. "Of course," he says anyway.

Kyle Nguyen deposits him in front of the dining room table. Baker gives Gene's baseball cap a jostle, somewhat noogie-adjacent. "Good," she says.

On the table, the cheesecake sits on a glass cake stand. Gene takes in the clumsy chocolate lettering, the crooked line of its homemade crust, and he forgets to worry about the things he's procrastinated on all offseason, about how he probably still won't hit any homers this year, about the five additional pounds he didn't manage to add, about the money, or his probable footnote of a career.

Today, it doesn't matter.

Today, his team has laid out one of his jerseys, facedown like a tablecloth, across the table's dinged-up wood grain. His name, IONESCU, arcs across the fabric, an open parenthesis around the cake stand. In rich Beaverton green and goldenrod yellow, with the Lumberjacks logo of their parent organization sewn into the sleeve, this jersey is home. He has to resist the urge to trace the even stitch of the hems, the letter patches, marveling at their existence.

"You guys are saps," Gene says. Like he doesn't love it.

Kyle Rivera, armed with a sizable knife and an even larger

grin, says, "You know it, big guy." He sticks the knife into the center of the cheesecake and starts to slice a piece before Vince protests.

"We haven't even done 'Happy Birthday,' you jackasses. Wait thirty more seconds," he says. They leave the knife there, teetering halfway through the soft wall of cream cheese and sugar, as if someone had attempted a quick cake murder before getting distracted.

Baker whips a lighter out of her backpack, the little handheld kind in vivid red. Someone turns off the dining room lights, and, as the flames ease their way down the candles' wicks, Gene's teammates sing, off-key and up-tempo. They press in behind him, jostle his shoulders, knock his glasses crooked, take his hat off to mess with his hair, ping-pong him a few inches in each direction like their collective little brother.

When they shout in the general vicinity of the final note, Baker's voice rings through the noise. "Make a wish before Kyle shoves his whole face into this thing."

Gene doesn't make wishes on his birthday. It feels like inviting cosmic jokes into his life, to ask for all the quiet things he wants most—on April Fool's, of all days. But his team is here. Maybe only because he stole thirty-seven bases for them last season, or because he hit over .400 in September. In the moment, it doesn't matter why they showed up for him. It matters that they did.

So he closes his eyes and lets a wish form. For the team, not for himself:

*To get Beaverton to the playoffs. To do whatever I can to help get us there.*

He blows, and the smell of smoke mixes with the tangy-sweet, graham cracker–based promise of his favorite homemade dessert.

"Dude," someone's voice interrupts. "Did y'all see this shit?"

Gene opens his eyes to find the Kyles crowded around one phone, Vince pulling his own cell out of his back pocket. Wordlessly, Vince holds it out to Gene, a push notification unopened on his screen.

Gene's hand doesn't shake when he takes the phone, but maybe it should.

A notification from *The Athletic* joins the one from the Major League Baseball app, then the *Oregonian*, all notifying Vince of breaking baseball news. Gene squints at the headlines, stacked up, and wills them to say anything but what they do.

**PORTLAND LUMBERJACKS ACQUIRE CATCHER ERNIE GONZALES & SHORTSTOP LUIS ESTRADA FROM ARIZONA**, and **PORTLAND SENDS PITCHING HAUL TO ARIZONA FOR PROSPECTS GONZALES & ESTRADA**, and **GONZALES & ESTRADA HEADED TO PDX IN LAST-MINUTE BLOCKBUSTER.**

The knife, having finally lost its balance, slides slowly out of the cheesecake until its handle hits the serving plate with a weak thud.

# 2

## APRIL

**Current record: 0–0**

**@JenWertherPDX: THREAD:** In a surprising (and potentially very exciting) last-minute move, the Portland Lumberjacks have sent a bevy of pitchers to Arizona in exchange for rising star Ernie Gonzales & former top-100 prospect Luis Estrada. Both will start the season with Triple-A Beaverton. (1/5)

**@JenWertherPDX:** With this move, Portland's infield plans gain some clarity. Both Gonzales & Estrada will need some additional minor league seasoning first, but the hope is that they'll slot in as the Lumberjacks' catcher and shortstop of the future. (2/5)

**@JenWertherPDX:** Gonzales, who signed at 17 out of the Dominican Republic, finished last season with Arizona's Triple-A affiliate team, the Reno Aces. His stellar reputation with pitchers and strong offensive profile make him the clear centerpiece of the trade for Portland, but . . . (3/5)

**@JenWertherPDX:** Estrada—son of the late Luis Estrada, Sr.—is an interesting add-on: since returning from an ill-timed off-field injury, his bat has been uninspiring, but he's coming off a Gold Glove year defensively, and some believe he's due for a resurgence at the plate. (4/5)

**@JenWertherPDX:** We'll have a full write-up soon, but a parting thought: with Gonzales & Estrada expected to remain at Triple-A this season, this won't pay dividends for Portland right away, but, at the very least, the Beavers should be plenty of fun to watch this year. (/end)

---

Opening Day, most years, attracts the biggest crowd of the season. It's the stink of hope that hovers over the game, even for a team with a lackluster roster and a long history of heartbreaking seasons. On Opening Day, anything can happen.

Gene, most years, loves that stink.

The people turning up to spend a tepid, verdant Oregon Tuesday in a ballpark that has no roof and is subject to rain delays more often than not in those early months. The bated breath, the waiting, the open arms of possibility—all of it the foundation of Gene's love for this slow, old, American sport.

Today, a small collection of cars has already started to fill the parking lot outside the stadium when he and Vince pull up. Cars Gene doesn't recognize, cars that belong to neither his teammates nor Jen, the reporter the *Oregonian* assigns to sporadically cover their games. Near the front doors, a small handful of overenthused fans wearing Portland jerseys waits for the gates to open. These are the truly hopeful ones, here to see the big league team's future, all for the price of a cheap minor league ticket.

Most days, Gene would give them a smile on his way past,

welcome them to the game. Today, he skirts around them, careful to stay out of view until he and Vince are behind the stadium and Gene can swipe into the heavy staff entrance doors. Today, he has an unfamiliar churning in his gut, nerves and apprehension and every other variety of *I don't know how I feel about this.*

"You're panicking," Vince says.

"A little."

"It's going to be fine." Before Gene can voice his worry, Vince tries to alleviate it. "I'm sure they're just going to slide him over to second. We need a decent second baseman."

"Okay," Gene says, though he has his doubts.

Because the thing is, Luis Estrada is a shortstop.

And Gene is a shortstop.

And Gene doesn't have a Gold Glove. Gene doesn't have a former superstar dad. Hell, Gene doesn't even have a size-medium jersey. No, Gene has his dependable size small, and a dad who played for this same minor league team for a little over a decade before retiring without fanfare.

If someone needs to move to second, well, from an outside perspective? Most people would pick Gene. He's younger, less experienced, with a weaker arm and fewer accolades. Most important, when he and Luis shared a field in college, Gene *did* play second—it's an established pattern, the expectation.

But this is *his* minor league team, and he has more than held his own at shortstop. It's the de facto captain-of-the-infield position, flashier and more impressive, and for all that Gene tries not to care what anyone else thinks, he has always, *always* enjoyed impressing people. Surprising them. Shortstop carries more pride than second, however you slice it, and Gene has grown into that pride quite nicely over the last year.

All he can do is show up and hope, which is all he can do most of the time anyway.

Gene decided, in the days since the trade was announced, that he would give Luis a chance. He did *not* obsess over Luis's impending arrival, but maybe he did do a bit of reading.

Maybe he read Luis's whole Wikipedia page, and a slew of articles, none of which told him anything he didn't already know: that Luis Estrada was born in Los Angeles, the youngest of five and the only boy, a former Stanford student like Gene. That Luis started playing baseball with his dad—star shortstop Luis Estrada, Sr.—as a kid and that, after his dad died when he was eighteen, Luis took his senior season off from his high school team. That he was selected by the Red Sox in the fourteenth round of the draft after his junior year at Stanford, almost exactly a year after Gene first met him.

(Wikipedia and Baseball-Reference don't mention the phone call Luis never made to Gene after he got drafted, or the seven silent years that followed. They don't mention the way the Stanford team fell apart after Luis left, or the way some of his things still sat abandoned in his old locker stall when Gene came back for his sophomore year.)

And maybe Gene read about Luis's accident, the one he'd also heard about as it was reported in real time, almost two years ago, when Gene was still playing a few levels lower in the minors. His teammates' cell phones had lit up with the news that Luis Estrada, at the time still playing in the Red Sox system, was being called up to the majors to fill the roster spot of an injured infielder. Gene remembers reading the news, the way his pulse had jumped at it, excited and thrilled for Luis in spite of it all. But, while Gene had hit two doubles and a triple against the opposing team that night, Luis never made it to his own game.

Maybe Gene allowed himself a sliver of soft-bellied empathy when he revisited those same articles he read two seasons ago, about Luis's rental car hitting a wet patch of asphalt on his way to the stadium, about his weeklong stay in the hospital and the resultant months on the injured list; about the long road to recovery, and how Luis had never been the same hitter since.

The thing that stung the most, that Gene swallows down and promises himself he won't dwell on anymore, was that he hadn't gotten to be there for Luis when any of it happened. Because Luis had decided, without explanation and without ceremony, that Gene didn't need to be in his life anymore—that Gene would watch all the successes and all the hurt from the sidelines.

So Gene can be mature. He'll try to just think of Luis as a human being—not his competition and not his former teammate, though both are true. He'll play team-first, stay in the moment. He'll look on the bright side.

When he and Vince arrive in Beaverton's clubhouse, even hours before first pitch, its offseason staleness has been consumed by a buoyancy Gene hasn't seen in months, their teammates a sea of brown and pink-tinged skin, covered only in the laziest way possible by their Beaverton workout gear. For the first game—particularly the first game post–blockbuster trade—guys show up early.

On first glance, Gene sees neither Luis nor Ernie, but the clubhouse thrums anyway.

The Kyles have staked their claim on the locker room speakers, blasting a new playlist. Charlie Cooper, a minor league journeyman who has shifted to first base in his later years, is shucking himself of a Hawaiian shirt far too bright for such a dingy April day. Their third baseman, Trevor Ross, has set up shop in his stall, cap pulled low over his eyes while he takes his first prepractice nap of the season—the sleepiest man to ever handle the hot corner. Bench guys and relief pitchers and junior coaches mill around, their steps and shouts and head nods setting the rhythm for a new season.

Nestled in the corner of all that calamity, Gene finds his locker stall with ease. Vince, for his part, lies down on one of the benches, his sturdy legs stretched in front of him, crossed at the ankle.

"Feels good, right?" Gene asks.

Vince has been in far more impressive locker rooms than this one. Still, he nods.

Gene doesn't bother asking if Vince wants to run stadiums with him—he never does, hasn't in the full year Gene has known him, likely won't ever again before he retires. He has reached the point in his career where no extra pound of muscle can overtake time's slow assault on his bum shoulder. Having missed more than his fair share of time to every arm injury possible, Vince playacts at lazing, but Gene knows that when he comes back from warm-ups, Vince will be working with a physical trainer, deploying interminable ice packs and careful mobility routines to try to milk his left arm for all it's got.

So Gene focuses on his own routines. He holds up two pairs of cleats—one pair blue and pink and white, well-worn; the other high-top, a deep and brilliant green, never used. He barely considers before hanging his usual pair by their laces on a hook in his stall, the height and barely-there heft of the spikes familiar as they click against the wooden wall. If nothing else, when he puts his uniform on in a few hours, he will have stable ground under his feet.

Before he can get out to the field, Baker's voice comes from her office—crystal clear and well-projected. "Altzy, Nes. Get over here."

Vince makes a face—*How are we in trouble already?*—but heeds her request; he clears a path for them both, until they land in front of Baker's door. Behind her desk, she greets them with a nod before gesturing at the man sitting across from her.

"Boys," she says, as if Vince isn't closer to her age than Gene's, "this is Ernie Gonzales. Gonzales, meet Vince Altman and Gene Ionescu."

Ernie Gonzales is somehow bigger than Gene expected. He's seen the numbers—six-foot-three, 220 pounds. They don't exactly scream *compact*. Up close, he's solid, with thick legs poking out from his practice shorts, the prototypical catcher's ass rounding them out. But when he stands and turns toward them, it's his broad grin and enthusiastic nod that stick with Gene. He's big, yes, and *effusive*.

"It's good to finally meet you," Vince offers with his handshake. He's at ease, the way he always is around new people, and it's obvious why Baker tends to leave intra-team relationships up to him. She likes to say that, as captain, Vince is the babysitter—not her. "Been a big fan since we played you last year."

Gene extends his own hand. "Bigger fans now that we don't have to play *against* you anymore. You can call me Nes, by the way. Everyone does."

"Nes," he repeats, Gene's nickname already sounding at home in his voice, thickly accented and filled to the brim with an easy brand of kindness. "In that case, you can call me Gonzo."

"Deal," Gene says, and he shakes the hand of this man who is more than a foot taller than him, this man who is destined for something really incredible someday, and the trade doesn't feel half so bad if it means they get someone like Ernie playing for them. "It's great to have you here."

At that, Ernie pulls him into a hug, the kind perfected by men in locker rooms—a tug of the hand, one arm each trapped between chests, two solid and encouraging pats to the back—carefully calculated for minimum intimacy. When Ernie does it, it feels genuine.

"I'm gonna take him to meet the rest of the pitchers," Vince says.

"Team meeting in ninety," Baker says.

Vince waves his acknowledgment over his shoulder as he leads Ernie down the hall, and Gene swings himself into one of the two open seats in front of Baker's desk.

"So."

She leans back, feet on her desk, and holds up a hand to stop Gene's line of questioning before it can start. "I don't have the lineup ready. Don't ask."

Having Baker on your side makes a world of difference—it's the only reason he's here at all. Last year, she served as pitching coach, but this year, with their regular manager out on family leave, she's stepped in as interim manager. Gene played for other teams, lower in the minors, before coming here, but when he finally got to walk into this particular stadium, play for this particular person? It settled something in him. He feels safe here, in her capable coaching hands. Plus, part of him hopes it bodes well for his season—to have someone who gets it, at least a little bit, in charge.

So, he shoots two lazy finger guns and drops the subject. "You get any sleep last night?" he asks instead.

She raises two unimpressed eyebrows high on her forehead and laughs, a flat, humorless burst of a thing that has *Fuck no* written all over it.

"That good?" Gene asks.

"Just get your asses to the playoffs this season and make it worth my while." She seems almost genuinely pleased by that, the idea of her team getting to play into the fall, before she gets back to business. "But, listen—I called you in here because I need you to do me a favor."

"Shoot." Gene leans forward in his chair, hoping against hope that the favor might be something fun and not, like, *Can you move my Subaru into one of the shady parking spots?*

"I need you to give Estrada a tour of the stadium."

Gene sucks his lips between his teeth to keep from grimacing. *Positive attitude*, he reminds himself.

"Sure, yeah. Not Gonzo?" The whole endeavor would be significantly less awkward with Ernie's presence added to the mix.

"The pitchers have Gonzales covered. Just Estrada, thanks."

It's a dismissal of sorts, in her subtle but firm way.

When Gene goes looking for Luis, Kyle Nguyen points him toward the showers.

Gene elects to wait at the edges of the locker room proper, in the hopes it will make for a less awkward reunion than the showers might. When Luis emerges, though, he wears a towel and nothing else, and Gene regrets every decision that landed him in this locker room, in front of this man. There is no amount of googling that could have prepared Gene for the immediate, too-deep recognition that sucks every bit of oxygen from the space around them.

Luis is always shorter than Gene expects, borderline tall in any other company but almost small amongst athletes, his collarbone nonetheless distractingly eye-level for Gene. His skin is still that same bright and beautiful brown, his arms thoroughly tan-lined where a T-shirt might fall; his eyelashes are still long, his eyebrows still thick, his hair almost-black and, yes, still fucking perfect. He's handsome—has always been—but also? Almost pretty, in a way that photos just can't convey.

There are differences, too: broader shoulders, deeper eye bags, shorter hair, more of a beard. Somehow even less confidence than Luis used to project. When he opens his mouth, the left side of his lips remains unmoving in a way it didn't used to—nerve damage, courtesy of the same car accident that kept him off the field for a full season. And still, Gene recognizes him. More foundation-crumbling than that, though, is that Luis clearly recognizes *him.* The way Luis stares at him, the way his eyes slide a little to the left of Gene's ear when Gene stares back, makes

Gene feel eighteen all over again, breathless and tense and desperate for things to make sense.

It's not as if Gene has changed so much, really. Not like a shorter haircut and a few years of testosterone have altered him so fundamentally as to look like someone fully new. But Gene has separated his time at Stanford—those pictures of him and Luis in the same jersey, crowded at the mound when Stanford's ace pitched them into the College World Series, happy in a way that feels simpler in hindsight than it did at the time—so thoroughly from his time in the minors. It's jarring to have Luis here, suddenly belonging to both the before and the now—to have to reconcile those two versions of Luis, those two versions of himself.

When Gene finally manages to talk, his voice much deeper than last time they spoke, Luis's face does register the barest traces of surprise. That, at least, is satisfying.

"Baker asked me to give you a tour."

"Uh," is the first word Luis says to him in seven years.

"It won't take long."

"Can I"—he squints, shoulders raising up by his quite prominent ears—"put on a shirt first?"

His voice—which Gene used to know so well but which sounded so different in the video interviews he *definitely* did not watch last night—comes out as flat as his mouth.

Yes, it would be for the best if he put on a shirt, because—well. It would just be for the best.

"I'll meet you outside?" Gene asks.

When Luis walks out two minutes later, a dog trails behind him—a husky, his tongue lolling and mouth open wide, one eye bright blue and the other brown, with far too much fur for the summer. Luis has changed into the most nondescript outfit possible: a T-shirt, impossibly soft-looking; full-length track pants, tighter than they need to be and tied at the waist; a plain zip-up hoodie, worn open; and remarkably uncreased sneakers, the only pop of color.

"You good to go?" Gene asks.

Luis shrugs, like, *Sure, let's get this over with.*

Awesome. Perfect. Great start.

Gene points out the weight room, sparsely attended today while everyone enjoys the first-day-back-from-vacation atmosphere of the clubhouse. Luis nods. Gene shows him the equipment room, not yet completely stale this early in the season. Luis nods. Gene shows him the elevator up to the press box, where their announcers sit dutifully for each game.

"They're like local celebrities," Gene says. "Dan and Nancy?"

Luis nods, his expression unrecognizing.

"Well, *very* local celebrities. Like, pretty much just in the stadium."

Gene has listened to Dan and Nancy announce games for as long as he can remember, used to mouth along from the dugout while they announced his dad's name in the lineup. Dan and Nancy may be celebrities only to Gene, but they are celebrities all the same.

Luis nods.

Voice and shoulders already tired from carrying every bit of this conversation's weight, Gene leads Luis down the main concourse, the one with the visible metal beams of their bleachers' undersides. He explains that the stadium was constructed in the 1920s, making it by far the oldest stadium for a Triple-A team; its last major renovation was in the nineties, right before the Beavers moved in.

Luis.

Nods!

Gene can't bite back his grimace now. This has gone about as well as he expected it to, but it would help if Luis would, like—*say words.* At least his dog is smiling.

The thing is, Beaverton's field is home to Gene. It sits off Beaverton Hillsdale Highway, down the road from Beaverton City Library, across the parking lot from the Village Inn where he and his dad used to eat an occasional breakfast during the season. All the streets and landmarks that made up home when Gene was a kid. He wants to point to the cracks in the paint, to the hot-dog-and-pretzel stand, to the women's bathrooms where, at age eight, he hurled cotton candy while his dad held his hair back. He wants to laugh over how his dad apologized every time someone walked in and found one of Beaverton's players, still in his uniform, huddled over the trash can with his kid; he'd imitate his dad's Romanian accent—*Sorry, sorry, give us one minute please.*

He's not sure if this version of Luis would appreciate the humor or the heart of that story, so he keeps it to himself.

Instead, he takes Luis to the nosebleed seats and sits him down. If Luis has questions, he can ask them. Gene has already done more than the minimum.

A few silent minutes after they settle into their seats, someone starts to replace the letters on the lineup. Beaverton uses a green-painted wood scoreboard, with the game's stats manually posted in white numbers and letters. Every player's name, number, and position gets placed into the lineup before each of their games—the embodiment of classic, old-school baseball, where Gene should not but does belong.

Luis watches those letters just as Gene does, and Gene realizes, belatedly, that the name they're spelling up top of the lineup—batting *first*—is his own.

Gene Ionescu, number zero, second baseman, spelled out in those tall and incredible and improbable letters, all five-foot-two and 145 pounds of him. Up at the plate first. He'll take the season's inaugural swing, hopefully get his name notched next to the season's inaugural hit—

Wait.

Second baseman?

He looks again, squints until his eyes sting.

There it sits, next to his name: 2B.

"Well," Gene says. *Positive fucking attitude.* "Good news for you."

Luis takes this opportunity to speak up, finally. "Is it news? You're a second baseman."

Gene's eyebrows raise so slowly, so perfectly in sync with the turn of his head, that by the time Luis makes it into his line of sight, his eyebrows have completed their journey to his hairline. "Excuse me?" he says.

Luis manages, somehow, to look surprised by Gene's reaction. "I just mean, you've never really been a natural shortstop."

Every bit of Gene, every inch of him, wants to tell this guy that, when he left their college team, Gene held down the fort just fine for the next three years. That he had finished *second* in Gold Glove voting last year, thanks. That his glove always has been and will remain more than fine. He wants to ask if Luis would like to go down to the field and see who can sprint down a rogue ground ball faster.

He *wants* to ask Luis what he thinks a natural shortstop is, exactly, and why Gene can't be one. To ask if he knows that Gene still gets asked by hecklers if he got lost on the way to the softball field. He could yell his accomplishments until he went hoarse, and they wouldn't matter to the people who only want to mock him for not wearing a cup, that vocal and not-insignificant subset of fans who are upset that Portland would ever allow someone who looks like him to play in their system.

Luis's dismissal stings differently, though. He doesn't call Gene a gimmick, doesn't roll his eyes at Gene's presence; he just doesn't *care*, seems to now think of Gene like a piece of lint to be brushed from his shoulder.

The worst part, though, is that Luis is right—Gene was never going to be Beaverton's shortstop today. This lineup is exactly the one Gene knew to expect, much as he had tried to pretend otherwise.

He sucks his teeth, not gently, and nods once. "All right," he says. "That's the tour. See you at batting practice."

He leaves Luis sitting there in the stands. It's possible Luis can and will help their team this season, but what Gene hopes for most in this moment—what the selfish, petulant pit in his stomach begs for—is for Luis to fall flat on his face.

The first play of the season comes directly toward Gene, a simple pop-up off of Vince's third pitch—a breaking ball that the batter barely catches a piece of. It's an easy out for Gene, as if the guy had aimed right for his glove.

Or, at least, it *should* have made for an easy out.

Instead, Luis crashes into Gene from the right, much more solid than he looks. He makes no call, lays no claim to a ball that has sailed perfectly into Gene's territory—just tries to make the catch anyway, and fails. Almost as if he doesn't trust his teammate to make the simplest play imaginable.

They tumble into the dirt and lie there, tangled, Luis's elbow buried in Gene's shoulder, until Gene pushes up and forward and gets the ball in his ungloved hand. He snaps it to first and scrambles to cover second.

The opposing team's runner holds at first base. If the error gets charged to Gene and breaks his perfect fielding streak, he'll be pissed.

"Fuck," Luis mutters from the ground. His voice deep and even, unmoved and unmoving.

Out of begrudging sportsmanship, Gene offers his hand to him. As frustrated as he might be, it's nothing compared to the offense that bubbles under his skin when Luis ignores that hand and acts put off by its presence, standing up and sighing.

Okay.

Fuck this guy, maybe.

Vince turns and gives Gene a look that's part *Are you okay?* and part *What the hell.* Gene waves him off. He tries to do the same thing to his own sinking gut. Plenty of games get off to a shaky start, for plenty of reasons. He can't do anything but get settled into position for the next batter.

Still, by the time the ninth inning arrives, even Gene's hope has worn thin. With two outs and down by one run, he stands in the on-deck circle, willing Luis to hit the ball anywhere a fielder isn't. Take a walk. *Anything.* It just has to be enough to get to first, to give Gene a chance to tie the game up.

Luis strikes out looking on three pitches, his bat never leaving his shoulder. By the time Gene and Vince straggle to the locker room with a frustrated Baker, Luis has long since left.

# 3

## APRIL

**Current record: 0–5**

Objectively, signing a grubby baseball for a kid, minutes before a game starts, falls pretty high on the list of innocuous, nice things for a player to do.

Objectively, Gene gets that.

Subjectively, though, he hates how effortlessly Luis signs his autograph, how smooth the cursive looks on the dingy white of the ball, eleven letters collapsed into an L and an E and two elegant swoops. Luis has always been something of a perfectionist—compulsive in his practice routines, obsessive about his swing-tinkering, fastidious in his classes, and torturously private about his personal life—so it comes as no surprise that he would be careful with this, too.

Gene wishes he'd show an ounce of that perfectionism, that care, to the team Gene has built his life around. Instead, Luis has managed all of one hit in their first week, good for a 0.067 batting average. It's a small sample size, but Gene draws conclusions nonetheless. His conclusions:

1) Luis Estrada is his least favorite teammate, on both a personal and professional level, literally ever;

2) That's it.

Luis can cover his mouth with his glove—can spit a sharp and derisive and familiar *Fuck* into the leather whenever he makes a mistake—all he wants. Gene will start feeling bad for him when Luis decides to be less of a tool.

A better man than Gene might watch Luis pass the ball off to Ernie to sign and think it's nice that he wants to give the ten-year-old fan something special to take home. Said better man would notice that Luis goofs around with the kid while she waits to get her ball back—"Does your family come to games much? Do you want my dog to sign it? Oh, it was a joke, sorry. He'd just steal the ball and run away. But who's your favorite player? Oh, good choice. You want *his* autograph? That one I can get you for real."—and would be slightly charmed by this version of Luis, less uptight and almost kind.

But Gene does not want to be a better man.

He stares at Vince's iPad, skimming through a last-minute review of the same scouting reports they reviewed in depth before today's game. He stops only when a baseball gets dangled in front of his face.

"What?" Gene says, eyes still on the scouting report.

"Sign it."

Luis's voice, which Gene could identify in his sleep.

"Why?"

Luis points at the stands. "She says you're her favorite player."

When Gene looks over, it's the same girl from before, her grin the most wonky-toothed, genuine one he has ever seen. She waves, a broad-arcing thing. "She did not," he says.

"Sign the damn ball, Nes."

And Gene *is* Nes here, has always been Nes once he puts his jersey on. When his first name changed, Nes remained—eternal, comfortable, well-worn. But Luis hasn't earned Nes, not anymore. When the word comes out of Luis's mouth, it no longer feels like a twenty-one-year-old standing awkward in their dorm hallway after a late practice, suggesting the nickname and, in doing so, subtly dubbing Gene a part of their team a few weeks before he officially made the roster.

It's a faint reminder of that Luis, more like a haphazard outline of who he used to be. There are few things Gene needs less than that right now.

So he's been calling Luis by his first name, too. His nickname—Nada, because *nothing gets past him! Nada!*—used to slip so easily from Gene's lips, the rhythm of it familiar and friendly. This, though—first names only and a safe distance left between them—is easier now. Impersonal.

"It's Gene," he corrects.

Luis stares at him. "Okay. Sign the damn ball, Gene." He holds it in front of Gene's face again, perched delicately between his fingers like the leather doesn't agree with him.

Gene signs the ball. He has never perfected this; he gets asked a fraction as much as the other guys do. Most people who want autographs from minor league players want them so that they can resell the autograph later on, if the minor league player becomes a big name someday.

The minor leagues—especially Triple-A, the final stop before the major leagues—are nominally meant to serve as the last bit of seasoning before a player breaks onto the real stage. Their actual purpose is more multifaceted than that. Beaverton's roster, like every Triple-A roster, is also peppered with players who will never be or are no longer good enough to be full-time major leaguers, players who could be on the cusp of something big, and players with fat question marks next to their names: the used-to-bes—Vince; the should-have-beens—Luis; and the leftovers—Gene.

In other words, no one expects Gene to make it to the majors, so they don't expect his autograph to appreciate, so he has rarely needed to give it at all.

His signature comes out clumsy, out of place next to Luis's. He adds a smiley face like an apology.

"I know it's ugly," he says when he tosses the ball back.

"She's not going to care." Luis doesn't comment any further, doesn't even look at the ball before he's walking away and lobbing it back into the stands. He asked the girl who her favorite player was, then got Gene to sign the ball, and Gene is forced to believe one of two things: either she said he was her favorite player—improbable, leaning toward impossible; or Luis came over and asked him unprompted—so far beyond impossible it makes the first option seem almost *likely*.

When Luis returns to the bench and settles two careful feet away from him, Gene chooses not to think about any of it.

Luis has stayed at shortstop all week, despite posting defense far shoddier than Gene has come to expect from him—four errors in five games does not a shortstop make. Maybe, if Portland—perpetually desperate for infielders but never desperate enough for Gene's name to get called—didn't seem so publicly hell-bent on developing Luis to be their next franchise shortstop, Baker would move them around. Give Gene a shot, give Luis a rest. But there Luis's name is, up on that green board, batting ninth, SS next to his name.

Gene, no longer used to second base, has also played like shit. He and Luis have led the team to a rousing five consecutive losses. The only silver lining is that Luis *will* get called up someday, and, just like when Luis left Stanford, Gene will get to be shortstop again. He'll have room to breathe and space to play. His life might turn out less dream-shaped than Luis's, but it'll be his, and it'll be good.

But today, Vince will get his second start of the season, and there's a kid in the stands who likes the Beaverton Beavers enough to have a favorite player, whether or not that player is Gene. He can see no reason why they shouldn't try to win a game for Vince, for that kid, for Baker, whose always-short nails have been bitten to stubs as her team has shit the bed over the past week.

If they're going to win, he and Luis will need to play . . . okay, not *well* together, but competently, at least. Which they have accomplished precisely zero times thus far.

Gene takes a deep breath and begs it to steady him before he slides a few feet to the left, iPad held out and opened to the scouting report, until his elbow and knee bump up against Luis's.

At the contact, Luis jerks his leg away, his arm banging against the dugout bench's wooden back with a faint *thud*, followed by a frustrated "*Shit*," then an exasperated "*Jesus*," in rapid succession. Gene watches it all, somewhere between confusion and horror, and, while Luis settles back in a few careful inches away, Gene wonders how, exactly, Luis has survived this long in the notoriously close quarters of the minor leagues if he can't tolerate sharing a bench with a teammate.

Luis rubs at his elbow—not quite massaging it, just prodding, as if feeling for a bruise. An itch at the back of Gene's mind says: he might react this way only to Gene, and Gene hasn't gotten such a negative response from a teammate in years.

Luis Estrada is Gene's least favorite teammate, but the idea that Gene might be Luis's, too, bothers him in a way he doesn't expect. Like his skin has been pulled too tight.

They lose. So thoroughly that the only real thing to do when the game ends is hop in the showers and wash the whole thing away.

Gene shuffles into his usual stall and stands under the water while he waits for it to warm. Beaverton's stadium, as old as it is, still boasts the best showers Gene has found thus far in the minor leagues—generally at least semi-clean, with acceptable water pressure and walls that divide the stalls from each other. The stalls don't have doors, though, and as he turns to wash the soap from his back, Luis walks by.

Luis keeps his eyes to himself, but Gene doesn't.

Gene, in spite of the way his brain revolts against him for doing it, watches.

He watches Luis's careful, measured steps, the way he keeps his shoulders up by his ears. They're good shoulders, if Gene is honest with himself, which he would really rather not be about this, but there's the thought anyway, persistently gay: *they're good shoulders*. Not especially broad, but broader than the rest of Luis's body might suggest they'd be. Sparsely and darkly freckled.

He does not, Gene notes, have back hair, in contrast to what his chest hair would lead one to expect. Maybe he waxes. Maybe he lucked into a surprisingly hairless, absurdly sexy back.

It's that thought that makes Gene's skin go cold under the shower's warm spray. It's that thought that makes Gene turn around and face the wall, any remaining soap on his back be damned.

He does not find his teammates attractive, as a rule. Not a general rule—a firm one, with no exceptions to date. It keeps his too-big heart safe, never to get disappointed by the usually straight and always cis men who populate his day-to-day life. It also means that Beaverton's clubhouse has always felt comfortable to him—everyone, including Gene, can walk around as naked as they want, and no ounce of him needs to feel self-conscious about it.

At Stanford, Gene got ready in the women's locker room, cordoned off from the rest of the team until he came out two years after Luis had already left. While he noticed—lightly, casually, unobtrusively, of course—that Luis was at least semi-nice to look at, there was not much of an opportunity to care beyond that. Between the teammate factor and the then-impenetrable walls of Gene's own closet, he didn't consider it overmuch.

But tonight, with those walls gone and the shape and gentle curve of Luis's back instantly memorized, Gene *does* feel self-conscious.

Not because his body doesn't look like Luis's, or the rest of his teammates'—he's fine with that, is more comfortable about that in Beaverton than he's ever been anywhere else. No, he feels self-conscious because the possibility exists that Luis might *see* Gene's body now, that he might have an opinion about it, and some small, traitorous part of Gene wants that opinion to be positive.

Gene yanks the shower knob to the right, until the water runs so cold it's almost hot again.

When he eventually emerges, wrapped in his towel, his fingers pruny, he gets dressed as quickly as he can manage, the fabric of his sweatshirt and shorts sticking to his still-wet skin.

He finds Vince sitting in Baker's office, the two of them tossing a baseball back and forth. Luis's dog sits next to Baker's desk and watches the ball sail between them. Gene's dad and Baker played together a couple of seasons, so Gene knows few catchers' tosses better than hers. When he was six and she was twenty-seven, she would play catch with him by the backstop while his dad took fly balls in the field. Her toss hasn't changed.

He used to dream of *being* Baker someday—a woman, playing in the majors, in the same uniform and eye black as the guys. This was well over a decade before Gene realized that he was, after all, *literally* one of the guys, but the sentiment never entirely left him. Something about her being out there—crouched behind home plate and calling the game—felt like possibility.

She lobs the ball to Gene, silently inviting him into the conversation. The casualness of it amazes him, sometimes.

"Shit game tonight," she says, from her office in the stadium where she coaches, and he plays, and that amazes him, too.

"Yep," he agrees. He pops the p.

He went three-for-five at the plate but got caught trying to steal a base. The latter fact, of course, will be the one that keeps him awake tonight.

"We'll try again tomorrow," he adds, because he really does want to believe that tomorrow will be different than today, than the days that led up to today. It's the way Gene approaches baseball—not just day-to-day, but inning-to-inning, play-to-play. The ability for one pitch, one hit to change the tide of a game has always made baseball special: it is a rare sport where, truly, the game doesn't end until it ends.

Baker gives him a mock salute when Gene tosses the ball back to her. Vince grabs his jacket and keys.

The night air is cooler than it was during the game, almost sharp. They're teetering on spring's precipice, these final weeks of unpredictability before they topple into summer's heady, nonstop heat. Gene likes these weeks best, when it's still easy to be an optimist. They've lost six games in a row, won zero, but a lot can happen with so much of the season still to go.

In the car, Vince tosses his phone into Gene's lap. "Pick a playlist?"

Gene clicks through Vince's music library, past a dozen albums any white dad might play on his way to the hardware store, until he lands on an option they can both enjoy. Vince turns the volume up, and Gene opens Twitter—logged into the nameless, locked account that Vince uses mostly to follow all his real-life queer friends. All ten of them, including Gene. Gene types his own name into the search bar, and, yep—there it is, from a Twitter handle Gene recognizes and wishes he didn't.

**@Lumberjax_Brandon71**: Thought Ionescu was supposed to be good at this??? lmaooooo

Which, okay, Lumberjax-underscore-Brandon—whatever. Not the meanest tweet Gene's ever seen about himself. What he wants, what he opened the tweet for, is the video linked beneath. As soon as he clicks on it, the audio comes through the speakers. Gene considers turning the volume off entirely, but the Bluetooth has already snitched on him.

"No," Vince says, though they both know Gene will ignore him. "Turn that off."

The video is shaky, taken on a cell phone, but it does the trick. Giving up on subtlety, Gene holds the screen as close to his face as he can, to watch his failed attempt to steal second base. Vince calls it self-flagellation, Gene calls it learning from his mistakes.

The thing is, the pitcher was a head-nodder.

People think that stealing bases is about raw speed, but it's about knowing your moment. In college, Gene memorized a video where the reigning MLB stolen base champion explained that you have to learn a pitcher's giveaways. You wait for him to give that infinitesimal nod of his head, or squint just so—that little thing he always does before he throws the pitch. And then, before the ball even leaves his hand, before his windup is even done, you go.

By the time anyone notices, you're already safe.

Gene took off the instant the pitcher's head declined, pulse hammering, his helmet falling off somewhere between first and second. He hasn't been able to stop reliving the pressure of the second baseman's glove on his back, the tag applied an instant before Gene's outstretched hand hit the base. In the video, the second base umpire squeezes his hands into fists to call Gene out.

"You're obsessing," Vince says.

Which, yes. Gene's ADHD fixates on things, plays them on a loop until they become so ingrained that he can't ever forget them. It's why he tries not to read Twitter, why he hates conflict. It is, Gene really does try to tell himself, why he can't stop thinking about the way Luis reacted to their elbows bumping in the dugout, why Gene hates the idea of being *anyone's* least favorite teammate so much.

For all that he loves to see the good, it has always been a conscious choice, a skill honed over many years. One born out of necessity. If he let himself do anything else, if he let himself think about the things people said and thought about him, he would never stop. He would start to believe them.

But he's human. Sometimes he fixates. "A little," he says to Vince.

"It's *fine*," Vince says. "It's not like one stolen base was going to fix that game."

"I know."

"Didn't you tell me you were going to stop going on Twitter?"

"I lied," Gene says, turning back to the video. He did delete Twitter from his phone, but he's noticed that he can find rude comments on Vince's version of the app just as easily as he could on his own.

"At least you weren't as bad as Estrada."

"Not a high bar." Gene presses play on the video again. This time, he sees it, a half-second before video-Gene takes off: a slight turn of his head toward their home dugout along the third base line, a barely-there delay before he runs. He scrubs backward, tries to recall what it was that pulled his focus away from the task at hand, but all he can remember is Luis staring back at him from the dugout.

Then, a notification pops up at the top of Vince's phone.

"You have a text from Jack," Gene says.

"Open it?"

Vince's text stream with Jack looks more or less exactly how one might expect two married, thirty-eight-year-old queer men to text each other. Heart emojis from Jack, a picture of their dogs, a text from Vince that reads, *I'm getting too old to be away from you and the kids this much.* The "kids" here meaning the dogs. He'd paired it with the breaking heart.

Jack's message is a link, captioned, *Price dropped!!*

Gene's thumb presses on the link before he asks if he should—he recognizes the Zillow logo when he sees it. Looking at the ridiculous, expensive real estate Vince and Jack always consider but never buy has become something of a pastime for Gene.

This particular house is the exact kind of place where a once-great baseball player should retire. Not too ostentatious, but gorgeous. The windows span most of the outside walls, and it sits in front of a backyard so big it might actually be measured in acres. There are five bedrooms—five times as many as Gene has ever had, and three more than he can possibly imagine having—but Vince and Jack do want to adopt, eventually, and they love having guests.

The house is perfect, except that, according to the ZIP code, it's in Bend.

"Is it the yellow one?" Vince asks.

"Yeah." Something about the way Vince perks up when he says it makes Gene ask, "Wait. How real is this?" He tries to sound casual about it, but his heart pounds, surprise making it hard to swallow.

"We're just talking about it," Vince says.

"When would you move?" he asks.

"In a year or two. When I retire."

Gene clings to the "or two" part of that answer, and says, "Bend is nice."

"Well, you know we want kids."

"You and me? I don't remember that conversation."

Vince rolls his eyes. "Jack doesn't want to adopt when I'm traveling so much." If the set of his shoulders is any indication, this involved a fight, which Vince and Jack have only rarely.

"Bend's probably a good place to raise kids. I mean, I know literally nothing about that, but it seems . . . pretty?" Gene guesses.

"It is. And it's only about three hours from here."

A road trip, to be sure, but a lifetime spent on buses packed with twentysomething-year-old men has somewhat numbed Gene to the idea of road trips. What's three hours? Vince is from a small town, Jack from a smaller one. It makes sense for them to move somewhere quieter.

"It's a good house," Gene says. He adds, half-joking, "You pick a bedroom for me? The beige one?"

Vince says, "The beige one is the guest room. Yours is picture twenty-four."

Picture twenty-four shows a room that opens up, via glass-paned French doors, onto a weathered back porch. The light through the windows makes it look sunny. Spacious. Gene says, "Not too shabby."

"We're thinking about putting in an offer," Vince says, eyes firmly on the road ahead of them. "But obviously we wouldn't move until after the season."

Gene always knew the ice packs and physical therapy wouldn't be enough to keep Vince pitching forever. He shouldn't be surprised that he's considering retirement, but The Yellow House and the mention of an offer have made Vince's inevitable departure feel real in a way he can't bring himself to face just yet.

Gene doesn't know what he would have done when people started paying attention to him if Vince hadn't been there to remind him that no one else's opinion mattered. He doesn't *care* to imagine playing without most of his teammates, but he *can't* imagine playing without Vince. A small part of him digs its bitten nails into the idea that they will always play together, but an athlete's career ends when it ends.

If this is his last season with Vince, he sure as shit doesn't want to spend it trying to convince Luis Estrada not to hate him. The sooner they can get Luis traded or called up, the sooner Gene can enjoy this year for what it is: his last chance to help get Vince to the playoffs, to share a team with the guy who made this place feel like home.

# 4

## APRIL

### Current record: 0–11

Luis wears a long-sleeved shirt under his jersey to every game, one with a high neck that covers his Adam's apple and ends just below the perfect, trimmed line of his beard. He also wears a cross, less than an inch long and strung on a thin gold chain, which he keeps on top of the undershirt but tucked under his jersey. A lot of guys who wear crosses kiss them when they step up to home plate, but Gene has never seen Luis do that. His sits between his collarbones, untouched.

He has a small waist, leading into nonexistent hips, leading into impossibly long and curveless legs. The only curve Gene *can* find on him is that one at the small of his back, enough of a dip to fit a hand, if said hand were on the small side. Gene has caught himself thinking about that dip more times than he can count.

The fact that Luis has the audacity to have gotten *hot*—and not even yeah-he's-fine-for-a-straight-guy hot, but *legitimately* hot—in addition to being the world's biggest pain in the ass?

Gene doesn't care for that shit at all.

"You're staring."

Gene slides his eyes over to Vince. "I am not."

"I'm surprised you're not drooling," Vince whispers, though he's never been a great whisperer.

Gene gives an exaggerated wrinkle of his nose. Okay. No more locker room glances, then. They might not have been as glance-like as Gene intended.

"Don't be gross," he says. He finishes doing the buttons of his jersey, all the way up to the top. He tucks it neatly into his knee-length pants, before replacing his glasses with contacts and checking that the piercings that line his ears are firmly in place, none of them begging to be snagged. He is careful, as he does so, to look anywhere but Luis's corner of the locker room. In the final moments before they take the field, he smears eye black on his cheeks, a little unevenly.

Vince watches him the whole time. He won't pitch today, so he has plenty of time to nag at Gene.

"You want to talk about it?" he asks, when the team has started to filter down the dugout tunnel.

"I don't know what you're talking about," Gene says, while he squeezes life into his glove.

"He's nicer to look at than his dad was," Vince muses. "If you're into skinny guys." Luis Estrada, Sr., an international signee out of Mexico, had played his final season during Vince's first, right around when Gene got old enough to start keeping track of players other than his own dad.

Gene chances a look across the locker room. Luis pulls a hat on over his hair, facing away from his teammates and toward the wall. Gene can see his shoulders rise, then fall, as he takes a pace-setting breath and tucks that cross into his jersey.

Luis heads into the dugout tunnel, and Vince digs an elbow into Gene's side. "Hey, do you think he's—"

"I don't think about him," Gene lies. "So I don't know."

The implied question being: *Do you think he's queer?*

Well.

Unclear, but the thought may have crossed Gene's mind. Never long enough to decide on a guess, though. But regardless of what the answer might be, Luis isn't the first teammate Vince has asked this question about. He always means it in the most innocuous, just-curious kind of way and would never ask anyone who isn't Gene. They've both played with other queer men—bi men and gay men and men who don't label it but aren't straight. Most of them don't outright say it, and none of them say it publicly, but it's there, not exactly a secret.

Gene and Vince are open about it, in their own ways—Vince to the team and Gene to literally anyone who asks, and plenty of people who don't. That openness has given Gene one of the closest friends he's ever had.

No amount of closeness, however, would make Gene want to talk to Vince about Luis's potential queerness. A good thing, too, as they make their way out to the Reno visitors' dugout and join the rest of their team. Vince shifts effortlessly into his more team-appropriate demeanor, a subtle change. He replaces nosy questions with slightly dad-like teasing and a handful of sunflower seeds. This Vince is still Vince, just through a different filter.

Gene has never excelled at filtering himself like that, and he stopped trying sometime around his senior year of college, right around when he came out and gave up entirely on being drafted.

Twenty-year-old Gene would be amazed by twenty-six-year-old Gene. That thought is enough to distract him from the small of Luis's back and the cross he doesn't kiss, at least for a little while.

"Okay, odds on us pulling off literally one goddamn win?" Vince asks as he settles onto the bench next to Gene.

"Tonight, or ever?"

Eleven games into the season, they remain wholly unvictorious. Vince doesn't sound as sad about it as Gene would expect. "Either," he says.

Gene pretends to consider. "One hundred percent chance."

"Which one?"

"Both. We're going to win tonight," Gene says.

"You've decided?"

"I've decided, yeah."

Some games, he gets a feeling that something special is on the way. Tonight, the only feeling he has is that they're all overdue for some dumb luck.

"That's not how it works," Luis says as he inches between Gene's knees and the dugout railing to get to the watercooler.

Vince laughs. "Now we're definitely going to."

Luis's eyebrows lower, so Vince explains.

"I swear to God, if Nes says he's decided to do something and someone else says he can't, it happens. Every fucking time." Vince points at the air, emphasizing the words. "*Every* fucking time."

Luis looks at Gene, unconvinced. Gene takes it as a challenge.

Maybe Luis has a Gold Glove and a dash more power in his swing. Gene makes contact more; he's faster, better at stealing. Most important, Gene has an optimistic streak where Luis has instead cultivated an unimpressed, unenthused mien. Gene is bolder, more bullheaded, in the way that befits a baseball player.

Maybe everything feels like a competition, maybe Gene can't stop thinking about him, and maybe that has frayed Gene's fragile focus down to a single, tenuous thread. But he will drag this team into the win column all the same.

---

NANCY: How long of a leash do you think Steph Baker plans to give Estrada before we see Ionescu get a start at shortstop?

DAN: I think this is the lineup we'll be seeing for a while. Ionescu hasn't looked much better at second, I can't imagine that switching them makes for a particularly tempting alternative right now. Estrada's Gold Glove is bound to show up one of these days.

NANCY: I hope you're right.

DAN: We've got Ionescu leading us off again today—

NANCY: He's shortened up his swing pretty considerably since last fall. He's not a power hitter by any means, but he looks more solid this year. He takes strike one, a heater down the middle at ninety-eight.

DAN: Now, you say Ionescu's not a power hitter—

NANCY: Listen, I think we'd all love for him to turn into the sort of guy who hits fifteen homers a year, but—

DAN: Fifteen! Sure, who'd say no to that?

NANCY: —*but* I don't think that's going to happen. Five or ten, however, isn't out of the realm of possibility.

DAN: Caught a piece of that one. Fouls it off down the line.

NANCY: Missed his timing a bit on that, but not by much.

DAN: Down to the last strike. Ionescu's batting .355 out of the leadoff spot so far this season.

NANCY: Right, a lot of growing pains at second, but he's off to a hot start offensively. He's also leading the league in walks and stolen bases. Certainly making up for that lack of power with a great eye at the plate. He takes the third pitch for ball one.

DAN: It's not a surprise Steph Baker isn't giving Ionescu a day off—not much production coming from the rest of this lineup outside the first two batters.

NANCY: Agreed, Gonzales has more or less lived up to his reputation, though he's had a bit of a strikeout problem himself—

DAN: *Ionescu barrels it up—right into the gap—*

NANCY: They'll hold him at first, and it's a leadoff single for Gene Ionescu.

DAN: Good at-bat from the kid.

---

"What did I *say*?" Vince yells while the team thunders into the clubhouse after the game. He carries Gene in a celebratory piggyback ride. "Twelve to three? That's not a win, that's a *slaughter.*"

It wasn't just Gene, either. Ernie hit his first home run of the season, a towering, undoubted bomb of a hit. Their starter kept them in the game through six efficient innings. Even Luis managed to make it to base twice, which in and of itself was something of a miracle—something Luis should but won't celebrate, because he seems incapable of celebration, opting instead to quietly pack his bag as the rest of the team devolves into cheers.

It was a lazy mid-April matchup, but when Baker tells them to grab drinks before their early-morning flight, they listen.

Because he and Luis used to play for Reno, Ernie picks the bar, and they pile into a few overcrowded cars. It is a sign of his inimitable lovability that, when he shows up in a new team's gear, having thoroughly trounced his old club, the bartender still cheers when Ernie leads Beaverton into the dive bar.

That doesn't surprise Gene. What surprises Gene is that, when the last car empties, Luis gets out of it, hands shoved deep into the pockets of a bomber jacket and his dog's leash looped around his wrist.

"What the hell is he doing here?" Gene asks Vince.

"The dog or the man?"

Gene stares at Vince.

"I think you'll find he plays for our team," Vince says with a levity that Gene does not appreciate. Then Vince tips his head back and yells, "First round's on me, boys," and it's hard to be all that upset.

Gene didn't party much in college, but years in the minors and an undying need to be liked have taught him all of the go-to drinking games, and how to participate without getting completely trashed. The trick: if you win, it's a slower descent into drunkenness, and you can tap out as soon as you get tired, bragging rights firmly established.

That's the plan for tonight.

"Nes, you're my partner," Vince announces as they set up for beer pong.

Gene has served as Vince's drinking-game first mate since the first time he ever went out with the team, selected out of kindness that first night and out of competitiveness each time after. He has the gentle wrist flick and the ball's perfect rainbow arc down to a science. When he takes his rightful place at Vince's side, he gives a lazy salute to the captain.

"Gonzo, you picked the bar. Get a partner, you're up first," Vince says.

"Nada," Ernie says. "Will you do me the honors?"

"Bold choice, going without a pitcher," Vince taunts.

"Nada has a more accurate arm than any pitcher I have ever caught," Ernie argues.

Gene resists the urge to roll his eyes. Luis fucked up a routine throw literally last night.

Luis, sitting on one of the stools at the bar, shakes his head. "I'm good," he says.

The team's complaints come immediately, a chorus of "*Ah, c'mon.*" Gene joins in without hesitation. The chance to beat Luis at this meaningless game is far too tempting to resist.

When Luis drags himself to stand next to Ernie, Vince leans in close to Gene and, loud enough for everyone to hear, says, "They don't have a chance."

Just as Gene has an uncanny ability to predict a baseball win as it storms into the stadium, Vince has yet to call a drinking game wrong, perhaps because Gene has never seen him lose.

"Y'all can start us off," Vince offers. "Newbies first."

Ernie nudges Luis's side with an elbow and flicks his eyebrows up—*Go ahead*, those eyebrows say.

Luis sinks his first shot into the top cup of Gene and Vince's pyramid with ease. He doesn't even have the goodwill to play it off as beginner's luck. He simply stares Gene down as Gene lifts the cup and, to the cheers of his team around him, downs it in two solid gulps. When he sets the cup back down, Luis is still staring.

Gene means to throw him a wink, just to be a shit, but he's sidetracked by Vince's own perfect opening shot, so exact that the beer in the receiving cup barely moves. If Gene stares when Luis drinks, well, Luis stared first.

He and Vince do win, though not as handily as they usually would.

"Good game," Luis says, the praise as perfunctory as possible.

"Don't take it too hard, man. You put up a way better fight than your dad did back in the day," Vince says.

It's an offhand remark, said in passing before Vince starts calling for their next challengers. But Luis's face shutters, and he ducks into the crowd as soon as the attention shifts away from him. Gene, usually good for at least three rounds and the equivalent one-point-five beers it would amount to, taps out, too.

"Seriously?" Vince asks.

And because Gene can't say, *Yes, if I catch Luis Estrada staring at me like that again, I'm going to combust. Also, can you sue someone for being that annoying and that hot? Asking for a friend,* he says, "I gotta piss."

Vince shrugs and ropes one of their relievers into taking Gene's spot.

In the interest of maintaining appearances, and because he really does need to use the bathroom, Gene scoots down the narrow back hall, praying for a single-stall situation. He's not in the mood for a drunk man with bad aim trying to suss out his whole deal while also trying to locate the urinal. Gene never hates being trans, but the cramped, under-cleaned stalls of a men's bathroom put that fact to the test every time.

Still, when he emerges—single stall; Gene must have some good karma today—and finds Luis standing against the wall, hands shoved in his pockets, he would actually rather go back into that bathroom than face the awkward shuffle of trying to get past Luis in a hallway this minuscule. Never mind about that good karma.

"Sorry," Luis says, nearly squeezing himself into two dimensions to get around Gene. The saving grace of his, well, *everything* is that nobody seems less happy when Luis walks into a room than Luis himself. That's one thing he and Gene can get on the same page about.

Out of curiosity, albeit of the masochistic sort, Gene waits around while Luis uses the bathroom, scratching absently at Luis's dog's ears until Luis reemerges and startles at Gene's presence.

"Question," Gene says, while Luis picks up his dog's leash.

"Oh," Luis answers. "No thank you."

Before Gene can react to that answer, Luis beelines toward one of the sunken couches in the back corner. Gene follows.

"Do you still not drink?" he asks. Luis never did in college, instead seeming to avoid anything that might risk revealing his humanity. No drinking, no smoking, no staying up past two in the morning and spilling a secret or two. For all those hours they spent together on roadie buses or crammed onto dugout benches or hanging out in teammates' dorm rooms, Gene knows so few secrets about Luis.

"I said no thank you," Luis says. As soon as he sits, his dog lies across his feet.

"Yeah, but that wasn't what I was going to ask earlier. This is a *different* question."

He'd wanted to ask if it bugs Luis to get compared to his dad so often, but drinking is a safer topic anyway.

Luis's mouth flattens. Gene had thought it quite flat before, but this takes its flatness to new non-heights. "That is a loophole at best."

"Yes."

"I drink sometimes. Usually not lukewarm beer from a pitcher, but mostly I just don't like"—Luis twirls his finger in the air—"big groups. Or parties. Or . . . loud places."

It's the most words Gene has heard Luis string together all in one go since he got traded. He speaks with the same stilted lilt he used to, if a little more pronounced now—not an accent but a peculiar pattern of pauses, like he thinks everything through before saying it. It's not altogether charmless.

"Okay," Gene says. "So you hate parties and groups and loud

sounds, and you still picked a career that involves playing a game—"

"I'm aware of the irony—"

"—in a big group, in a loud stadium, literally every day."

Luis raises his eyebrows. Sunken into the cushions, even without one of his larger teammates nearby, he looks . . . small. "I am regretting that choice," he says, and Gene almost wants to laugh. Part of the appeal might be that it's at Luis's expense. Still, though, the barest hint of a sense of humor exists in Luis's voice. So faint it's like someone's cologne sticking around in an elevator when they themselves disembarked three floors ago, but it smells so nice that you wish they'd stuck around so you could ask the name of both the cologne and its owner.

Gene does not laugh. Instead, he reasons, "You didn't have to come tonight, you know."

"Gonzo asked me to. Have you ever tried to say no to Gonzo?" Luis sounds like someone who has known Ernie for years and has long since given up on disagreeing with the man.

"I have not," Gene admits. "But I think if you stick around for, like, ten more minutes, you've officially met the bare minimum of polite teammate duty."

"Thanks. I'll start a timer."

"For real?" Gene asks.

For real, indeed. Luis sets a timer. He opens his mouth to say something else, but before he can, Vince's voice interrupts from across the room.

"Nes, get over here. We have challengers," it says, buoyant.

Luis's mouth snaps closed.

"Sorry," Gene says. He's not sure what he's apologizing for. It can't be for leaving Luis's side, because Gene gets the distinct impression that Luis prefers his side to be vacant.

"I'm leaving in"—Luis checks—"nine minutes and thirty-eight seconds, anyway."

"Pro-tip? Don't tell Altzy you're dipping, or he'll convince you to stay another hour."

"Got it."

When Gene takes his usual spot next to Vince, he almost turns to check if Luis is watching him from the corner couches.

But sometime in the fifteen or so minutes Gene spent away from the table, Vince has tripped toward tipsy. It sharpens his beer pong skills but mildly hinders his ability to stand up straight. Gene acts as something of a buttress, his shoulder jammed halfway into Vince's armpit to keep him steady. He has done this for Vince plenty of times, but never this early in the night. He makes a mental note to ask him if he's doing okay when they get back to the hotel room they always share on road trips.

In the meantime, they kick Kyle Rivera's and Cooper's asses in a perfect six throws, made all the more impressive by both Gene and Vince using their respective glove hands.

When Ernie asks to tap back in, he trades Gene's ping-pong balls for a deep brown, chilled bottle. A peek at its label tells Gene that it's not beer but cider.

"You didn't have to bribe me. I wanted a break," Gene says.

Ernie shakes his head. "No, this is from Nada. He told me to give it to you when he left."

Gene can't help it. He looks at the door like he might catch Luis on his way out. He stares at it, as if the worn-down wood grain will tell Gene why *this* guy, *this* teammate makes him feel like his stomach is falling out his ass.

He sits on a stool, holding the drink Luis bought him, and reminds himself why he can't trust that moment of ease between them.

Luis's team-worst batting average could be excused, but not the fact that he has done seemingly nothing to improve upon it. Every time he steps into the dugout after he strikes out, his bone-deep, palpable displeasure makes the team wilt. He distracts

Gene from enjoying what could be his last five months playing with his best friend.

More than any of that, two minutes of half-pleasant conversation can't negate Luis's sudden departure from Gene's life all those years ago, or how inconvenient it is to have him here again; it can't make Gene forget how it felt when Luis shrank away from him on that bench, how he'd brushed off the very idea of Gene playing shortstop like it had never been a real possibility. His dismissal and discomfort have snagged at Gene's equilibrium and left a quiet resentment where any new trust might have been able to grow.

It doesn't matter if he signs baseballs for kids before games. It doesn't matter if he still has some semblance of a sense of humor hiding somewhere in there. It doesn't matter—because Luis is going to leave again, and this time, Gene is determined, his life will be better for it.

Gene sets the cider on the bar, untouched, and joins the crowd of Beaverton Beavers at the beer pong table, cheering on both teams at once.

# 5

## APRIL

**Current record: 3–15**

**@JenWertherPDX:** As April draws to a close, @BeavertonBeavs shortstop Luis Estrada leads the Pacific Coast League in fielding errors and all of Triple-A in strikeouts. Expect an off day soon for the former top prospect.

---

They lose their first game against the Rainiers, their quasi-rivals by proximity-based default, unsurprising but still deflating. Luis—who spent the four hours on the roadie bus from Portland to Tacoma with headphones on and his dog stretched out on the seat next to him—is similarly silent on the way back to their hotel.

When they arrive, Gene and Vince stick around outside so Vince can have his solitary daily cigarette he very decidedly is not supposed to smoke, and which Jack very decidedly has asked him not to smoke, and which Vince still very decidedly smokes every day.

Baker sticks her head out the automatic front door and, without really looking at them, yells, "Ionescu, get your ass over here."

Gene gives Vince a grimace. *How do you think she's going to kill me?* that grimace says.

Baker is reading something on her phone when Gene joins her inside the hotel lobby. In moments like these, facing down a growing string of mediocre games made infinitely worse by his and Luis's clumsy teamwork, even Gene's optimism gives way to anxiety. A tiny sliver of stubborn pessimism, sharp in his chest, insistent that he's getting sent back down to Double-A or cut entirely, unlikely as that may be.

He stands in front of Baker, amidst the rancid vibes emanating from her general vicinity. She does not like to lose. No one does, but she has made both a career and a personality out of this fact. Her lead-blowing, rubber-bat-toting, limp-gloved team lands, therefore, pretty damn high on her shit list at the moment.

"Hey," Gene ventures, in case she's waiting on him to cross the uncomfortable silence.

But she holds up a long finger and continues to read. She has almost a foot of height on Gene, and he feels every inch of it in that annoyed finger.

"I'm reading," is all she says.

"Got it." *Then why did you call me over?* Gene wants to say, but could not be paid enough to *actually* say.

"Bit of a change of plans," she says. She finally locks her phone and meets Gene's eye, giving him the hard look she gets whenever she has to deliver bad news. Like she's trying to silently remind him that it isn't her job to coddle.

This is it. Okay.

Gene holds his breath, and she says, "You're rooming with Estrada tonight."

He exhales, immediate relief at not getting sent down. Then, when the realization hits him, it's a panicked hand around his throat, not quite firm enough to stop his protest from escaping.

"You can't be serious," Gene says.

She holds a room key aloft. "I'm not in the mood to hear any complaints today. You two need to figure your shit out on your own time. I'm not watching my infielders fumble Little League–level grounders anymore."

Gene is stubborn, but not nearly stubborn enough to put up a fight against Baker. He has yet to meet someone who can. Still, the prospect of sharing a room with Luis—sharing a room with Luis after *that* game—is so completely unappealing-slash-intolerable that Gene drops his bags in said shared room, makes only the briefest of eye contact with Luis, then turns and marches across the hall to Vince's. His bags can stay with Luis. *He* will stay far away.

Is it mature? No.

Does he feel a bit bad? Yes.

But Luis hasn't spoken to him once since that night at the bar, and Gene can't believe he briefly entertained the idea of Luis sucking even a tiny amount less than Gene originally thought. He *still* avoids working out when Gene does, *still* intrudes on Gene's wedge of the infield while neglecting his own, *still* refuses to let his leg so much as drift into the general vicinity of Gene's on the bench. Whenever Gene gets onto the bus or walks into the locker room after Luis, Luis keeps his eyes firmly affixed to the ground.

So no. Gene's opinion has not much improved, and the idea of lying in a double bed three feet away from Luis's double bed—he can't. Not today.

"First he won't swing at meatballs," Gene says to Vince, jabbing his finger into the open palm of his opposite hand to emphasize each point he makes, "and *now* he's chasing way out of the zone. He should still be batting ninth, not sixth."

"Theoretically, I agree with you, but it's not like we have a ton of great hitters to replace him with. You need to cut him some slack," Vince says, sprawled out on his bed and scrolling through his phone as he pays attention to only every other word Gene says.

"The best thing he did today was get hit by a pitch," Gene says, because no one is listening anyway.

Except the door beeps as the words come out of Gene's mouth, announcing the arrival of Vince's new roommate. Ernie stands in the doorway, eyebrows raised.

This is the kind of conversation Gene would prefer not to have in front of any teammate who isn't Vince, so he snaps his mouth closed with a decisive, slightly painful *click*. He doesn't need teammates to know that, sometimes, he does have kind of a shit attitude.

The version of himself that he brings to the stadium is the purposeful, manicured one who sees every game as a potential win. That version of Gene isn't a lie. But, also, fuck, sometimes he needs to complain for a few minutes.

"Sorry," Gene says. "Long day."

Ernie shrugs, dropping a very nice duffel onto the room's desk. "No worries, I get it."

Gene cannot imagine Ernie, of all people, having a bad enough day that he would be happy a teammate got beaned by a pitch. To be fair, though, Ernie would probably have said the same of him until ten seconds ago.

"He isn't a bad guy once you get to know him," Ernie says. "He bugged me when I first met him, too."

Gene considers a retort—something along the lines of, *Yeah, just don't get too attached to him*, maybe—but he settles for, "I'll take your word for it. How's the wrist?"

Ernie holds his hand aloft. He took a ball to the wrist last week and has landed on the injured list. "Doing okay," he says.

"Feeling any better?"

"Not much, but don't tell the trainers I said so."

With that, Ernie flops onto the empty bed.

Even the most cursory of glances around the room tells Gene that he has become the odd man out here. He has never stayed with someone other than Vince while playing for Beaverton, but there is literally no room at the inn.

"Okay," he says, willing someone to offer to let him sleep in the armchair. "I better head out."

Vince tosses his phone to the side and raises an eyebrow at Gene. "Text if you need anything?" he asks.

"Yeah," Gene says, though, like—what would he say: *Nothing to report, I'm just not mature enough to sleep this close to my literal teammate?* No. "See you guys tomorrow."

Rather than heading straight to his room, he takes the stairs of the Holiday Inn Express two at a time on his way to the front desk. Carpeted, patterned grooves worn into the fibers by years of tired feet. At least they're less air-freshened than the elevator.

The same sullen woman who checked the team in—who is, somehow, always the poor sucker in the lobby when the team comes to Tacoma—stands behind the desk. She looks unimpressed when Gene asks if they have any Sour Patch Kids in the sundry.

"You can take them," she says. "I'm not counting the till again."

When he comes back up the stairs, perhaps still filled with dread but strengthened by the free, stale pack of candy, Gene sends up a silent prayer that Luis will already be asleep with his big, obnoxious headphones on. Amen.

He dips the key card in.

A quick scan of the room informs him that Luis is not, in point of painful fact, in bed. Beyond the weak light of a single nightstand lamp, the room is dark, the sheets untouched save for Luis's duffel on top of the comforter. The bathroom light is off, too, the door almost closed. Gene wants to believe that, by some miracle, he has timed his appearance for the exact moment Luis needed to use the bathroom. He wants to crawl into bed and pretend to fall asleep before he needs to interact with Luis, then get up so early the next morning that he'll have left before his roommate has even woken up.

But—he hears an almost-sound sneaking out from under the bathroom door. It's the near absence of noise. The too-obvious held breath of it all, followed by the inevitable exhale trying to keep itself quiet.

That exhale shakes. Gene knows that exhale. He knows its shake. Gene knocks on the door's motel-quality wooden face, and, when no answer comes, he pushes the crack wide enough to slip through.

The bathroom lights are off, leaving the room dim and heavily shadowed, the lamp in the main room filtering in just enough light for Gene to see. Luis sits in the bathtub, fully clothed except for his long and bare and hair-dusted feet; his hair sticks to his temples, his forehead pressed against his knees. His dog lies curled on his feet, looking up at Gene but not moving from his station.

The room smells distinctly of sweat—the anxious, claustrophobic kind that sours faster than any other. Luis doesn't react when Gene walks in, so Gene closes the toilet lid and sits, crossing his legs.

Luis's phone lies on the lip of the tub, open to Twitter. The most recent tweet is from a familiar, chronically online Lumberjacks fan, with a link to a recent *Oregonian* article, captioned:

**@Lumberjax_Brandon71**: Shit, Luis Estrada is the best prospect we have? Lumberjacks really are screwed, huh?

The link displays a picture of Luis fumbling the ball at second, his eyes squinted shut as if he's scared of the thing. Gene is just out of frame, yelling at Luis the exact same way the camera does. In the moment, he was *furious* that Luis hadn't trusted him to make the play, but looking at it in picture form, Gene can see it on Luis's face: he is floundering, and he is *miserable*.

It probably doesn't help to have a teammate shouting at him from two feet away, seconds from colliding with him. Guilt settles in Gene's chest, all that blame he's been aiming at Luis suddenly turned back in on himself, much harsher than he realized. Maybe that's why Ernie was so unsurprised to walk in on Gene's ire earlier. Maybe Gene hasn't been hiding his shit attitude nearly as well as he wanted to believe.

To crush a teammate under the same bad-faith anger strangers have turned against him more times than he can count—Gene is ashamed to have let that hypercritical version of himself out, to have let it win for weeks.

But then there's the tweet in the center of Luis's screen, above a cut-off picture of Gene and Baker in the dugout:

**@JacksFan1989**: Wow, Luis Estrada sucks even on the girls' team.

As soon as he's read the words, Gene locks Luis's phone. He goes to get up, give Luis some space, sit on one of the hotel beds until he's sure that Luis won't spend the whole night curled up in a bathtub.

"I don't think you're a woman," Luis says into his knees, roused by the click of his phone locking. His voice, for the first time since the season started, has real emotion in it—because he's crying, and Gene has to admit that he likes that Luis doesn't try to hide it. "I'm sorry people write that shit."

Gene sits back down.

"I know," he says. He hadn't known, not for sure. There were worries—but now that he's said it, Gene trusts that it's the truth. "You're not the one who wrote it."

"Not that you couldn't play if you were. But—I don't want you to think I've been sucking because I'm transphobic or something."

"Okay."

"I just suck because I suck."

Gene, hypocrite extraordinaire, says, "It would probably help if you stopped searching your name on Twitter."

He might see a smile at the very edge of Luis's lips. To his horror, Luis's dimple is still visible underneath his beard. Gene would love to pretend he's never considered the life-ruining qualities of that dimple, but, well.

This is much worse than the crying.

"People are really fucking mean to you on there," Luis says.

"Well, yeah. I'm a trans person on the internet." He takes out his own phone, scrolls for an album he hasn't played in years.

Out of the corner of his eye, he sees Luis extricate his head from between his knees to say in the direction of the shower tile, "I'm still sorry."

Gene shrugs. "Don't be. They're not too keen on you, either."

He clicks on the song he was looking for. He can't tell, exactly, whether Luis wants him to stay, but he has no idea what the right thing to say is here. Gene has anxiety—which this bathtub breakdown and a season's worth of observation would imply that Luis has some form of, too—but everyone reacts differently. Some people need to be held, some people need to be talked through it. Some people need a dark room, no sounds, a meditation podcast. Maybe that's what Luis is always listening to on those big headphones.

But he doesn't know what Luis needs, so he settles for teasing. Tried and true.

"I hope you still like Kermit," he says, setting the phone on the lip of the tub. "Rainbow Connection" strums its banjo introduction out, the volume as low as Gene can get it.

Luis glances over at him. Gene notes that Luis's grip on his elbows has darkened from white-knuckled to a few shades closer to his usual brown. Progress.

"Oh, fuck you," Luis says, and Gene can't help but crack a smile about it.

"So you *do* still like Kermit?"

Luis sighs the kind of put-upon sigh, a little huff of annoyance, that betrays that he does find Gene at least mildly amusing. "I do not have a crush on a Muppet."

Gene doesn't smile a secret little smile. "Sure," he says. "Totally. It's just that, that's exactly what a person who has a crush on a Muppet would say." Even if he thinks about how, seven years ago, he would have appended a teasing "*Nada*" to that, he doesn't say it.

When the conversation fizzles and Luis's breathing steadies, just a little, Gene fishes in the pocket of his sweatshirt for his Sour Patch Kids and rips the bag open. He lays three layers of tissues on the lip of the tub. One by one, he picks out each of the greens.

"You still do that?" Luis asks.

"I hate them."

"So why do you buy them?"

"I like the other flavors," Gene says, setting another green atop the sugar pile.

Luis squints at him.

Gene shrugs. "It's like the mean tweets. If you want to play, those sort of come with the territory. Sometimes there's shit parts of things you love."

"So it's a metaphor?" He sounds unconvinced.

"No, I just hate the green Sour Patch Kids. *You* wanted a deeper reason."

In the conversational lull that follows, Gene gets his first good look at what a mess Luis is. The bags under his eyes can't have come from one good crying session—they have a depth, a permanence that betrays bone-deep exhaustion. His normally perfect hair has broken loose from its pomade, curling at his temples, a messiness that signals the sheer effort he puts in to get it to look as good as it usually does. At the pulled-loose neck of his T-shirt, there are hints of nail marks, pink-brown, like he has itched the skin of his collarbone raw.

"So," Gene attempts.

Luis's eyes slide closed. "I don't want to talk about it."

"Okay."

"You don't have to stay."

"Okay."

"Can I eat your greens?"

"Okay."

"You know other words. I just heard you use other words," Luis says.

Gene gathers the green Sour Patch Kids like a bundle of bread and cheese in a fantasy movie, the tissue gathered at the top to create a small pouch. When Luis holds his hand open, Gene dumps the tissue out, the little lime monsters shedding a film of sugar coating onto his palm. The dog immediately perks up, resting his nose on Luis's bent knees.

"Thanks," Luis says.

And they sit, the only sound the crinkling of Gene's candy bag, the occasional bite taken, and a dog's eager sniffing. It's too quiet, too easy to think.

The thing is, Gene can guess why Luis was hyperventilating in the bathtub. Gene has done it himself; he will do it again. It's a lot of pressure, doing something people don't want someone who looks like you to do.

Maybe Luis isn't trans, but he's shorter than your average player, with a significantly less imposing frame. More to the point, he's Mexican, with deep brown skin and a distinctly Spanish name—neither of which are *uncommon* in baseball, but shitty people are always going to have shitty opinions about someone who looks like Luis playing America's sport. They're always going to judge him faster and harsher than they would if he were white, if he were built like someone who could hit forty homers a year.

Their situations are different, their lives marked by their identities in decidedly different ways. Gene knows this. But he can understand, at least to some extent, how lonely it can be sometimes to look different—to *be* different—from the person you'd expect to find on a baseball card.

"Do you think they're gonna trade me again?" Luis asks.

"Don't take this the wrong way? It wouldn't be worth it."

That gets a wet little laugh from Luis.

"Also, you aren't our best prospect. That'd be Gonzo," Gene adds. "Maybe it'd help if we could, like . . . make one routine play. This is a novel idea, but we could try to catch the ball."

Luis clicks his tongue. "That's the dream," he says.

A plan begins to unfurl itself in Gene's mind. Something tempting. Something that, if it worked, would mean a lot more of Luis for a while, and then absolutely none at all. Something that might prevent Luis from looking this tired, from having panic attacks after games.

It would be best if he could avoid Luis entirely. But he's here, on this team, playing Gene's position and tanking the team's playoff dreams. The best option would have involved Luis playing in a different team's system, their never sharing a locker room again—but the next best thing is to get him called up as soon as possible. Which would mean Luis needs to start playing a lot better, and soon.

"Here's a thought," Gene says.

"I could quit," Luis suggests. There is an unexpected, unjoking tone to the suggestion.

"No."

"We could both quit?"

Gene is taken aback by the speed with which Luis fires back at him. "I don't want to quit," he says.

"Everyone wants to quit sometimes."

"I don't," Gene says, and he means it. He wonders, distantly, whether Luis's comment was genuine, too.

"What's your thought?" Luis asks.

"We should start our extra practices again."

Luis considers. Maybe. Or he's looking at the grout mold, Gene can't tell. "Why?"

"Because if you're going to make it to the majors, you have to stop sucking so bad."

Luis lets out a bubbling, self-deprecating "*Ha!*" "And what do you get out of it?"

"I want to get Beaverton to the playoffs." A half-truth.

"Not Portland?"

"I don't play for Portland."

Of course, there is the possibility Luis will say no. That he and Gene will keep on doing exactly what they have been for the past three weeks, until one or both of them gets traded, sent down, or released from their contracts.

But Gene knows, as certain as a person can be, that Luis will say yes.

"Okay," Luis says.

"Fucking—'*okay*,'" Gene says, pitching his voice down to imitate Luis's. "I thought we weren't allowed to say 'okay' anymore."

"That is not what I sound like," Luis argues.

"Listen, testosterone did his best, but my voice is what it is. I'm working at a deficit here."

Luis smiles—the crooked, laugh-laced one he never offers in photos. It's dangerous, that smile.

"Tomorrow?" Gene offers.

Luis sticks his hand out to shake. His wrists are strong but surprisingly delicate-looking for someone who makes the routine throws Luis makes. Gene can, to his horror, imagine running a thumb across the hard ridge of that wristbone.

It might be the worst idea Gene has ever had, but he shakes Luis's hand anyway.

# 6

## APRIL

### Current record: 3–16

The next morning, on his way out of the hotel, Gene runs into Vince, standing exactly where they had yesterday and smoking what Gene has started to suspect is a more-than-once-daily cigarette.

"You're up early," Gene observes.

"Gonzo snores."

"So do you," Gene says, which gets him a dismissive flick of Vince's wrist.

"Where are you going?" Vince asks.

"Uh," Gene says. "Practicing with Luis, actually."

Vince's eyebrows, sleepy as they and he may be, shoot toward his hairline. "Seriously?"

"Yeah."

"Well, then I'll see you later if you haven't killed each other," he says.

"I'll do my best."

"To kill him or not to?"

Gene shrugs. Mostly, he's going to try not to have any thoughts, feelings, or opinions about Luis this morning. He's going to get through the next two hours of his life, and hopefully the team will have a better infield in return for their efforts.

"Let me know how it goes?" Vince asks.

"Definitely."

Vince gives him a two-fingered salute with the hand holding his cigarette.

Gene sets off across the parking lot in the direction of the bus stop. Pretending it's an afterthought, he yells over his shoulder, "I'm gonna tell Jack I saw you smoking."

"You wouldn't dare," Vince says, but he puts the cigarette out in the standing ashtray, and that's all Gene really wanted in the first place.

When Gene gets to the stadium—on time for the agreed-upon 9:30, to avoid running into any Tacoma players—Luis is already in the dugout, one leg up, ankle rested on opposite knee, his jersey swapped out for a T-shirt, too tight on arm muscles Gene would prefer not to notice. When did Luis get so goddamn noticeable?

He'd left by the time Gene's alarm went off, but Gene assumed he'd gone to breakfast. Instead, he appears to have taken the time for a shampoo, condition, and pomade just to sit there and look sour. Gene feels like a frizzed-up mess in comparison.

Luis's baseball cap rests on the bench next to his hip. Add in the dog curled at his feet, and Luis looks like an all-American boy, but actually attractive. If you ignore, like, 85 percent of his personality and the pinched way he holds his mouth.

Gene drops his bag in the dirt in front of the dugout, his bat clattering against the ground. "Sorry, didn't realize I was late."

"No problem," Luis says. He sounds annoyed.

Struggle as he might with punctuality, Gene was careful to be on time today—and, in fact, was only apologizing so Luis could apologize in turn, for being so obnoxiously early. "You didn't have to wait for me to get started," he says.

"I said it's not a problem."

Gene can't keep the frustration out of his voice. "It sounds like it's a problem."

"It's not." Luis slaps the loop of his dog's leash against his open palm—impatient or nervous, Gene can't tell.

They used to do this in college. After Gene managed to squeeze his way onto the roster and into the starting second baseman job, Luis, a junior to Gene's freshman, helped him. He stayed late, or came early—taught Gene how to predict the way the ball would bounce in the grass, and never much excelled at small talk. In an effort to alleviate Luis's foremost deficiency, Gene gets them started. "What's your dog's name?" he asks.

"Dodger," Luis answers.

Gene can't help but laugh. It's the most Angeleno thing he's ever heard.

"What's funny?" Luis asks.

"Sorry." Gene schools his face. "I just didn't realize we were allowed to bring pets on roadies. How old is he?"

Luis visibly bristles, any vestige of patience or interest in this conversation sapped in an instant. "Look, can we just get started?"

Gene—worried that he's offended Luis, mad at himself for his nosiness, and annoyed that Luis has the gall to be frustrated by such an innocuous question—pushes his jaw forward before he says, "Fine."

"He's two."

"I said it's fine."

"But you asked."

Gene takes a breath, one far huffier than necessary. "I was trying to be polite."

"So I answered your question," Luis says, his voice rising.

"Yeah. Thanks."

"Look, I don't know what you want from me. You asked a question. I answered it."

Gene pulls a hand down his face and does his level best not to let out the screech building in the back of his throat. He has never had this hard of a time talking to a teammate, and it isn't even because Luis is Luis, or because Gene has, inconveniently, finally realized that he's beautiful.

It's because he's impossible.

"Thanks," Gene eventually manages. "He's very cute."

"Thanks."

"Great."

"Great."

A pause, Dodger's panting loud and almost comical in between them.

"Let's just practice?" Gene asks, finally.

"Fine."

"*Great.*"

And so they do.

Luis does his stretches with the kind of focus most players save for the game itself. He sits on the field gingerly, like the idea of grass stains offends him, legs straight ahead and body folded precisely in two. He places his long fingers in the gap between his cleats' spikes, and, briefly, he looks almost at ease. The illusion falters every time he shifts into a new stretch and pairs it with the world's deepest sigh, each of which elicits from Gene a fresh eye roll.

Gene considers asking him how far, exactly, the stick up his ass is wedged, and if maybe the case is terminal. But instead, he does his own stretches a few arm's lengths from Luis, a little more dedicated than he usually is about getting limber.

Luis looks out of place in Tacoma's stadium. He has looked out of place in every stadium Gene has seen him in this season.

Even if it weren't for his flirtation with a major league tenure three years ago, even if it weren't for his once-superstar dad, even if it weren't for his (alleged) preternatural ability to predict the ball's path as it smokes its way over the infield dirt, Luis looks wrong on a minor league field. In spite of his recent struggles, Luis is still promising, polished, *pretty*. Too good to belong somewhere so small.

Tacoma's field gets mowed more often than Beaverton's, and their seats are more recently replaced. The stunning view of Mount Rainier on the horizon, beyond the farthest reaches of right field, gives the whole place an air of importance, but even this stadium, like Beaverton's, seats a fraction as many as a major league one.

Luis looks too good for all of it, the luster of his prospect status untarnished by his performance the past couple weeks. It makes Gene self-conscious. Like Gene should feel bad about the home he worked so hard to find.

He hates that. Years of fine-tuning his confidence, wrecked by a few weeks with Luis Estrada.

But they do their warm-ups, and with Luis next to him, it's easier for Gene to talk himself into one more set of push-ups; it's easier to run—*really* run—when Luis does the same, pushing himself a step ahead of Gene, then falling behind, a repeating cycle that they maintain until they finish their laps. For the rest of their time, they hit lazy grounders at each other, so easy they really *could* have handled them in Little League, and Gene can almost tell himself it's simple.

It's a far cry from fielding together, from turning routine double plays as well as they need to, from trusting each other to be solid enough at bat to sneak in a stolen base. They'll have to work back up to that. Still, by the time they finish, Gene almost doesn't regret coming. He feels readier for the game than he does when he practices alone, and that's not nothing.

Luis drops onto the dugout bench, arms held out for Dodger to jump into. "What's the verdict?" he asks.

"What do you mean?"

Luis looks up at him, the bottom of his face pressed against Dodger's fur. "You think this will solve our problem?"

Gene shrugs. "Maybe? You looked decent out there."

Luis raises his eyebrows.

"Like—baseball-wise," Gene clarifies, which makes Luis tilt his head, which makes Gene wish he'd said nothing at all, at any point, ever.

"I assumed that's what you meant. You just usually don't compliment me."

"Do something worth complimenting, and maybe I'd do it more often," Gene says. It comes out flirtier than he intended. He should keep his mouth closed, and also probably run as far away as his post-workout legs can carry him.

"Are we doing this again?" Luis asks.

Instead of saying, *No, actually, I plan to avoid all further opportunities to make an ass of myself in front of you,* Gene says, "Sunday?"

"I can't do Sunday mornings. Tomorrow?"

"Sounds good."

It does not sound good. It sounds like another night Gene will spend awake, another morning he will spend uncomfortable and trying too hard. But, until Luis gets called up to the majors and Gene gets his position back, he will show up. Because—and this really is what Gene tells himself—the faster they stop needing these practices, the faster Luis leaves. The faster Luis leaves, the less Gene has to think about the tug of his perfect back muscles on his too-tight shirts, about how his beard might feel to the touch, about his voice and the terrible urge it gives Gene to try and make Luis keep talking.

---

NANCY: We're here in the bottom of the sixth at Cheney Stadium, the game is tied, Tacoma and Beaverton with two runs apiece.

DAN: Estrada grounded into a double play to end the top of the inning—what do you think about what we're seeing from him? It doesn't seem like he's heating up at the plate at all.

NANCY: Right, it's interesting to see him hitting middle of the order—he's oh-for-five in this series so far. Beaverton's certainly missing the pop from Gonzales while he's been out.

DAN: Still looking at a week or so there before he's ready to come back. Steph Baker is not getting much to work with.

NANCY: I think it's safe to say this team is a far cry from the one most of us were hoping for.

DAN: Well, you've got your catcher out and his replacement is a little on the young side—

NANCY: Right, a twenty-year-old is going to struggle to set the tone, get his pitchers in line. And then with the keystone falling apart, it's not a pretty picture out there—

DAN: —And that's another missed cue between Ionescu and Estrada on what could have been a clutch double play.

---

After they give up their second game, a surprisingly close one, to the Rainiers, Gene drops his shit on the floor of his and Luis's room and flops facedown onto his bed.

"Are you going to bed?" Luis asks.

"I'm lying down. Can't a man just lie down anymore?" he says into the comforter.

"Got it. Sorry."

A pause barely has time to settle between them and slow Gene's insistent heart before:

"Rough game today," Luis says.

Gene sighs. He rolls over onto his back and squints at Luis. Gene's glasses sit crooked on his nose, the natural result of his miniature temper tantrum, but he can still see Luis's borderline-earnest face, waiting for Gene's response. He hasn't seen that open look on Luis since college. It's impossible to ignore him when he looks at Gene like that.

"Could have been worse," Gene says.

"Yeah, but you hate losing in extras."

This is true. Gene has long harbored a love for extra innings. It's an optimist's paradise, to start—anything can happen with a tied game and tired teams. And, practically speaking, it's free baseball. Gene has met a lot of players who hate free baseball because it means they're stuck at the stadium longer, but never once, not even in the worst blowout losses, has Gene ever wished he could leave the ballpark faster.

The fact that Luis remembers that Gene hates this particular brand of loss most of all—

Well, it probably doesn't mean anything. No one likes losing in extras.

"At least we kept it close," Gene says. "Sorry you had to stay late—I know you need your beauty rest."

Luis laughs, but it comes out more like a dribble, like he's not sure if he wants to commit to it.

Gene grabs for the remote on the nightstand between their beds and fumbles for the power button. If he can turn something on, he won't have to look at Luis, and he won't have to stay up all night thinking about the dimple that lurks under Luis's beard when he laughs. He flips mindlessly through channels for a minute or two. He can feel Luis looking just as pointedly at the TV, can almost feel him thinking, too.

Finally, on some ESPN offshoot, Luis says, "Oh, this is a good game."

Gene sets the remote down. Baseball it is.

It's an old game, a sea of teal on a bright green field. Gene recognizes the tight, full-length pants as hailing from either the late nineties or the early aughts, but Ichiro's presence in the outfield signals that it's the latter.

Only baseball's harshest critics could resist one of Ichiro's rookie season games, however old it might be. In life, as in baseball, Ichiro is forever.

"Did you know he and Griffey were apparently, like, best friends?" Gene asks. He read an article last week about the brief period when both men played for the Mariners, when the Lumberjacks were still relatively new.

"I was actually just talking to Ritz about that last week," Luis says.

"You still talk to Ritz?" Gene asks before he can stop himself, the mention of their old teammate—Tracy Ritter, dubbed Ritz, far more Luis's friend than Gene's, but a good guy just the same—piquing his interest.

"He and Max are letting me crash at their place for a while."

Gene stares at the TV a bit too hard. "They still live in Portland?"

"Yeah, they moved back after graduation."

Well. No one told Gene that.

"I read that he made ties with Griffey's face on them once and had the whole team wear them," he says, desperate for a subject change before Luis can notice how much he hates that he's always the last to hear news about his former teammates. "Ichiro. Not Ritz."

"To be fair—" Luis starts.

"That's also, like, absolutely something Ritz would do."

"I'd honestly be surprised if Ritz *doesn't* have a Griffey tie," Luis says with a chuckle.

It's only a chuckle, sure, but Gene jots it down in the success column anyway, though he's not sure what he's trying to succeed at. He just knows Luis's laugh is a good sound.

He presses his lips together, as tight as he can, to keep himself from drawing the conversation out. He can't tell if he wants to keep talking because he lacks impulse control, or if he maybe likes some small, *very select* parts of Luis's personality off the field, but he takes his phone out and types the things he'd like to ask. *Where do Max and Ritz live now?* and *Do they have you sleeping on the couch?* and *Do you do anything fun in your free time, or is it just baseball games and baseball re-runs 24/7?*

He has a curious mind.

And, just as he starts to unstick his lips from each other and let one of the questions spill out, the chime of his phone interrupts. His sister's name—JOEY, with the queen and yellow heart emojis—displays across the top of the screen.

"*Shit,*" Gene says.

When he answers the call, the screen shows his nephew, Mattie, eight years old and decked out in the Double-A T-shirt Gene gave him the last time they came to see one of his games, back when he was playing in Ann Arbor.

He went to visit them in Gowanus last offseason, before he started with the Beavers. That he has lived an entire year in a new state, on a new team, without his family seeing a single inning—he can feel every ounce of missing them at the back of his throat, scratching and sad. A season without your own people in the stands can feel interminable.

"Hey, Mattie," he says. His voice is bright, because it has to be.

He can hear Joey in the background, somewhere past Mattie's head, as loud as she's always been: "Did you forget to call us?"

"Sorry, Jo. I lost track of time."

She pops up behind Mattie's head for a beat to say, "Good game today." That means she checked the box score and nothing else. A 5–4 loss doesn't look so bad if you don't look under the hood, which Joey never does. Gene appreciates this about her. It hides a world of ills. Much as it's sweet that his dad watches the grainy game feed whenever he can, an indication of the sheer devotion he has to Gene's career, Gene almost prefers this type of family support. Love without the details, he has always found, is easier to receive.

For the next thirty minutes, he sits listening to Mattie talk about, in turn: his Little League team as a segue, from which he moves on to the science fair, then his school's annual writing magazine, then a poem he wrote about a worm he found in the yard, and finally, unrelated to any of the preceding topics, the merits and demerits of various mac and cheeses.

"Can I have the phone, bub?" Joey says. Gene gets a quick view of her cluttered counter and feels a pang of homesickness for the closet-sized kitchens of his hometown, a feeling that only grows when Joey's face appears.

When their parents started dating, Joey quickly perfected the art of thinking Gene a nuisance—the irritated older sister to Gene's irritating younger brother, more than a decade before any of them realized Gene was a brother at all. It's a slightly unusual family, theirs. They're related only by marriage, and it shows—she's heavier, her hair smoother, her skin still winter-pale while Gene's has started to tan—but there's a similarity in the way they hold themselves. Tired, but honest. Wide-open smiles. In all the ways that count—in all the ways that make him miss home enough to start to regret everything that landed him so far away—she is his big sister.

"You know, he misses you," she says.

Gene's stomach roils with guilt. "I'll set an alarm next time so I don't forget, I promise."

"Don't worry about it. You're busy," she says, waving him off.

Gene glances at the TV, which is playing the same old game it was playing when Mattie called, except that Luis has muted the volume and put on his headphones. Gene can't exactly call this "busy." How much of one sport can he possibly consume and still convince himself that it's necessary? He has yet to find his limit.

"I guess," he says.

"Let's talk again soon. Call when Mattie's in bed sometime?" She's trying to get off the phone.

"How's Tuesday?"

"Whenever," she says with a shrug.

"I'll call Tuesday."

Joey waves him off. "Fine. Tuesday."

"Bye, Jo."

"Bye, dude."

She hangs up, and Gene locks his phone as quickly as he can, so as not to wallow. No point in it. Before he can think overmuch about all the things he isn't wallowing in, he reaches for the remote and unmutes the TV.

"Sorry, I didn't know if you wanted me to leave," Luis says.

"It's fine."

Luis takes the hint and doesn't ask any follow-up questions. At least, on the bright side, Gene's temptation to talk has exited the building.

Ten minutes or so later, Luis looks at his phone, grabs a key card, and leaves the room. Gene wonders if he has a date or something, then wonders why he wondered that, then puts a firm lid on that train of thought.

Luis comes back a minute later, carrying a take-out bag stamped with the Frisko Freeze logo, grease already staining its bottom. From the bag, he pulls a single fry, offered to a whining Dodger. Then: a burger, an order of onion rings, two orders of fries, a milkshake, and a soda. Gene wonders how one man can eat all of that *and* run stadiums the next day, but then Luis sets the milkshake, one of the wax paper packets of fries, and the bag of onion rings on Gene's nightstand.

Gene stares at them.

"I wasn't sure what you'd want," Luis says, then hands over a fistful of condiments—mustard and barbecue sauce and ranch and plenty of ketchup—without further comment.

Gene eats his portion in silence, with gratitude he doesn't quite know how to express, through the rest of the game and into the movie Luis flips to afterward. He wonders whether Luis might have accidentally left the burger out of Gene's order, or if he had simply managed to remember, seven years and a meager handful of half-civil conversations later, that Gene doesn't eat meat. Either way, he can't stop picturing Luis, hunched over a take-out menu, thinking of Gene and picking out things Gene might want.

# 7

## APRIL

### Current record: 3–17

Gene doesn't sleep through Luis's quiet trill of an alarm like he did the day before, so he's conscious enough to hear Dodger's collar jingling, Luis's bare feet shuffling across the carpet, and the spray of the shower turning on. Gene can't fall back asleep, which is, possibly, less about the noise and more about the unignorable presence of Luis on the other side of the bathroom door.

These extra practices are a means to an end. Gene knows this.

But he also knows that Luis ordered him food last night, that Luis had asked for a second practice, that Luis had looked at him with something shockingly like earnestness last night when they got back from the game. Something almost like hope.

And what the fuck is Gene supposed to make of that? That they're friends again?

He spends five minutes overthinking it, palms far too sweaty over such a simple question, until Luis turns the shower off.

Before Luis can find him awake and neck-deep in this thought spiral, Gene shoves his feet into his untied sneakers, chucks his unzipped duffel over a shoulder, and grabs his breakfast from the room's minifridge. At the last second, he grabs a second serving and tosses that in, too.

Now, sitting in the dugout, waiting for Luis, he regrets bringing the extra bagel.

To save money on the road, he makes them ahead of time and packs enough to last the first few days of each road trip. He probably won't *actually* give it to Luis. As he watches a layer of Pacific Northwest mist settle on the field, the bagel seems like an embarrassing reminder that he had, for a moment, thought of Luis's name in the same sentence as the word "friend."

No, not friend. Something between colleague and friend. Colleague you sleep in the same room as sometimes, and also spend nearly all your waking hours with. Is there a word for that?

*Fucking weird* could work.

"You left early."

Luis drops his bag at the top of the dugout tunnel. His eyebrows are pulled so low they graze his eyelashes, but he almost looks like he might . . . smile?

Gene grins, half-grimace. "I didn't know if you wanted to walk here together."

"So you left without saying anything?" Luis says, his smile becoming less deniable.

"Yes," Gene admits.

Luis unhooks Dodger's leash and plops onto the bench next to Gene. Dodger doesn't move until Luis gives him a nod of approval, then he takes off at a run, tongue flopping and fur blowing back. "Okay, a better question."

Gene gives him a single finger gun. "Shoot."

"Did you ever consider just asking?"

"I was worried that would be awkward," Gene says.

“And this”—Luis gestures between them—“isn’t awkward?”

“Oh, this is the shits.”

Luis really does have a good smile—mostly unmoving on the left side, but when he wants, it stretches wide on the right, and it stretches now. *Fuck* that smile, for real.

“We can walk together next time if you want. Or not. Whatever,” Luis says, while Dodger, on the field, flips onto his back and starts rubbing the grass into the white of his fur. “Jesus. He’s gonna be green for a week.”

They run their stadiums without further preamble. Gene finds it easier to run with an excitable dog in front of him, setting the pace, and an offensively hot man at his back. Maybe he’s identified the trick to getting baseball players to do their training.

After, they drop into post-run stretches. They agreed last night—after the food incident but before they went to sleep, Luis giving him a stilted good night and flicking the nightstand lamp off in a way that made their beds feel infinitely closer than they were—that they would attempt some actual infield drills today. Not much talking to do during infield drills, which Gene appreciates, because with every minute he spends around Luis, it gets harder not to talk to him.

Like, for example, when Luis folds over into his first stretch, Gene says at his back muscles, “So if you didn’t play baseball, what would you do?”

“What?” Luis asks the grass.

It’s the kind of question you ask the other team’s first baseman to distract him when you’re trying to steal a base, not the kind of question you ask a teammate.

“You studied physics and history, right? So what was the backup plan?”

“How the fuck do you remember that?” When Gene doesn’t give him an answer, Luis responds, “Divorce lawyer.”

Gene rolls his neck, feeling the pull in his shoulder. "Very funny."

The look on Luis's face says it wasn't a joke.

"Oh. Got it," Gene says.

"What?" Luis asks. The outside edges of his voice sound offended.

"That's the most depressing answer I've ever heard."

"Well, fine. What would you be?" Luis asks.

Most people had assumed Luis would get drafted eventually. Son of a superstar? Potential for days? Sure. The only question was when it would happen—what year, what round. But no one expected Gene to get drafted at all, no one expected him to sign undrafted, and, honestly, no one had even really expected him to make his college team. He *needed* to have a backup plan.

Eventually, when his contract runs out, Gene will need to dust that backup plan off and see if it still fits.

"A wedding photographer," Gene says.

Luis sucks his lips between his teeth, like he's trying to bite the laugh off of them. "Jesus Christ," is what he says.

"What?" Gene says, mock-innocent.

"A divorce attorney and a wedding photographer? You're messing with me."

"I absolutely am not," Gene says. "I was a second shooter for a hot minute. The woman I worked for mostly did graduations and stuff, but I got to help with a few weddings."

"When?"

"Summer breaks," Gene says. "And for like two months right after I graduated, before I signed with Portland. And in the offseason."

Luis sits up straight. "Wait, after you graduated? You weren't drafted?"

He sounds surprised, which irritates Gene. They weren't talking anymore by the time Gene graduated college. His four years of solid play weren't enough to entice a team to overlook his transness—thirty teams and seemingly interminable rounds of the draft, and his name never got called—until Baker, still in her scouting days, came along and offered him a tiny free agent contract and half a chance.

Gene needs to not talk about this, not now, not right when he feels the first inkling of comfort around Luis. He needs not to explain himself.

He stands, brushes the grass from the seat of his shorts, and offers Luis a hand up.

Luis, to his credit, drops the subject and takes the hand.

When they look at the lineup card, taped to the side of a bank of locker stalls, Luis's name sits right below Gene's for the first time all season. Batting second. Gene doesn't like the thrill that gives him, but, when he steps up to the plate in the top of the first and Luis steps into the on-deck circle behind him, his heart races in spite of himself.

He turns, makes eye contact with Luis, and holds up two fingers.

A *double*. He's calling his hit.

Luis yells back at him, "Prove it."

Maybe they're not friends, but Luis has started to feel like a bona fide teammate all the same. And maybe Luis *is* a better shortstop than Gene, when his head's not up his own ass. Gene is still the better batter. Today, he wants to prove it.

This pitcher, Gene surmises as the first pitch of the game sails toward him, has not done his research. The pitch sails straight into the middle of the strike zone. Guys *always* throw Gene meatballs, because no matter what his batting average says, they take one look at the sixty-two inches of him at the plate and assume he's the safest batter to throw junk to.

Today, though, as the pitch winds its way toward him, Gene focuses on the surprise on Luis's face when he asked whether Gene hadn't been drafted. Gene—as if in answer to that face and to this insulting, garbage pitch—scoops the ball out of the zone and over the opposing infielders' heads.

The ball drops right into the gap between Tacoma's too-old right fielder and their too-young center fielder, far enough from either of them that Gene has time to make it to second standing. He claps his hands and points at Luis, a grin eating the full bottom half of his face. Luis, getting his own bat ready, rolls his eyes, but he grins right back.

---

DAN: So—something's different here today, don't you think?

NANCY: Well, we got some classic Ionescu with that leadoff double in the first, and then the fly ball from Estrada to advance him to third—maybe Steph Baker was right to try this new one-two combination out.

DAN: We'll have to see if they look more comfortable in the field, though, whenever Altman finally lets some more balls in play. He's struck out half the batters he's faced so far, with his fastball sitting mid-nineties. He's walked two batters here in the fourth, though—

NANCY: Oh, and that's a pop-up to Ionescu—Estrada lays off it, Ionescu makes the play with ease.

DAN: What do we think, Nancy? Their signals going to stay uncrossed today?

NANCY: Hopefully! The Beavers sure could use a double play here with Lopez coming up to bat for the Rainiers. He's been on fire recently, went ten for twenty last week, and he can do some real damage, too—

DAN: Oh, ouch. Altman catches Lopez right on the shoulder with that one. Looked like the ball got away from him there on the windup.

NANCY: Lopez recovers well; he'll take first. Loads the bases with just one out.

DAN: Not what you want with the heart of Tacoma's order coming up.

NANCY: You have to figure Vince Altman's feeling pretty grateful for that early run support today.

DAN: That's ball one—looks like a rare sinker.

NANCY: Spikes it right into the dirt, a good play from catcher Mark Moore, filling in for Ernie Gonzales, to get a glove on it. We've seen Altman get this team out of some jams, here's hoping he can—

DAN: Oh, that's smoked.

NANCY: High fly ball to dead center field.

DAN: Rivera's not going to be able to get after that—

NANCY: That's a grand slam well past the fence. Four–three, Tacoma with the lead in the bottom of the fourth as Moore calls for a mound visit.

---

When Gene reaches Vince and gives him a reassuring clap on the ass, Vince covers his mouth with his glove.

"They need to pull me," he says.

Moore shakes his head. "Four runs isn't so bad. It's fine, we just need to focus." Ernie might have said more or less the same thing, but when Moore says it, it lacks the authority. It comes out hesitant, like a question.

"No," Vince says, lifting his arm. Gene expects him to twist it in a wide circle the way he does when his shoulder is bugging him, but instead he straightens it out. He winces, tries it again, and hisses, "*Fuck.*"

That is not—to put it lightly—good. That is worst-case-scenario shit.

"Get me the fuck out of here," Vince says. He doesn't even bother covering his mouth with his glove to hide it from the crowd.

Gene can't tell if it's frustration or pain that's making his voice strain that way, but either way, Baker and a trainer jog out, Vince is pulled less than thirty seconds later, and Beaverton's infielders are left staring at each other across the mound.

"*Shit,*" Luis says.

"Shit," Cooper says.

"Shit," Ross says.

Eddie White—their resident long-relief guy—starts warming up in the bullpen. His stuff looks fine, but he is no Vince. He's a career minor leaguer, the guy you throw in when your starter absolutely beefs it and you need someone to eat some innings—not the guy you throw in when you want to win.

"Fucking *shit,*" Gene concludes as White jogs in and the infielders take their places again.

This isn't even the thing that's supposed to take Vince out. He has a bum shoulder, not a bum elbow.

After Gene's dad retired and they moved back to Brooklyn, they still watched Portland play whenever they could. They had to set up a special subscription for it, living as far away from the team as they did. But the Ionescus loved the New York Mets and the Portland Lumberjacks like family—one team or the other's game serving as background noise in their house more often than not. Gene had never been much for pitchers, but he bought his dad a Vince Altman jersey for Father's Day during Vince's rookie season.

They saw the game where Vince tore his UCL. For some pitchers, it's a twinge—then a surprise when they find out they need Tommy John surgery. When it happened to Vince, it was a sudden thing. He kneeled on the mound—this solid, thick-bearded guy, in his early thirties at the time—with his straightened, extended arm tucked between his knees and his mouth wide open in pain. Every single person in that stadium, every single person watching on their TVs, figured he would miss the rest of the season and most of the next.

Gene's only comfort, when they have to tuck back into this game and do their best, is that Vince's reaction this time was far more subdued, if just as panicked.

He looks across the expanse of second base, not sure why until he finds Luis looking back. If it were possible for a heartbeat to slow down and race at the same time, Gene's would.

He nods, and Luis nods back, and at least they can finish the game. They can do that.

In the end, they eke out a win, but the mood in the dugout is moribund. Vince returns from the clubhouse in the eighth, an Icy Hot strapped to his elbow. If it worried Gene less, he would laugh. An Icy Hot—slapped on top of muscle and veins and skin and a torn-up nerve—is not going to accomplish a damn thing.

---

**@JenWertherPDX**: Vince Altman (left elbow) will undergo an MRI tomorrow. An injured list stint seems a foregone conclusion, but we'll see what the team says. Altman underwent Tommy John on the same elbow five years ago—here's hoping it's a minor issue this time.

. . .

Sometime around midnight, it becomes clear that Gene won't get any sleep. He'd hardly had time to shower before Vince left to catch a flight home, and, though the trip from Seattle to Portland takes less than an hour, Vince still hasn't responded to any of Gene's texts.

Around the ten thousandth time he checks his phone, he hears a sigh from Luis's side of the room.

"Am I bugging you?" Gene asks.

"It's fine."

"I can't sleep."

"You're just," Luis says, sighing again, "moving a lot."

His voice is unfortunately devastating at night—deeper, slower, the sort of thing Gene wants to tuck away to think about the next time he's back in his own room.

Gene sets his phone facedown as quietly as he can on the nightstand. He lasts less than a minute before he checks it again, careful to make as little noise as possible.

Still, Luis flops the comforter off his body with a decisive snap. In spite of the month or so Luis spent looking like he'd sucked on a lemon and sat on a stick, it still comes as a surprise to see him this annoyed.

"Shit, sorry," Gene says, sitting to slide his glasses back on.

Luis gets up, grabs a pair of jeans from the floor, then tosses them to the side in favor of a pair of track pants and a logo-less black T-shirt. Even in the dark, it looks soft. He grabs Dodger's leash from a coat hook in the closet.

"Are you coming, or did you just want to pout?" Luis asks.

Gene eyes him. "Coming where?"

"Wherever's open."

"You're not gonna kill me, are you?"

"For what?"

"Keeping you up."

Luis shrugs. "I can't sleep, either. And I'm pretty sure you could kick my ass if you wanted to. You have crazy eyes."

He points his first two fingers at his own widened eyes to emphasize his point, then takes the liberty of digging in Gene's duffel. Gene turns the light on, watches him bypass the Tupperware container of testosterone supplies and hold up a foil-wrapped bagel that Gene very much forgot was in there.

"What is this?" he asks.

"The bagel I was going to give you this morning," Gene admits.

"Why were you going to give me a bagel?"

"Because I had an extra."

Luis peels the foil back. "Chances it's still okay to eat?"

"Nonexistent."

"Damn." Dodger, upon realizing Luis has food in his hands, shoves his face as close to the bag as he can get it. "Wait, where did you get a good bagel in Tacoma?"

"I made it," Gene says.

"You made me a bagel?"

Gene gets out of bed and takes it from Luis's hands. "No, I made *me* a bagel, and I felt rude not sharing. Why are you going through my bag?"

"Because I'm hungry."

"And you thought you'd find food in my duffel?"

"Well, to be fair, I did find food in your duffel. But I was looking for your sweatshirt."

"Why?" Gene leans over and plucks his Lumberjacks sweatshirt out of the side pocket of the bag, where he keeps anything he might need easy access to.

"Thought we could go get some food."

"It's midnight."

Luis tugs on a sneaker. "Is there not a Denny's in Tacoma?"

There is, indeed, a Denny's in Tacoma.

As at all Denny's locations, a sheen of grease covers the tables, the booths, the silverware, probably their skin the second they step inside. It smells of stale fries and bad pie, of growing up without much money and going to cheap diners once a month as a treat. Comfortable and familiar.

They sit against the window, the sky outside so dark that all Gene can see in the glass is their reflections—Luis looking at the menu like something might appear that appeals to him, Gene sitting with his legs pulled onto the booth, crossed so each foot balances on the opposite knee. Dodger sits under the table, his presence unquestioned by the overnight staff.

Luis wrinkles his nose at the menu.

"It's the same shit as it always is," Gene says.

"No, yeah." He looks disappointed, somehow, by the glossy pictures that in no way represent the actual food.

"Are you too classy for Denny's?"

Luis doesn't answer. When the server comes by their table, he orders a stack of pancakes and a ginger ale, and Gene asks for fries and the thickest chocolate shake the cook is willing to make at midnight. Then, when they're alone, Luis says, "My mom owns a diner."

Gene blinks. He has only ever really known the barely skimmed surface of Luis: his hometown, his college major, his sibling count, and his apparently everlasting propensity for late-night greasy food. The least vulnerable parts, the safe parts, and the things he can find out online just as easily as he could ask the man himself. If he's being fair, he hasn't asked Luis much. Not on Stanford's roadie buses, not on Beaverton's; not at practice, not in the sparse and memorable handful of times they hung out alone in someone's dorm room or the dining hall.

He's never told Luis much about himself, either.

"Like a bougie diner?" Gene asks.

"No, like a normal one. I mean—it's better than a Denny's."

"Everything is better than a Denny's. Sorry," Gene adds, to the server who has come to drop off Luis's already-sweating soda.

"Oh, I hate it here," the server says, which . . . is fair. Gene has a certain nostalgia for the place, but he'd never claim the food or the ambiance was "good," per se.

Luis laughs, ripping the wrapper off and dropping the straw in amongst the bubbles. "Well, that settles that."

"Where's her diner?" Gene asks.

"L.A." He says it as if no other city exists, which Gene finds annoying and charming in equal measure.

"Is that the one on the hat you're always wearing?" Gene regrets the question as soon as he asks it, the admission that he pays enough attention to Luis and his outfits to observe a pattern.

"Yeah," Luis answers. "My sisters and I used to wait tables for her."

Gene nods, then decides to dig his hole a little deeper, albeit in a different direction. "I'm surprised you had to work. You know, with your dad—"

Luis gives him a look, and Gene stops in his tracks. So, okay. They're not there yet.

"Got it, never mind," Gene says. To divert the subject, he says, "My dads own a little grocery store."

Luis's eyebrows raise.

"In Carroll Gardens," Gene says.

Luis scratches his beard, a nervous tic Gene has tried not to notice. He likes the *scritch-scritch* sound Luis's close-cropped nails make on the hair.

"That's in Brooklyn," Gene adds.

"No, yeah. But did you say 'dads'?"

Gene grabs Luis's straw wrapper and starts folding it neatly in on itself. People are entertained, sometimes, by the unusual makeup of Gene's family, but no one ever looks more surprised by the existence of actual, run-of-the-mill gay people than male athletes.

He tries to judge, before he answers, whether he's ready to get into this with Luis. Gene is out, yes, but over the years, he's learned to lean on the silent kind of tolerance that makes his presence on a team full of cis, straight men possible. If he plays well enough, they don't complain. When he's lucky, he finds guys like Vince and the Kyles, coaches like Baker, who genuinely want him there, who revel in his noise and his joy and his difference.

He never thought of Luis as one of those people, never gave him the chance to be. But now that they're here, now that they've ventured into this conversation, he *does* want to let Luis in—just a little, if only so there's someone else to fill this quiet with him.

In the end, Gene confirms: "Dads."

"Oh."

"My dad and my stepdad."

"So—"

"My dad and the man he married, yes."

Luis nods, a little more slowly than necessary. "Cool."

Encouraged by Luis's quick adjustment, Gene leans his elbows on the table. "Dude, you know *I'm* gay, right?"

"Well."

"Oh my God," Gene laughs. "*Look at me.*"

"I didn't want to assume!" Luis says with a slightly self-deprecating grimace.

"You could have googled it."

Luis shrugs. "I figured you'd tell me if you wanted me to know."

"So you didn't keep tabs on me at all?"

"I mean," Luis starts. "I heard some stuff. Ritz follows you on Instagram, so I knew you'd signed with Portland."

"You got reports on me from Ritz?"

"Not by request."

"And Ritz neglected to mention I'm gay?"

Luis drags a finger through the condensation on his glass, refusing to meet Gene's eye, half a smile playing at the crooked corner of his lips. If it weren't for the beard, Gene could almost mistake this Luis for the one he used to know.

"He totally told you," Gene says. He resists the urge to tap Luis's shin with his toes, instead keeping a hand on his ankle and his legs on the bench seat, where they're safe.

"Look. I don't like reading stuff on Wikipedia. It's weird. We used to know each other."

"Ritz isn't Wikipedia."

"I wanted you to tell me if you wanted me to know." *Now* Luis looks at him. It's a serious look. Deep brown eyes and diabolical eyelashes and no more smile.

Well. Fuck Gene sideways.

"Well, I googled *you*," he says, as if that'll help the situation.

"Why?"

The thought *Because you're playing my position* seems too immature to admit, *Because you're possibly the hottest guy I've ever seen* too honest, and *Because maybe I missed you even when I hated you* too vulnerable. But the real reason does lie somewhere in the intersection of those three things.

"I was curious," Gene says.

Luis smiles. Does he know what that smile does to a defenseless homosexual? "Why?" he asks again.

If Gene didn't know better, he'd say that smile constituted at least one unit of flirtation. But he knows better.

"Because I always google my teammates," Gene says, which is true.

"Oh." Luis sits back. "So, like, what does Google say about Vince?"

The server drops their food off with little ceremony. Gene adds an extra dash of salt to his fries and, as he dips the crispiest one he can find into his shake, says, "I don't have to google Vince—I literally live in his house. Plus, he's Vince fucking Altman."

"You live in Vince's house?"

Gene regrets the self-inflicted reminder of Vince, of his overextended arm, of the string of unanswered texts Gene has sent him. Both now and on the field earlier, Luis's presence has distracted him in a way he's not yet ready to pick apart and analyze. He would prefer to enjoy the calm and not to think too hard about its source.

"What are your sisters' names?" Gene changes the subject.

"That's what you want to know?"

Gene shrugs. "Google didn't say."

He taps one finger against the table for each name. "Jamie, Sabrina, Dani, and—"

"Mia," Gene finishes, because Luis used to mention her, and apparently that piece of information got stuck somewhere in the cracks of Gene's shit-awful memory, stubborn and unmoving, like everything he's ever learned about Luis.

"Yeah. My turn?" Luis asks, dumping an unconscionable amount of syrup onto his pancakes.

"For what?"

"To ask a question," Luis says around his first bite.

"What's the question?"

"Your dad's Franklin Ionescu."

"Not a question."

"But he is?"

Gene raises his eyebrows. His family could afford to fly out for just one game his freshman year, and Luis had met them only in passing. Not long enough to talk minor league careers with Gene's dad. Franklin Ionescu certainly wasn't ever a household name the way Luis Estrada, Sr., was, either, so there's no real reason for Luis to know, and yet—

"Ionescu isn't that common of a name," Luis clarifies.

Fair. He pronounces Gene's name right, starting with a *Yo* instead of an *Io*, three syllables rather than four, subtly different from the way most people say it.

"Yeah. That's my tata," Gene confirms. Then, he clarifies, "My dad. I call him my tata."

"I remember. Romanian, right?"

Gene doesn't want to peel apart the layers of revelation here, doesn't want to think too hard about the things Luis remembers, or about how they maybe knew each other better than Gene wanted to admit. "He's my uncle, technically," Gene says. This isn't something he usually talks about with his teammates, or with most people at all. His dad is his dad, and he doesn't like to think about what came before that.

"Your uncle?"

"He's my birth mom's brother." He doesn't mean to tell Luis these things, but they spill out, each word a little too easy. "She drank a lot. Eventually she left."

"Oh."

"Then my tata adopted me, when I was really young. And he didn't leave."

Luis pokes his fork at a pancake. "My dad was gone a lot, too. I know it's not the same."

"No." But the way Luis never talks about him makes more sense in this context. "Still sucks, though."

"Well," Luis says, "for what it's worth, your tata was a good player."

Gene shrugs. He's grateful for the subject change. "*I* thought so. You're the first person who's ever asked me about him, though."

"I went to a lot of minor league games when I was a kid. I saw him a couple times," Luis explains. He slides a small bite of pancake off the end of his fork and holds it under the table for Dodger, muttering a very quiet, "Gentle," as he does so. Gene definitely does not notice the way Luis's voice goes just as soft as the word it says.

"I bet I went to more games than you," Gene wagers. "And I was probably at the same ones you were."

"I mean, probably not. They were in California."

"Yeah, my tata homeschooled me for all of elementary school. So I traveled with the team."

"Shit. So you and Beaverton go way back."

"Yeah. After I turned five, my tata used to let me sit in the dugout whenever he played."

"Seriously?" A hint of jealousy sneaks into Luis's voice, but it's padded considerably by amazement.

"Up until he quit to be gay."

Luis sets his fork down. "Is that really why he quit?"

"Sort of. He wasn't making enough money. Homeschooling was getting harder, and he was worried I wasn't spending enough time with other kids. Plus, he had a boyfriend back in Brooklyn, and being a queer man in sports can be the absolute pits sometimes."

"But you're doing pretty well for yourself," Luis reasons. "Not a lot of guys who go undrafted make it as far as you have."

"Baker did it."

"And it was impressive when she did it, too."

Gene dips another fry in his shake. He's not sure he trusts Luis enough yet to get into the nuances, the ways being out—being the only openly trans person in every room he walks into in this league, not to mention the only fully out gay man—can still make things so complicated. Still, "impressive" sticks with him, even as he changes the subject.

"Can I make an observation?"

"About me?" Luis asks.

"Yes."

"Well, now you have to." He looks nervous.

Gene points the fry at him. "You should try to hit a homer every once in a while."

"What?" He laughs when he says it. He sounds a little relieved.

"Like, you're still kind of skinny—"

"Gee, thanks."

Gene barrels on, "—but you have a great fucking throwing arm. You must have some power in there."

Luis shifts. "I've never been a huge homer guy."

"I know. I'm telling you that you should try to change that. You've got surprisingly good legs—"

"Surprisingly?"

"Surprisingly. And a decent swing." Gene checks each of these qualities off on his fingers. "You should utilize your pull side more. You're trying to hit for average and you're psyching yourself out. Fix your follow-through and smack the leather off the ball every once in a while. You could get twenty, maybe even twenty-five dingers a season."

Luis wrinkles his nose. "I've never even cracked fifteen."

"And?" Gene grins. "Try to surprise some people. It's fun."

He rests his case.

Luis takes a long sip from his ginger ale, considering. "You're too stiff at second."

Gene raises his eyebrows and blinks, as slowly as he can manage. "Excuse me?"

"When you dick around with the other guys before games, you're really good. Like, you move so easily. You never had the arm for short—"

"Excuse me?" Gene says again, this time with more emphasis on the *You should stop talking right now* subtext of the question.

"Okay, wait. Don't get offended yet. You're way faster than me.

You're athletic and you're energetic, and that's more important at second. Plus, it doesn't matter as much if you don't have the arm there. You need to stop trying to move like a shortstop. You just have to get the turn and the snap down faster. You have it during drills, but you're trying too hard during games. I never got why they moved you off second in the first place."

Gene slides his jaw forward, slightly to the side, ready to chew Luis out. Like fuck he doesn't have the arm to play shortstop.

But . . .

Okay. Luis didn't yell at him for *his* unsolicited advice.

Gene takes a deep breath.

"I'll take it under advisement," he says.

"You were a good shortstop."

"I *am* a good shortstop."

"Sure. Yes. But you're a *great* second baseman."

Gene tries not to blush at that compliment. He tries very hard not to blush at the fact that Luis has been watching him this closely, that, underneath the mild insult, he has picked out the things Gene is most proud of as a defender, as a player, and put it all on display.

"No more advice tonight," Gene decrees, because if Luis looks at him like that any longer, if he notices him like that anymore, Gene is going to sink through the linoleum, into the ground, and never come back out. "Can I give Dodger a fry?"

# 8

## MAY

Current record: 9–20

For a matinee game, Baker expects the team to show up no later than ten for check-ins and lineups and a quick strategy meeting. She sends the scouting report ahead of every series—one which she charitably pretends is written by the actual scouts and not herself, at midnight. Almost no one reads it. It's hard to find the motivation when they play the same teams on a loop all season, every season. Even when the series is new, it's not.

The morning of their first game back in Oregon, Gene and Luis arrive at seven. *They* read the scouting report. For the first time, they work their way through their extra practice with something bordering on ease: practice grounders hit and fielded cleanly, the twist and flick and muscle-memory tosses of a mock double play executed without issue. A white bucket full of baseballs sits at first base, concrete evidence of sweat spent and progress made.

Maybe that's why the win feels predetermined from the first inning.

Gene hits a triple, one that likely should have been a double. He squeezes in the extra base out of sheer gut instinct, made possible by a particularly strong sprint and an outfielder who possesses what Gene knows to be a rather weak arm. Luis brings him home with a single, swung on the first pitch and dropped into left field. For the first time all season, Luis has batted Gene in.

The opposing team's pitcher—a Triple-A stalwart who has played for the El Paso Chihuahuas for four years—then proceeds to issue two consecutive walks. To wrap up the scoring, with no outs and the bases loaded, Ernie—who talked Baker into letting him start after finally getting reinstated from the injured list—hits his first Beaverton grand slam, a no-doubter over the right field fence that brings all two hundred or so Beaverton fans to their feet with an excitement rarely felt in this stadium.

Less than thirty minutes in, they possess their first 5–0 lead of the season.

In the bottom of the fourth, Gene sits sandwiched in the dugout between Vince and Luis while Cooper battles his way through a ten-pitch at-bat on the field. Vince reads the scouting report again, as if it will open up and tell him how to de-age and un-injure his arm. He's barely a week into his stringent rehab plan. The idea is to keep him from needing any kind of surgery, but he will need to do the impossible to accomplish it—that is, resist running onto the mound to take over for the latest of their young, painfully inexperienced starters.

Luis, for his part, seems to focus on pressing as much of his thigh against the outside of Gene's as he can physically manage. So much for those careful inches he used to leave between them.

Gene misses those inches, and also, *fuck them*, because he wishes he had known sooner exactly how exciting Luis's uniformed leg pressed against his own could feel. Like the fabric is too tight, like Gene might rip the seams apart through sheer force of will.

He may have let things get a *bit* out of hand here, in his fantasy world.

"Anyone else think it's gonna rain?" Gene asks. He clings to it, that mundane question.

"Yep," Vince says, scrolling through the heavily annotated PDF on his iPad screen.

Luis looks up from his crossword. "There is one cloud."

"You haven't lived here very long. You'll see." Gene points at the open air above the stadium. While Luis isn't wrong about the mostly blue sky, the feeling in the air says rain. "I give it ten minutes."

Luis holds his phone out. "The weather app also says there's exactly one cloud."

"The weather app is delusional. We're gonna get rained out."

"I bet we don't," Luis says, challenge inching its way into his voice.

Gene raises an eyebrow. "Oh, yeah, Nada? What are you betting?"

Luis gives him a confused look, like he might not have heard Gene's question right. Then, "Dinner," he says, with a grin wider than a simple bet can justify.

At this, Gene raises the other eyebrow, doing everything in his power to act normal about this. Vince sets the scouting report aside, almost audibly tuning his attention in to the conversation.

"Whatever you want, on me, if it rains," Luis continues.

"And if it doesn't?"

Luis shrugs. "You can let me bat leadoff next game."

"*Ha!*" Vince barks. "Fat chance Baker will let that happen."

Luis leans around Gene. "We could ask her," he says.

Baker, watching Cooper foul off another pitch, says, "I don't give even half a shit."

Luis points at her, satisfaction written on his face. "See?" he says. Then, to Gene, he says, "So?"

Gene hasn't batted lower in the order than Luis since college. He very much does not intend to start again now, but he is also one *hundred* percent sure it's going to rain today, and even more certain he'd like to find out what a real, intentional dinner with Luis looks like.

"Does it have to be a rainout, or will a delay do the trick?" he barters.

"Rainout," Luis says.

Gene holds his hand out for a shake, and Luis's meets his halfway.

Cooper swings through his third strike, ending the inning. As the team grabs their gloves and filters out onto the field, Vince holds Gene back, grabbing the back of his jersey the same as he would the scruff of his dog's neck.

"What the hell?" He squints at Gene, then Luis's back as he jogs away, then back at Gene. "Last I checked, you hated each other."

Gene shrugs. "You told me to cut him some slack."

In the top of the fifth, their pitcher finally finds his rhythm, right as the clouds roll in. One out later, those clouds have broken, producing a steady stream, each drop plump against the brim of Gene's hat. Luis looks across the second base divide at him, his smile wry and disbelieving. Gene winks.

No sooner has their pitcher thrown the third strike for the Chihuahuas' final out of the inning than the grounds team starts pulling the tarp across the field. Where Portland has a state-of-the-art roof, constructed with the rest of the stadium when the team was founded in the nineties, Beaverton has open air. Not the best idea in its particular geographic location, but an inevitability of playing for a low-budget team.

They pile into the dugout, most of the team putting on Beaverton-green windbreakers. Luis leans back against the dugout wall, his legs stretched out in front of him. Where a lot of guys wear the full-length style of pants now, Luis wears the same as Gene: old-school, just past the knee, tucked into his high, vivid green uniform socks. With his eye black and trimmed beard, his firm shoulders, the way his hair always manages to stay perfect, no matter how long it's under his cap, he looks exactly like the kind of guy Gene would like to stick on a baseball card and frame.

Maybe he always was.

"Not a rainout yet," Luis says.

"Give it ten minutes," Gene assures him.

"Mhm."

Twenty minutes pass, and there they all still are. Packed into the dugout, restless to the point of annoyance.

"I'm *bored*," Kyle Rivera groans. He has taken to lying across the dirt, his legs and arms starfished. Gene shudders to think how many sunflower seeds and dried-up tobacco puddles he's lying in.

"So entertain yourself," Baker intones.

Luis looks at Gene, flicks his eyebrows up, and it gives Gene an idea.

"Hey," he says.

"Yeah?"

Gene wiggles his eyebrows.

Luis narrows his eyes.

Gene widens his.

"*No*," Luis says, realization beginning to dawn.

"How would you feel about a round of—"

"—fucking *Cavalry?*" Luis finishes.

"*Fucking* Cavalry," Gene agrees.

Without another word, Luis ties Dodger's leash to the dugout bench and gathers an armful of the unassigned bats in the corner. He sticks a hand out from under the dugout roof to get a feel for the rain and shrugs when his palm is coated in seconds.

While he sets up boundary marks on the field—one his glove,

the other a spare cap—Gene explains the rules to their teammates.

"We need at least two more guys," he starts.

In the end, they get eight volunteers. Gene gets paired with Ernie, Luis with Kyle Clark. Gene and Ernie make for a sturdy team, if not particularly tall; Luis and Kyle are all lithe limbs and long reach.

"Okay," Gene announces. "Wild-card round, then we'll do a two-round tournament. Winner gets the Dad Hat."

The Dad Hat is given to the most valuable player in a game that the team wins. The hat reads BEST DAD EVER and is adorned with a 1995 Beaverton Beavers patch that reads—and this is the important part—BEAVER POWERED. Between wins, said player gets to keep said hat in their locker stall until someone dethrones them. It belongs to Kyle Nguyen at the moment, in honor of a particularly good home run robbery to cap off their most recent win in Salt Lake City.

"We're all clear on the rules?" Gene asks.

Nods. One "Hell yeah," one "Yep."

Luis tips his head toward the dugout. "We need a referee."

Gene twists. "Altzy, get your sweet ass out here. We need an ump."

Vince groans, but he drags himself into the rain. Even in the worst of moods, Vince has always been down for some tomfoolery.

"First team to hit the ground loses," Gene says.

"Got it," Vince says.

And, with that, Gene clambers onto Ernie's shoulders for the first round.

"You good up there, Nes?" Ernie asks. He has opted for the ankle hold over the knee hold, a bold strategy—less stable, but better for last-minute saves.

Gene approves. "All good, big guy," he answers. He appends it with a quick squeeze of his thighs.

"Be careful, you could crush a watermelon with those things."

Gene laughs and gives Ernie's head an extra squeeze for good measure.

Cavalry goes like this:

The players on the bottom—the horses—lock their arms around their riders' knees, and the players on top—the riders—accept a baseball bat, helpfully proffered by someone not otherwise occupied. One team begins at the glove, and the other team begins at the hat. They are approximately, eyeball-measuredly fifty feet apart. When the referee yells "Go!" the horses take off.

The goal for the horse goes as follows: don't drop your rider.

The goal for the rider, armed with a baseball bat and a foolhardy will to win: knock the other rider off.

Cavalry is, put simply, jousting for bored baseball players with no horses. Chicken, without the pool. Batting helmets and catcher's chest plates are mandatory for riders, and all other safety precautions must be approved by the referee, lest they provide a competitive advantage.

In the end, for the final round, it's Luis across from Gene, bats leveled before anyone can say "Go!" Luis has doubtlessly lost their bet from earlier, but he has a chance to win the Dad Hat, and Gene can tell he won't go down without giving it his best shot.

Gene yells, pointing to the mud beneath them, "Get ready to eat shit, Nada!"

And there's that confused look again.

Gene ignores it. He doesn't have time for distractions with Cavalry glory on the line.

Kyle Clark is faster than Ernie. That much is certain. But he's also top-heavy, made all the more so by Luis's presence atop his shoulders—a weakness. If Gene can get them to wobble *backward* rather than at a sideways tilt, he and Ernie are golden.

So, when the "Go!" sounds and Ernie takes off in his bear-style run, Gene readies the top, flat end of his bat, aimed at the center of Luis's chest rather than his shoulder. It's a subtle enough adjustment, one that Luis won't notice until they're far too close for him to dodge it.

As soon as he and Ernie come within a couple feet of striking distance, Gene notices the smile playing at Luis's mouth. Wide enough to show Luis's uneven bottom teeth, utterly devastating.

Gene, possessing a reckless gay heart that refuses to listen to his smarter, equally gay head, falters.

He and Luis hit each other at the exact same moment. They tip off the shoulders of their Cavalry partners, into the stinking mud that has formed in the foul territory where they've been playing, a tumble and a tangle and Gene laid out across Luis's torso.

The air knocks out of Gene's lungs, it's true. He doesn't know whether it's the fall itself or if it's Luis's beautiful smile hiding behind the cheek guard of his batting helmet. More likely than any of that, it is the warmth of Luis underneath him, the way Luis doesn't move to push him off, the way his pulse thunders loud enough for Gene to hear it over his own.

Gene lies a breathless moment in the muck, helmet mostly off his head, rain falling directly onto his face, the realization hitting him.

He has made a serious miscalculation.

He has, somehow, had more fun today than he's had on a baseball diamond in years. And it's Luis—under him, laughing and groaning and overwarm and so stunning it hurts—who has made it so.

Gene, pushing himself off Luis and more fully into the mud, has the horrifying, sobering thought: maybe he doesn't want Luis to get called up. Maybe he doesn't want him to leave at all.

Before he can chase that thought down, capture it, and smother it, Vince leans over him, blocking the rain and the cloud-muted sun.

"Yeah, man, I can't tell who won," he says.

"Me," Gene and Luis say in perfect unison.

Vince holds his hands up. "You told me to be impartial. I can't tell."

"No, I told you to pay attention, which you patently did not do."

Baker approaches, her hood pulled on over a baseball cap. "Go home," she yells, shoving a thumb over her shoulder.

"We can't give it twenty more minutes?" Gene says, having hauled himself to sitting but not yet managing to stand. He'd lose the bet if the ballgame started again, but he's having too much fun to care. Fuck a leadoff spot—he doesn't want the day to be over.

"Too damn wet. Field's a mess, even with the tarp. Lightning's starting soon, too—don't want any of you jackasses getting fried."

It takes a whopping two minutes for the field and dugouts to clear. They made it through four and a half innings, and it will be recorded in the books as a win. Not exactly a pretty way to get it, but with the way they started the season, no one will take issue with it. A win is a win is a win.

As he and Luis—the last two stragglers to leave—slump in the dugout, its bench creaking under their combined weight, Gene takes stock: mud has started to seep up into his underwear, dirt splatters both of their socks halfway up their shins, and Gene's hair drips from his temples to his neck. He tries to dry his face on the front of his shirt, but it does absolutely nothing to help the situation.

"Well," he observes.

"You live nearby?" Luis asks.

"Not too far, but I was planning to walk home. Well, to the

MAX station at least." Vince had a physical therapy appointment after the game, so Gene's usual car pool plans weren't an option.

"Even though you knew it was going to rain?" Luis asks, slightly incredulous.

"Yeah." Gene shrugs one shoulder.

"Why would you do that?" Luis gives the brim of Gene's hat a decisive flick of disapproval.

"I don't have a car. And I like the rain," Gene says.

"Why?"

"Because *I'm* not from California."

"To each his own, I guess." Luis squints out at the downpour and takes a sizable pause before offering, "Do you want a ride?"

"Best ballpark snack."

"Popcorn."

Gene wrinkles his nose. They sit at the start of Vince and Jack's long driveway, the engine of Luis's run-down truck long since turned off and neither of them making any move to leave. Dodger dozes between them, and they have rolled the windows down in spite of the rain, to keep them from fogging.

"Oh, come on. Popcorn is universal," Luis protests.

"Pretzels!" Gene argues.

Luis waves him off. "They're always stale."

"Maybe in *your* shitty old stadium. Not ours. Timmy makes them fresh every day, baby!"

"I guarantee Timmy takes them out of a freezer like at every other ballpark pretzel stand."

"Do you like playing here?" Gene asks. They've been trading questions for the better part of an hour, but none of the others have been remotely serious. He doesn't know he's going to ask this one until it has already left his lips. It sounds like a nonsequitur, maybe, but to Gene, the two feel connected—the frozen and thawed and, yes, slightly stale pretzels in Beaverton's stadium are special not because they're especially good, but because they're in Beaverton. Because Gene knows Timmy, has been getting the same frozen pretzels from the same stand for nearly his whole life. He's curious whether Luis could ever see himself feeling that way, too.

Luis thinks. "Yeah. I may not have tried the pretzels yet, but it's a good stadium."

"It is *not*," Gene says. He may love it, but Gene's love does not a good stadium make. "But I meant, like, are you having a good time? Are you glad you wound up here?"

"Yeah," Luis says. Nonchalant.

"I'm asking because you've never been very good at having a good time."

"I'm aware."

"So. You are, though?" Gene asks.

Luis shrugs. "I don't know. Could be worse. Hate getting traded, but this isn't the worst place to get traded to. I used to like playing in Beaverton."

"Used to?"

"Like, when my team would come here. I liked it."

With his feet up on Luis's dashboard, Gene turns away from the row of tidy shrubs along the side of Vince's driveway to look at Luis. "I used to like playing here, too."

"Used to?"

"Yeah, and then this asshole came and wrecked my shit."

There is a split second where Luis doesn't laugh, where Gene worries that he might not realize he meant it as a joke. And, to Gene's surprise, he really did mean it as a joke. But then Luis's face splits, and he kicks Gene's foot.

And then, "My turn?" Luis asks. "You got like three in a row."

"Shoot."

"It's a little personal. You don't have to answer if you don't want to."

That caveat rings every warning bell Gene has. Coming from most people, it always precedes a question far beyond the personal, something in the territory of *Only your doctor should ask*.

"Okay," he says anyway.

"When did you come out?"

"Gay or trans?" Gene asks.

"Come on. I'm serious."

"So am I! It changes the answer."

"Never mind," Luis says. "You don't have to tell me if you don't want to."

It's a level of consideration precious few have given Gene. He toys with the idea of not answering the question just to take in the simple joy of having that option at all.

Instead, he says, because he finds that he actually does want to tell Luis, "Senior year."

"Did you know before?"

"Like," Gene says, testing the question in his head before he finishes it aloud, "when I knew you?"

Luis nods.

Part of him did, maybe. The part that ached every time he had to get ready for games in the girls' locker room, though he tried to shove that ache down. He used to tell himself he just felt left out, distant from his friends. But then Ritz and Max graduated, Luis got drafted, all of Gene's friends on the team were gone, and the ache remained.

The part, too, that has reared its inconvenient head again in recent weeks: the way his breath has always gone clumsy, his palms sweaty, around Luis. Back then, even if he wouldn't admit it—and he wouldn't, absolutely couldn't until just now, as he sits in Luis's truck and enjoys the ease between them—he wanted *so* fucking badly for Luis to look at him twice, to notice him and like what he saw. But he also couldn't imagine anything more horrifying than a straight teammate having a crush on him. At the time, he wanted Luis to be gay, to like him. Not gay-with-an-exception. Not "gay *but*." Gay *and*.

Those feelings make a lot more sense now, in hindsight, but he's not about to admit them to Luis.

"I don't know. Not consciously," is what he says.

"Was it hard?" Luis asks.

"Coming out? I mean, it wasn't great." Stanford's announcers never did stop calling him by his deadname, and his teammates were only marginally better. *They* got his name right, sure, because they just kept calling him Nes. But in that last year at Stanford, the seat next to Gene's on every roadie bus stayed vacant. No one slapped his ass after a win, invited him to parties, asked about his life. It'd been the same in the minors, until Vince had dragged him out to post-win drinks for the first time and made Gene feel like there was space for him.

"How so?" Luis asks.

"Like—when you got scouted, they were nice to you," Gene points out.

"Sometimes. The ones who were interested, yeah."

"I only got scouted twice."

"Okay," Luis says, like a question.

"Once by Baker—that was fine; obviously it worked out. The other time, the guy was like . . . he watched me for the whole game—I went three for five, by the way, with a stolen base—then he met me after and told me, 'If we're ever looking for a gimmick, I'll give you a call.'"

Luis sits up straighter, his face twisted into something between shock and disgust. "He did not."

Gene doesn't broach the rest of the story, the part where their coach still shook that scout's hand and thanked him for coming, still asked if he wanted to grab drinks later. The part where that same coach never apologized to Gene, never asked if he was okay. The part where Gene spent an hour staring at the bulletin board full of Stanford players who'd gone pro—Luis's photo among them, handsome and shining as always—and realized he'd never make it onto that board. Worse, that no one had ever expected him to.

Gene shrugs. "Eh. I'm over it."

He isn't. But he hopes Luis understands why he doesn't want to talk about it anymore.

When Luis asks his next question, it's an easier one. "Are you glad you did it?"

"Yeah," Gene says. "I am. I know some people say, like, they didn't have a choice *not* to, and I get that. But for me it was always a choice. It was just, the other option sucked so much worse than whatever shit I was going to get for coming out."

Luis nods. "You've changed a lot."

"I mean, yeah. Four years of testosterone will do that."

"No. Well, I mean, yeah, that too. You look—"

Gene raises his eyebrows, half-curious, half-wary.

"—really good, obviously."

"Oh, 'obviously'?" Gene says, a little smug.

Luis rolls his eyes, but the sound of "really good, obviously" replays in Gene's head, the syllables lining up with "Dinner, whatever you want," Luis's voice a loop driving Gene dizzy with all the things he won't let himself think.

"I mostly just meant," Luis interrupts, "you seem happier now."

"Happier?"

"You never used to talk this much. At least, not with me."

And that—*that* means more to Gene than any comment Luis could make about how he looks. Because he *is* happier. This version of him—louder and less closed off and far worse at keeping his biggest feelings tucked away in the name of making other people comfortable—is happier than he ever imagined he'd get to be.

It's hard not to like Luis for caring enough to notice.

"It's a lot easier to let people in now that I'm not trying to keep *myself* in. You know what I mean?" Gene asks.

Luis—to Gene's surprise—nods.

Gene—to his surprise—believes that nod.

"Why do you ask?" Gene asks.

"Just curious, I guess."

Luis stares out the windshield, his dog's chin resting on his leg. Luis has some mud behind his ear, somehow missed in the shower, and bags under his eyes, and he looks *tired.* It seems like there might be more of a reason, but Gene returns the favor—he doesn't press the issue.

"My turn for a personal question?" Gene asks.

"Sure."

"You don't have to answer if you don't want to."

"Okay."

"How come you get to bring Dodger on roadies?"

Luis, as if by instinct, sets his hand between Dodger's ears and scratches, absentminded. He doesn't answer at first, the pause long enough that Gene almost rescinds the question. Then, he says, "He's an emotional support dog. I have, like"—he clears his throat—"really fucking bad anxiety."

Gene nods. "And he helps?"

"Yeah, I guess. He's consistent at least." When Dodger flops his head back, farther onto Luis's leg, Luis adds, "It helps to have to take care of someone else. And he's a total diva, so. Plenty of work to distract me."

It isn't a surprise that Luis has anxiety. Gene has always sort of known. The set of Luis's shoulders, the way he leaves every celebration early and almost never talks if he doesn't have to. But to be invited in to this, to know it because Luis shared it, is different. It's like Luis said back at Denny's: Gene wants Luis to be the one to share the things he wants Gene to know.

"Thank you for telling me," Gene says.

"Thanks for asking."

"Oh, I love being nosy."

"It's just"—Luis fiddles with Dodger's collar—"this stuff is hard."

"What is?"

He gestures between them, a hand on his chest and then toward Gene, like there's something there, connecting them. Invisible but enough. "This. Getting to know people. Talking to teammates." He takes a deep breath. "Being a person off the field. If that makes sense."

Something in Gene aches at that. Because it does make sense. People—teammates, coaches, fans, if you have them—watch you when you play, and they expect you to be that same person always. The version of yourself who steps onto the diamond and has all the rules memorized, all the right moves rehearsed. It's hard, sometimes, to find the people you don't have to rehearse for.

The years Gene spent moving up through the minors, carving a niche for himself on a new team every year—*knowing* that most of his teammates held assumptions about him long before he stepped foot in the locker room—was harder than the baseball itself has ever been. He never considered the possibility that Luis might share that experience, in his own way. Anxiety and uncertainty and expectations make for a potent combination.

"Well," Gene says, "I think you're doing okay right now. For what it's worth."

"I don't know about that. Pretty sure half the team wouldn't know my first name if it weren't for my dad," Luis says.

"Gonzo likes you."

"Gonzo likes everyone."

*I like you*, Gene almost says. *Against my better judgment. It's sort of impossible not to.*

Instead: "The guys here are a good group. You should get to know them sometime."

Luis sucks air through his teeth. "We'll see. But thanks."

Gene nods. "So, can people pet emotional support dogs? Asking for a friend."

"You can pet him."

Dodger's fur is fluffier than it looks, somehow, but the real treat is the quiet look Luis gives Gene while Dodger grins between them.

"Okay, can I ask another question?" Gene asks. "It's a very serious matter."

Luis sighs and looks at him, expectant.

"Which mascot would you fuck if you had to fuck one of them?" Gene asks.

Luis rolls his eyes so hard his head tips back against the headrest. "That's so gross, dude. You had that question ready."

Gene wanted to let Luis set his discomfort aside for a moment. This gets the job done. "It's gotta be the Phillie Phanatic," Gene says.

"Disgusting."

"Why?"

"What even *is* he?"

"Doesn't matter. It's about the extendable tongue," Gene says.

"*Stop*. Fucking nasty. This is a gross question."

But he's laughing, so Gene presses on. "My second choice? Thank you for asking. It's Mr. Met."

"Jesus God. Not even the Portland Lumberjack?"

Gene points at him. "So that's your answer?"

"I'm just saying, at least he's a *human*."

"Is it the flannel shirt that does it for you? Because if so, you're living in the right city, my friend."

"You're a pain in the ass," Luis says.

He doesn't drive Gene down the driveway until late in the afternoon, until long after their game would have ended, when the rain has broken into something like a gray brightness.

When, at the end of the driveway, Luis sees Vince and Jack through the living room window, he asks, "Who is that?"

Jack is not a secret on their team. But, then again—if Luis barely talks to anyone, who would have told him?

"Vince's husband," he says.

"Got it," Luis says.

Gene waits for further reaction, but none comes. If Luis is surprised to hear that one of the best pitchers of the last two decades is gay-married and playing on their team, he doesn't show it.

"Okay," Gene finally says. "Well, thank you for the ride. And for hanging out."

He slides off the seat, his feet hitting the fine gravel of the driveway. Right as he closes the heavy door of Luis's truck, Luis says, through the still-open window, "One more question?"

"Shoot."

It comes out in pieces. "If I were also gay—like. In theory. Is that something—we could talk about? Sometime?"

It is all Gene can do to keep breathing.

"You don't have to answer yet," Luis says. Before Gene has the option, Luis turns the engine on and backs out of the driveway, a few ticks too fast to be called anything but reckless.

# 9

## MAY

**Current record: 10–20**

Gene has never been to Baker's house, and before today, he would have guessed that she might live full-time at the ballpark. Not that he assumed she would have nothing in her life but her team, but—certainly he didn't expect this little house in Troutdale, with her Subaru out front and a motorcycle parked under an awning, visible through the side fence. He *very* much did not expect a pink-and-orange-and-white flag in the window, five shades of A Lesbian Lives Here. He didn't, most of all, expect a decidedly un-Baker woman, in a *sundress,* to answer the door when Gene knocks at ten in the morning on their day off.

Listen. He knew Baker was a lesbian the exact moment he met her. She doesn't hide it. But he didn't expect this kind of lesbianism—the crunchy-granola kind, the literal-Birkenstocks kind, the Vitamix-and-bougie-coffee-beans-on-the-counter kind, but, well, here they are.

The sundressed woman leaves when Gene arrives, and Baker

calls him into the kitchen, where she's sitting at the dining room table.

"Help yourself if you want some coffee," she says. She has her laptop in front of her, watching what sound like scouting videos. This, at least, lines up exactly with what he pictured.

"Is she your wife?" Gene asks, popping open her fridge to check if she has any kind of creamer before he pours himself a mug. Grabbing the carton of oat milk, he adds, "Also, are you vegan?"

"No," she says.

"To which question?"

She stares at him.

"Okay. I was expecting someone . . . butcher."

Baker takes a sip of her coffee—black, hot, no sugar, of course—and says, "I have that base covered. Was I supposed to wear something special for this?"

She has on the most formal version of her usual—button-up shirt, short-sleeved, untucked over the most androgynous jeans imaginable. She has paired it with a bun, high enough that it shows off the undercut at the nape of her neck. It needs a trim, but they've officially reached the point in the season when everyone's hair needs a trim.

"This is fine," Gene says.

He promised to take headshots for her weeks ago, when Vince showed her the pictures Gene took for his dogs' birthday and Baker asked, "You have a camera?" As if that were the single requirement to take a decent headshot, which, Gene reasons, it sort of is.

Now, sitting in her house, she seems to regret asking at all.

"What are these for?" Gene asks.

"Headshots," she says.

"No, I know. What are you using them for?"

"Just this thing I do every year."

"Okay."

"A camp. For girls who play baseball."

Gene nods.

She finishes the bottom inch of coffee in her mug and starts passing it back and forth between her hands, in the same rhythm as a baseball smacked into the waiting palm of a glove. "And this year, they asked me to run it, or whatever. So I need a headshot for the website."

"Oh, shit, Baker. That's really cool."

"It's a bunch of administration. I hate it."

Gene begins to sit across the table from her, coffee in hand.

"No, don't sit down," she says. "I want to get this over with. Can we take them in here?"

"Uh," Gene says, "no. I figured we'd go outside, use the natural light."

Baker points at the window. "I can open the blinds."

"Let's go outside," Gene suggests again.

She pinches the bridge of her nose. "Fine."

"It'll take ten minutes."

"I'm holding you to that."

They pick a spot against the railing of her deck. Her backyard is a hodgepodge of projects: a raised-bed garden half-planted and surrounded by waiting seedlings, a small shed with open doors, its contents overflowing onto the unruly grass. The deck, also messy but in a far more contained way, is the easiest spot for Gene to frame a photo to exclude the chaos.

"How do you want me to stand?" she asks.

"However you're comfortable."

She raises an eyebrow.

"Okay, here." Gene points at her elbow. "Can I?"

She lets him position her elbow on the railing, conveniently waist-height. He appreciates being able to help her with something for once, rather than the other way around.

"Why do you hate admin?" he asks while he takes a practice shot.

"I do this so I can coach. If I wanted to deal with a bunch of bureaucracy, I'd have looked for a front office job."

"Are we talking about the volunteer thing or Beaverton? Also, can you tilt your head back a little?"

Baker gives the most awkward smile imaginable. "Both."

"You don't have to smile if you don't want to."

She doesn't. She does tilt her head, though, and Gene was right, the sun catches her cheekbones better this way.

"Do you get to coach, too?"

"Yeah. Shouldn't I stop talking? For the pictures."

"I'm trying to get some candids," Gene admits.

"Oh. Well, yeah. I get to coach. I wouldn't have agreed to run it if I didn't."

"That's cool. I don't think I could do that."

"As well as I do? No," she agrees.

The shutter of Gene's camera clicks another dozen times while they laugh, before Baker sobers.

"Did Vince tell you I'm interviewing for a job with U of O?" she asks.

Gene's finger stalls on his camera, frozen until he manages to muscle past the shock and ask, "What's the job?"

"Head coach."

Gene snaps a single, final picture, between the words "head" and "coach," the perfect space for Baker. The University of Oregon, while obviously not a professional team, is a Division I school. The sort that wins actual games and actual championships sometimes.

"It'd pay me more than three times what I make now. Better title, better office," she adds.

"Probably a better team," Gene says.

"*Definitely* a better team."

It's said with love, so Gene nods. "Baseball or softball?"

He is possibly the only person who can get away with asking Baker this question. It's the implication behind it, not the sport itself, that grates, but they both know Gene has fielded this question just as frequently as Baker. He spent high school on his school's softball team. It's different—hard, wonderful, electric in the ways Gene loves best about baseball, yes. But still different.

After a pause, Baker answers, "Baseball."

"So? Are you going to take it?" It's almost impossible for Gene to imagine her leaving Portland's system, but the uphill battle of dealing with Major League Baseball's bigotry gets tiring sometimes. He would not—*could not*—blame her for being tempted by a better offer from a place that might give her the respect she deserves.

But, "God no," Baker says, and he can't say he's surprised. "And you wouldn't, either."

"How do you know?"

"Because you're loyal," she says. "It makes you a good teammate. Even when it fucks you over, you're loyal."

Gene flips through the pictures he's just taken. "How do you figure?"

"All those extra practices aren't getting *you* any closer to the majors," she says.

It's the truth, but Gene doesn't want it pointed out.

"I don't think that's loyalty fucking me over," Gene says.

"Sure it is. A team only needs so many infielders. He plays shortstop, you don't. He gets called up, you don't."

Gene pauses on a picture of Baker looking confident, at ease. One of the ones he took right before she mentioned the University of Oregon job. "I kind of like second, actually."

She narrows her eyes.

"You want my advice?" she asks.

"Not really."

She gives it anyway, because the coach DNA runs deep. "You wanted to be the first openly trans man to play professional baseball, and you did it. You wanted to play shortstop, and you did that, too. If you wanted to play in someone else's shadow, you would have picked a quieter position."

He does not point out that she makes out the lineups, that she's the one writing "shortstop" next to Luis's name before every game, that Gene doesn't really have a say in the matter. Instead, he turns the camera around to show her the picture he thinks she should use. "This one is good."

Baker takes half a glance at the screen before waving him off. "Whatever, just email it to me."

"I need to edit it first," he says. He'll fix the lighting a little, make sure her backyard projects aren't peeking into the frame. He won't touch her flyaways, or the slight curve of a double chin she has always had, even when she was in catching shape.

"Whatever. But listen, no one has ever done what you're doing. You should do it the way *you* want to. If you give up now, no one else is ever going to get the chance to try. Keep your eye on the ball."

Maybe it's that overzealous loyalty, but Gene can't make himself believe that taking care of your teammates, that wanting good things for them, is naive; he doesn't ever want to be the sort of player to put his pride above his team. And Luis, Gene has realized in the past two weeks, is not his competition—he is his partner, his teammate, someone Gene wants to root for.

"I didn't want to be the *first* one," Gene says. "I wanted to be *a* trans man playing professional baseball."

"And may there be many more after you. But you're the first, whether you like it or not."

Maybe she's talking as much to herself as to him: after all, he and Baker, each the first of their kind in their own way, neither of them by choice, will, more than likely, stall out in Beaverton.

"When did you interview for the Oregon job?" Gene asks.

"They reached out to me in March. Their current guy is retiring at the end of this season, so they want to get someone lined up before then."

"Well, they did their research. You're the best in the area. Probably the whole coast."

"At their budget? Best in the country," she says. Modesty is not her strong suit, nor should it be.

"But you're sure you're going to say no?"

"I'm going to see if I can leverage this to get on Portland's coaching staff."

She should. It probably won't work, but she should.

"And if you can't?"

"Then I guess I'm back in Beaverton next season."

Gene slides his camera into its bag. "You know Vince is thinking about retiring after next year?"

She yanks open the sliding glass door and keeps her hand on it, as if holding it open for Gene to walk in first. Her face barely registers any emotion—more or less acknowledgment that Vince has talked to her about this, too, and that his retirement is, therefore, really, *actually* happening.

"Next year?" she asks.

The tone of her voice makes Gene's stomach sink. It must show on his face.

"He doesn't have another season in him," Baker says. "He doesn't really have *this* season in him."

"I know," Gene says, because he doesn't want to admit how deep in denial he's managed to burrow.

"You should talk to him about it."

Gene grimaces. "I have no idea how to start that conversation."

"It'll be fine, Nes. Beaverton will look different next year, but it'll be fine. I've watched plenty of people leave, and I'm still standing. You get used to it. The trick is not to get too attached," she advises.

"Easier said than done."

"I recommend getting a hot girlfriend," she says with a shrug.

"So she *was* your girlfriend!" Gene says, delighted to be let in on this small piece of her non-baseball life.

"It really softens the blow. But girlfriends might not be in your wheelhouse."

"They are not," he confirms.

"A boyfriend, then. Or a hobby. Something other than this." She waves a finger in the air, "this" meaning *the weird-ass lives we've chosen to live.*

"I'll think about it," Gene says, as if he knows how to do that. It's one thing to take a few headshots. It's another entirely to consider the possibility of a full life outside of baseball.

She squeezes Gene's shoulder, an affirming kind of gesture that Baker rarely makes but which lurks under the persistently irritated surface of her personality. She cares. Maybe that's why she sticks with her team, even when it fucks her over.

What Gene meant to do was: have an apparently overdue heart-to-heart with Vince, the one he had been subconsciously stepping around since Vince first brought up that house in Bend.

What happened instead was:

"You should invite Estrada to dinner."

Gene, after passing Jack in the Altmans' garden and letting himself in the unlocked front door of their house, found Vince in the kitchen. Now he stands staring at the man, trying to discern whether he should be concerned.

There is a slim possibility that Vince is cooking something. The measuring cups and various cutting boards on the counters would certainly imply that cooking has happened or will happen soon. The kitchen smells faintly of dish soap, in spite of the fact that every single dish the Altmans own is dirty. By neither sight nor smell can Gene fathom what monstrosity will appear on their plates that night, but, if Vince cooked it, a monstrosity it will be.

Most important, Vince is wearing an apron, clearly a gift from Jack, which reads MR. GOOD LOOKIN' IS COOKIN'.

Gene resists the all-consuming urge to tease him about that apron. Vince is clearly having some kind of injury-induced midlife crisis in the form of . . . Dutch babies? The cast-iron pan and powdered sugar are out, but Gene has serious doubts that Vince could even tell someone what a Dutch baby is.

"Why?" Gene asks.

"Because it's bullshit you haven't told me that you're dating him."

Gene laughs, sharply. Perhaps too sharply. "I am not dating Luis."

"Fine, then you have a new best friend."

The implication that Vince is the former best friend in question is wrong. He *is* Gene's best friend, no past tense, even factoring in recent developments.

"I do not," Gene says.

Vince might look relieved. He masks it with another jab. "I'm supposed to believe you're not friends *and* you're not sucking his dick? You're just—driving around together in his truck? Just because?"

Gene shuts down that train of thought as quickly as he can, but not nearly quickly enough. The image of it lingers, heating Gene's face. All he says is, "Stop spying on me, man."

"You got home a half hour after me, and *I* had PT." Vince opens and closes a drawer, mostly empty by the sound of it. Gene, looking at the counters, can take a guess where the drawer's previous occupants have gone. "That's a long-ass time to hang out with someone if you're not friends."

"I didn't say we weren't friends at all. I said we're not *best* friends," Gene says.

"Great. So invite him to dinner."

He can't exactly tell Vince that Luis came out to him last night, because it's not Gene's information to share. So he can't say that he's giving Luis space, because then Vince would ask why, and Gene has never been much good at lying.

"Fine," Gene says. "I will invite him to dinner."

He takes out his phone and types, deletes, retypes, lather-rinse-repeats the text five times before sending it. In the end, it reads, *You free for dinner? Altzy invited you.*

Makes it clear that the invitation is not for a date. Doesn't come across too clingy. Puts the onus of the invitation on someone else, so that if Luis ignores the text or turns him down, Gene doesn't have to spiral about it.

Hopefully. Hopefully those seven words do all that.

When he sets his phone down, he takes another look around the kitchen. "Okay, but what are you even making?"

"I am not entirely sure."

"Why the sudden interest in cooking?" Gene asks. He plucks an apple—Honeycrisp, because Vince and Jack buy all the best shit—from the fridge, and grabs a spoon and the jar of peanut butter. As they talk, he takes a small scoop of the peanut butter and slathers it directly onto the skin of the apple before each bite. Protein and vitamins, or whatever.

He sits on one of the barstools Jack keeps tucked neatly under the breakfast bar, and Vince plops onto the one next to him with a click of his tongue. Gene hadn't noticed earlier, but Vince is wearing literal khakis. Or chinos. Something in the khaki family, something which one might purchase at The Gap, something which Vince—who wears more knee-length athletic shorts than any gay man Gene has ever met—would never usually buy, let alone wear.

"Jack said I was getting on his last nerve," he says.

"Why?"

"He said I was"—he throws up air quotes—" 'puttering.' "

"Okay, well. Were you puttering?"

Vince drops his face into his hands. "I'm so fucking bored. My brain is melting out my ears."

"You've been injured before."

"Last time I was gonna be out for this long, it was right when I started dating Jack. I had a distraction."

Gene wiggles his eyebrows. "Pretty nice distraction."

"Shut up," Vince says. "That's my husband—don't be gross."

"I'm being gross *because* he's your husband."

Vince sighs. He has gotten dangerously close to perfecting the put-upon-dad vibes. At least he has that part down for when he and Jack adopt. The cooking, though?

"Do you know how to make spaghetti?" Vince asks.

Gene looks around. "There is not a single tomato in here."

When Vince groans, Gene leans around and tugs open the junk drawer, the one full of old-school take-out menus he and Vince have trawled plenty of times post-game in desperation for a restaurant that stays open past ten o'clock. Resting on top of the stack is a familiar folder, pale yellow and beginning to wear thin where the folded edge strains against its contents. In Jack's handwriting, it reads ADOPTION, in all capital letters. On all the dozens of occasions Gene has seen this folder, though, he's never seen the sticky note that sits on top of it now. Neon green, with a name and an address and a time written in Vince's scrawl. A date, two weeks from now.

Gene opens his mouth to say something about it—to ask who this "Melissa" is, if they've met with her already, whether she's a kid or someone who can help them adopt one. Maybe Gene could ask how Vince feels about it, even tell him dads don't have to know how to make spaghetti. But with half the contents of the

Altman kitchen spilled around them, it doesn't feel like the moment. Vince has gone back to reading recipes on his phone anyway. It's easy enough for Gene to pretend he didn't see.

Vince will tell him eventually, right?

He bypasses the folder and fans the menus for Vince, like cards. "Pick a restaurant, Mr. Good Lookin'. It's on me."

Luis, as it turns out, already had plans for the night, and by the time Gene hears the truck pulling up outside, the Altmans have made their way to bed. Even so, Gene feels cheated of the hours he has come to expect to spend with Luis. They haven't had an off day without travel in so long, Gene has forgotten what it feels like to pass a day without him. A month ago, he would have loved the break—he would have begged it to stretch longer.

But tonight, he finds himself rushing down the stairs and leaning his elbows on Luis's rolled-down truck window to ask, "Do you want to stay and hang out for a while?"

They take the outside stairs up to the attic apartment, the wood dried out for the coming summer and creaking under them while Dodger bounds ahead. Gene tries to remember what state of disarray he's left each room in and, hence, how embarrassed he should be. The bathroom, cleaned two weeks ago, is overdue but not outrageous; the living room, thoroughly unused in recent weeks, might pass for clean, other than the unbuilt coffee table; the kitchen, scrubbed this morning, shines; his bedroom, completely covered in laundry, does not contain a bed frame, but this is thoroughly and mercifully irrelevant.

"Sorry it's sort of a mess," he says as he opens the door.

Luis shrugs and follows Dodger inside. "That's fine."

Still, it's not really the mess but the minutiae that make it so nerve-racking to open his door to a new person. The fact that he can't get himself to put his apartment together, yes, but also the little one-inch-high plastic baby figurines on his mantel, with their hats shaped like vegetables, that he used to get at the bookstore in Bryant Park with Joey. His dad's old baseball jersey, which Gene wears to bed sometimes when he's homesick. The framed posters—of Freddie Mercury in drag, *Little Shop of Horrors*, a painting of the David statue where the artist has added top scars and removed the dick, which he loves but which seems painfully twee now that someone else can see it. It has been almost a full year since Gene last went on a first date, and this is not a date at all, but he gets the same nervous feeling over someone seeing his private space—the life he has and the person he is when no one is looking.

Luis takes his sweet time looking, too.

When he does finally speak up, he points at David. "Like your tattoo," he says.

The David on Gene's arm is surrounded by a small collection of other tattoos—a tree, a blackberry bramble, a stick-and-poke dog on roller skates. The beginnings of a mostly intentional half-sleeve. But the one Luis is talking about sits on the upper inside of his arm, such that when he wears his jersey or a T-shirt, everything but the tattoo's legs and feet get covered by the fabric. It's the sort of tattoo Luis would need to really look for to notice.

The moment passes as quickly as it came, unremarked upon, Gene making a mental note to fixate on it later.

"Do you want to watch a movie?" Gene asks, which is maybe the most date-like activity he could have suggested without getting naked. If Luis were any other teammate, Gene wouldn't think twice about watching a movie, but, alas—he is not any other teammate.

"Sure. Can I take off my shoes?"

Luis takes a minute to get comfortable, his demeanor resembling something more along the lines of someone about to get a teeth cleaning—apprehensive, trying to hide it. But Dodger curls up on the couch, a cloud of white and black and gray, and lets loose a whine-like howl until Luis settles next to him.

Luis looks good there. Arm resting on Gene's throw pillow, dog in his lap, socked feet, and his T-shirt tucked into jeans.

Gene turns on the TV and hands over the remote. "Pick whatever you want—I'll make snacks." Anything to put off the *How many couch cushions is the normal number of couch cushions to leave between you and a friend whose face you definitely don't want to suck?* dilemma.

From the next room, he hears Luis, in the distracted tone of someone scrolling through streaming services: "Question."

"What else is new?" Gene yells back, though the apartment is not nearly large enough to necessitate yelling.

"How the hell do you afford all of these? What kind of signing bonus did they give you?"

Gene peels open the plastic casing around a bag of popcorn, remembering their conversation about preferred ballpark snacks. He slides it onto the glass tray in his microwave and waits to hear the first pop before he leans in the doorway between kitchen and living room. "Promise not to get jealous when I tell you?"

Luis nods, mock-solemn.

"It was three thousand entire dollars."

"And you're using it all on streaming services, apparently."

"Vince pays for them," Gene says. Luis will see for himself when he logs in to one of them and sees Vince's name there alongside Gene's, sporting whatever ridiculous icon Gene most recently assigned him.

"Is he, like, your platonic sugar daddy or something?" Luis asks.

"No. Just my friend."

"Well, his house is insanely nice."

"I'm sure you can see the rest of it in the morning if you want to," Gene says, before he can convince himself not to offer.

"The morning? I'm staying over?" Luis asks.

"If you want. The couch is comfortable."

Luis leans back against the cushions. "Okay," he says.

"Okay? What, okay?"

"Okay. The couch is comfortable." He smiles. "Follow-up question?"

Gene flops down on the couch, popcorn bowl in hand and two sodas slotted into the crook of his arm. Luis appears to have chosen *The Muppet Movie*, which he's paused on the opening credits. "'Are we going to watch the movie?' Is that the question?" Gene asks.

"No. Why is your stuff in boxes?" To punctuate his point, Luis nods his head to the cardboard-cluttered corner, where Gene has stacked all the furniture he hasn't built and all the boxes of things he has nowhere to put until he builds said furniture. Gene doesn't know how exactly to explain how hard it is to get himself to start a project, how much he *knows* his life will be better if he just does it, and how he can't make himself take that first step, so he never gets to the last one.

"Ah," Gene says. "Because my brain is broken."

Luis raises his eyebrows. Waits.

"I have ADHD," he explains, "and it's super hard to get myself to do projects if I don't have a hard deadline. Plus, it's like—I don't know, you get tossed around so much in the minors, from place to place, I guess I didn't totally trust that I'd get to stay here." Gene hadn't admitted that part of it to himself, but now that he says it aloud—that was a factor, too. Maybe bigger than the other stuff. "You know? I mean, I guess you've been in Triple-A for a while."

"Yeah. Getting traded three times sort of complicated things, though." Luis chews on a piece of popcorn. "I'm still living out of suitcases. So, I get it."

"Are you going to get an apartment?"

"I can't afford one. Beaverton's hardly any cheaper than Portland."

"You could find a roommate." If Gene had a second bedroom, he'd offer it, but as is, he can't exactly offer Luis the second half of his floor mattress.

Luis shrugs. "Maybe. I still think you should build your furniture regardless."

"Oh, I mean. I one hundred percent think I should, too. Just—usually no one else sees it, so it doesn't really matter."

"So you live alone?" Luis asks.

Gene cracks open Luis's ginger ale and hands it over. "Are you asking if I have a roommate?"

"Or something else."

Gene looks at the TV. "No. My boyfriend used to come over sometimes, but he dumped me last season." He's not sure why he added that last part. It's not relevant.

"What? Why?"

Gene shrugs. "Didn't care about baseball, didn't get why I care about it, hated the travel schedule. I don't blame him." He plucks up whatever small shred of self-respect he has and slam-dunks it into the trash so he can ask, "Why?"

"Just curious," Luis says.

"Okay, '*just curious.*'" Gene gives a bad impression of Luis's voice.

"I don't really date much, either." Luis pulls a bag of Sour Patch Kids from his pocket and rips it open. With the very tips of his fingers, he starts removing the greens and laying them in a pile on one of the coasters Jack gave Gene when he moved in.

"No?" Gene asks.

"Not since before my accident." Luis hits the play button before Gene can respond to that, popping another piece of popcorn in his mouth and chewing as quietly as a piece of popcorn can be chewed. The notes of "Rainbow Connection" start strumming out of Gene's TV.

If Gene isn't mistaken—and he isn't, but it feels almost impossible to believe—Luis mouths the lyrics in perfect sync.

"How many times have you seen this?" Gene asks.

Luis slides another stack of greens onto the coaster. "I'd rather not say."

"Can you do a Kermit impression?"

Luis sings the next line—"What's so amazing that keeps us stargazing, and what do we think we might see?"—in a surprisingly sweet voice, the best Kermit that Gene has ever heard outside a Jim Henson movie. Then he shuts his mouth like it never happened.

Gene stares at Luis while Luis stares at the bag of Sour Patch Kids, and—goddamn if that didn't charm every last bit of him. "What the fuck?" he asks.

"What?" Luis says.

"How'd I not know you could do that?" *How'd you get so cute, and why didn't you warn me?*

"Didn't I ever tell you? Before I wanted to be a divorce lawyer, I wanted to be a Muppeteer."

"You absolutely did not."

In that perfect Kermit voice, Luis says, "I think you'll find that I did."

Gene sort of wants to kiss him over that, but Luis hands over the de-greened Sour Patch Kids first, and so, instead, Gene says, "Seems like you're pretty decent boyfriend material to me."

"I don't think a good Kermit impression ranks that high on most guys' priority lists when I'm a closeted gay baseball player, and not even the rich kind."

"I thought you just *might* be gay '*in theory.*'"

"Oh, no," Luis says, so much of the nervous energy he had

yesterday dissipated in a haze of popcorn and Muppets. "Gay for sure. It's just—my life's not really set up for it."

"How so?"

"Like, I have a panic disorder and can't even brush my teeth without gagging."

Maybe Luis is experiencing the same marvel as Gene—the sudden post-outing ease of talking to someone you don't have to hide around. Still, Gene laughs, surprised at the bluntness of it. "Well, I can suggest a solution for that last one, at least," he says without thinking. "Dating-wise."

"I'm all ears."

Luis does have those prominent ears, poking out even as his hair has started to grow a little shaggy around them, absurdly charming. Those long eyelashes, too, and eyebrows that stray past the outside corners of his eyes, toward his hairline. His nose is almost straight, with a bump at its bridge that makes it curve gently down. His mouth—eminently distracting. Even with the light of the TV, slightly blue-tinged and static-fuzzy on his profile, drowning out the warmth of his skin, Luis is—

Fozzie and Kermit start singing on-screen. "Movin' Right Along," indeed.

Baker suggested he get a boyfriend. Not ask his closeted gay teammate if he might want to make out on Gene's couch for a while.

Maybe he *should* start looking for a hobby, or a better vibrator, because, *shit.*

He spends the rest of the night with Luis's shoulder pressed against his, watching Kermit and Miss Piggy—

("Do you think Kermit is gay and Miss Piggy is his boyfriend's drag persona?"

"Pay attention to the movie, Nes."

"Okay, but you're laughing.")

—and Gonzo and Fozzie. The conversation drifts away from

the riskiest topics, but everything Gene would like to say sits there, pressed into the minuscule space between them, threatening to spill out again.

By the time they finish the third entry in their impromptu Muppets marathon, *Treasure Island*, it's going on one-thirty. Gene's arm cramps from keeping it locked in position, touching Luis's but not *touching* Luis's. Even four hours in, Gene can feel every bit of the contact, has nearly bitten through the inside of his cheek about it.

"You really can stay here if you want," Gene offers. "It's late."

"Well, I heard the couch is comfortable."

Before Gene can say something else impulsive and ill-advised, and before he can think any more about Luis pressing other, non-shoulder parts of himself against Gene, he gets sheets and a spare pair of sweats for him. While Luis changes, Gene throws the sheets over the couch as best he can, and then unmakes it just so he has something to do with his hands. Dodger stares at him the whole time, panting with his mouth open so it looks almost like he's poking fun at Gene.

"I know," Gene says, a whisper, like Dodger can understand him. "I'm a mess. But your dad is killing me."

He's about to unmake and remake the couch for the third time when Luis shuffles out of the bathroom. Gene's sweats hit him mid-calf, his ankles out for all the world to see. Gene has the unbidden idea that he'd like to kiss the inside of one of those ankles.

If, of course, Luis weren't his teammate, and if he weren't probably going to get called up to the major leagues while Gene stayed in the minors. Gene was too much of a baseball player for his last boyfriend—he'd like not to be too little of one for the next.

And that's all assuming Luis has any interest in him at all, which, as far as Gene knows, he doesn't. It's too much to risk—

this tentative friendship, the understanding he feels when Luis talks, the rhythms they have finally started to find. Gene can't throw that away just because his second-ever queer teammate is easy to talk to, with strong wrists that Gene would like to put to good use.

"Well," Gene says, heading that train off at the pass. "Good night."

Luis, sitting on his couch in those too-short sweats, kissable ankles and all, looks painfully soft. When Dodger lays himself across Luis to go to sleep, Gene very nearly has to clutch his chest.

"Hey," Luis says as soon as Gene tries to make his escape. Gene's heart picks up its stuttering, hoping against hope that maybe Luis is going to ask to share his bed. But Luis says, "If you ever want help"—he gestures toward the disassembled coffee table pieces in the corner—"putting together the rest of your shit?"

Gene raises his eyebrows.

"I don't mind. I think it's relaxing," Luis says. "We could watch a movie or something while we worked on it."

Which is maybe the worst thing Luis could have said, worse than asking to share his bed, because it's *romantic*, and *thoughtful*, and it isn't even intentional.

"Thanks," Gene says. He doesn't like to ask for help, but he thinks he might appreciate it in this case. "Maybe next week?"

Luis nods. There's a smile on his lips when he lies down, when he says good night. Gene closes the door to his bedroom, rests his forehead on the wood, and screams silently until he runs out of air.

And when he lies down on his own frameless mattress, he wishes he were a little braver. Enough, at least, not to care about all the reasons he shouldn't ask Luis to join him in here. That, or significantly *less* brave, so that the idea wouldn't have even crossed his mind. He wishes his imagination would stop running the image of Luis hunched over instructions, carefully slotting the wooden joints of a table together, on a loop through his head.

As it is, Gene stares at the ceiling, quilt pulled up to his chin and his fingers dancing on his arm, tracing the outline of his half-hidden tattoos and wondering when Luis started looking enough to notice them.

# 10

## MAY

Current record: 22–26

Vince has caught Luis coming into or leaving Gene's apartment no fewer than five times, each of which Gene knows about because Vince texts him a question mark and nothing else.

Three weeks after Luis woke up in Gene's apartment for the first time, they take a roadie bus all the way to Sacramento. Under normal circumstances, the team would spring for a plane—commercial, at six A.M. or earlier, most of them squeezed into middle seats—for a trip this long, but, because the series starts on a Tuesday, they spend their free Monday driving.

The drive takes nine hours with no traffic and no stops, so in actuality, it takes closer to twelve. They start at the ass-crack of dawn, industrial-sized coffees and travel pillows in hand, their bags chucked into the bus's undercarriage. Gene selects the seat across the aisle from Luis's, a choice which Vince gives only the barest of eyebrow raises before settling into the seat next to Gene for his morning nap.

Three hours into the trip, everyone's self-contained entertainment plans grow stale.

Six hours in, they have taken two rest breaks and completed a full round of Two Truths and a Lie, a game at which Gene excels and at which Luis absolutely bombs—he guesses, for example, that the lie in Gene's selection is that he knows a hairless cat named Garbage, and not that he was a photography major in college.

"Technically," Gene says, "her name is Spazzatura. Which is Italian for garbage."

"You were doing photography when I left," Luis argues.

"Yeah. I ended up majoring in stats, though." He briefly entertained the idea of going the front office route into baseball, as if he'd ever had any interest in the off-field parts of an organization.

Luis smiles, too fondly. "I feel like that was a trap. How was I supposed to know that?"

"That's the point of the game," Gene says.

"Then I want to play a new game."

"Because you're bad at this one?"

Luis, who has, for once, kept his headphones off the whole trip, nods. "Yes."

"Sore loser."

"Yes."

Ernie pops his head up from the row in front of them. "Alphabet Roast?" he asks.

"Perfect, yes," Gene says. "We need a twenty-sixth."

Their roster holds twenty-five men, so alphabet-based games are almost perfect. They can generally rope Baker in, and today is no different.

She says, at her normal volume, which carries to every seat in the bus, "A is for anemic, which is how Ross has looked at the plate this week."

Ross, half-asleep and mostly tuned out of the conversation until this point, gives a weak "Hey" from where he has sunken into his seat. He follows it up with, "B is for balls, which Keats can't stop throwing."

Luis leans across the aisle, his mouth infinitely too close to Gene's ear, and says, voice low, "I don't know anyone here well enough to play this."

Gene shrugs, if only to cover the way he shivers at Luis's lips being that close. "Do me. Like, say something about me, I mean."

"What if someone else gets to you first?"

"Guess you better hope that doesn't happen."

So, when Ernie says, "E is for all the extra bases Nada can't hit," Luis doesn't look insulted at all. He's too busy grinning, a little too widely, at Gene.

"Go ahead, then," Gene says.

"F," Luis starts, and Gene can think of a lot of words that start with that particular letter that he'd like to hear Luis say, "is for Nes having the fattest ass on the team."

A chorus of *whoops* erupt, punctuated most distinctly by Gene's half-manic laugh and Ernie's very loud, "*Amen!*"

"I don't think you understand the game," Gene says. "These are supposed to be *bad* things."

The way Luis looks at him, Gene thinks maybe he doesn't care what the point of the game is.

Gene clears his throat. "G is for geriatric, which is what Altzy is."

They have Vince penciled in to make his first post-injury start today, but he needs to throw a bullpen and check in with a trainer before he gets the green light. He's tense about it, has been tense about it for days, but no matter how many times Gene attempts to bring it up, Vince shuts the conversation down. Assuming he makes the start, they'll limit him to sixty or so pitches, to ramp him back up to a full workload, but it's a good thing. It's progress, promising, enough to tempt anybody's hopeful streak. At least, enough to tempt Gene's.

But Vince, next to him, doesn't even bother flipping Gene off. He just gives him the flattest possible look, adjusts his travel pillow, and closes his eyes again. Not ready to be teased for this, then.

"Okay," Gene says, in an effort to cover up the awkward moment, "I'll do yours for you. H is for the hour Kyle spends on his hair."

No one has to clarify which Kyle Gene means. Kyle Nguyen says from the middle of the bus, "Okay, but my hair looks good, doesn't it?"

"It does," Kyle Rivera agrees.

Gene's phone goes off in his hand.

When he checks it, a text from Luis reads, *Do you think they're dating?*

Gene texts back, *Kyle & Kyle?*

*Kyle & Kyle & Kyle.*

Gene bites his laugh down. *GOD I hope so,* he responds. He then follows it up with, *Why, jealous??*

*No. Too tall for me.*

Okay, well—that's a neutral fact. So he likes guys shorter than the Kyles. Most guys are shorter than the Kyles.

Gene types out, *You have a thing for short kings?*

Luis smiles at him, but he doesn't respond to Gene's text. He settles back into the game, and Gene spends the remaining six hours of the trip wondering whether that was flirtation or a rejection, not quite sure he wants the answer.

---

NANCY: So, it's no secret Beaverton had a rocky start this season, right? But—five games away from a winning record!

DAN: Still a ways off from ending that playoff drought, but it's nothing to sniff at. These guys have put together a really special run.

NANCY: They've won twelve of eighteen since their rainout at home.

DAN: Most of those by only one run.

NANCY: Luck seems to have been on their side a bit, especially today, getting Vince Altman back.

DAN: Right, he was officially taken off the injured list yesterday. Good timing, too, Nate Parker was really struggling to fill in for him.

NANCY: Big shoes to fill, that's for sure. Now, you mentioned—

DAN: —the drought, I know.

NANCY: We'll have to wait and see if this is their year, but something good is happening here either way.

DAN: My dad watched a game! The man missed the birth of his grandkid to watch a Lumberjacks game, but he missed last Friday's blowout loss against Miami so he could watch the Beavers.

NANCY: Now that's an accomplishment. These guys should feel proud, for sure. And let's talk about the guys—Estrada's batting .310 over the last three weeks. He was hitting barely over a buck-fifty before this stretch.

DAN: An incredible turnaround since they moved him up in the order.

NANCY: I almost hope Portland doesn't notice. I'd love to

see what he and Ionescu can do for this team with some more defensive work and a few months with a healthy Ernie Gonzales and Vince Altman. Assuming none of them get dealt to another team before the July trade deadline.

DAN: That's a lot of ifs.

NANCY: We're dreaming big here. Why not?

---

The entire team shows up to watch Vince's bullpen session, during which he throws what look suspiciously like vintage Vince Altman pitches into Ernie's waiting glove. His command looks good, better than it has all season. His velocity has raised a tick, too—not to his Cy Young levels, but better than it was in April.

Gene can't quite tell where he and Vince stand after the comment on the bus, but the bullpen session encourages him. His job may always be just the quieter cousin of most players' dream careers, but he has started to love playing again. He might have a little bit of a massive thing for his teammate, but that doesn't scare him as much today as it should. Because—damn if this doesn't all feel special anyway.

This is a messy team, in a messy year of Gene's usually very straightforward life, but when they put their jerseys on to the sweet, ridiculous sounds of Cooper's Margaritaville music taste, it really feels like they could get all the pieces in place this year to make a run at the playoffs.

"You know, I was thinking," Gene says, as they wait in the dugout for their names to get called.

"Yeah?" Luis asks.

"You owe me dinner."

Luis grins. "Tonight?"

"No takeout."

"No, no takeout."

Over the speakers, Sacramento's announcer reads Gene's name with little enthusiasm, mispronounced. Gene shrugs, *What're you gonna do*, at Luis before jogging out to join their lineup.

He has a good feeling about this game. He gets those often—he seeks them out, revels in them, no matter how small—but this one is the same as before the rainout, the game that turned the tide on their season.

So, when he works a ten-pitch walk to start the game, Gene settles in.

He shoots Luis a nod from first—half-flirt, half-promise. He thinks about sitting at Denny's, past midnight, telling him to hit a homer or two. He thinks about the disbelief in Luis's eyes, and about how he never doubted for a second that Luis could do it, even when he most wanted Luis gone, when he wanted those homers out of spite, to get Luis called up sooner.

Now, when Luis swings on the first pitch he sees and makes solid, feel-it-in-your-teeth contact, Gene wants it because Luis is his teammate, because Gene wants good things for all of his teammates. Because he wants good things for Luis, specifically.

Gene forgets to run. He watches that ball arc its beautiful path all the way past the outfield green, into the stands, until Luis, coming up behind him, urges him on. They round home, Gene barely ahead, and the congratulatory slap he gives Luis's ass almost stings. It startles a laugh out of Luis and a cheer from their dugout, and, eleven pitches in, they have a lead.

But the real victory comes in the third.

After Vince gives up a single to Sacramento's right fielder, Ernie calls for a mound visit. Vince sighs as they gather around the bump, his glove over his mouth.

"What?"

"You feeling okay?" Ernie asks.

"It is the third inning. I'm fine," Vince spits. While he is always efficient, today he has been almost *harsh*. His pitches are coming out sharp, laced with anger in place of his usually laid-back focus.

Ernie studies him, a little suspicious, but it takes a lot to get Vince Altman off the mound. So, instead of trying to, Ernie holds his glove up to his mouth. "Up and inside. Six-four-three double play."

Nerves drop, unceremoniously, all the way down to Gene's feet.

"You better not fuck this up," Vince says, eyes first on Luis and then, a little more firmly, on Gene. He has never spoken to Gene like that, but Gene won't get his feelings hurt. Not now, not on the field, not in a game.

"Aye-aye, captain," he agrees.

Vince throws his slider exactly where Ernie asks him to—so far inside it's nearly on the Sacramento catcher's wrists. When he swings, it smokes up the gap, setting up a play most infielders could only dream of making.

But Luis dives.

He gets his glove on the ball, plucks it with ease from his palm as Gene sprints toward second. His foot hits second base the same moment Luis's throw finds its way into his hands.

*You need to stop trying to move like a shortstop. You just have to get the turn and the snap down faster. You have it during drills, but you're trying too hard during games.*

Gene doesn't try.

He twists and unleashes the throw to first. The way he would in drills, the way he would when he and Luis field increasingly unlikely grounders before full-team practice, each in an attempt to impress the other.

Gene may not have a cannon for an arm. But he can do this. He can show up at second when Luis needs him there, can twist himself into whatever shape the team needs from him to make the play.

Maybe Vince doesn't celebrate when they make that tight double play, and maybe it shouldn't be such a big deal. But Luis jumps to high-five him as the inning ends, punctuating it with a slap to the ass—repayment for Gene's congratulatory gesture earlier—and Gene feels, finally, like things have settled into place, if only a little.

They win. Vince lasts only one more inning, but he turns in a solid start that their bullpen brings home with ease.

He sits in the locker room after the game, long past when most everyone else has left.

"We can do dinner another night," Luis says to Gene, duffel bag slung over his shoulder.

Vince tips his head back against the wall of his stall and sighs, echoing in the empty locker room.

"Yeah," Gene says. "I'll meet you back at the hotel."

Barely within Gene's line of sight, Vince rolls his eyes. As soon as the door closes behind Luis, Gene stands in front of Vince.

"You didn't have to cancel your date on my behalf," Vince says.

Gene doesn't bother correcting him. "Like fuck I didn't. You and I are getting dinner and you're going to tell me why you've been so fucking miserable all day," he says.

"I'll take a rain check."

Gene doesn't hesitate. "No."

He grabs Vince's bag for him and slings it over his own free shoulder. Vince is the kind of man who will allow himself to be gay, to marry another man, to reject *some* societal expectations, but still will not let himself get caught crying or asking for help. All those years surrounded by meatheads rubs off on a guy, apparently. He still will not let someone else carry his weight, literally or figuratively.

Gene, however, is not in the mood to coddle that part of Vince tonight.

Gene has spent a good many years ridding himself of the idea that, just because he has admitted to himself that he's a man, he should do things the ways cis men do them. He has picked and chosen the parts of manhood he enjoys and skipped over the rest, like a boy buffet. Short hair? Please. Spicy deodorant? Excellent. Cheaper toiletries and an abundance of useless sports trivia? More of those, please, yes, though he was partaking in men's shaving cream and Baseball-Reference Dot Com long before he ever considered injecting testosterone in his body.

But then, he still buys his jeans from the women's section, because no amount of said testosterone can rid him of his famed fat ass, not when he's doing the sheer quantity of squats and stairs he does. Sometimes, he cries easily, but so does his exceedingly cis dad, so, well, whatever.

Mostly, he's a man because he says he is.

And he's never understood why Vince won't let other people help carry his shit. So Gene picks up the damn bag for him.

"I'm not hungry," Vince says, sounding distinctly like a child when he does.

"Tough shit."

"Fine," Vince says. "But I'm driving."

"You don't even have your car here. I'm calling one for us."

"Fine. I'm paying."

Gene pats his cheek, because it will bug the shit out of Vince, and sometimes that's the best way to get him to snap out of a mood. "Sure, big guy. You can pay."

Gene holds open the door out of the locker room and into the hall that leads to the parking lot. Vince is crankier than he would usually be about an impromptu Tuesday night dinner, and certainly crankier than he can justify being after a solid win behind the best start he could have hoped for—but otherwise, it's the exact same as it would have been any other night.

They go to a little Korean place, less than fifteen minutes away, the one with the bok choy and noodles that Gene likes, the barbecue that Vince likes, and the exceedingly good beer they both like. Comfort food—warm and familiar. It's what Gene would want if he'd had a bad day, which Vince seems intent on having.

"What'd Teresa say?" Gene asks.

Teresa came in to replace the team's old physical therapist last year, and while she does apply an abundance of ice packs, she knows her shit. No way she'd let Vince pitch without a lengthy check-in.

"That I'm getting old," Vince says.

"Okay, well, the calendar could have told you that."

Vince takes a long drink from his beer. "You know I'm not that old? Thirty-eight is not that old."

"Well—"

"Plenty of guys keep pitching past thirty-eight."

"Plenty" is a massive exaggeration. Not to mention, most of those guys didn't make it to the majors at nineteen or have to fight to stay off the injured list since the day they crossed the thirty-year threshold. Though Vince may only be thirty-eight, athlete ages are different, and he has the arm of someone twice his age.

But he doesn't need to hear those things from Gene.

"So what does she recommend?" Gene asks.

"Retirement."

"Right now?"

Vince shrugs, watches their food get set down with an apathy Gene has never before witnessed from him about anything.

"End of the year," he says eventually.

So, that's that.

To his surprise, Gene doesn't find himself half as upset by that as he would have been a month ago. What upsets him—what makes his voice come out sadder than he means for it to—is that Vince has deflated.

"Well, that's still a few months. And then you get to adopt, right? Have a kid in that big fancy house?" Gene says, forcing cheerfulness into his voice.

Vince squints at him. "What do you mean?"

"I saw the folder in your kitchen. You had a meeting about it last week, right? I'm really excited for you." He grins, and he means it, even if Vince is leaving for real. Even if Gene will miss him. He *is* excited for Vince.

But: "What's there to be happy about? We're two gay men closing in on forty—you really think they're going to just hand us a baby on the first try?"

Gene's smile falters. "I could write you a letter," he offers.

"A *letter*?"

"People do that, right? Like, I can say you're a great team dad, so you'll be a great dad-dad."

Vince drops his chopsticks, just aggressively enough that the couple at the next table glances over. "Oh, come the fuck on. I'm not your 'team dad,' I'm the *captain*. I want to play, not sit on the sidelines like I'm coaching your Little League team."

"You are playing," Gene says, because it's the only part he trusts himself to respond to without crying, and he doesn't want to cry in front of Vince when he's like this.

"Yeah, and what's the point?"

It takes Gene aback. "What does that mean? Like, you're quitting?"

"It means it wouldn't matter if I did."

"Of course it would. The team needs you."

What Gene means, of course, is that *he* needs Vince.

For Gene, it has never been a crisis of confidence. Not in his skills, at least. Three years into this career, he has yet to feel overwhelmed or outmatched on a baseball diamond. This is his game—one that lives in the deepest parts of him—and he is *good.* That much, at least, Gene has never questioned. What he *has* questioned is whether this game could be good to him in return. He'd always doubted that, until he came to Beaverton.

He owes this in part to Baker's presence—to the trail she blazed, even if it wasn't the one Gene has followed.

But no small part of his success here—no small part of the reason his teammates celebrate his successes, no small part of Gene feeling completely welcome and wanted in Beaverton's clubhouse—is Vince. He treated Gene like a little brother the instant Gene walked in. In a sport so dependent on confidence, on optimism, on trusting the person batting after you, that vote of support can't be overvalued.

And Vince knows that.

So when he says, "Well, it's not *your* career that's going to shit, is it?" Gene knows Vince means it exactly as personally as it sounds.

The other thing is—Vince is the reason Gene plays the way he does. Vince is the reason Gene is a people-first player, the reason he knows a game doesn't end until the last out is made. Because Vince will look at a team full of absolute lemons, complain about them until he goes hoarse, and still believe they can cobble together a scrappy win every night.

He invited Gene into that stubborn determination, and Gene has made his home in it.

"Okay," Gene says. It's all he can say.

But Vince isn't done.

"Do you know what the worst feeling is?" he asks.

*This, probably.* "No."

"Not being needed. I'm supposed to be the fucking captain, and you guys went and got better without me playing."

"You got us through tonight's game," Gene points out. "You could get us to the playoffs if you wanted to."

It's a long shot. But it's Vince's fondest hope—to pitch in the postseason.

"If we make it to the playoffs, it'll have nothing to do with me. I'm going to retire in the minors, with a bum shoulder and a breaking elbow, and no one is going to care. And you don't get that, because you're twenty-six with your whole career ahead of you."

It's a selfish way of looking at things, and utterly untrue to boot.

Most of all, it makes Gene angry. To be talked down to, dismissed like he doesn't know anything about feeling irrelevant. Like his body has never kept him from the things he wanted most.

It's fucking insulting.

Gene takes a crumpled twenty out of his wallet and sets it on the table.

"That's all I have," he says.

Vince stares at that twenty-dollar bill like it spat in his food.

"Stop snooping in my shit," Vince says. His voice is painfully even. "And stop trying to fix everybody else's problems. I don't want a letter, I want my career back. Can you fix *that* for me?"

Gene scoots his chair away from the table, the scraping abrupt and loud against the dinged-up hardwoods.

"Text me the receipt, I can pay you back the rest," he says.

And he waits to cry until he's a few blocks away, sitting on the curb and dialing Luis's number before he can overthink it. Luis picks him up twenty minutes later, both of them packed into the back of a taxi so Gene doesn't have to take a car alone, at night.

Luis gives Gene a box of tissues clearly stolen from the hotel bathroom. He puts his hand on top of Gene's, briefly, on the seat between them, and squeezes. He doesn't mention the dinner they were supposed to get. He doesn't ask if Gene wants to talk about it. But he sits in the quiet with Gene all the same.

# 11

## JUNE

Current record: 38–34

NANCY: I want to talk for a minute about Gene Ionescu.

DAN: Please, do.

NANCY: *Twenty-four games.*

DAN: It really is incredible, isn't it?

NANCY: For those of you who maybe haven't been keeping track of Beaverton until recently, Ionescu is working a twenty-four-game hitting streak. He's twenty-six years old, barely more than five feet tall, from Brooklyn, New York. But his dad played in the Portland system for about a decade.

DAN: I think we can call him a hometown kid.

NANCY: I think so. He is also—

DAN: —Yeah, I was going to say—

NANCY: —the first openly transgender person to play professional baseball in the . . . in the country, right?

DAN: In the country, that's right.

NANCY: Had you heard of him before last season?

DAN: No.

NANCY: Okay, so I'd heard rumblings that he was pretty good, but no one told me he was *this* good.

DAN: Right, he's batting almost .350 on the season.

NANCY: And now playing better defense than half the guys in the big leagues, next to Luis Estrada, who was acquired in the Arizona deal this spring. Portland has made it pretty clear they're hoping to call Estrada up sometime in late summer, after the All-Star break.

DAN: They certainly need another infielder, but he and his glove will be sorely missed here in Beaverton.

NANCY: That they will. We might not see *either* of these guys around here next spring.

DAN: It'll be interesting to keep an eye on, for sure. Ionescu was good last season as well, but he wasn't quite this caliber.

NANCY: Right, finding a rhythm with Estrada up there in the keystone has helped, and he's really flourished in the leadoff spot.

DAN: With the Futures Game coming up next month, you have to wonder whether they might get the chance to show off their stuff with the best of 'em.

NANCY: It'll be interesting to see who gets called up first.

DAN: Who's your guess?

NANCY: I'd have to go with Estrada. That glove is something special.

DAN: All right, well, I'm rooting for Ionescu, then.

NANCY: Just to be contrary?

DAN: Just to be contrary. Seems like a good kid, too. It'll be interesting either way.

NANCY: Here's to keeping that hit streak alive, huh?

---

Thinking about streaks and averages and strikeout rates—it doesn't help. You can't stress yourself into being a good baseball player—you are or you aren't, and even if you are, you need a healthy dose of luck in order to actually see results.

*This* is what Gene thinks about while he steps up to the plate for this fourth and possibly last at-bat of the night. He needs to take every at-bat as it comes, not as the be-all and end-all of some useless statistic. What *matters* is whether his team wins.

And, currently, Beaverton is not winning. They are not-winning by exactly five runs.

So he does what Vince always tells him to do. Vince, who isn't pitching tonight, who has hardly talked to Gene since that dinner in Sacramento almost a month ago, who Gene misses more than he can say, even now, while he can hear the ghost of Vince's words.

What Vince always tells him: *wait for your pitch*. Many people have said this before him, of course, but Gene has always felt, somehow, like the advice meant more coming from a pitcher of Vince's skill. He knows how to work a count better than anyone

Gene has ever met, and he used to be a decent hitter in his heyday.

So Gene will work his count. He'll wait for his pitch.

He gets two balls—junk pitches, nowhere near the strike zone—first. Never in his career, up until these last couple of weeks, has Gene ever gotten pitched around. Even with the tear he's been on recently, he isn't a power hitter. He hasn't hit a home run since college. Pitchers aren't scared of him.

But today, Reno's pitcher walks him on four pitches, none of them even close to the zone. It's a cop-out, refusing to give Gene anything remotely hittable. It won't help his streak, but it'll help the team the same as a hit would.

Two innings later, Gene watches from the on-deck circle while Beaverton's number nine hitter works a full count, which turns into a walk one pitch later, on a borderline call.

Two outs, bases loaded, down by three. Bottom of the ninth.

He might not win this game for them, but he can keep it alive. If anything, Gene has been better this season when the team is under pressure than when it isn't. It's the excitement, the stakes, the opportunity to turn his optimism into real results.

This guy—blond and bulky, a cookie-cutter kind of guy—pitches around him, too. The risk of walking in a run is more appealing than the threat of the bases-clearing, game-tying double they both know he's capable of.

But his third pitch—

His third pitch barely misses Gene's head.

Gene ducks back with such force that he stumbles and falls into the dirt. The pitcher, rather than give any sign of apology, spits into the dirt and accepts the ball his catcher tosses back to him.

Maybe it's the heat of this game, the score much less close than it feels, but Gene yells at him, "*What the fuck?*"

The pitcher yells back, words sharp enough that they'd hurt Gene if he hadn't heard them so many times before: "Get up, *bitch.*"

When he does get up, Gene can hear Baker's voice behind him, a harsh "If he hits one of my guys, I swear to God," followed by Ernie's, far less kind than it usually sounds: "Hey, watch it, asshole!" Luis, in the on-deck circle, has taken one step closer to the batter's box, his bat forgotten at his side.

Gene waves them all off behind his back.

And then the pitcher throws a pitch down the middle, a little high but painfully easy for Gene to see.

Gene takes one swing at that pitch and sends it sailing over the outfield wall.

It's a magnificent fucking thing, that swing. That home run. It's no four-hundred-footer; it doesn't tower. But it moves so fast, at such a perfect angle, that not one single person in that stadium must think there's any chance of it remaining in the park.

When Gene rounds third base, he gives the pitcher the same point he might give a teammate, one that says, *Thanks for that, dude.* And when he crosses home plate, half the team waits to mob him. Even Vince stands at the edge of the dugout, and behind the flat expression he's worn for weeks, he may even look proud.

Gene's batting helmet stayed on for his jog, but now, just past home, it falls off in the pile-on. He is jostled every way a person can be jostled, and when he finally escapes to jog toward the dugout, Luis gives him a sound smack to the ass that makes Gene tip his head back and laugh so loud it rings in his raw throat.

He has never been much good at wanting things, Gene. It's a foreign feeling to him. Hope? Hope is comfortable, well-worn. His favorite, most familiar feeling. But hope isn't selfish; hope is so easy to turn in someone else's direction. Wanting, though. Wanting has always felt presumptuous—to ask for something,

something unlikely and rare, and then actually, really hope to get it? All for himself? He doesn't do that.

Maybe, before tonight's game, Gene knew that a tiny, secret little part of him wanted the dream that every kid wants, and that some never grow out of—to play in a packed stadium, in the majors. To make the playoffs, win a World Series. He doesn't care about getting his face on the big, fancy electronic boards. But to have his name—his dad's name—on a Portland jersey, in that beautiful green and blue: he has thought about it. He never admits to this. He never treads into the territory of real, visceral, disappointment-inviting *want.* But it has crossed his mind.

Now, tonight, with these people—having his name on a Beaverton jersey feels just as good. Maybe even better.

Every Friday, Gene lines up the supplies for his testosterone shot along the edge of the bathroom counter, his hands freshly scrubbed and his shorts made of stretchy fabric so he can lift the leg up high enough to get the needle in safely. The actual shot often doesn't get done until the wee hours of a Saturday morning, whenever he finally gets freed from the Friday evening game. It's reliable. The steadiest habit he has.

All of this happens exactly the same, on this night in mid-June, an hour after Gene's walk-off grand slam.

Except tonight, Luis has joined him.

Even after Luis signed a lease on a two-bedroom apartment with Ernie a few weeks ago, he has continued to make visits to Gene's a more-than-weekly occasion. A few pairs of his socks are buried somewhere in Gene's clothes hamper, kicked off and left behind, and Gene has started keeping ginger ale in his fridge just in case. Little reminders that Luis was here and will be back.

When Gene called him at one in the morning, long after their evening game ended but still reeling from the adrenaline, Luis came over. Now, an hour later, Luis sits on the closed toilet lid while Gene gets his shot ready. He keeps his eyes closed, his hands clenched between his pressed-together knees. Dodger sleeps, curled up, on his feet.

While Gene felt self-conscious about Luis seeing his posters, he is oddly at peace about this. Luis is the first person since Gene's ex-boyfriend—who was also trans, and understood this better than most of the people Gene has to spend his days with—to show any interest in this part of his life without crossing the very firm barrier into invasive curiosity.

It's the first time since his fight with Vince that Gene has felt really at home in this house. It's still not perfect, won't fix the awkwardness when he and Vince cross paths, but this? Luis, joining him for the quietest part of his routines? He looks good here, in the nooks and crannies of Gene's life.

"You do this every week?" Luis asks.

"Every Friday, yeah," Gene says. "Shabbat shalom to me."

It's really the only kind of observance he has time for during the season, a harried ten minutes. But it's his. If he treats it like a tradition instead of a nuisance, he finds, it reminds him how hard it was to get here, how lucky and happy he is to get to be a part of making himself.

"You're Jewish?"

Gene rubs a fresh alcohol wipe on the sealed rubber lid of the testosterone vial. "Yeah."

"Does the league give you shit for that?"

"Being Jewish?"

"The testosterone. Like. Is that considered a PED?"

Without a diagnosis, yes, technically testosterone counts as a performance-enhancing drug. But Gene isn't the only guy in the league who has what Major League Baseball tactfully calls "low testosterone levels." There are plenty of cis men with the same prescriptions he has, under a fraction of the surveillance.

"They have me do a blood test once a week," Gene tells him.

"Once a *week*?"

Gene flexes a halfhearted muscle. "Gotta make sure I'm not getting too jacked."

"Are they allowed to do that?"

"There aren't really rules about what to do with trans players, for obvious reasons. So they kind of wing it. They mostly check that I don't have more testosterone than your average cis guy, and, like, make sure they inconvenience me once a week so I remember what a freak I am."

Luis peeks one eye open to find Gene with the leg of his already-short shorts rolled higher, then closes it immediately upon seeing the needle in Gene's hand. He clears his throat, whether out of wooziness or discomfort, Gene can't tell. "You're not a freak," Luis says.

"Only in the fun way."

Luis clears his throat again. "So has it been an issue? Like, is it ever too high?"

"No. Literally not once," Gene says. He closes one severely astigmatic eye to bring the syringe's measurement lines into focus so he can pull the right dosage.

"And you still have to do it?"

"Yep."

"That sucks."

"I'm not a fan," Gene admits.

"Does it hurt?"

"The shot or the test?"

"The shot," Luis says.

"Not so bad. They used to have me do it in a fat deposit, which was easier because it was a thinner needle. Now it's in a muscle, which hurts a little more."

"I could not do that." Luis tips his head back and takes a deep breath. "I'm not great with needles."

"*No*," Gene says with sarcastic emphasis. "I never would have guessed."

"Very funny."

"You'd get used to it, too," Gene says.

"Probably not. I tried to get my ear pierced sophomore year, and I passed out at the piercing place."

"You wanted to get your ear pierced?" he asks.

"Yeah," Luis says. "I was kind of hoping it would get girls to stop flirting with me."

"Oh, boo-hoo. I'm Luis Estrada and I'm so hot, girls just *can't* resist me," Gene teases.

"Well. Maybe it wasn't that extreme."

Gene scrunches his nose at the pinch on his thigh. "No?"

Luis grins. "Okay, I mostly wanted Max's gay roommate to flirt with me."

"*Kelly?*"

"Yeah. Why so surprised?"

Gene shoots him a teasing look he won't see. "He's . . . so *British*." He pulls the needle out of his thigh and adds, "So? Did he? Flirt with you?"

"Yeah. We actually dated for a while."

Gene's chest suddenly feels strange and concave, despite the fact that almost a decade has passed since Luis's sophomore year. He drops the needle into his sharps container, then sticks a Band-Aid on his thigh, in the middle of the bald patch where his weekly Band-Aids have ripped out most of his leg hair.

"And? Was he worth passing out over?" Gene asks.

Luis shrugs. "We're friends now. So, I guess."

"How long did you date?"

"Can I open my eyes?"

"Yeah, you're good," Gene says, slipping the sharps container back under the sink and collecting his various wrappers.

"End of sophomore year, beginning of junior."

"So, when I knew you?"

"Partly."

Gene nods, a little slowly. "I didn't realize."

"Well, I didn't tell you. We didn't really tell anyone at the time."

"Why'd you break up?"

"I was closeted," Luis says, with a single shoulder shrug. He slides a hand into Dodger's fur, something Gene has noticed he does whenever he's nervous. "And confused. And also I kind of liked someone else."

The word "Who?" threatens to blurt from Gene's lips, a curious and almost hopeful impulse stopped by the fact that he knows better. He considers, for a moment, letting himself say it anyway, but he'd rather live in a world where the dinner invitations and soft looks and secrets shared could mean something, where "someone else" could translate to *you*.

Before Gene can respond at all, though, Luis says, "Speaking of college—Max and Ritz say hi, by the way."

Gene blinks. When he was a freshman, Max and Ritz had seemed otherworldly cool. Seniors, co-captains of the baseball team, surprisingly welcoming. It never really surprised Gene that he and they lost touch—he'd had time to prepare for their graduation, so it had stung significantly less than the unexpected loss of Luis—but still. He has missed them. He just never considered the possibility that they might miss him, too.

"To me?" Gene asks.

"Yeah. They're going to come to a game next homestand and wanted me to ask if you'd come over for dinner after." Luis gives the spot behind Dodger's ear a scratch and doesn't meet Gene's eye when he adds, "If you want. No pressure, obviously. I warned them you're busy."

It probably isn't a big deal. Probably, it's just a casual invitation, genuinely offered without pressure. And still, Gene has to swallow around his happiness, around the joy at being included, being remembered. Being welcomed into a space where his presence isn't needed—just wanted.

"Yeah, okay," he says when he can get the words out. "That sounds good."

Luis grins. "Cool."

"Cool."

Then, before Luis can see how thoroughly the invitation has affected him, Gene says, "You're sure you want to give up on the ear piercing, though? Because honestly, you'd look hot with, like, a little George Michael earring."

"Thank you. But I'm not willing to pass out in front of another piercing artist."

"I could do it for you." Gene points to one of his piercings, the third on his right earlobe. "I did these ones."

"Why the hell would you do that?"

Gene tries to sound as nonchalant as he can. "I get lonely sometimes. And when I get lonely, I get bored. And when I get bored, I get impulsive. This was a relatively safe impulsive thing to do."

"When did you do it?"

Gene counts backward. "When I was playing in High-A. So, three years ago."

Luis stares at Gene's ear a little too long. Who knew Gene could feel bashful over an earlobe? "I can't," Luis eventually says.

"Okay. That's fine."

Gene packs up his extra needles and slides the supplies back under his sink. When he goes back into the kitchen to check on their late-night freezer pizza, Luis follows.

Halfway through the pizza, Luis says, "Out of curiosity, though?"

Gene smiles.

"You've done it before? And it's safe?" Luis asks.

"I have plenty of extra needles and alcohol wipes. It's all in sterile packaging. I have gloves, too, and my sharps container to throw the needle away."

A long pause, then Luis says, "Would you mind?"

It's a little impulsive, a little chaotic, the exact opposite of Luis's usual measured decisions. Gene loves that measuredness, loves the way Luis is careful with people. But he loves this, too. He loves being a part of Luis's little gay rebellion.

Gene gathers the supplies, just slowly enough to give Luis a few minutes to change his mind if he wants to, but not too long. He sets Luis up on the couch—a soft place to catch him if he passes out.

"Feel okay?" Gene asks.

"Feel like I'm gonna puke, but yeah. Are you doing it on the gay ear?"

Gene bites back a grin. "I mean, either ear can be gay. It would be gayer if you, like, dangled a rainbow flag from the hoop or something."

"Are you making fun of me?"

"No."

And he isn't. He understands wanting to look queer. It has made his life harder, but it has also made everything in him quiet in a way he never thought he'd achieve. It's why he wears earrings, why he usually keeps his nails painted; it's why he doesn't hide his top surgery scar in the locker room, or pretend to need an athletic cup.

Gene lines up his supplies for the ear piercing, just like he does for his shot, all in a row: gloves; a fresh needle, still in its plastic casing; one of his favorite old stud earrings, thoroughly sanitized; two foil-wrapped alcohol wipes; and a new bar of soap to catch the needle as it exits Luis's ear. He sets them on the coffee table Luis helped him put together last month, while Gene introduced him to *Rocky Horror*, and he tries not to feel unbearably domestic about it all. It was so much easier, almost comically so, to get the thing built when he had Luis there to make him laugh and read the instructions with him.

"Feeling good?" Gene asks, the question directed at both Luis and himself.

"No," Luis says.

"Okay, but—"

"I'm sure."

Gene adjusts himself on the couch, attempting to find a comfortable way to sit. He nudges Luis back against the cushions so his head can rest. Gene had pulled Luis's hair away from his face with a stretchy headband, and he looks offensively cute like this. Men as hot as Luis should not legally be allowed to look this cute.

"Okay, suggestion," Gene says.

"You anesthetize me while you do this."

"No. But is it too familiar if I—"

Gene tries to demonstrate straddling Luis's lap.

"It's hard to get a good angle when you're sitting," he explains.

"Do you need me to stand?"

"Not if you're okay with me getting real personal for a minute."

Luis shifts a bit before he says, "That's fine."

So Gene slings one leg over Luis's lap, and finds the whole ordeal much easier to manage from this angle. He sits high on his knees, so they barely touch, until Gene tilts Luis's head to the side, finally feeling that beard under his fingers, so surprisingly soft Gene could scream.

Even with so little contact between them, Gene marvels at how different this is from how Luis pulled his elbow away from him in the dugout, or even from the way they lie in their hotel beds so many nights, a few careful feet between them. Gene has thought about this—admittedly without the ear-piercing aspect, and with significantly more touching—but now that he can feel the rise of Luis's chest as he breathes, it's altogether *more*.

"Okay?" Luis asks.

Okay, so Gene has been staring too long. He pretends he hasn't. "I should be asking you that."

Luis peeks one eye open. He is keeping his hands tragically to himself. "It's just that you're being a lot quieter than you usually are."

"I can be quiet."

"I've yet to witness that."

"Nada. Shut up and let me focus."

Gene tries very hard not to note the way Luis swallows. He really does.

In the end, the actual piercing occurs without incident: one last "Sure?" followed by a nod, before Gene presses the needle through Luis's ear, as gently and quickly as he can manage. Luis lets out one small gasp, but the color never drains from his face, and Gene will remember that gasp forever

"Do you want to look?" Gene asks, once he's placed the earring and slid the protective cap back on the needle.

Luis stares back at him, and Gene absolutely could have extricated himself from Luis's lap by now. But then Luis's gaze slips, falling somewhere closer to Gene's lips. It lingers there a little too long, and for a brief, insane moment, Gene thinks—

"Do you know that you call me Nada sometimes?" Luis asks.

Gene's face and the back of his neck heat all at once, so quickly he goes almost light-headed.

Of course Gene calls him Nada sometimes. How could he not? How could he not speak about Luis in the fondest, most familiar way he knows how?

But in a much realer way, no, he very much did not realize that he does that.

"Do I, Nada?" Gene asks, consciously testing it out. It's just right in his mouth, the weightless lilt of it.

Luis smiles, no teasing, and who gave him permission to be so soft? It makes Gene's ribs too small for his heart.

"Nes," Luis says, and that's also exactly right, like his name was made to be said in Luis's voice. How had Gene ever thought that voice, that beautiful mouth, was flat?

Luis's hands, kept so politely to himself the entire time Gene has crowded into his space, lift, tentatively, a question, and Gene nods. They slide onto Gene's thighs, warmer and broader than Gene imagined, and Luis pulls him forward, their chests and noses bumping against each other.

Like this, Gene is taller than Luis, and he relishes it.

Gene could say it's the residual game adrenaline, but it's not. It's Luis. Even without his baseball pants to sway Gene's opinion, even with his eye black washed off and his perfect hair pushed off his forehead, he is entirely too much. Tonight, Gene is dizzy over Luis the person, Luis his friend.

"Nes," Luis says again.

"Nada."

"I'm going to kiss you now."

When Luis leans in, Gene holds his face, wants to feel every part of this—Luis's breath against his lips and his nose against Gene's cheek, and the way Luis's jaw falls open, just barely, when he leans the rest of the way in.

He tastes like ginger ale, but so does Gene; his lips are overwarm, but so are Gene's. But then he slips a hand around the back of Gene's neck and slides his mouth open just enough. He tilts his head *just enough.* He is half-smiling into the kiss, and Gene can't help but curl his fingers, relish the surprising softness of Luis's beard.

And *God*, Luis can kiss. *They* can kiss. It's the same as playing with him, in their best moments—he moves exactly in time with Gene, their lips in sync and no conversation needed, really, because they each know what the other is going to do, what he wants.

Gene pulls Luis's bottom lip between his teeth, and Luis laughs—he laughs!—and pulls Gene down, fully onto his lap, and Gene is laughing, too, and it's stupid. It's definitely stupid.

But it's also exactly right, exactly perfect, exactly *exactly* what Gene wanted tonight, and every night—Luis's lips and his laugh and the hard press of him against Gene.

"Nes?" Luis says.

"Nada." It might be the only word he remembers, will ever remember.

"Are you avoiding my question?"

Gene rolls his eyes, his forehead against Luis's. "I have fully forgotten the question," he says. He leans back in, intending to kiss Luis again (and again and again), when his phone rings on the cushion next to them.

"Do you need to get that?" Luis asks.

"Absolutely fucking not," Gene says.

But then, while Luis's hands fall to the dip of Gene's waist and his mouth strays toward his jaw, the phone rings again.

Then its text notification sound goes off once—twice—and then *Luis's* phone rings. Dodger takes this moment to jump off the armchair and stick his cold nose on the back of Gene's thigh.

"Christ," Luis laughs. He digs his phone out from his pocket, and he holds it so Gene can read, too.

A text, from Baker.

*You, Nes, + Gonzo picked for Futures Game.*

Gene stares at that message for long seconds, willing the words to feel even remotely real.

Then, a follow-up: *Call for deets.*

Gene doesn't need to check his phone, but he does. He calls Baker back, then pretends not to be in the room while Luis makes his own call to her.

He can't quite make it make sense—he, Gene Ionescu, is going to play in the Futures Game. So is Luis. They're going to play in *the* game where they send *the* real prospects, the ones they think will be real—*legitimate, good*—major league players someday.

And, in an instant, kissing Luis becomes a much worse idea than it was five minutes ago. No matter how much he likes Luis the person, Luis is still Luis Estrada, Baseball Player, the same as Gene is Gene Ionescu, Baseball Player, and if they're going to have all those extra eyes on them, Gene Ionescu, Baseball Player should probably remove himself from Luis Estrada, Baseball Player's lap.

So, when Luis leans back in, says a quiet and smile-laden "Congratulations, Nes" and presses his lips to Gene's again, Gene takes it in for half a breath. Tries to remember what Luis's lips feel like—happy, full of possibility, and perfect in ways Gene never could have imagined—before he slides off Luis's lap.

"We probably shouldn't," he says. And, as if he doesn't want the exact opposite, he adds, "Right?"

There's a small chance Luis looks disappointed, but he just says, "Oh. Okay." Not an agreement or a disagreement. Just "Okay," his hands suddenly pressed between his knees and his shoulders up by his ears again, in that way Gene has come to love for its vulnerability and hate for the discomfort it signals.

He has never been much good at wanting things, Gene, but something incredible has been put in front of him, his for the taking.

How could he risk all that for a kiss?

PART TWO

# The Futures Game

# 12

## JULY

**Current record: 49–38**

The night before they leave for the Futures Game, Luis sees Gene's bedroom for the first time.

He sits promptly on the floor, crosses his legs, and holds his hand out for the instruction packet that came with Gene's as-yet-unbuilt bed frame. He doesn't blink twice at the mattress on the floor, or the pile of clean laundry that Gene haphazardly tried to fold before he came over.

Gene's apartment isn't *dirty.* He keeps it perfectly clean. It's just that he goes through cycles of messiness, wherein his apartment will be without clutter for two weeks, and then one day he'll inevitably be too tired to fold a load of towels and underwear, and everything goes downhill from there. The clean laundry in the hamper quickly overflows, taking over the armchair and then the top of his dresser, and if it's already this messy, he might as well leave six half-finished books on the nightstand, too.

Luis pays no mind to any of that, attention turned in full to the task at hand, so thoroughly that Gene can almost forget about the thing they're avoiding, the conversation they aren't having. That night after they kissed—after Luis fell asleep on his couch and Gene tried so hard to shove the memory of those lucky minutes into storage, to be taken out and examined at an easier time—Gene wondered if things would get weird, but instead they've been the same, just with an invisible barrier between them, Luis back to keeping his leg a careful few inches from Gene's on the bench. They're still themselves, but a little less honest.

On the field, at the stadium, it seems like the smart move, but every time Luis comes to his apartment, Gene wishes he could let himself keep the honesty.

After two hours of exhausted fumbling—and one *Sorry about all the noise I swear I will be done soon* text typed out and unsent to Vince, the most recent text in their thread a curt congratulations from a few weeks ago, after the Futures Game news—Gene has a bed. Luis helps him heft the mattress into place as Gene tries to find something to look at that isn't Luis's arms, or the very tempting bed between them, or the satisfied way Luis likes to look at a job well done.

He doesn't *succeed.* But he sure does try.

When Luis tips forward onto the mattress, though, and lets out the longest, most moan-like sigh Gene has ever heard? Gene gives the fuck up.

He climbs onto the other side of the bed and tries not to take it personally when Luis folds his elbows in closer to his ribs. Dodger tucks himself between them, like he knows they need that extra barrier tonight. Even so, the second Gene's back hits the bed, he knows what it feels like to lie on a mattress dipped by Luis's weight, to see the rhythm of Luis's breathing out of the corner of his eye, tantalizingly close. Paired with the knowledge of Luis under him on the couch, the way his hands felt exactly right on Gene's thighs, how he felt pressed against Gene—

"What time did you want to leave for the airport tomorrow?" he asks Luis. A reminder of where they're going, and why that last kiss had to stop. Why Gene can't kiss him again.

"Like, three? If that's okay?"

Their flight leaves at six A.M. sharp. Gene agreed to let Luis sleep on his couch tonight, as he has done so many times before, so that they can carpool in the morning without needing to make an extra stop. Gene checks his phone.

"Okay, so you need to wake up at . . . ?"

"Two."

He turns his phone toward Luis and his chest absolutely does not swell at the sight of Luis looking at him from the other side of his bed. "That is in ninety minutes."

Luis groans at the ceiling. "Perfect," he says.

"I'm so sorry," Gene says. "I didn't realize how long it would take. In my defense, you offered to do this."

"It's fine." Luis yawns. "I probably wasn't going to get any sleep tonight anyway."

He doesn't look like someone who plans to stay up all night. When his eyes droop closed, they stay that way, his eyebrows uncharacteristically unfurrowed. He stretches, a devastating, stomach-revealing thing, and Gene presses his own eyes closed.

"How far are your dads from the hotel?" Luis asks.

They have settled into their seats for the nonstop flight to New York. Gene is sandwiched in the middle seat between Luis (window, made necessary by his anxiety) and Ernie (aisle, made necessary by his broad shoulders).

Like every player invited to All-Star Week, the three of them will stay in a Manhattan hotel. Gene, however, plans to spend whatever spare time he has with his family in Brooklyn. While invitations to the Futures Game are hard-won, an immense honor for minor league players who receive them, the game itself is still by far the quietest part of All-Star Week's festivities. The warm-up event. The focus will land solidly on the shoulders of the major league stars, the household names who will be competing first in the Home Run Derby and then in the All-Star Game itself. As invitees, Gene, Luis, and Ernie will get tickets to both of the marquee events, but the spotlight will have moved on to bigger things by then.

Gene's dad, however, is immensely proud, as if Gene himself is the main character of the week, the headliner for every event this year, and the next, and all the events to come, forever. When Gene texted the family group chat to tell them he'd be coming to town for the break, that he could even get them tickets to see him play, it was past four in the morning in Brooklyn. Even so, his dad had called him in seconds, screaming to Gene and all of Gowanus that he always knew he'd see his son play at Citi Field, then to ask if he could pick Gene up from the airport.

"They're in Brooklyn," Gene says.

"And Brooklyn is . . . far?" Luis asks.

Gene laughs. "Have you guys ever been to New York?"

Luis and Ernie shake their heads.

"Not *far.* Just inconvenient," Gene sums up.

Luis lets out a puff of air. He popped a Xanax pretty much the minute they sat down, with Dodger in a crate under the plane. Under different circumstances, Gene might be tempted to give Luis's hand a comforting squeeze.

"You brought headphones?" Gene asks.

Luis holds up the same ones he wears on every road trip, the ones that Gene used to wonder so much about, until he found out that travel just makes Luis anxious, and that without the headphones or another distraction, he would have to stew in that anxiety.

"Yep," Luis says.

"Downloaded some podcasts?"

"Approximately a thousand. Yes."

Luis made a packing list the day after they found out they'd be taking this trip. He doesn't need Gene checking in to make sure he hasn't forgotten anything, but Gene does it anyway, because Gene is a worrier, and it's easier to worry about someone else than it is to worry about himself.

For his part, Gene has armed himself with a backpack full of books he likely won't have any time to read, a liter-sized water bottle, and snacks enough to last five plane trips. His backpack barely zips closed and doesn't come close to fitting under the seat in front of him, but he's prepared. He doesn't usually travel like this, but this is not the usual kind of trip. This is the *Futures Game*, the most important baseball experience of his young career. He will go into this eyes wide open, well-hydrated, and snacked up.

The flight is five hours long, with no layovers, which feels like a luxury compared to the roadie bus. Sure, they have no legroom here, and sure, each of them is hopped up on nerves strong enough to power the plane, but in spite of it all, they would be hard-pressed to find anything worth complaining about.

By the time they touch down in New York, Gene has almost talked himself out of worrying. It's not like he ever thought he'd get to play here. It's all he can do to try his best, and if his best isn't enough, well, that's what he expected anyway. Just on a bigger stage than he ever thought he'd get.

JFK's concourses are enough to make anyone regret coming to the city—grimy, packed with the world's crankiest people, perpetually stuck in the limbo between too rushed and too slow. It's purgatory, if you believe in things like purgatory, which Gene doesn't. Except for when he's at JFK.

But then his dad is there, with a bouquet of flowers, and JFK is the best place in the world, actually, if only because it contains

Gene's dad and his dorky bouquets. When they hug, Gene's bag falls to the ground, and he lifts his dad off the ground a few inches, enough to make him squawk.

"You got bigger," Franklin says, as if Gene didn't stop growing a good decade ago. His accent is as thick as ever, and he has started to gather grays. Gene can't believe his family has the gall to get older without him there.

"Did I?" Gene says.

"Maybe you just look bigger because you never come home anymore."

"Aw, Tata. Come on."

" 'Tata'?" Ernie asks.

"That's what he calls his dad," Luis says.

Franklin wipes his cheeks on the neck of his shirt before he picks Gene's bag up off the ground and offers to take one of Luis's.

"No, it's okay," Luis says. "We have to get to the hotel."

He insists. "I'm driving you. Now give me your bag."

They follow Franklin out and into the parking garage, where his old Volvo waits. Gene sits in the front, and Luis and Ernie pile into the back with a delightedly free Dodger sandwiched between them. Gene gives Luis a smile in the rearview, which makes Luis's cheeks tinge pink.

Oh, God.

"Tata, what're we doing for dinner tonight?" Gene asks to distract himself.

"Oh, Art started cooking this morning. Your friends are welcome to come, but they will have to be okay with a lot of questions."

"How good is the food?" Ernie asks. Luis punches Ernie's arm. "What? I want to know if the questions are worth it."

"It is very good food," Franklin assures them.

"Nes, you look *just* like your dad," Ernie says, tapping Gene's shoulder over the back of his seat.

"Maybe if you grew the mustache," Luis says, touching his top lip when Gene turns around to look at them. He looks very pointedly north of Gene's lips. "Then you'd match."

Franklin, taking the on-ramp onto the highway, points at Gene. "I have always said you would look good with a mustache."

"Tata, you told me one time I would look good with a pierced eyebrow."

"Because you're my handsome son. You always look nice."

Gene rolls his eyes, but there's no dedication to it. Being here, with his dad—being told they look alike, from some of his favorite teammates, some of his best friends? He hadn't realized how much he wanted that kind of normal thing.

When they pull up to the hotel and unload their bags from the trunk, Gene says, "We can meet you at the apartment in a few hours? Around six?"

"Five," Franklin counters.

"Fine. We will be there at five."

"Or four-thirty."

"Tata!" Gene laughs. "We smell. Let us shower."

He considers. "Fine. Five, and not one minute later."

He gives Gene a kiss on the cheek, then gets back in his car. He's yelling at the honking cars behind him before he's even peeled away from the curb.

Gene can't begin to imagine how much a night at this hotel must cost—at least as much as a monthly payment for the car Gene wishes he had. Maybe double.

They check themselves in with an air of amazement, Gene and Luis receiving key cards to the same room and Ernie to one down the hall, which he will share with an old Double-A teammate. It's weird, being in a hotel when they don't have to hustle to a game in an hour. Sure, they'll play in two days, but until then, they have *time*. Actual time. It's become a foreign concept to Gene in the past few years.

At hotels on the road, they're lucky if the room comes with two beds and a couple of outlets. Before that, when Gene was in High-A and Double-A, he was lucky if the cleaning staff remembered to stock the toilet paper before smoking their cigarettes half out the window and half onto the bedsheets. But this room has tall windows bracketing a sliding glass door, and a small outdoor balcony with a table. It has a mini-fridge that appears to be younger than Gene's nephew, and a room service menu set out next to the *literal couch*. It has space to hang up clothes, and a whole separate room for the beds. Gene looks around the corner, whistling low and admiring the taut pull of the bedding before Luis passes him and starts pulling it up from the bottom edge.

The sight is familiar, so much so that Gene has to hold back a fond smile. "I highly doubt *this* place has bedbugs," Gene says.

"Any hotel can have bedbugs."

Gene lets his bags drop to the ground. "I admire your vigilance. But this hotel rules."

"It's just as dirty as any other hotel," Luis says.

"It objectively is not."

Luis lifts the mattress up at the corner to peer underneath.

"What's the verdict?" Gene asks.

Luis lets the mattress fall back to the frame. "Clear."

Gene jumps onto the comforter. "Perfect," he says, his voice muffled by the bedding.

"Okay, I've told you: they only wash the sheets. They don't wash the comforter. You're breathing in other people's grime right now."

Gene holds his middle finger up over his head.

Seconds later, the water turns on, and instead of thinking about Luis undressing in the bathroom—he has seen Luis in, quite literally, every state of dress and undress imaginable and has mentally explored every possible iteration thereof—he reads the room service menu.

By the time they've emptied the plate of fries Gene orders, Gene has taken his own shower, letting his hair air-dry. Luis's, too, has gone a little curly—when he doesn't style it, it has some wave to it. It looks softer this way.

"We should grab Gonzo," Gene says. "It'll take us almost an hour to get to Brooklyn."

"Because of traffic?"

Gene looks at him like he's lost it. "We're not driving. We'll take the train."

"Like, underground?" Luis looks wary.

"I thought you'd like that. You hate being on a plane."

"I hate being in a metal tube in the sky, so you thought I'd like being in a metal tube underground?"

"Yeah, kind of."

Luis lets out that same little puff of air he did earlier. "Fine," he says.

"If you hate it, we'll ditch the train and grab a cab."

"I'm holding you to that."

Luis does, in fact, hate it, but not enough that he's willing to admit defeat. Gene offers three times, and Luis shakes him off each time, so he leaves Luis alone to his controlled breathing.

They've all dressed up for the dinner, somewhat. Gene is in a button-up that he hasn't buttoned anywhere above the bottom of his ribs, along with the same jeans and Docs he wears more or less everywhere. Ernie wears the most straight-guy dress-up outfit imaginable—khakis, untucked blue button-up—but he has, at least, rolled the sleeves of his shirt to his elbows and added a nice watch. Luis wears a white T-shirt, tucked into his nicest black jeans, which in turn are tucked into the ankle boots he is so fond of wearing. Gene's family probably won't bother to put on shoes, so even a plain blue button-up will look fancy; it still means something to Gene that they all, independent of each other, decided to make an occasion of the night.

"Okay," Ernie says as they walk from the train station, a very separated O and K. "You were adopted."

"Yes," Gene says.

"By your uncle."

"Bingo."

"Because your mom was a hot mess."

"Dude," Luis says.

"No, that's fair," Gene says. "Yeah."

"And your uncle-dad is married to a man," Ernie says, drawing imaginary lines in the air like he's trying to connect the lines of Gene's family tree. "And *that* man has a daughter from his last marriage. So now she's your sister. Am I forgetting anything?"

"He has a nephew," Luis says. "Mattie."

"Oh, I won't remember any of these people's names," Ernie says.

They laugh as they round the corner onto Gene's dads' street.

When he was in college, Gene did not feel proud to have grown up in Gowanus, which he'd learned was known outside of New York mostly for its dirty canal. Now, with Luis and Ernie trailing behind him, he feels a sort of unexpected affection—not just for the neighborhood but for how comfortable he is here, and how well he remembers how to get from the station to the squat three-story building in which his dad and stepdad live. That bone-deep knowledge that he will never lose.

It isn't exactly glamorous, but it's his place, and his people, the same as Beaverton.

"Where's Vince?" Art calls from the kitchen, as soon as Franklin opens the front door for them.

Gene doesn't answer that question. "Hey, Art. Good to see you, too."

Art—Franklin's husband, Gene's stepdad since he was sixteen—comes into the living room holding a dripping spoon and embraces Gene. He always smells a little like tomato sauce and garlic, like the Italian grocery store he owns, and Gene takes in a deep whiff. The man gives better hugs than anyone Gene has met, literally ever, and he gives them liberally. When he gets ahold of Luis, Gene has to laugh. He looks something like a green bean next to Art.

They serve dinner family-style, in large bowls in the center of a table that wasn't built for this many people and which only gets more crowded when, halfway through the salad course, Gene hears a shout from down on the street.

"Is that—"

"Go see," Franklin prompts him, and Gene nearly knocks over his chair in his haste to stand up. When he ducks into his old bedroom—set up the same way it was when he lived here—to look out the windows facing the street, he sees Joey and Mattie on the sidewalk, both of them waving so hard their arms might rip out of their sockets.

He bounds down the building's stairs so fast he half-slides down the last two and bursts onto the street just as enthusiastically. He is met by a hug to rival Art's, Joey's arms around him as the door closes.

They only let go when Mattie worms his way between them. He's tall enough now to nearly reach Gene's armpit.

"This should be illegal," he says when he hugs Mattie. "If you get taller than me, I'm going to be so mad."

"Well, I guess you're going to be mad," Mattie says.

"Wow. Rude. I think we need to start giving you coffee. Stunt your growth a little like my tata did to me."

"Is there food inside?" Mattie asks.

"*Is there food inside?*" Gene repeats. "Has your Papa ever *not* had food ready when you came over? You silly little man."

In the excitement, Gene has locked them out, and the building's buzzer hasn't worked in years. He tips his head back and yells toward the open window until Luis comes down to let them in.

The seven of them eat what could charitably be called a disgusting amount of food. Even once they've all gotten through their seconds and thirds and slipped Dodger enough bites to constitute nearly a whole plate of his own, Art has plenty left over to insist they take back to the hotel with them later, in case they somehow manage to find room in their stretched stomachs.

Luis gets along great with Mattie, if only for the simple fact that he doesn't talk nearly as much as Gene's family does and therefore makes for an ideal audience for Mattie's monologues. Luis and Franklin end up in the living room, listening to a lecture on Mattie's newest LEGO sculpture, while Ernie excuses himself to meet up with some of the other guys playing in this weekend's game.

Gene is left in the kitchen with Art and Joey, an assembly line for the dishes. Gene is on rinsing duty, sandwiched between Art, the scrubber, and Joey, the drier.

"So," Joey starts.

Gene tries to cut the conversation off there. "I know."

"Luis Estrada got hot."

"Stop. Your dad is right there."

Art shrugs, handing Gene the heavy, ancient, enameled Dutch oven in which he makes sauce three to five times a week. Gene maneuvers it carefully under the spray of the water.

"He's cute," Art says.

"Gross, Art."

Art holds his hands up, innocent. "Not for *me*. Just a general observation."

Gene hefts the pot onto Joey's waiting towel. "You guys aren't the quietest talkers in the world, so if we could talk about literally anything else, that would be great."

"But you admit it," Joey says.

"I didn't say anything."

"Your crush is not and never was subtle." *Rude,* because he's trying his fucking best. She gives a low whistle. "And shit, I get it."

Gene shoots her the exact same look he would have given her when they were younger, if Joey had tattled on him to one of their dads: murderous.

"What?" she asks. "Who wouldn't?"

"Motherhood has not matured you."

"I'm a fun mom."

"You're an ass is what you are."

Art hands over a knife, pointedly pointed at both of them. "Cool your jets. Be nice to each other."

Joey drops the subject, if only because they're both adults and reprimands from a parent have gotten a bit more embarrassing since high school. Even so, she gives Gene a little knowing look, accompanied by a smirk that makes Gene's face heat.

When they finally take their leave, exhausted and jet-lagged and having accepted no fewer than two plates of leftovers apiece, the clocks have crept up on midnight without any of them noticing. They take the train back to their hotel, just him and Luis.

One stop into their trip on the F, Luis leans his head against the window, and by the time they get to Jay Street, he's asleep, his head tipped to the side and onto Gene's shoulder. It's the first time they've touched, outside a high five or a congratulatory ass slap on the field, since they kissed, and it warms Gene from his shoulder to his cheeks, down to the gay swoop of his stomach. Luis breathes steady now, mouth open and cheek buried against the fabric of Gene's shirt. He isn't a snorer, but he makes these sounds in his sleep, sort of content and painfully sweet, that make

Gene wish they had to take the train all the way up through Manhattan and deep into Queens.

It almost hurts, how soft Luis's head feels there, how vulnerable he looks and sounds when he sleeps. Gene is supposed to spend these few days making a commitment to his baseball career, not falling further into whatever this is he's feeling for Luis, but baseball means Luis, and Luis means a whole mess of these thoughts Gene doesn't want to name, and so, if Gene wants baseball, he has to take this, too.

When they get back to the hotel, Luis crashes into bed much as Gene did earlier: face-first, ass up, a full-body flop. He smiles at Gene, an eyes-half-closed little look, before he falls back asleep, still wearing his ankle boots and black jeans. Gene peels the boots off for Luis and lines them up just so in the corner of the room while Dodger curls into a donut at Luis's back.

To cope with the sleepy sounds Luis makes and the way he clutches a pillow to his chest, Gene takes a picture and sends it to Joey, captioned, *If I did have a crush, how fucked would I be?*

He receives a string of exclamation marks in response, so many they spill onto a second line. He tosses his phone onto the bed next to him, not bothering to plug it in.

# 13

## JULY

Current record: 49–39

The distinct feeling of having barely slept hangs over Gene's morning: heavy limbs, headache, a Luis Estrada–shaped pain in his ass.

They have practice at one in the afternoon so they can get to know the guys they'll share a roster with tomorrow. The results of the game won't count for anything in the standings—it's an exhibition game, played for pure enjoyment and the honor of being recognized—but no one likes to lose. If they did, they probably wouldn't have gotten picked for this.

Even considering their bodies' insistence on West Coast time, and the resultant sleeping in that they did this morning, they have time to kill before practice starts.

Normal people would enjoy the city. Gene and Luis, however, take the opportunity to haul their asses out to Queens a couple hours early, so Gene can show Luis Citi Field. It was Gene's second-ever major league stadium, following Portland, and the one he spent the most time in after his dad stopped playing. When Gene was in high school, and later college, his dad would get them season tickets, and they would trek out to the stadium two or three times a week to sit in the nosebleed seats. Gene spent half his money from his first job buying them soft pretzels and cheese dip.

When they walk up to the stadium—towering, beautiful, unceremoniously constructed at the intersection of two highways and across the street from a muffler store—Gene grins, not at the brick arches but at Luis taking them in.

"Well, I mean, points docked for the Mets playing here"—Gene jabs his elbow into Luis's ribs for that—"but damn."

Gene cranes his head back to look up at the familiar name in big letters over the arches; they're a couple yards away now. "Are you nervous?" he asks.

Luis gives a tight laugh, one that says *Yes* better than any collection of actual words ever could.

"Perfect. Same," Gene says.

On an impulse, he reaches out to give Luis's hand that comforting squeeze that's been tempting him since yesterday. Before he can, Luis reaches into his pocket, grabs the ID an MLB representative gave him at the hotel, and scans it.

They're the first ones there, as far as players go, but a whole staff of people are getting things set up. He and Luis bypass the locker room and walk down the tunnel, past the dugout Gene has seen some of his favorite players sit in countless times, out onto the field.

The dimensions are not so different from their own stadium. Just basic, expected variance. But something about the embrace of this many seats, rows and rows of them, somewhere in the neighborhood of forty *fucking* thousand, makes the field itself feel bigger, too. It's the bright white of the foul lines, the perfect evenness of the dirt at home plate, the brilliant green of the grass.

"I almost want to, like. Lay down in it," Luis says.

"So do it." Gene gestures, an invitation.

"I don't want to get caught."

"Nada, they absolutely do not care," Gene says.

To illustrate his point, he drops onto the grass, falling neatly on his ass and then tipping his body fully horizontal. The sun is warm, barely on the good side of harsh. He pats the spot next to him.

When Luis lies next to Gene, his breath evens out. Gene can almost hear the second it happens.

"Wow."

"Fucking wow," Gene agrees.

"I mean, it's no Dodger Stadium"—Dodger perks up at the mention of his name— "but what can you do?"

Gene kicks his leg out until it makes light contact with Luis's shin, but he grins up at the sun, taking it all in. The stadium and the impending practice and tomorrow's game and his own place here, and Luis.

Neither of them starts the Futures Game the next day, but Gene can't imagine caring. As long as they get put in at the same time, get to play at least one inning together, it could not matter less to him.

Their opportunity comes in the sixth.

The funny thing about games like this: literally everyone is good. It's no All-Star Game, but every one of the players here has a chance of playing there someday. Gene doesn't consider himself a part of that group, really, but when they put him in to pinch-hit, he doesn't feel completely out of place anymore.

At his back, Luis yells, "*Let's go, Nes!*"

Gene can tell by the focused sound of Luis's voice that his hands are cupped around each side of his mouth, the O drawn out and joyous.

The pitcher throws Gene a slider, absolutely filthy, but Gene manages to drive it into the gap, a couple dozen feet away from the nearest outfielder. He slides into second, and Luis subs for the next hitter. His batting stance, once he settles into it, is easy, with very little movement. Gene uses Luis's steadiness to even out his own breathing, wandering just far enough off second that it becomes a risk.

This guy is a nose-wrinkler. The best kind of giveaway, because it's the kind the pitcher almost never even knows he does. The second the tip of his nose twitches, Gene takes off toward third, sliding feetfirst and not even looking up to check where the ball is. He hears it smack into the palm of the third baseman's glove a full second after his foot touches the base.

And it doesn't really matter anyway, because Luis redirects the next pitch over the outfielders' heads.

Gene has never understood why athletes sometimes yell in each other's faces. And then Luis crosses home plate, and it might only be the sixth inning, but Gene claps his hand together with Luis's, and he yells, and he *yells*, and Luis yells, and Dodger howls from where his leash is tied up in the dugout, and their team is up two runs, and okay—Gene gets it now.

When the last out lands in Gene's glove less than an hour later, Luis lifts him into the air, not one bit of hesitation to it, arms locked under Gene's ass and Gene's legs thrown around his waist, glove hoisted in the air until the rest of their team joins them.

Maybe it doesn't matter for Beaverton that they won, but this game still mattered, still meant something; to Gene, at least, it's his first intoxicating glimpse of something he has never let himself dream of. And maybe he doesn't let himself want it—maybe he isn't there yet. But with Luis holding him up and the ball shifted into his ungloved hand and guys he met yesterday clapping his shoulder in the middle of the field he used to go to with his dad? He doesn't fully believe yet that a life this big is available to him. But he knows, now, that it's out there. That this feeling exists, and he is capable of feeling it.

Luis's laughter drifts up, and he doesn't let go of Gene until he absolutely has to. Gene is, he realizes on that baseball diamond, a little in love with that laugh, and a little in love with Luis.

That feeling exists, too. He is capable of feeling it, too, so much and so thoroughly that all he can do is laugh along.

After their post-game celebrations, the hotel room's manufactured silence is a shock to the drumming in Gene's chest, his fingertips. Luis leans against the wall, his shoulders perfectly relaxed, and he smiles at Gene. Crooked. Heart-stopping. An invitation. Gene can imagine a dozen ways for this night to go, but in every one that he likes, it's him and Luis, and the dizzy way he felt when Luis kissed him on his couch.

Gene steps toward him, chases the feeling of Luis lifting him on the field and holding on to him for dear life, and Luis's smile doesn't falter. If anything, it grows, and Gene has never felt more sure that Luis will be there, ready to make whatever play Gene has in mind.

Gene looks at Luis's earring for a second, a reminder of the last time they let themselves be a little reckless. He nods down at Luis's unmoving hands. "Are you going to touch me or what?"

"You're the one who wanted to stop last time," Luis says.

"Was I?" Gene asks, regretting that decision now more than ever.

Luis nods, nearly closing the distance between them, more than confirmation enough for Gene that he's not the only one tiptoeing up to this precipice. With his lips almost against Gene's, Luis says, "You gotta touch me first, Nes."

Gene doesn't *want* to find that unbearably attractive. He really doesn't. But Luis, hands pressed against the wall behind him, his hair air-dried and curly after his post-game shower, a smug smirk slung across his lips . . . well, shit.

So he leans back enough to meet Luis's eyes, willing himself to look less giddy, more confident than he is, and, with Luis watching him, he slides his hand down, cupping it against the front of Luis's pants. Before he can ask if that's what Luis wanted him to do, Luis tips his head back against the wall and honest-to-God moans.

"Fuck. Okay," Gene says, whatever lingering hesitation he may have harbored chucked out the window, dispelled by Luis's moan and the way he presses into Gene's hand.

Gene might not let himself want things very often. He has practiced un-wanting for years, practiced tamping down every errant desire until he can ignore it.

Except, he wants Luis. He really fucking wants Luis, and if Luis's face and voice and body are anything to go by, the feeling is mutual.

So Gene, for the first time in years, lets himself want.

He moves his hand to the back of Luis's head and pulls him ever so slightly down. He stands on his toes and lines their lips back up, and he doesn't need to kiss Luis, because Luis kisses him first.

If Gene thought they had moved in sync last time, this is something else entirely. When Gene opens his lips, Luis's open just the same; when Gene laces his fingers together on the back of Luis's neck, Luis is already stooping lower to get a better angle. When Luis moves his head to the left, so does Gene, and their mouths slot together so well, it makes Gene's fingers curl against the nape of Luis's neck.

It's the same as when they're on the field together, or an extension of it. "Easy" isn't the right word—*easy* could never begin to cover the way Gene feels with Luis. That would imply that this feeling has no teeth to it; no. It isn't easy. It's natural—heady and hot and all-encompassing. Gene understands the way Luis thinks, anticipates the way he moves. It makes them good teammates—the best teammates—and, Gene learns as Luis finally touches him, it makes them pretty damn good at this, too.

Luis's hands find the small of Gene's back, firm and steady and fucking maddening, and then, when Gene has almost recovered from that, Luis slides them farther down. Gene smiles against Luis's lips.

"Be my guest," Gene says. It comes out like a dare.

Luis scoops him up, the same as he had an hour earlier, his hands under Gene's thighs, and turns, until Gene's back presses against the wall. Luis has eight eminently noticeable inches on him, but Gene makes up for what he lacks in height with solidity. While he would not call himself brawny by any measure, no one could accuse him of being slight. He has short, strong legs and enough back muscle to hold his own in any pull-up contest. Before today, he had no doubt that *he* could pick *Luis* up, but vice versa? Color him moderately surprised and painfully turned on.

He moans about it, tips his head back about it, gets his back pressed against the wall about it.

Luis—whose kisses were focused and intense moments before—now trails those kisses along Gene's neck. *These* kisses come teeth-first, a little sharp, tongue and soft lips following close behind like an apology. Gene didn't need an apology, by any means, but he appreciates the slide of Luis's tongue against his throat. Likes a reminder that he makes Luis desperate, too.

When Luis runs his teeth against the hollow under Gene's fallen-open jaw, Gene's fingers curl again, this time harder, tugging on Luis's hair, and Luis makes that sound again—approval, or relief, or desperation. Whatever it is, Gene makes a mental note to remember that for later.

"Nada," he says, keeping his hands firmly in Luis's hair.

Luis doesn't have to ask what he means. With Gene's legs wrapped around his waist, he moves them a few feet to the right, through the door to the bedroom.

"Sorry, dude," Luis says to Dodger when he closes the door, but Gene kisses the spot where Luis's neck meets shoulder, and Luis doesn't sound all that sorry.

He drops Gene—not gently—onto his bed. Gene half-bounces, something between a laugh and a gasp rolling past his lips in surprise.

The comforter on Luis's bed has remained peeled and folded at the foot of his mattress since they arrived, and the flat sheet is smooth against Gene's skin as he props himself on his elbows. Luis stands at the edge of the bed, nudging Gene's bent knees apart. They each reach for the necks of their shirts, tug them over their heads, and, grinning at each other, throw them to the side.

Gene reaches out and pulls Luis in by the belt loops, tugging him until he tumbles onto the bed, a mess of limbs. When he lands on top of Gene, between his legs, arms bracketing him, Luis wastes no time getting back to kissing. He kisses with intent. His mouth open, focused, determined, the kind of kissing that makes Gene feel like he might be losing his mind one small movement at a time. Their chests pressed together, hearts *going* as if they just finished a run, almost the whole of Luis's weight on top of him. Gene can feel how hard Luis is, and he pulls Luis in by the hips, in case they can get closer, somehow. When Luis rolls to Gene's side, leaving one leg slotted between Gene's, Gene curves his body to get the contact back, blatantly desperate.

Luis holds Gene's face and leans back in, a smile insisting at the edges of his lips.

"Don't laugh at me," Gene complains. He should have known the months of half-aborted imagining would be nothing compared to the real, human weight of Luis on top of him. But here he is, shocked into shallow breaths over it.

"I'm not laughing."

"Good," Gene says, even though Luis is lying a little bit.

"I promise," he lies again, but this time, when he says it, he slides a hand down Gene's stomach and between his legs, to rest high on the inside of Gene's thigh.

"You're still doing it," Gene tells him, head light and not really caring. Because no matter how much of a hard time Gene might give him about it, Gene likes that Luis laughs. He likes that Luis—this nervous man, this man who manages to be anxious about everything—laughs at this.

"Only a little," Luis says. His hand has not moved, and doesn't move, until Gene nods at that hand's implicit question, and Luis moves it up.

Gene's shorts don't last long, and his briefs last less than a second longer. It has been nearly a year since someone saw Gene naked outside a locker room, and it has never been a constant in his life. Sex has always been so far down on his overcrowded priority list that it often gets bumped off entirely. In Gene's experience, it has often come laced with nerves, the odd experience of sharing a body he is supposed to be ashamed of but has taught himself to love instead. He doesn't love the way people see it sometimes, the way they judge it, but *he* loves how his body looks, loves its transness most of all.

He expected to be nervous, falling into bed with the first man he's ever slept with who doesn't have a body like his own. But he isn't. It's different, but it was always going to be different; with Luis, at least, that doesn't feel like a bad thing. With Luis, it feels like he has exactly the body he should, because it knows how to move with Luis's. It has nothing to do with any of the mechanics and everything to do with Luis himself, and with Gene, and with their uncanny way of understanding each other. And that's what matters, really.

Lying there, as naked as he's ever been, next to Luis—who's

propped on an elbow, his pants unzipped and pushed halfway off his ass, looking Gene up and down with ease and interest—Gene has never felt better about himself.

"Do you know what you're doing?" Gene asks, not because he doubts him but because Luis likes to be teased, and because he likes to tease Luis.

"More or less," Luis says. He runs a hand up the inside of Gene's leg.

"So, more, or less?" Gene tries to say it like a test, but it comes out more like a shiver.

His hand has strayed higher, teasing at the coarse hairs at the highest part of Gene's thigh. "Well, will you let me know if something is bad for you?"

"Yes."

"And will you let me know"—he pauses and waits for Gene's nod again—"when it's good for you?"

What Gene means to say is, *You're so full of yourself.*

But when Gene nods, Luis moves his hand to where Gene has been wanting it for months. With Luis watching Gene's face as he runs his thumb against Gene's clit and slips a finger in, slowly, to the second knuckle, gauging Gene's reaction before he really throws himself into it, Gene possesses no thoughts whatsoever other than *okay*, but in all capitals, yelled with the most enthusiasm he has ever felt in his life.

Like: *OKAY! FUCK! OKAY!*

Because, as far as Gene is concerned, Luis does know what he's doing. Gene can't tell if it's because Luis actually is that good, or just because Gene has never in his life wanted someone so badly, but it makes no difference. When Luis curls a second finger inside him, their next-door neighbors must hate them, but Luis grins at the sound Gene makes, and fuck the neighbors, actually.

It doesn't take long for Luis to get Gene off the first time that night, and Gene would be embarrassed by how quickly it went if he had any capacity at all to be embarrassed about anything at the moment. Instead, he laughs, relieved and a little dizzy, and holds Luis's face a bit too tight.

"Shit," Gene says. "Yeah, okay, you can keep doing that."

Luis, in flagrant disregard of Gene's request, removes his hand. And then, with no trace of the hesitation or nerves he usually has, he says, "Do you want to sit on my face?"

And, okay, *now* Gene has never felt better about himself.

He nudges Luis onto his back and peels off Luis's jeans and briefs—Calvins, navy blue, the same as they've looked every time Gene has seen them in the locker room, except tonight they strain, indecent and perfect.

He gets his first real, full-bodied look at Luis then. He takes the time to pause, to marvel at him. The best part isn't even his long legs, or the comfortable set of his shoulders, or the barely raised mole on his hip that Gene will kiss as soon as he gets the chance. The best part isn't Luis's dick, though Gene does plan to enjoy it. No, the best part is how his laughter has morphed into a soft and tentative smile, waiting for Gene's reaction, and how he looks nervous but not anxious. That distinction is a miracle for Luis, and Gene wants to live in the feeling of being trusted like this.

"Can I?" Gene asks, wanting to get his hands on Luis and to get it right.

Luis, propped on his elbows, his cheeks impressively red, nods. "I don't know what you're asking for. Whatever it is, yes."

Gene grins and straddles Luis's thighs so he can reach between his own, just long enough to slick his hand. He reaches for Luis and raises his eyebrows.

Luis's jaw goes slack when he nods, when he circles his fingers around Gene's wrist and pulls his hand closer. Gene wraps a loose hand around him and matches the rhythm of Luis's hips, tests a flick of his thumb and wrist and watches Luis's head tip back against the pillows.

"Fuck, Nes," Luis gasps. Luis's voice gets higher and a thousand times more expressive during sex, and Gene will probably spend literal hours touching himself to those two syllables later. Luis is also louder than he looks like he'd be, and what a pair they make.

"Wait," Luis says when another gasp stutters its way through his lungs. He moves his hand back to Gene's wrist and stops it with a bitten-off gasp.

"Bad?" Gene asks, but it obviously wasn't.

"God, no. Come here?"

Gene knee-walks his way up to Luis's waiting face, pausing with his legs on either side of Luis's neck, such that he sits more on Luis's chest than his face. He has kissed those lips and tried his best to commit their particular way of moving to memory. He loves how uneven their pressure is, nearly all concentrated on Luis's right-hand side but all the more enthusiastic for it. What Luis wants is more intimate, though, far closer than kissing, far more dedicated than two exchanged handies in a hotel room. The craziest thing, the thing that hitches Gene's breath, is not that Luis wants him, but that Gene wants to let himself be wanted.

He couldn't put that into words if he tried, so he says, "You're fucking gay."

The look on Luis's face—one part thrilled and two parts unabashedly impatient—is certainly that.

"Yes," Luis agrees.

Gene wonders, for the few seconds he takes to get situated, whether this moment is something Luis has imagined, if Luis has spent nights wanting this the way Gene has. That possibility alone makes Gene's knees weak, and then Luis is plucking Gene's hand up from where he has it braced on the headboard and sliding Gene's fingers into his hair, and then he pulls Gene closer, his hands on the backs of Gene's thighs.

His mouth is warm, and wet, and so is Gene. The sound is absolutely absurd in its dedicated loudness, but Luis's eyebrows lower in concentration, and Gene could stay here for as many hours as Luis would let him, for as long as Luis wanted him.

When Gene's legs start to shake, and he laughs again, he tightens his fingers in Luis's hair; at that, Luis gasps against him. Luis's shoulder starts to move, and without looking, Gene can tell he has wrapped a hand around himself. Luis doesn't slow in the slightest, his tongue and lips insistent—and God, yes, enthusiastic.

For the next however-long, nothing else matters. Just Luis and his hand on Gene, and his hand on himself, and his tongue in Gene—and the feeling of his voice, desperate and pressed close, when he lets himself come.

Gene lies on top of Luis, head on his shoulder and their legs a tangled, wet, sweaty mess. In the corner of Gene's line of sight, Luis swipes the palm of his hand on the—admittedly already-filthy—sheets, and Gene wrinkles his nose.

"*Nada*. Gross."

Luis laughs, and Gene feels it in his ribs, and it's a beautiful, musical thing. Looser and happier than Luis usually sounds.

"You weren't supposed to see that," Luis says.

"Well, I did, and you're nasty."

Gene props himself up to look Luis in the eye and God, what a sight: Luis—face wet and sloppy, lips darker than usual, beard looking like he lost a very enjoyable fight with Gene's pussy. His hair stands straight up, clumped together where Gene grabbed it.

"Oh my God," Gene says.

"Do I look good?"

"You look like a hot mess."

But he scoots far enough up to kiss Luis, to taste himself on Luis's lips, and now that he's allowed himself this, he's not sure that he can unlearn how good the last hour felt. And he's quite positive that he doesn't want to forget anyway.

"Wash your face," Gene says, into their kiss.

"You want to take a shower?"

He shouldn't. He really should not give himself one more thing to love about Luis, not when things are this complicated and this unbearably good.

But, he justifies to himself as he nods and rolls off of Luis, nothing is set in stone. Never mind that Luis will get called up and Gene won't. Never mind that one of them could get traded to another team, and they have no say in the matter. Never mind that Luis has shown no interest in coming out, and that Gene has never been much good at hiding anything about himself. Never mind that the short drive from Beaverton to Portland will feel a lot longer when they have near-opposite travel schedules and a three-hour game nearly every single day, six months of the year. Never mind that Baker told him to get a distraction, not to fall in love with the worst idea imaginable.

Never mind all that.

Because Gene rolls out of bed, and he slips one arm under the crooks of Luis's knees and the other arm underneath Luis's back, and he hefts Luis in one easy motion, carrying him to the bathroom as Luis throws a halfhearted, fake-annoyed fit.

Because Gene thinks—as he leans his cheek against Luis's back in the shower, as Luis washes clean his beard and the hair on his stomach, as they collapse into the clean bed, wrapped in their towels and each other while they debate what food to order—he is in love with this man. Luis—neurotic and talented and kind and terrible at first impressions. Luis—concerningly sweaty and unbelievably, unfairly gorgeous. Luis—who Gene didn't want at all and now can't imagine losing. He can try to logic that away as much as he pleases, but there it is—the fact of it, warm and steady and, in the end, not at all surprising.

And Gene wants every weird, complicated bit of that.

# 14

## JULY

**Current record: 50–40**

They fall asleep in the same bed, never quite managing to come down from that post-game, post-sex high. They stick together along nearly the full lengths of their bodies, laughing every time they try to move, and are rewarded by the slightly suction-cup sound of their skin peeling apart. At some point, Luis lets Dodger back into the room, and the night passes without an abundance of sleeping. Instead, stubbornly half-awake, they roll increasingly on top of each other, until the three of them lie in a crowded pile.

By the time morning arrives, Gene's eyes sting a bit, and his limbs feel as if his muscles have, perhaps, fully fallen out from under his skin. Their shower—almost like a continuation of thc one they shared the night before, though this time with more shampoo and marginally less kissing—does little to wake him up. He loves it all the more for its quiet. When Luis leans out from behind the curtain to grab the iced coffee he bought Gene earlier in the morning, Gene takes it in grateful hands. He offers Luis a sip, which Luis accepts, and when they kiss again, it tastes like coffee and cream and no sugar at all, and Gene smiles into it. He can't seem to stop doing that.

They meet Gene's family for breakfast, a meal at which Gene and Luis do their best impressions of people who woke up in two separate beds. Whether or not the Ionescus believe them, they make it through the meal without incident.

The next morning, when they're getting ready for the Home Run Derby, Luis watches Gene button up the Portland jersey the team gave him to wear this week—mint-shouldered, made of slick fabric, with a row of trees printed along the bottom in a deep green, so that they look like the silhouette of a forest when the shirt is tucked into Gene's shorts.

As soon as Gene twists the final button into place, Luis tugs him in by the waist. "What are the chances you'd be willing to undo some of those?" he asks.

"High," Gene says.

Luis grins and reaches to help. Gene could maybe get used to the sappy, unfamiliar feeling that spreads through his chest every time he makes Luis experience even a modicum of happiness.

Luis says, "I have to ask you something."

"Take the whole thing off?"

"Oh, that too, later."

Luis looks too focused, too purposeful. Gene puts a hand on one of Luis's. "What's up?"

"I want to visit my family," he says.

"Okay."

"Like, before the break's over. I bought a ticket to go after the All-Star Game tomorrow, and"—he takes a deep breath—"I was wondering if you'd come with me."

*Oh.*

"Do you want me to?" Gene asks.

"Yes."

"Then yes."

Luis fiddles with one of Gene's undone buttons.

"I want to come out to them. Well, the rest of them. Mia already knows. She's bi, so it wasn't that hard to tell her." He takes a deep breath. "And I just think it might be easier if I'm not alone."

It's an awfully boyfriend-like request to make, and Gene is quite certain one night doesn't make them *that*, but he doesn't particularly care. Not when it comes to this, at least. He would go with Luis even if they'd never kissed, even if they never planned to. If Luis wants him there, Gene will come.

Luis starts again, "But it would mean one less day with *your* family, so I'd get it if—"

Gene cups his face. "Send me your flight number."

"I already bought you a ticket. Just in case. I didn't want the flight to sell out."

"How much? I'll send you money."

"I used miles," Luis says.

"Can you send me the information?" Gene asks. "I need to change my name on the reservation."

Vince is always telling him he should get his name change done, but it's expensive, and time-consuming, and complicated, and, frankly, it doesn't bother Gene enough to overcome the ADHD paralysis. Still, it makes his airport experience a little weird. His ID has a picture of him from right before he came out, same short hair but a rounder face; it says his deadname, which isn't a big deal to him, but he does try to angle it away from his teammates when they fly. They could probably find it on Google in five minutes, but they wouldn't do that. He changed his name because he loved being called Gene, not because he hated his old name. He's lucky in this way, in so many ways.

He explains this to Luis as they log in to Luis's airline account.

Luis still looks away when Gene types it in, as if he hadn't known Gene by that name first.

While they pack their things, Gene asks, "Any reason you're doing this right now?"

"Why? Do you think it's a bad idea?" he says.

"No. But I don't want you to do it on my account."

"I think they sort of already know about me. But I just—wanted to actually tell them, while I have a chance to do it in person but before I have time to lose my nerve again. And if I have you there, I think it'll feel a little less scary?"

Gene tries to ignore the low-grade firecrackers in his chest, the warmth and the spark and that wild joyous burst about being included in this. "Okay," he says. "It went well when Mia came out?"

"Yeah."

"Does that make you feel less nervous?"

"I always feel nervous," Luis says. It comes with an exhausted eyebrow raise, a quirk of his lips, but Gene understands: there's something a little freeing in admitting to yourself that something will scare you no matter how well you prepare.

The next night, just as the flight attendant tells them to put their phones in airplane mode for the flight, Gene's lights up with a message—a link from Kyle Clark, in a group chat with Gene and both of the other Kyles. It's followed up with a text from Kyle Rivera: *You were all great!*

Kyle Nguyen adds: *Tell Nada & Gonzo we say congrats & also they need to give us their numbers, lol*

Gene texts back, *Will do!! Love you guys*, then clicks on the link.

It leads to an article from the Portland Lumberjacks SBNation blog, but before Gene can even read the headline, his eyes are drawn to the picture, which, for a second, makes him wonder if he might need to clean his glasses. Because surely he can't be seeing right.

But there he is, hoisted high in Luis's arms, Luis looking up at him with that honest, beautiful smile. Ernie stands at Luis's back, jostling his shoulder and yelling in delight.

*Futures Game Inspires Glimmer of Actual Hope for Once*, the headline reads, although Gene is starting to tear up and can't be completely sure. He blinks twice—long efforts that don't quite save him—and looks again. Underneath the picture, the caption says, *Ernie Gonzales (left) joins the celebration with Beaverton teammates Luis Estrada (center) and Gene Ionescu (right), following the National League's Futures Game victory at Citi Field.*

"Holy *shit*," Gene says. It's the first time he's seen his own face headlining an article about anything other than his transness. As he scrolls down, he catches a sentence here and there, praise upon praise for the season he and Luis and Ernie have put together so far, representing the bright future of Portland baseball. Like it's a given. Not once before has Gene read words like this, written about him—assertions that he doesn't only bolster his teammates' playoff hopes, but that he could also give that hope to people he's never met and will never meet, who have rooted for the Portland Lumberjacks for years and have next to nothing to show for it.

He has also rarely seen a trans athlete so unequivocally celebrated for the things they bring to the field. In some ways, the quiet presence of his blue-and-white-and-pink cleats in that picture matters more to him than seeing his own face there.

"Please turn your phone to airplane mode," the flight attendant says.

"Sorry. Yeah, of course."

As soon as she has passed their aisle, Gene returns to the article, taking screenshots of the whole thing before he gets in trouble again.

"Holy *shit*," he repeats, because it bears repeating.

Luis, for his part, is halfway to incoherence already, having taken his requisite preflight Xanax when they sat down. He rests his head on Gene's shoulder, and Gene turns the phone to show him.

"That's us," Luis says.

He falls asleep by the time the plane takes off, already working on the beginnings of a drool patch on Gene's shoulder. Gene puts his headphones on and starts his music while he reads on.

The article goes pretty far into the weeds of Gene's batting and fielding statistics, which Gene marvels at, because at no point in his baseball-playing career has anyone ever written about his actual on-field metrics so thoroughly, or in so positive a light. The article mentions that he's trans only one time, and then proceeds to systematically pick apart what kind of a player he is.

This, more than the Futures Game, more than any of it—this is what makes Gene start to think there might be a chance, however slim, that he could make it.

As they cross over the New York border, Gene slides his hand under the sweatshirt Luis has draped across himself like a blanket. He laces their fingers together, and, even in his sleep, Luis squeezes Gene's hand. For a minute, for a moment, Gene lets himself imagine what it would be like if they both made it. If they got the whole damn dream.

# 15

## JULY

### Current record: 50–40

"You know, it didn't hit me until right now that I'd be staying with my twenty-eight-year-old friend at his mother's house," Gene says as they turn onto Luis's mom's street in Pasadena.

He'd paused before "friend," having backed himself into a corner, trying to find a suitable word and landing on a safe, completely insufficient option.

"And my abuela. And Dani."

"Right, right. Even better. Very romantic."

Luis takes his foot, somehow, even farther off the gas. "Do you want to get a hotel?"

"Nada, no."

"I thought this would be more comfortable. But you're right, it's weird." His shoulders have started hunching toward his ears again.

"It's not weird," Gene insists. "I mean. It is weird, but I like it."

"Really? Because we can—"

"No. I want to stay here. I mean, I'm going to tease you for it, don't get it twisted—"

"That's only fair—"

"—but I want to stay here," Gene says. He means it. He wants to see the place where Luis grew up.

Luis grips the steering wheel a little tighter and stops the car entirely, his stare locked on a house two doors down.

Gene knows Luis wants to visit his family, that he wants to do this, because, like Gene, Luis suffers from a severe case of decision aversion—for Gene, it's the ADHD, but for Luis, his brain takes him in logic loops about everything. Gene has watched him hem and haw between a white and a black T-shirt, the same brand and size, for ten minutes.

So, the fact that he bought these plane tickets, that he brought the idea up to Gene at all—it means he wants to do it. Even if he does lean so far forward Gene worries he'll honk the horn, anticipation curling his spine.

In a fit of softness, Gene reaches over and rubs a circle into the back of Luis's shoulder. He scratches at the short hairs at the nape of Luis's neck, the ones that have grown long enough to start forming the beginnings of curls. He keeps his hand there, resisting the urge to touch his earring, that little gold reminder of Luis's trusting Gene with the softest parts of himself.

When Luis's posture relaxes a bit, Gene asks, "You okay?"

"Yep."

"You don't have to do it today," Gene says. "You know that, right?"

"I don't want to do it tomorrow morning."

"I just mean, they're excited to see you. You don't have to come out to make a visit worthwhile. If you want to wait until the season is over and you come home for longer, that's okay, too."

Luis widens his eyes and inhales a little too deeply, his mouth a perfect line. "I guess," he says, which Gene knows is Luis code for *If I don't do it now, I am never going to do it,* solely because Luis has said so at least a dozen times.

The Estrada house is a single-story building, simple and painted a pale buttercup yellow. The windows are old, single-paned, and plentiful, and the house has only a single-car garage, meaning that Luis's sisters' cars are parked in a cluster in front of the house and their neighbors'. There's a bench in front of the window, on the porch, where a scarecrow sits, either very late from last fall or a little early for this one. In the center of their yard sits a mature lemon tree, splashes of yellow fruit popping out from amidst the leaves. Even with the car windows rolled up, Gene swears he can smell them.

"Nes," Luis says, pulling his attention away from the house.

"What's up?"

"I feel like I'm gonna pass out." He leans his forehead on the wheel.

"You won't."

"How do I say it?" he asks the dashboard.

" 'Hi, Ma. I like to touch men sexually. What are you cooking, you need any help?' "

"No."

"Do you want to practice?" Gene asks.

"No. I'm just going to try to stay upright."

"If you have to pass out, you can land on me."

Luis gives a mock-serious nod, and Gene gives him a salute in return.

"See you on the other side," Gene says.

Luis tugs open his door and grabs their duffels from the backseat, sliding Gene's over the roof of the rental car to him. Dodger bounds out of the car and up to the door before Gene and Luis can even get their bags on their shoulders, right as the front door opens and a bevy of Estrada women spill out.

They'd spent the drive reviewing the basic makeup of Luis's

family so Gene wouldn't make an ass of himself: there's his grandma, queen bitch (her words) of her poker group, who moved in after Luis's dad died a decade ago; his mom, who makes the best omelets and can't sing for shit but always sings anyway; his two oldest sisters, Jamie and Sabrina, old enough that Luis says they feel almost like aunts; Dani, the middle sister, who Luis says will want to talk about the associate's degree she recently finished, and her boyfriend, specifically in that order; and Mia.

Gene has heard about Mia—who is a year older than Luis and crops up in two of the three total photos Luis has posted to his Instagram—many times. Luis looks by far the most like her: the same brown eyes, and the same loose, smooth curls. They each have a nose so straight and so beautiful it looks aristocratic, almost severe. They have the same small bump at the ridge, right where their noses wrinkle when they smile big enough. Or, like now, when Luis gives an anxious wince as they walk up to the house.

"Can I hold your hand?" Luis asks, strained and quiet.

Maybe this is Luis's way of saying it. Wordless, simple, a gesture of connection with a person he cares about, made in front of the people who raised him. Quiet and trusting.

It suits him.

So, Gene holds out his hand and says, "If you want to. Of course."

Luis laces their fingers together, and if Luis weren't having a bit of a capital-M Moment, Gene would have one of his own. Because Luis's hand is warm, familiar, slightly callused, and Gene has never met a man's family like this, but Luis squeezes Gene's hand like he really means it.

When Gene turns to the rest of the Estrada family, still waiting in that doorway, they look to him, to Luis, to their hands between them, and there is no grand moment of revelation. Just a slow unfurling of smiles and an all-at-once movement forward to meet their grandson, son, brother halfway up the walk. As he and Luis take those final steps into Luis's family, Gene feels every bit of the early-morning sun.

It's Mia who pushes through the wall of her sisters first. She is taller than Gene expected, closer to Luis's height than Gene's, and when she hugs Luis, she squeezes so hard the air rushes out of him on a grunt.

Gene could swear he hears her say, "I'm proud of you, dude."

She hugs Gene next, crushingly tight, before she lets the remaining Estrada sisters and matriarchs have their turns.

"Uh," Luis says, blinking away what might be tears. He points in turn. "Nes, this is Mia, Dani, Sabrina, Jamie, Ma, Abuela." Then, he points to Gene. "This is Nes. Gene."

Luis's mom takes his bag and hands it off to the closest sister, Dani—by far the shortest of the siblings, a woman with Down syndrome and an impossibly thick braid of almost-black hair—who promptly hands it back to Luis.

"I'm not carrying your bag," she says. "Even if you do have a boyfriend."

Luis laughs, and then he really does cry a little, just before his mom pulls him into a hug. It takes her until the end of the hug to realize she hasn't introduced herself to Gene.

"I'm Lydia, honey. It's good to meet you." She has a sweet voice, even quieter than her son's, and when she hugs Gene, it takes effort for him not to cry, too.

Inside, it smells like French toast and horchata, all cinnamon and sweet, and Luis picks up Gene's hand again; when they finally make their well-embraced way to the dining room table, Gene notices that something in Luis's face has opened up. Partly, Gene is sure, it's the simple act of being home. But the other part, the part that queer people maybe understand better than anyone else, is the act of a parent changing the shape of their home so it can fit you, and loving you as much as they always have. More, because they know you better now.

That night, when Sabrina and Jamie have gone back to their own houses and the oldest two Estrada women have headed to bed, Gene and Luis sit on the couch with Mia and Dani, their legs curled up on the cushions with them. Dani nods off between sentences, waking up in bursts only long enough to correct Mia when she gets bits and pieces of one story or another wrong.

"We should probably get to bed," Mia says, tipping her head toward Dani.

"Are you sleeping here tonight?" Luis asks.

"Yeah. Ma set up my old bed in me and Dani's room. I wanted to see you guys tomorrow before you had to take off again."

Dani yawns, her face pressed into the couch's back cushion. "It's my room."

Mia rolls her eyes. Then she looks at Gene, her eyes so appraising that Gene mentally runs through a catalogue of things he could apologize for.

Finally, she points at Luis. "He has had a fat crush on you for years," she says. "And I'm telling you this because it'll piss Louie off."

She grins then, and kisses Luis's cheek, right where beard meets blushing skin. She says, quietly but not too quiet for Gene to hear, "Let yourself be happy."

Then she hauls Dani to bed.

Gene watches them disappear down the hall. He raises his eyebrows at Luis.

"No," Luis says.

"*Years?*"

"*No.*"

"No, you *don't* have a crush on me, or no it hasn't been years?"

"Okay," he reasons, pressing his palms together and gesturing with both hands, "here's the thing."

Gene leans in close, lowers his voice as much as he can. "Because you eat me out pretty enthusiastically for someone who isn't into me."

Luis's nervous smile turns into something looser, far more lopsided. "Fair."

"Can I see your room? Since you have such a crush on me."

"I'm a grown adult. I did not use the word 'crush.'"

"No? What would you call it?"

Luis presses his lips together, trying to smother all that giddiness that's come out tonight. "I don't want to incriminate myself."

"Oh, please do."

Instead, Luis kisses Gene, a solid and purposeful kiss. Gene forgets what he was asking. He forgets what he was teasing Luis for. He forgets everything but Luis's lips on his, his tongue a tease against Gene's.

Luis breaks the kiss off, and Gene chases it down, eyes closed, until Luis tugs on his hand.

"My room is down the hall. If you still wanted to see it," he says.

Gene does. He does want to do that.

Nothing in Luis's childhood bedroom tells Gene anything he didn't know about him before. He keeps every space he occupies neat, and clearly did so in this room before he left it, too. Everything in it is blue: the comforters, the Dodgers posters, the pale blue paint on the walls. The pillowcases are blue, the hangers in his closet arc blue, and a copy of Joni Mitchell's *Blue*, on vinyl, is hung on the wall. Gene wonders if, were he to take it down, the paint under it would be darker than everywhere else, blocked from the sun-bleaching that has affected the rest of the walls.

"So how do you feel?" Gene asks. "They took it well."

Luis thinks. "Weird."

"Yeah. It feels like that sometimes."

"It's just . . ." He shrugs. "I didn't really think I'd ever get to, like—date, or whatever. And I definitely didn't think I'd get to tell anyone about it. Not if I wanted to have a career. So it's weird that they know. But—good."

"That's good. That's really good, Nada."

On Luis's desk, a picture of them and Ritz and Max sits in a frame, Gene's cheek pressed to Luis's so they could all fit in the photo, their Stanford uniforms grass-stained after their championship win. Gene remembers that game perfectly, and remembers even better the way Luis's cheek on his had made him feel—halfway in his grave in a distinctly breathless, sweat-slicked palms kind of way. Luis's hair is longer in the picture than he wears it now. Gene's, too—the same curls he has now, but chin-length and bobby-pinned back in a million places under his baseball cap. He thinks, if he squints at the picture, he's wearing mascara. The picture and all its memories slam into him all at once, a wall of affection for these kids who tried so fucking hard and didn't even know what they were trying for.

"I'm surprised you kept that," Gene says.

"Why?"

Gene picks the frame up, traces the cheap wood grain. "Like, why not a picture from draft day?"

"Winning the College World Series was a lot cooler than pacing in the living room while we waited for the phone to ring. Sorry, though." Luis taps the frame. "I know it's an old picture. I haven't lived here in a long time."

"It's fine."

"I can get rid of it."

Gene shrugs. "I know it bugs some trans people. But I don't mind. That's still me."

"We can get a new picture."

"Great. Then you can put them both up." His grin is smug and broad when he adds, "So did you already have a crush on me in that picture, or not yet?"

"Oh, shut up. I'm going to put it in the drawer."

"No, don't do that. I'll stop teasing."

"You won't."

"Probably not."

Luis picks the picture up and stares at it for a second. "I had a crush on you way before this."

"Before I came out?"

"I told you, it was a confusing year for me." He shrugs again, then gestures to Gene. "A lot less confusing now that I know you're just as gay as I am."

"Sorta like you knew before you *knew*-knew."

Luis nods, then sets the picture facedown on his desk.

"No!" Gene protests. "Why? I really don't mind."

"You might not mind, but I look fucking awful in that picture."

This is categorically false. Luis is handsomer now, by every measure, and the beard helps him in the jaw department, but happiness has always looked good on him, and he looks happy here. Gene wonders, for a second, if this is what Mia meant when she told Luis to let himself be happy. He wonders what happened between this picture and Luis getting drafted and the call Luis never made to tell him goodbye. He wonders what turned this man—young and gangling and awkward, yes, but joyful, too—into the panic-ridden version of himself Gene met three months ago.

It feels too heavy for such a hopeful night to ask when and why Luis got so much sadder. And then, there's a part of Gene that doesn't want to know why Luis stopped talking to him back then. He just wants to enjoy that he was important enough to Luis for this picture to make it onto his desk and that he gets to be that important to Luis again.

Then Dodger shuffles past them and plops onto a dog bed, in the perfect outline of himself, before letting out a put-upon sigh.

"We're up past his bedtime," Luis says.

"Apparently."

Gene points to the ground, where someone has blown up an air mattress and helpfully placed it next to Luis's bed, both mattresses twin-sized and the air mattress looking like it might have a small leak somewhere.

"So, do I have to sleep on that?" he asks.

"No, we can share my bed."

"The twin?"

"Is that too cramped?" Luis asks.

Gene tries to imagine a world in which he wouldn't want to share any size bed with Luis, but he can't, so he says, "No. Not at all."

Luis sits down on the edge of his narrow bed, pulling Gene in by the wrist until Gene lands in his lap, their legs pressed together and hands trying to find anywhere to rest in the bed's scant space. Luis gives up, sliding his hand around Gene's side, onto his back, and tips him until they have to bend their knees to fit on the mattress. Gene hits his head on the wall when he moves to lie down, getting an instant headache for his trouble.

"Shit, sorry," Luis says, his face pressed to Gene's shoulder.

"This is karma's way of getting back at me for never having sex in college," Gene says, rubbing the spot he hit. Luis looks at him, confused, so Gene clarifies, "Never had to maneuver my way around an extra-long twin."

"Got it."

"Was it worth it?"

"In college? Not really. Now? Yes."

Luis gets up to lock the door and slide a chair underneath the doorknob for good measure, and Gene gets why people like that little dash of rebellion. He wishes sneaking around to kiss Luis could always be like this—harmless, risk-free, just stupid enough to be sexy.

Back at home, it won't be. But tonight it is, and tonight it's good, and tonight he pulls Luis back into bed. Tonight, they press together in their pajamas—Luis in sweats, Gene in boxers he never wears during the day—and let their hands wander.

Gene holds Luis's face and pulls him in, a little slower, a little softer, hoping that if Luis notices the shift, he doesn't comment on it. They lie chest to chest, one of Luis's legs slotted between Gene's, pressed up close against him, kissing without any direction at all until Gene starts to rock his hips.

"Is that okay?" he asks. He reaches for the waistband of Luis's sweats, tugging it gently.

Luis nods, his forehead on Gene's.

So Gene moves his hips again, spits indelicately into the palm of his hand, and wraps that hand around Luis's dick, falling into an easy, unhurried rhythm while Luis gasps against his lips. It's good: the slide of his boxers against him, wet enough he won't want to sleep in them; Luis's leg held firm, even when his arms start to shake; and the weight of Luis in his hand, perfect enough to make Gene wonder how he'd feel in other contexts—in Gene's mouth, in him.

That thought alone is enough to speed Gene's hips, his wrist. Luis's mouth is insistent and sloppy at his jaw, and Gene taps his shoulder until Luis looks at him.

He didn't get to see Luis's face last time, buried as it was, and he'd like to see it now.

It's weird, how comfortable Gene is with him, as he watches Luis's mouth fall open, hears the stifled sound Luis makes, and feels Luis finish, pressed between them. Gene has the passing thought that it's intimate in a way he has never been with someone before. It's completely messy sex, distinctly young in its clumsiness, and all the sweeter for its lack of pretension or pressure.

Luis kisses Gene, then kisses his slick palm as Gene gets himself off, so relieved when he does that he laughs quietly against Luis's lips as his muscles unspool.

"Shit, Nes," Luis says.

"What?"

Luis props himself up over Gene, looks him in the eye when he says, "Can I say something?"

"Shoot."

"I love that you laugh when you finish."

Gene tries to catch his breath, unsure whether it's the sex or that word or the fond look on Luis's face that has knocked every bit of oxygen out of him. He shoves his face into the crook of his elbow. "Stop that."

"Why?"

"Because you have a Selena poster on your wall, and she's watching me get flustered."

Luis nudges Gene's arm off his face. "Well, you look good flustered."

"I look like a mess," Gene says. He gestures to where Luis came on his stomach.

Luis gives Gene a kiss, almost a peck, and says, "I'll get a washcloth."

When he gets back, he wipes Gene's skin and peels his boxers off for him. He leaves a kiss on the inside of his thigh, this one much more lingering, until Gene taps the side of his face.

"I'm way too tired for that, Nada."

Luis leans his forehead on Gene's thigh. "Got it. You have extra shorts in your bag?"

"Yeah."

"I'll grab them for you."

After they've cleaned up and pulled themselves somewhat together, after they brush their teeth, after they turn the lights off and start to climb into bed, Luis asks, "Will you lay on top of me?"

Gene raises his eyebrows.

"It helps me sleep," Luis explains. "It's, like—"

But Gene has already rolled, shifting until his body covers almost the entirety of Luis's, just half of Luis's shins and his feet poking out from underneath Gene. He settles in, Luis's chest hair a little coarse against his own skin, and if this helps Luis sleep, he would happily do this every night.

Only if it helped Luis, of course.

"Hey, did you notice Dani called me your boyfriend today?" Gene asks, because the sound of it has stuck in the back of his head, tantalizing.

Luis lies perfectly still. "Yeah."

Gene props himself up to look at him. "You didn't correct her."

"I mean," Luis starts, and he lifts a hand to touch Gene's chest. He waits for Gene's nod before tracing along the curved line of the scar that runs, horizontal and unbroken, across Gene's chest, bisecting his rib cage. "Would you want to be? In theory?"

What Gene wants is to melt into this touch. He wants to feel Luis's breathing and weight and thereness underneath him, every night, ideally until he forgets what it's like to sleep by himself. He wants to memorize exactly how soft Luis can be with him, how desperate Luis's voice can get, how good it feels to fall into each other. He wants Luis to be the first and last person he talks to every day, because no one has ever been so easy and so interesting to talk to. Gene has never loved someone's voice and wanted to live in it the way he wants to live in Luis's.

That's all much harder to admit, a lot more vulnerable and true than anything Gene has ever allowed himself.

"I'm not very good at wanting things," he admits.

"What do you mean?"

Gene shrugs. "Like, I try not to do it."

"But you're the most optimistic person I know," Luis says. He plays with one of Gene's curls, his finger gentle as he twists Gene's hair around it, letting it go when the tension starts to pull.

"I'm an optimist. I hope. That's different from wanting," Gene says.

"I don't get how."

"I have a theory."

Luis raises his eyebrows, waiting.

So Gene takes a deep breath, and lays out for Luis something he has never said aloud. "Hope can be selfless. But wanting feels selfish, and wanting means disappointment."

"Hope doesn't?"

"Hope and optimism, are, like . . . shots in the dark. Wanting is specific, and it's hungry. It's nuance."

Luis is clearly unconvinced. "Okay, Nes. Then I *hope* someday you let yourself *want* something."

"That is a loophole at best," Gene says, the same thing Luis said to him at the bar in Reno, the first time in years he had let himself find Luis charming. It's hard to remember, now, what it was like—feeling anything but affection for this man.

Luis nudges his chin until Gene kisses him, and Luis tells him he's ridiculous. They lie on that old twin bed, kissing just to kiss, Luis's arms loose and languid around Gene's waist, for as long as they can keep themselves awake. And when they can't hold their heads up anymore, Gene lays his on Luis's shoulder. They listen to an unseasonable California rain as it refuses to slow outside, until they eventually make their way to sleep.

In the morning, Gene can't quite remember drifting off, but he tries to remember how Luis looks here now, sun-dappled and warm. It seems to Gene they were awake and then waking, with nothing in between, exhausted and bright-eyed.

PART THREE

# The Playoff Chase

# 16

## JULY

**Current record: 50–40**

In the top of the first, Luis and Gene take their usual places. Gene looks across the short distance of second base to grin at Luis, working his glove back into shape, as if a year, rather than a week, has passed since he last wore it. Luis's eyebrows raise, a small flick of acknowledgment, and he nods his head just enough that Gene knows Luis has seen him.

When they landed back in Portland, Luis continued to hold Gene's hand, stopping only when they had to stand up. Luis texted him this morning—*Morning, Nes. I'll see you at seven?*—even though they confirmed their practice plans last night, and when Luis's name popped up on his lock screen, it did so over Gene's new background—that picture of him and Luis at the Futures Game, Ernie in the frame enough that Gene can maintain some semblance of plausible deniability.

This bad idea may have snowballed a bit out of his control.

He hasn't let something get out of his control in years. It feels good.

He throws Luis a wink, a flirty, dorky thing that no one but Luis is close enough to see. Luis turns a little pink across his cheeks and along the tops of his big, inelegant ears. Gene loves those ears. He loves how they make Luis look more human, how they give his intimidatingly pretty face a tinge of friendly approachability.

Gene would like to kiss those ears, right where they run pink.

"Stop that," Luis yells.

"Stop what?"

"You're a twit."

Gene shoots him a finger gun with his ungloved hand as Vince finishes his warm-up pitches. Gene keeps expecting the sting of Vince's quiet to wear off, for his absence to feel less unbearable, but it hasn't. He misses his friend and his dependable presence, their twice-a-week dinners and morning car pools.

In the month and a half since their dinner, Vince has been nothing short of a miracle on the mound. When he readies his first real pitch, Reno's batter at the plate, the energy on the field shifts. Their captain is manning the ship, and they can get serious.

Gene adjusts his hat on his curls and gets into a ready stance: knees bent, feet light, glove ready. Gene may not have been literally born on a baseball diamond, but close enough. He was raised on one, with a glove on his hand as soon as he could hold it up.

This is his place, and Luis and Baker and the rest of the team—even Vince, even when he doesn't want to be—they are Gene's people.

The first pitch Vince throws comes back into the infield on a sharp, concerning crack, a laser trying to make its way through the gap. Gene, without any conscious thought, judges its angle, its velocity, the way he and Luis practice again and again until it's rote. He dives to catch the ball, and when it hits the back of his glove, no part of Gene is surprised.

Luis is at his side faster than Gene would think possible, if it were anyone but Luis. Without looking, Gene lobs the ball up. Luis catches it in his ungloved hand and fires it to first—that smooth, effortless throw that will probably make him a real, genuine star someday—dead center into Cooper's glove. A line drive like that, for any other team, would have turned into a guaranteed single.

But they are not any other team, and Gene and Luis are not any other keystone.

When Gene stands up, Luis gives him a high five, and Gene smacks his glove against Luis's ass, and maybe Gene is imagining it, but it feels different. They played well together before, yes. For months now, and for a whole college season, he trusted Luis to be exactly where he needed him, and he returned the favor to Luis in full. But today, he didn't have to look where Luis was—he knew. He didn't need to *trust* Luis would be there—he *knew*.

Gene never worried much about being good—he knew he was, he had always been, and he felt, most of the time, like he would always be—but when he plays alongside Luis, he can consider the possibility of being great.

When Luis starts walking away from him, to his spot in the shift, he gives Gene the same wink Gene has been giving him all morning, except clumsier, somehow even dorkier, and it's a miracle Gene's grin doesn't split his head in two.

Then, from first base, Cooper gives a short whistle. "Guys," he calls, pointing to the stands. Gene and Luis and Ross all turn, taking it in with their first baseman.

And with a start, Gene realizes what Cooper's talking about.

The stands, usually barely more than barren, are emanating *noise*. The real, honest-to-God *sound* of cheering. The seats, many of which haven't held actual people in years, creak in that charming, scary way of an old ballpark. The team has made all of one out, on one pitch, and people are cheering for them.

"Holy *shit*," Gene says.

Maybe they're just disappointed by the big league team this year. Maybe it's a celebration of Vince, the onetime hero of Portland baseball. Maybe it will last exactly one game, or maybe they'll all leave after three innings. Gene doesn't care. This is Oregon baseball, loud and green and excited, and he is a fucking *part* of it.

They lose the game. It happens, it's never fun, but the stands don't empty out until the game ends, and that encourages Gene more than any win ever has.

He lingers longer than everyone else, the way he does after most every game. For once, he doesn't spare a thought to the standings, or to whether or not Tacoma won their game a few hundred miles away. Those things can wait for tomorrow. Today, he wants to keep the feeling of Beaverton cheering in his chest, overfull to the point that his ears ring from the pressure.

He would be the last one hanging back in the locker room, except that Luis's leg is pressed against the side of Gene's, each of them watching the door as the last of their teammates make their way out. As soon as the door closes behind Vince, Gene nudges Luis's shoulder, this time with intention. He cranes his neck to see what Baker is up to—packing her bag, tucking tomorrow's lineup into a folder on her desk—and wiggles his eyebrows at Luis.

"Good night, Baker," Gene calls, to make sure she's really on her way out.

"Go home, Nes," she responds, flat and subtly amused.

"Yeah, yeah." Gene turns to Luis and, much more quietly, says, "You in a rush to leave?"

Luis flicks his eyes down Gene's chest, his look lingering low, just below where Gene's uniform belt rests. When Luis's gaze drags back up, the warmth in Gene's cheeks travels downward, as if moving in reverse of Luis's gaze. When they make eye contact again, it takes every bit of self-control Gene can muster not to sling one of his legs over Luis's lap and set up shop there for the rest of the night.

Instead, he stands, peels off his uniform pants, and shucks them and his jersey into his locker stall. He grabs his towel, slips his feet into the same battered flip-flops he's been subjecting to the team shower all season, and tips his head back in the direction of the showers. It takes Luis all of ten seconds to pluck the cup out of his compression shorts, strip the shorts and pants off, wrap his towel around his waist, and jog halfway to the showers. He leaves Dodger, tuckered out from the long game, napping on the dog bed in the corner.

Clad only in his briefs and his towel, Gene pops his head in the doorway to Baker's office.

"Better take your own advice," he says.

She slings her backpack over one shoulder. "If you would stop slowing me down with all this talking, I could."

Gene mimes zipping his lips closed and throwing away the key, because it's silly and cheesy and the exact sort of thing that makes Baker roll her eyes at him. He watches her leave and waits for the metallic *clunk* of the door closing behind her. The water turns on down the hall.

When he rounds the corner into the showers, Luis is waiting for him, his towel already discarded and hung on a hook.

Gene has seen him naked at least a hundred times, but the effect is rather different when he looks at Gene the way he does now. Like he's been waiting for this, for Gene. Like perhaps Gene was worth the wait.

Gene hangs his towel next to Luis's and reaches in to turn the water on in the open stall to the right of Luis. Then, while he waits for the water to heat up, Luis is there. Standing behind him, hand sliding around to lie in Gene's stomach hair, his voice teasing against Gene's ear when he says, "What's with these?"

To punctuate his point, he snaps the waistband of Gene's underwear, the sound emphasized by the tiles' acoustics.

"I was trying to be polite to Baker," Gene says.

"Towel's not good enough?"

"Towels can slip."

"If Baker was fazed by a stray ass-cheek or two, she would have found a new career path."

"Fair point."

"And she's gone now."

"Even fairer."

"So." Luis tugs on them. "Can I?"

And *that's* why Gene had left his underwear on. He likes the intentionality of this, likes the confirmation that Luis wants him enough to ask.

Gene nods. He turns around to face Luis, to give him a half-challenging look while Luis tugs the briefs until they fall to the ground with a slightly shower-humid, muffled sound. Gene steps out of them, kicks them into the corner, and plants his hands on Luis's hips. He walks Luis backward until his back presses against the tiles.

"In the showers? Really?" Luis says, though he makes no effort to remove himself from the wall. The water has started to wet his hair, and he pushes it off his forehead. With his other hand, he slides his fingers into Gene's hair, right at the nape of his neck.

"Sorry, do you need more ambiance for me to blow you?" Gene asks.

Luis appears to forget his indignation, opting instead for tipping his head back against the tiles and letting his mouth fall open slightly. Gene takes Luis's closed eyes as an opportunity to even out his own breathing.

"See, that's more the reaction I was expecting," Gene says. He presses a kiss into the crook of Luis's neck, and then the center of Luis's chest, and then, moving to his knees, the sharp angle of Luis's hip. He might love that spot. Almost as much as he might love the spot where Luis's thigh meets the rest of his body, that soft and slightly difficult-to-access part of him, where Gene trails his next kiss. And he loves none of it so much as the sounds Luis makes at each kiss. Each time Gene's lips meet skin, Luis grows louder.

And Luis is not a loud man. Not talkative or particularly emotive, not with anyone but the people he trusts most, and, as Gene meets his urging glance, Gene delights that he can count himself a part of that group.

When he finally gets to take Luis into his mouth, he can't help but smile slightly at the way Luis reaches for his head, to hold and to steady himself.

"Nes, oh my God," he says, his voice slightly raspier than usual, and a few steps higher.

When Gene looks up to meet Luis's eyes, Luis's hips tip forward, not at all elegantly, and Gene doesn't bother trying not to feel smug about it. He will be smug about this until he dies, thanks very much.

Minutes later, as Luis's gasps speed up, the lights in the locker room proper flicker back on.

"Shit," Gene says. Luis opens his eyes at that, in time to see Gene stand up and brush his own wet curls back.

"What?" Luis asks, half-laugh and half-desperation, and if Gene hadn't already felt so damn confident in his handiwork, that plea of a question would have sealed the deal. He'd like to get back to that sound, and the pressure of Luis's thumb on his cheek and the slightly rhythmless stutter of his hips, later.

But for now—

He nods his head to where the light has come on and, without any further comment, ducks into the stall next to Luis's. He pretends to partake in a standard post-game shower because he can't imagine that "getting caught by Baker" or "giving the cleaning staff a real nice show" are items on Luis's career trajectory plan.

They dry off a few minutes later, and Gene says, "Okay, so, locker room sex: not the best idea."

"I wouldn't go that far," Luis says. He looks over Gene's shoulder.

"Should we go check?"

"I guess. Do you have plans tonight?"

Gene raises an eyebrow and shrugs one shoulder, an attempt at nonchalance. "Depends."

Luis wraps his towel around his waist. It hides what it needs to hide. "Oh yeah? On what?"

Gene flicks a look down Luis's body, and suddenly Luis's towel doesn't hide quite as much.

"Jesus Christ," Luis says, tipping his head back to stare at the ceiling.

"Sorry," Gene says, although he absolutely isn't. "I'll meet you out there?"

"Yeah, give me a minute."

The lights in Baker's office have been turned back on, and there she sits, at her desk, hat still on and keys in hand, the phone pressed to her ear. She looks up at the sound of Gene's flip-flops on the tiles and points to the phone. Gene nods in acknowledgment, an assurance that he won't interrupt the call.

He won't interrupt, but he *will* attempt to eavesdrop.

All he can hear, though, are "Uh-huh" and "Yep," repeated several times, a scattered pause here and there while she listens. Not nearly enough substance for Gene to figure out who might be on the other end.

"Yeah, I'll send that stuff over tonight," she says.

That, while vague, perks Gene's ears. If she's sending something—documentation, probably on a player, to someone whose phone call was important enough for her to answer on a Friday night—then someone is almost certainly getting traded. The trade deadline, scheduled each year for the end of July, looms in their clubhouse every day, but Gene has done his best to ignore it up to this point. If they start plucking guys out of the clubhouse to send to other cities, it will become markedly harder to pretend it isn't happening.

When Baker hangs up the phone and relocks her office door, she leans against the wall for a second.

"Estrada leave?" she asks, as though she can't see Dodger still asleep in the corner.

"Is he getting traded?"

"They don't ask my opinion on trades, Nes."

"Okay. Have you heard anything, though?"

She looks toward the showers. "Is there something you want to tell me?" she asks.

It's pointed. Enough that Gene wonders if she came back earlier than they realized.

He could admit it. He could ask her for advice.

He could ask what he should do if he's maybe in over his head.

"Nope," he says.

She considers him, lips pursed and eyes narrowed, until they hear Luis coming down the hall.

"All right," she says. "Drive safe. I'll see you tomorrow at two."

"We'll be here."

He catches it after he says it. "*We*," not "*I*."

Back at Gene's apartment, he wastes no time pulling Luis into his room, where he sits him on the edge of the bed. Gene gets to his knees and nudges Luis's apart, intent to get back to what Baker interrupted.

He runs his nose up the inside of Luis's thigh, and Luis almost leans into it, until he says, "What did Baker want? She left pretty fast."

Gene wants to say *Nothing*, but he has a harder time lying to Luis than to anyone else. Not only because Luis would notice faster, mind more, but because Gene finds that he doesn't want to keep things from him.

"She asked if I wanted to tell her anything," Gene admits.

Luis's eyebrows raise.

"I think she might have—heard some stuff."

"Oh."

Gene hoists himself onto the bed next to Luis, not particularly interested in having this conversation from between Luis's legs.

"So," he says.

"So," Luis agrees.

"What do you think about that?"

Luis takes a deep breath, so long that Gene worries he'll never let it out. "I'm not as worried as I thought I'd be. Like, she knows about Vince, right? And that hasn't been a problem."

"That's true," Gene says. A small, itching part at the back of his mind says, *Vince is a former Cy Young pitcher. His husband doesn't play on our team. Our coach isn't always going to be Baker.*

And then Luis says, "I mean, I want this. If you do."

*Luis is going to get called up*, that insistent voice says, *and you won't, and maybe you should tell him what happened with your ex-boyfriend—how baseball will always eat up your life, and you're not sure you know how to want another person the way you want this career, challenges and all. Maybe you should tell him that it scares you to admit that you want these things at all, because you've been told a thousand times by a thousand people that you don't deserve either.*

Gene studies his face, searching it for the tension he has come to expect, but what he finds is Luis, solid and exquisitely *there*. For a moment, Gene can't bring himself to be afraid of that.

When Gene leans in, Luis's mouth on his is steadier, headier, more insistent, and when he holds Gene's waist, there is no shake to his hands. His heart beats a frantic rhythm when Gene pulls him down to kiss at his pulse, but this time, rather than the thrum of anxiety Luis usually gives off, it's happiness, relief, and want.

When Gene pulls Luis on top of him, he makes quick work of Luis's belt and zipper, sliding his hand under the waistband of Luis's pants and pressing it against Luis's straining briefs, and says against his lips, a giddy smile of a question, "You want me?"

This time, Luis doesn't hesitate. He nods. When Gene kisses him, open-mouthed and purposeful, he holds Gene tighter.

"Nada."

"Nes."

Gene takes his hand out of Luis's pants and rests it on Luis's shoulder. He wraps his legs around Luis, using his heels to pull Luis's hips in closer, so they match up with Gene's own. Pressed together like this, Luis shifting against him with his mouth open against Gene's and his eyebrows furrowed, Gene has never been more turned on. He has never felt so completely, overwhelmingly in love.

"Do you want me?" he asks again. He moves his hips once, pointedly, in case Luis hasn't caught on yet, but, of course, he has.

Luis nods, and Gene's head moves with his. Always in sync.

"Are you sure?" Luis asks.

Gene grins and grabs his face, relishes Luis's beard under his fingertips. He wants to hold this tightly to Luis all night, possibly forever. He wants to be as close as physically possible, and there are so many ways to achieve that, but this—Luis on him and in him and everywhere—is the one he wants tonight.

"Absolutely fucking positive," Gene says.

"Thank God."

Luis holds on to Gene's legs to keep them wrapped around his waist and knee-walks up the bed, until he can tip Gene onto his back again, head on the pillows and shirt rucked up on his ribs. He tugs Gene's pants off in one go, waiting for Gene's nod before he does the same to Gene's underwear. He undresses himself next, his belt jingling as he tosses the whole mess of layers onto the floor. Gene tugs his shirt over his head, so that when Luis settles back on top of him, they're wearing nothing but the residue of eye black that their showers didn't manage to remove.

"Glasses on or off?" Luis asks.

"Off."

Gene is nearsighted anyway, and he doesn't plan to let Luis get far enough away that he would need them.

Luis takes them off far more gently than he did any of their clothes, folding them and setting them on the nightstand before he leans down to kiss Gene and slide a hand under one of Gene's legs. While their lips slide against each other—desperate, wet, smiling—Gene lets Luis guide his legs back around his waist, locked at the ankles and holding Luis against him.

"Shit, Nes," Luis says. Between their bodies, Luis touches from the soft and tattooed inside of Gene's arm, to his shoulder, to the dip in his throat, down and across Gene's scar, his fingertips gentle and each touch more maddening than the last.

Luis kisses along Gene's collarbone, his head ducked as he runs his tongue along every spot where he sucks hard enough he might leave a bruise. He holds himself just high enough above Gene that he can reach the places Gene loves to be kissed most, and then, when Gene's moans turn into something closer to a plea, Luis shifts so he can slide a hand between Gene's legs.

"I'm good," Gene says, his voice pleading even to his own ear. He'd laugh at himself if he could. "I'm good whenever."

"What, I can't take my time?"

Gene shifts his hips up, pointed. He loves that Luis always wants to touch him in every way possible, but tonight, impatient and wanting and more than thoroughly kissed, he says, "I'd prefer you didn't."

Luis grins. "You're always teasing me. Let me have my fun."

"This is *not* how I tease you."

"Too bad."

He barely even touches Gene, his hand so delicate about it that Gene might dissolve into the mattress. When he finally does slip one finger exactly where Gene wants it, moving in an infuriatingly slow circle, Gene twists his hands into the short, soft curls at the nape of Luis's neck.

Luis waits until Gene's fingers tighten, until his breathing goes shallow and useless, before taking his hand away. When he moves it to Gene's back, it's wet, and Gene half-whines at its absence.

"You good?" Luis asks.

"You're getting the sheets dirty," Gene says. Anything to draw attention away from that sound he made, and the fact that he's going to make it again if Luis doesn't put his hand back soon.

"Oh, that ship has sailed."

Gene bites the inside of his bottom lip, and he feels far too good to be really embarrassed, but when Luis settles his hips back between Gene's legs, Gene can't quite hide his reaction.

"Hey, Nes?" Luis asks.

"Nada."

"Do you want me?" He lets his voice lilt the same as Gene's did on the question, a terrible but adorable imitation.

Gene rolls his eyes, nodding when Luis leans in to kiss him. "Yes." He kisses Luis again. "So hurry up."

Luis rolls off Gene and the bed to dig through the duffel bag he dropped by the bedroom door. He emerges with a condom and a small bottle of lube. He holds the latter up and looks at Gene, his eyebrows a raised question about where, exactly, Gene would like Luis to fuck him. If Gene had any doubts, Luis's dependable consideration would have done away with them. But he doesn't. Not about Luis, not about doing this with Luis, not about any of it.

"I'm good without that. If you are," Gene says.

"I'm very good with literally whatever you want." And that's perfect—the confirmation not just that Luis wants him in theory, but that he wants the actuality of it, that he will take what Gene offers and that he will have that goofy, thrilled look on his face about it the whole time.

Gene can't help his own smile, so big it almost hurts. "Then get back over here."

Luis drops the lube and rips the condom packet open while he walks back to the bed. Gene, watching him, can't help but say, "Okay, confession."

Luis, teeth still on the very edge of the condom wrapper, raises his eyebrows. "Am I going to like this confession?"

"The whole time you helped me build this bed, I was, like"—Gene presses his palms together, like a prayer—"dying for you to fuck me on it."

That makes Luis—well, "beam" might be the only word for it, before he schools his features into something closer to confidence. Gene wants to shake him until he beams again. "The feeling was extremely mutual," Luis says.

Gene holds his hand out.

"Can I?" he asks.

He props himself up on an elbow, Luis kneeling between his legs, and takes the ripped packet. Gene has never had this kind of sex with a cis man, but he knows enough to know how to put on a condom. He has to admit, it's a hell of a lot better rolling it onto Luis than it was when he had to practice on a banana in high school. It's better with Luis pressing into his hand, watching Gene and biting his lip and steadying himself on Gene's shoulder.

"Good?" Gene asks when he's done and Luis has taken a moment to catch his breath.

"Yeah."

Gene lies back down on the pillows, a hand in Luis's happy trail until Luis lies back down, too. He holds himself over Gene with one hand, the other on Gene's hip, pressing him down just barely into the mattress.

"Are you gonna fuck me or what, Nada?"

"You are the most impatient little shit I have ever met."

Gene wraps his legs around Luis one last time. He *is* impatient, and he'd like Luis to do something about it. So when Luis puts a hand on himself and looks up to check on him, Gene nods. Luis kisses him and presses in, slow at first and then all at once, gasping when their hips bump against each other.

For all the talking they usually do, they both lie there, silent and clinging to each other, for what feels like full minutes before Luis says, "Are you good?"

His voice comes out more strained than Gene has ever heard it. His arms shake with the effort of holding himself up and holding himself steady, and Gene can't blame him, because his own legs are weak, even just lying there.

"I'm perfect," Gene says.

Luis slides a hand under Gene's back, and Gene is so hyperaware that this one extra point of contact is almost too much all on its own.

"Can I?" Luis asks.

Gene nods. He emphasizes it with a roll of his hips that makes Luis gasp again. His lips crash into Gene's, and neither of them can keep from moving after that.

With Luis's face buried against Gene's shoulder, Gene turns, his lips nearly touching Luis's ear when he says, earnest and honest, "I want you, too, Nada."

Luis makes a bitten-off noise against Gene's skin and moves his hips faster, and maybe he says Gene's name and maybe he says "Please" and maybe he says "Fuck" and maybe Gene's short fingernails still manage to bite into Luis's shoulders, and they don't last all that long, in the end.

And Gene is right. It's fucking perfect.

Late that night, Luis lies with his head on Gene's chest, his breathing heavy. They didn't necessarily agree that Luis would sleep there, but at almost one o'clock, with Luis dozing off—well, Gene wanted him there anyway. He has started to sleep worse at home than he does on the road, but he has a feeling that more nights like this could alleviate the problem.

When Luis's silenced phone lights up, Gene plans to let the call go to voice mail. Until he reaches to flip the phone over, sees Baker's name on the screen, and instead drops it onto the floor, waking Luis up in the process.

Gene winces, holds back a laugh at the confused look on Luis's face, the small puddle of drool he leaves behind on Gene's skin.

"Huh?" Luis asks, ever dignified.

"Baker's calling," Gene says.

"You?"

"You."

That wakes Luis up.

Gene isn't the only one in that bed who knows what a one A.M. call from a coach usually means. In fact, if anything, Luis knows much better, having received said call once from Boston, once from San Francisco, once from Arizona, and now, it seems, from Portland.

He makes no move to pick it up.

"You're not going to answer?" Gene asks.

"It can wait for the morning."

But then Baker calls again. And again. From the floor, the phone fills the room with an insistent light, a reminder that, as much as Luis might want to put off the inevitable, it won't go away.

"You should answer it," Gene says.

"I don't want to get traded again." And there's that familiar tension, that exhausted tilt of Luis's eyes.

"It could be something else."

Luis looks at him. He doesn't have to say what they both know.

"Maybe they traded you somewhere good. Someone noticed you enough to want you." If Gene's voice cracks, well, they don't have to talk about that. "You have to answer it regardless," he adds.

Rip the Band-Aid off and all.

Luis reaches over, the blankets pooling around his waist, stark white against his skin even in the dark of Gene's room. Gene reaches out and holds him around the waist; he tells himself it's to give Luis a small bit of stability. The real reason is much more selfish, much less easy to admit to himself: he might not get another chance.

"Hey, Baker." Luis's voice comes out a croak.

Gene can hear Baker on the other end of the line, never much good at talking at any volume below a bark. She says, "Everything okay?"

"Sure."

"Took you a while to pick up. You busy?"

"I was sleeping."

Technically the truth.

"I'll be quick."

If it were Gene, he would just ask where he'd gotten traded, and when he had to get on his flight. Luis waits for Baker to say it.

"So," she starts.

"Yeah."

"I have some good news."

Luis's eyebrows lower, and he looks at Gene, a little confused. Trades usually don't get framed as "good news."

And then it hits Gene, a moment before Baker says it.

"Portland's second baseman took a pitch to the ribs tonight, and he's going to be out for a while. They need an infielder," she says.

"You're getting called up," she says.

"They want you in Portland tomorrow morning at eleven-thirty," she says.

"Congratulations, kid," she says. "I'm sorry I couldn't tell you earlier, with the team there. They hadn't finalized everything. But we're all gonna be rooting for you tomorrow."

It hits Gene in waves.

First: he is so fucking proud. Like, eyes-prickling, heart-swelling kind of proud. *No one deserves this more than him, and he's going to be incredible* kind of proud. Luis has wanted it for as long as Gene has known him, and many years before. He's stayed closeted for this, forgone dating for this, worked his skinny, beautiful ass off for this, and Gene can't think of a single damn person he'd rather see succeed.

Second: maybe, in the most terrible pit of Gene's gut, he is jealous. Maybe he was jealous when Luis got drafted, too, when Luis had the option of leaving for something bigger. Maybe, in the parts of him he's most ashamed of, he wonders why his phone didn't ring, too.

But, third: it doesn't matter. That small seed of jealousy is something he'll work past on his own, on his own time, because Luis has gotten the dream. That impossible dream that everyone in the minors harbors to one degree or another—Luis has accomplished it.

And, fourth: Portland isn't nearly as far away as some of the places they could have sent Luis. This is not Luis getting drafted to Boston and leaving without comment—Portland is manageable. Hell, Gene can take the train to Portland. He can see Luis play on his off days. They can, if Luis wants, keep honest nights like this one, wrapped up in Gene's sheets and each other.

Fifth:

Fifth.

Maybe Luis won't want to anymore. Maybe, on a stage as big as Major League Baseball, it will be too much for him. Maybe a man who left his last boyfriend to be closeted won't want to stay with someone for whom the closet was never an option.

But when Luis hangs up the phone, he still leans in to kiss Gene. He still lets Gene wrap his arms around his waist, still lets his head fall into the crook of Gene's neck, and still whispers, "Holy *shit*."

"Holy fucking shit."

Luis laughs, a weird and lopsided sound that Gene still loves.

"I'm getting you champagne."

"It's one in the morning."

"Okay, then I'm getting you whatever I have in my fridge," Gene promises, voice wet with happiness, with worry.

"Fine."

"Congratulations, Nada," Gene says. He gives Luis a kiss before extricating himself from his arms.

In the kitchen, he allows himself a moment of pause. He sets two bottles on the counter—hard cider, technically, but whatever, it bubbles—and stares at their labels. He had intended these for a regular night, to drink with Luis while they sat and watched a movie. If he'd known they would be celebrating something so monumental, he would have sprung for a nicer brand.

If he'd known yesterday's game together would potentially be their last, Gene would have lingered in the locker room longer.

He would have taken a better mental picture of the way their field looked with Luis to his right. He would have kept Luis up later kissing.

As it is, he grabs both bottles by the neck, in one hand, and takes a steadying breath. Or, rather, he takes a breath and wills it to steady him before he walks back into his bedroom. When he pushes the door open, he expects Luis in the same position he left him—half-covered in blankets, leaning back against the pillows, hair messy and smile a little dreamy, a little nervous.

But instead, he has his knees hugged up to his chest, his head shoved between them, his knuckles waxy white where he grips his elbows, his arms making a bracket around his body, as if to protect himself. Dodger nudges his head against Luis's hand, but Luis doesn't seem to notice, his shoulders rising and falling far too rapidly. Gene can see where his tensed muscles strain under skin.

He looks almost how he did in the bathtub back in their hotel in Tacoma, after that particularly awful game, but magnified.

Gene sets the ciders down on top of his dresser and closes the door. He turns his fan on, in the hopes that the white noise will help Luis the way it usually helps Gene. He sits down on the mattress and doesn't touch Luis, waiting for some kind of signal that he can.

"Are you okay?" he asks.

"My chest hurts."

"Do you need to go to the doctor?"

"No."

"Can I get you a cold washcloth?"

Luis straightens his legs out in front of himself and swings them over the edge of the bed before Gene can react. Looking at Luis's face, he has to disagree—Luis definitely needs a doctor. He's pale, and, in the mere minute since Gene left him alone in the room, sweat has plastered his hair to his forehead. He massages one side of his chest—the concerning side, the side you do not want a person to need to massage.

"Let me get you a washcloth," Gene says.

"I got it."

"Let me—"

But Luis stands up, and then promptly tips over and crashes to the floor.

# 17

## JULY

**Current record: 50–41**

After he falls, Gene is convinced for one terrible minute that Luis has had a heart attack and died on his bedroom floor, decidedly, completely naked. If not for the circumstances and the deep pit of worry eating its way through him, he would find the whole scene a little funny. Once he realizes Luis only fainted—"only" being a relative term—he checks for bumps on Luis's head and, when Luis comes to thirty seconds or so later, fetches him some clothes.

"What are these for?" Luis asks.

"I'm taking you to the hospital." Not a question.

"No, I'm fine."

But he puts the pants on when Gene hands them over and lets Gene usher him into the passenger-side door without any fight, so, Gene reasons, he must really feel like shit.

They take Luis's truck—no one has money for an ambulance, particularly not a twenty-six-year-old and a twenty-eight-year-old whose jobs only pay them their shitty salaries six months of the year. Though, Gene notes while Luis ducks his head between his knees and continues arguing that he doesn't need a doctor, Luis is about to get a pretty significant pay bump.

"This happens all the time," Luis says.

"It absolutely does not. Do your seat belt."

Gene has seen and heard about more than a handful of Luis's panic attacks, and while hyperventilating and mild chest pains have made frequent appearances, fainting has not.

When they get to the hospital, Luis waits in one of the plastic chairs while Gene talks to the nurse behind the emergency room desk. Luis keeps the cool washcloth Gene got him pressed against the back of his neck, a lot less cool now. He has on a pair of Gene's sweatpants, too short in the legs; the shirt he borrowed has damp armpits and a stripe of sweat down his back, as if he just finished a workout rather than a panic attack.

The doctors get to him alarmingly fast. Gene has been told many times that, while waiting is the pits, you *want* the doctors to make you wait, because that means you're probably fine. When they call Luis's name a mere ten minutes after they get there, Gene's own pulse starts racing.

He can't go back to see the doctor with Luis, so he paces. When he put his shoes on in a hurry, he neglected to grab socks, and now his Docs rub against his ankles in the most unpleasant way possible. On inspection, the friction has eaten through the top layer of skin, and his heels have begun to bleed. He sits, his laces loosened, and jiggles his leg hard enough to shake his seat until Dodger sets his chin on Gene's knee to still him.

In the end, it takes three hours before Luis walks out, eye bags even heavier than usual, his usually perfect hair a hot mess.

"What's the verdict?" Gene asks.

"I have anxiety. Shocker."

"That's it?"

"They said that I should, and I quote, 'try to be less anxious.'"

"Awesome."

Luis shrugs. "Apparently I was also dehydrated, so at least they fixed that. So glad my insurance makes me pay a hundred and fifty dollars for a doctor to tell me to drink water and get an easier job."

Gene winces. "Sorry. I thought you were having a heart attack or something."

"It's okay. Thanks for driving me."

Gene takes him back to his apartment, because there's really no point in Luis's going home. They throw yesterday's warm-up clothes into the wash so they'll be fresh when they get up, and Luis squeezes in a single hour of sleep while Gene lies, staring at the ceiling, next to him.

A call-up is better than a trade, he reminds himself until he grows tired of hearing the words in his head.

So why does he have this terrible, insistent feeling in his gut?

"He *fainted*?" Baker says.

Gene closes the door to her office. As far as he can tell, no one in the locker room heard her, but it's possible they're just being polite.

"A little," Gene confirms.

"Is he okay?" Real concern laces her voice, and not just of the *Can he still play?* variety.

"The doctor who checked him out said he's fine, yeah."

"And you picked him up to take him to the hospital? Why didn't you call him a fucking ambulance?"

Okay, so he fudged those particular details a bit. But he needed someone to tell him he'd done the right thing, and he couldn't exactly admit to Baker that Luis had fainted naked on the floor of his bedroom. So he told her that he received a call from Luis shortly after she herself had hung up with him and that, halfway through said phone call, Luis had started to complain of chest pains, and Gene went to check on him.

There's no way Baker believes him, but he hopes she doesn't mention it.

"Because ambulances are expensive," Gene answers, which, at least, isn't a lie.

"The team would have paid for it."

"I don't think he wanted the team to know. He didn't want to get benched." At least, that's how Gene would have felt had he been in Luis's position.

"He's still *playing*?" Baker asks, incredulous. She reaches for her phone, and Gene realizes he's made a serious error in telling her anything, no matter how many details he fudged.

He jolts forward to stop her. "You can't call them!"

"Like hell I can't."

"Baker, come *on*, you know he can't just—"

"He will get another chance," she says, tapping in a number she has long since memorized.

"Not necessarily."

"Guys like Estrada get second chances. He will be fine."

Gene doesn't agree. Luis has caught a lot of flak in the last few years, flak that might have landed a little softer were he white; for guys who are straight, and white, and cis, it takes longer for fans' and coaches' and executives' goodwill to wear off. Gene has seen the things people say every time Luis falters; this opportunity was hard-won, and Baker knows that as well as Gene.

"Baker," he says.

She sets her jaw. "We have to keep our players safe. He can't play if he went to the hospital last night. What kind of coach would I be if I didn't say something?"

"What kind of coach would you be if you held your players back?"

Baker puts her phone down.

"Do I trust you to do your job?" she asks, voice frighteningly level.

Gene bites his tongue, quite literally, until he trusts himself to answer truthfully. "Yes."

"Even though you're screwing your teammate?"

Gene blinks at her, the fact of his and Luis's relationship—whatever that relationship is—thrown in his face like it could be a bad thing, something to be used against him. It stings, in his throat and behind his eyes.

"But that's none of my business," she says. "Just like this decision is none of yours."

She points at her door. A dismissal. Gene slams it on his way out.

"Check the fucking attitude, or I'm scratching you," she yells through the glass.

His warm-ups—stairs, laps, push-ups, the parts he can do without Luis—go by much faster today. He did this pared-down version of their routine for years on his own, but it doesn't sit right with him anymore. He feels unprepared for the day. The energy he usually burns off running down grounders bubbles in him, speeding his breath and urging him to do another set of bleachers. He resists it, but when he sits on the bench in the dugout, he can't stop himself from jiggling his leg so hard it might register as an earthquake on some scales.

It's an unseasonably cold day in Beaverton. One of those odd summer days that make you check the calendar.

He knows the following: he probably fucked Luis's chances of playing today; Luis has probably found out by now that Gene fucked his chances of playing today; Luis fainted in his room less than twelve hours ago, and Gene isn't completely convinced that Luis *should* be playing anyway; and, loudest and most selfish of all, he misses Luis for more than just their warm-ups, like someone took a sharp knife to the most important part of his life and sliced it out.

He texts Luis—*Where do they have you batting?*—desperate to hear that he hasn't ruined this opportunity for Luis by opening his fat mouth. He stares at his phone and wills it to light up with an answer.

Instead, the bench creaks to his left, and when Gene looks, it's Vince, his beard grown out over the past months in a way that makes him look less polished, more intimidating.

"Baker's pissed at you," he says. It's the first thing he's said to Gene since Sacramento that wasn't directly baseball-related.

Gene swallows around the feeling of relief, just at Vince talking to him, even if he's said nothing good or even surprising yet. "Did she tell you why?" he asks.

"No. You want to?"

Vince isn't pitching today, but he has an ice pack strapped to his shoulder anyway, has shown up hours early for this game. Captain, through and through.

"Everyone's pissed at me," Gene says.

"I'm not."

Gene laughs, horrified that it comes out wet. Vince has never been a fan of crying, certainly not turned in his direction. Gene tries to pretend it didn't happen, wills the tears away.

"I'm really not," Vince says. "I'm fucking jealous, because you're twenty-six, and you have your whole career ahead of you."

"It doesn't really feel like it. You're leaving. Nada got called up this morning—"

"I saw that. Should have been you."

Gene shakes his head. "He deserves it."

"You can still be jealous, Nes."

"I don't want to be." And it's such a small part of the problem, really. That Luis has gotten something Gene can't have. The problem is that Gene wants to be there, at his side, while he does it. He wants to hold Luis's hand and play a little to his left; he wants Luis Estrada, Baseball Player, to bat him home, and then he wants Luis Estrada, the person, to take him home.

He can't say all of that, can't admit to Vince this aching want he has let into his heart, the tender bruises it has given him on its way in. But Vince pulls him in, gives him a side-hug like the dad he will be someday, and drops a kiss into the middle of Gene's curls. His ice pack leaves a cold spot against Gene's T-shirt.

"I know," Vince says. "But sometimes we're jealous. Sometimes our bodies won't let us fucking win, and it sucks, and you're allowed to hate it."

"I missed you, dude."

"I'm sorry I threw a fit."

Gene nods. "I'm sorry I didn't want to let you be upset. I wanted to fix it."

"Because that's the kind of person you are."

Gene clicks his tongue. "I know it can be annoying."

"It's the absolute worst," Vince says, but Gene can hear the humor in his voice, and it's the kind of ribbing they used to do, so familiar it hurts.

"What am I gonna do when you leave?" Gene asks. He says it like a joke, but he means it, utterly and entirely.

"Not replace me with Luis Estrada, I hope."

"You have got to get over that. I can have two friends," Gene says.

"*Friends*," Vince says, like there should be air quotes around the word. "Not ready to get into that yet?"

"Absolutely not."

Vince lifts his hands, palms out in front of him, and tilts his head like *Fair enough*. "I can respect that."

"Thank you."

"Don't thank me yet. I'm going to have to tease you for this eventually."

Gene tips his head against the back wall of the dugout. "Please wait until I'm less fragile."

"Deal. One question."

"No thank you," Gene says, the same as Luis did all those months ago, because he's thinking of Luis, because he always is.

"Were you two an item in college? Is that why you've always been so obsessed with him?"

Gene wrinkles his nose. "I'm not obsessed." He is. "And no, we weren't."

"And now?"

"So why haven't they called you up yet?" Gene asks, desperate to move the topic away from himself. "You've been tearing it up."

Vince shrugs. "Oh, who the hell knows? What're you gonna do."

"Did you ask?"

"About a million times, yeah."

"Nothing?"

"Crickets." He shrugs again, but this time it seems a little more genuine. "As long as we can get Beaverton to the playoffs, I can retire happy."

"Yeah?"

"Well, that's what I told my therapist, at least."

Gene laughs. "We'll get you that postseason start, Altzy. Who cares if you do it in front of forty thousand people or eight thousand?"

"Eight thousand is a little generous for our crowds."

Gene stands up, walks to the ledge of the dugout and leans over its railing, marveling at the empty plastic-and-metal stands around them.

"I don't know," he says. "Beaverton might be turning into a baseball town."

. . .

"Fucking brutal," Gene says as the Beavers make their way down the dugout tunnel after an excruciating, double-digit loss.

"Absolute dogshit," Ross agrees. He struck out, almost mercifully, to finally end the game.

"We'll get 'em next time," Gene says. "Yeah?"

Ernie gives Gene a shoulder nudge as he walks past, smile just as bright after a tough loss as it is after the most electric of wins.

Ross gives a halfhearted nod of agreement. "Let's just hope Nada fared better than we did, right?"

Gene usually leaves his phone in his locker during games, to force his full, fickle attention onto the game. Tonight, he brought it to the dugout with him, checked it about a million times, until the battery finally died on him. Last he saw, Portland was in the third inning. The walk from the dugout to the locker room has never felt so long, and Gene itches to check the score more than he has in years.

When they pour back into the clubhouse, Ernie sees him first.

"Nada!" he yells. The team, as if drawn up by the same string, stands straighter, trying to crane their necks around to see.

Sure enough, Luis sits in front of his locker, in the same sweats he borrowed from Gene that morning, his T-shirt swapped out for one of his usual—plain, black, a little on the tight side. He has a Beaverton cap on, the one he thinks draws attention away from his ears, tipped back in the way he prefers. He has shoved his hands into the pockets of his jacket, and he looks far more relaxed and infinitely happier than he did that morning.

"What the hell are you doing here?" Vince asks.

Luis shrugs. "Guess I'm finishing up the season with you losers," he says, to which a chorus of cheers arises from the team. Gene, for his part, can't quite bite back the smile that insists at the edges of his lips. It's laced with confusion, but there it is: he wants Luis here. Or rather, selfishly, horribly, he wants Luis next to him, wherever that may be.

Almost as badly, he wants Luis for the team. He wants never to have another game like this one, and Luis can help them toward that goal. He'll ask Luis later what happened, but for now, he's happy. Completely, face-split-in-two happy.

"Shit game tonight," Luis says, dropping the side of his fist onto Gene's shoulder.

Gene should worry, maybe, about how obvious and ridiculous his smile must look at that insult. But he beams, unashamed. "Thanks. Try and beat that next game."

"Oh, don't worry. I will."

What had seemed five minutes ago a lost-cause night has transformed into something better, unexpected, and Gene figures he should probably assume that it won't last. But Gene is an optimist, and he wants to give himself this.

Baker has other ideas.

Usually, after a game this sloppy, she bangs into the locker room and brings with her a bone-deep unpleasantness, her jaw set and her face red. She has never needed to give them the postgame, you-all-suck speech, because the disappointment that surrounds her says all that she needs to say.

So, tonight, they watch her progress across the room in complete silence, expecting her to walk straight out. Instead, she stops outside her office, arms folded, face surprisingly neutral.

"All right," she says. "Not the outcome we wanted. New series this week, though. We'll give it our best."

A tentative feeling of relief starts to nudge its way in at the corners of the room. They wait while Baker considers her words, all of them exhausted in the way only a four-hour blowout loss can make you.

"I'll let you go in a minute," she says. "Off day tomorrow, and I'm keeping practice optional, so if you want to take the chance to rest up, do. We'll fly out to Albuquerque tomorrow night. If anyone's interested, we've set aside a bank of seats for the Portland game. It's a day game, so whoever wants to can catch a few innings before we head to the airport."

Her offer is met with a smattering of confusion. They've all been to their fair share of Lumberjacks games, and there's nothing particularly special about tomorrow's matchup, a sleepy Sunday matinee against another bottom-dwelling team.

"Are they that desperate to fill seats?" Cooper asks.

"Can it, Coop," Vince says, and Gene notices, belatedly, that he's filming the room on his oversized iPhone.

Baker holds her hands up, and finally lets her neutral façade break just enough to smile. "Hey, if you want to miss your teammate's major league debut, be my guest."

Everyone turns to look, confused, at Luis. Or, at least, Gene does, and he thinks he can feel everyone else doing the same.

But then:

"He's played here for almost two years, and we will miss him like shit, but goddamn if we aren't proud."

Luis hasn't played for Beaverton for two years. Before Gene can put the pieces together—

"Ionescu, I'm sorry to say you won't have tomorrow off. They need you in Portland at noon."

So everyone isn't looking at Luis. They're looking at—

"You're getting called up, Nes," Luis says, at which point the locker room erupts into the sort of cheering you only muster for a person you really love, and will really miss.

# 18

## JULY

**Current record: 50–42**

Since the Portland Lumberjacks franchise was founded in the early nineties, 502 players have suited up in some iteration of the team's uniform, from those early teal-and-red-and-cream days through the brief buffalo-plaid phase, up through the current palette of mint and greens.

Hours after he's told he'll be the 503rd, Gene turns the brightness on his phone down as low as it can go, reads every name on the all-time roster. Somewhere around the hundredth familiar name—long past Altman and Baker, into the G names—an arm slides around his waist, the weight an immediate comfort.

"What are you doing?" Luis asks. He starts drawing lazy circles on Gene's stomach, the backs of his knuckles dragging without aim through the coarse hairs there.

They each had a single celebratory drink with the team after Baker's announcement before excusing themselves a few minutes apart and going back to Gene's place together.

Gene had meant to ask why Luis was back in Beaverton, apologize for telling Baker about his trip to the emergency room, see if Luis was okay. But they'd had their own private celebration first, and then Luis had fallen asleep so quickly, and here Gene is now, hours later, still not sure how to say any of the things he needs to say.

"Sorry," Gene says. "I didn't mean to wake you up."

Luis deposits a kiss on the back of Gene's neck. "You didn't. Are you checking to see if anyone added your name yet?"

Gene locks his phone and sets it facedown on the bed. "Nosy."

He flips himself over, and Luis pulls him in until their chests touch. A few inches from Gene's, his face is so sleepy and so sweet that Gene almost can't take it.

"I have to tell you something," Gene says.

Luis's eyes open all the way, worry furrowing his eyebrows immediately. "Is everything okay?"

"I told Baker that I took you to the hospital. And I shouldn't have."

"Oh," Luis says. Surprise, and then calm. "That's okay."

"It wasn't my business to tell," Gene says, tracing a finger on the same side of Luis's chest Luis had held last night before he passed out. "I was just worried about you, and I didn't think. I'm sorry."

"Nes. I'm not upset with you. I told the Portland coaches as soon as I got to the stadium. I figured they probably wouldn't want me passing out on the field."

"Is that why they sent you back down?"

"Probably."

He says it so casually. If it was Gene getting sent back down, he couldn't imagine feeling anything but distraught.

"You're allowed to be upset," Gene says.

"I know. But I'm not."

"Why?"

Luis tips his head forward, until his forehead meets Gene's and his lips press into a kiss. "Can't I just be excited for you?"

Gene moves his head back until Luis can't reach to kiss him. "Nada."

Luis sighs. "I mean," he says, "I had a panic attack, Nes."

"I know."

"No, like—when they called me up the first time. That's how I got in my accident."

"Oh," Gene says. Insufficient, he knows. In an ideal world, he would be able to wrap himself all the way around Luis, entirely protected, so Luis could have the privacy he deserves and so rarely gets. As it is, it's all he can do to listen.

So he does.

"I was driving, and I had a panic attack. This was before I had Dodger. So I thought I could, I don't know. Drive through it, I guess?" Luis digs the heel of his hand into one of his eyes and flops onto his back. "I couldn't. Obviously," he tells the ceiling.

"Shit, Nada. I'm sorry."

"I just—I wouldn't have been a baseball player if it wasn't for my dad. He really wanted me to. And I realized in the car . . . like, y'know, he's dead, and I was still doing this thing *he* wanted me to, and I had never stopped to think if *I* wanted it, because it was always easier to just do what other people wanted me to. But I hadn't gone on a date in years, and it was all shitty and fucking *hard,* and as soon as I let myself think about how my life had turned out, it felt like everything was falling apart. I was gay, and I didn't know how to be, and I didn't really know how to be a baseball player, either. Like I was sort of shitty at both."

Gene takes a beat to process all of that. He tries, as well as he can, to give the hurt in Luis's voice the space it deserves before he says, "I think you're pretty good at both those things."

Luis laughs. "Thanks. You're a little biased." He turns to look at Gene, then adds, "I'd been reading about you. That day, after I got the call-up."

"I thought you said you didn't read about me," Gene says.

"I lied. I read about you sometimes. And I thought about you—fuck, a *lot.* Especially after Ritz told me you came out." He takes a deep breath, a little shaky. "And I was just thinking—*God, I fucked up*. Somewhere along the line, I fucked up. I was going to play in the major fucking leagues, and it still felt wrong."

Gene rests his thumb in the dip beneath Luis's bottom lip, traces underneath one side of Luis's mouth to the other, and lets Luis press a kiss to the pad of his thumb. "Because of me? How?"

"Sort of. I guess I just liked to imagine"—he tugs on one of Gene's curls—"that you were really happy. You know? You were out, and you were still playing, and that had seemed impossible to me. Then I got traded to Portland, and I was *so* nervous to see you again. You should have seen me that first morning, before I came to the stadium."

"Yeah?"

"I was a whole wreck. But then I got to know you again, and obviously realized it's a lot more complicated than just coming out and everything either being entirely terrible or entirely perfect."

"It is. But that doesn't mean you can't come out."

"I know. It's just—I don't know, Nes. I just," he starts, and then he stops. "This time, when Baker called, it didn't feel the same."

"Okay."

"I was just glad I wasn't getting traded. I don't think I could do that again. But then I started wondering what was going to go wrong this time. You know?"

Gene knows that feeling well, too well, and he wants to hug Luis so bad he can feel the need in his stomach, in the itching palms of his hands.

"Nada."

"So, I fell apart because I imagined some problems. Which is very on brand for me."

Gene pulls Luis closer. Always closer. Dodger, from his spot on Luis's feet, lets out a long sigh, as if waiting for them to go back to sleep.

"How do you feel now?" Gene asks.

Luis smiles, a genuine and easy thing. "Like I'm really excited to watch you play later."

"You know that's not what I meant."

"That's my final answer."

"You're not mad at me?"

"Why would I be?"

"Or disappointed?"

"No."

"You're not mad they gave me your roster spot?"

"Nes." Luis grabs Gene's face. "Stop. No."

"Because I was a little jealous when you got called up. And it would be okay if you were upset."

With a kiss, Luis says, "Then it's a good thing I'm a bigger person than you are, isn't it? Now, can you promise you're not going to worry about this tomorrow?"

"I absolutely cannot."

"Can you promise you'll try?"

Gene considers. And—yes. He's still worried. But he can trust Luis to tell him the truth.

"Yeah," he says. "I can do that."

"Good." Luis reaches over Gene then, grabs Gene's phone, and holds it out for Gene to input the password. He scrolls until he arrives at the I names, points to where *Ionescu* would be alphabetized. "That's where you'll be tomorrow, after the game," he says.

Gene takes the phone back, sets it on his nightstand, and, in an effort to calm his own frenzied pulse, buries his face in Luis's chest. Before he thinks about getting *there*—that page, that team, Portland—he tries to let himself just be *here*, in this familiar room, with Luis.

Luis and Vince drop him off early and cheer from the front seat of Jack's SUV all the way until the metal door of the staff entrance closes behind Gene with a heavy *thud.*

Gene's phone goes off immediately, somewhere from the confines of his duffel.

A text from Luis: *You're gonna be great today.*

Then, shortly after: *Call if you need anything? We're going to head out to the airport.*

He and Vince had offered to pick Gene's family up after their early flight lands, but they'd insisted on dropping Gene off at the stadium before doing so.

He texts back, *Thank you again. Sorry in advance for how nosy Altzy's gonna be.*

*Literally already asked when I'm moving in,* Luis answers.

Gene cringes, taps out another apology, and drops his phone back in his bag. It's early for Gene to be there, and the quiet is almost stifling, the nerves even more so. He's supposed to stop by the manager's office in an hour, to have his first official meeting with the head coaching staff.

For now, though, he takes a deep breath, and he walks into that stadium on shaky legs, with a shaky stomach and a shaky heart.

If Gene could only ever step foot in one major league ballpark for the rest of his life, he would pick Portland's. Not only because it was the first he ever visited, not only because of home-team loyalty. Settled along the Columbia River waterfront, the stadium is borderline downtown without being busy. It's just tall enough to feel intimidating, ivy-covered, with a retractable roof. On sunny days, with the roof open, it's airy and bright. Every seat, from the dugout-huggers to the nosebleeds, feels magical. It's the first place Gene remembers feeling the grandness of baseball, the way a crowd can swell together, can turn their collective wanting into something almost palpable.

He visits the familiar spots first.

Portland's stadium boasts some of the best baseball food in the league, the thoroughfares populated not by stalls but by food carts, rotated out seasonally. Gene walks past the old reliables (hot dogs, tacos, gourmet popcorn and pretzels, the ones that never seem to rotate out and always command a serpentine line) and the newcomers (waffles, fried rice, that fancy ice cream shop with the flavors that never sound good). He'd like to meet everyone who works at every cart, until this stadium's people are as familiar as Beaverton's. Until he can recognize every coach, every player. The photographers, the cleaning staff, the ball kids, the announcers, the ushers.

For now, though, he settles for walking out into the open air, taking in a view he has seen dozens of times, if not hundreds.

Across the outfield stretches an eight-foot wall, an even line between the foul poles. The grass, mowed in perfect stripes, intersecting in stretched-out diamonds, loosely resembles the buffalo plaid of their mascot. The ninety-foot white lines painted between each of the bases stand out crisp and bright against the perfect brown of the infield dirt, and Gene, for the first time in his life, imagines himself there, feet planted in that dirt, playing for the very first team he ever rooted for. He imagines the way the ground will feel beneath his cleats.

The picture he sends Luis encompasses the whole of the field and most of the stands, taken at the widest angle Gene can manage. When Luis sends it back, he has drawn a red circle over the empty middle infield.

*See you here in a few hours*, the text reads.

Over and over, Gene considers going down to the dugout, setting his bag down, and lying in the grass, the way he did with Luis before the Futures Game. It feels impossible. Like if he lets himself do it, the whole thing will dissolve around him, too good to be true.

So instead, ten minutes before his meeting with the manager is supposed to start, Gene ducks into a freshly scrubbed visitors' bathroom on the main concourse, and he kneels in front of a toilet, leans over as his stomach threatens to revolt.

*Are you nervous?* Luis texts, as if he can sense it in Gene's silence.

*No, I feel great. Like I could run a mile. Ten miles minimum*, Gene responds.

*Liar.*

Gene smiles, then remembers how close his face is to a public toilet, and sits back on his heels.

Luis texts again: *Your meeting's going to be fine. He's just gonna say it's good to have you here, and then it'll be over.*

Luis is right. The meeting will last five minutes, at most, maybe a quick photo op. But it's the subtext of the meeting that makes Gene nervous: *Are you worth the risk we're taking right now?*

Gene doesn't know how to answer that question yet.

*Promise?* Gene asks.

*100%.*

So Gene stands before he can remember to be nervous.

He doesn't know if the risk is worth it. He doesn't know if he belongs here. But the same as he did at eighteen, walking onto that very first baseball team, Gene slings his beaten and battered cleats—tied together by the laces—around the back of his neck, hefts his duffel over his shoulder, and lets himself want it anyway.

· · ·

The hallways that lead from the publicly accessible parts of Portland's stadium to its innermost rooms—the clubhouses and managers' offices—are wider, taller, quieter than the halls in Beaverton. They largely pass in a blur, concrete walls and painted murals, framed photos of some of Portland's all-time greats. Gene snaps a picture of the Altman shrine—a jersey, a signed baseball, an enormous picture of a pre-beard Vince receiving his first Cy Young Award, all hung in a place of pride—and saves it for the next time Vince needs a light teasing.

Because Beaverton plays in an old stadium that no one wants to pay to renovate, the walls block out almost no sound. The Kyles' pregame playlists carry through the cement and wood and support beams, seemingly permeating the whole of the building. Here, nicer and newer material holds back the bulk of the noise, and even once Gene pulls the clubhouse door open, everything feels almost muted. Like he has earplugs in, forgot his contacts—something.

He misses Baker folding her arms in the corner to size them up. He misses Vince kvetching about his aches and pains while Gene slings his bag into his locker stall. He misses Ernie bounding in, grin blazing, to report to the room his latest efforts to impress the Stumptown barista down the street. And what he misses most, of course, is Luis at his side as he walks in.

But Gene is *here*. So he walks across that room, his chest too full to breathe, and he sets his bag in his locker, in his clubhouse, in his team's stadium. A Portland Lumberjacks uniform is hung up with care. Size small, colors crisp, pants short the way he likes to wear them.

A closed fist lands on his shoulder, an encouraging bump. Portland's starting third baseman—young but established, the core of a team that should, in a few years, be far better than its current record would imply—grins.

And suddenly the noise of the clubhouse hits Gene all at once: their aging catcher in the corner reviewing heat maps with his starting pitcher; a song starting and stopping and turning over to something new, a small squad of relief pitchers singing along to lyrics they only half-know; a hitting coach announcing that batting practice will start in twenty, the answering clamor of cleats being dropped into lockers and warm-up clothes being pulled on. A well-oiled machine compared to Beaverton's haphazard routines, built out of so many voices Gene recognizes from interviews. Nowhere near familiar, but it feels like it could be someday.

Then, the squeak of a marker as an assistant coach finishes writing the lineup in large block letters on the whiteboard. There, batting ninth, number zero: starting second baseman Gene Ionescu—the name he chose for himself, and the one he inherited from his dad, one stacked atop the other, an announcement and a vote of confidence all in one. Right there in a lineup with the guys he watches in highlight reels, whose names he sees in the headlines.

It's terrifying, one of the most breathtaking things Gene has ever experienced. Like someone has dropped him in an ice bath the size of an ocean and asked him to swim.

Then, Portland's third baseman, leaning in:

"Congrats, man. We're glad to have you here."

Gene smiles. And he breathes.

Fifteen minutes before first pitch—after he makes it through an uneventful meeting with the manager and hitting coaches, after infield drills and batting practice, after Gene is introduced to a full roster of players he has watched from afar for years and does his best not to act like a starstruck buffoon about it—they walk as a team to the dugout.

Gene tries not to look into the stands, pulling his cap a little lower on his forehead than he normally would to block them out.

As the home team, they'll field first. In less than twenty minutes, he will need to walk onto that field and trust that his legs will keep him upright, that his body can hold firm.

As the Portland announcers read out the lineup—starting pitcher first, then leadoff hitter, all the way down the lineup until they reach Gene's name—he barely hears the words. His hands shake, his throat constricts, and he briefly considers running back down the dugout hallway, out of the stadium, all the way back home to the safety of his bed.

Before he can, a voice to his right asks, "Has Baker made you guys wash her car yet this year?"

Gene pulls his attention away from the field, where Portland's center fielder is making his entrance.

The voice came from Ken Kelly—K.K. Slider to his teammates, named as such for three reasons: his initials, his wicked breaking ball, and his truly impressive eyebrows, much like the cartoon dog from whom the nickname was filched. A onetime mainstay in Beaverton's rotation, whose breakout season last year had landed him a spot on Portland's roster.

K.K. has a wad of pink bubblegum tucked in his cheek, good for a bite or two every few seconds. Gene has always found it distracting, the way he pokes it around from side to side with his tongue, but he's grateful tonight for a distraction.

"Uh," Gene says, the pinch of anxiety in his gut momentarily forgotten. "Yeah."

"Cleanest Subaru in Oregon."

"Which is saying something."

K.K. tips his head back and laughs. "You ever have to do it?"

"Not since last year," Gene says.

"Good for you. Staying out of trouble." Then K.K. points up, as if indicating the voices over the public announcement system. "I think that's you."

And sure enough, as they've talked, the rest of Portland's lineup has taken the field, and that's Gene's name, so loud he can feel it in his teeth.

He doesn't have time to think.

He walks up the steps and jogs to second, and as soon as he passes through foul territory and his cleats hit the grass, the sound fades away. There's the clean white paint of the first base line, the raked-out infield dirt, second base exactly where it always is, stalwart. That subtle give of the bag, sat in the center of it all.

And the crowd: so many of them, thousands upon thousands. All those people—the ones Gene knows and the ones he doesn't—can see him. A healthy number of them are aware of why Gene's presence on that field is such a monumental deal, and some of them love that and some of them hate that, and there are probably people out there in Portland jerseys who are hoping he fails.

It's too much.

He never wondered why Luis had a full-on panic attack about this shit. Not for one second. Even still, now that he's working life into his glove, getting his hat set just right, he understands it a lot better. Luis—as always—simply thought things through better than Gene did, realized faster how achingly terrifying this would be, and his body shut down over it.

Gene didn't blame him then, and he doesn't blame him now. But it's this—that thought of Luis, the image of him in the stands behind home plate, sandwiched between Vince and Baker, of Mattie watching from Art's shoulders, Joey whistling sharp and clear, Gene's dad yelling his name—that makes him steady his goddamn legs and stand up at second.

When he looks, squints until the stands come almost into

focus, he can see them. At least, he can see blurs where they should be, can see the way their arms move as they clap, as they cup hands around their mouths and cheer. Gene thinks he might see a few other people standing, too, but it's this half-row of his family and some of his Beaverton teammates, all there for him, that he cares about.

He'll play without them tonight, but he can play *for* them all the same. A little for Baker, a little for his dad in the stands, a little for Vince, and a lot for Luis. And with whatever's left over after all that, Gene will play for himself.

Twelve innings and a walk-off win later, Gene's family takes him out to the same diner Gene and his dad used to eat at to celebrate every big win. The Beavers left halfway through the seventh to catch their plane, and the game didn't end until their flight had already taken off.

Gene gets a FaceTime call sometime around midnight, NADA all in capital letters on his screen. He flops into bed before he picks up.

"You should be asleep," he says by way of greeting.

"Like fuck!" Luis says.

"Who're you rooming with?"

"Who am I rooming with? *That's* what you want to talk about?"

Gene grins. "I like knowing what's going on in your life."

"Altzy." Luis turns the camera to show a brief glimpse of Vince on the other bed before his own face reappears. "I can't believe you *stole home*. I'm so mad we missed it."

"Skip told me to grab a bag," Gene says in the most nonchalant voice he can manage. It was chaos at home plate when Gene slid in, safe, his formerly crisp uniform now lovingly decorated with infield dirt. There might not be a home run ball for Gene to keep, but there *is* a photo of him on the Lumberjacks's Twitter account, his teammates pressed in around him, a crush of Portland uniforms, Gene's batting helmet half-toppled off his head. There is his new team holding him aloft to a sparse but joyous Portland crowd. There is that bone-deep joy that Gene will never forget.

"We were watching the replays the whole way to the hotel," Luis says.

He sent Gene a few videos from the bus, his old teammates just as boisterous as the new ones. Gene saved every last one to his phone.

"Yeah, I liked the part where your finger was over the camera for half the video," Gene says. "You're the oldest twenty-eight-year-old I've ever met."

Luis grins.

"And I love that about you," Gene says before he can overthink using that particular word in this particular context, to this particular person. "Is Altzy sleeping?"

"Not yet."

"Getting there?"

Vince, from what sounds like a few feet away, answers, "If you two could stop yapping."

Gene grins. "Tell him hi."

"I'm happy for you, Nes, but I've been up since six. I'll congratulate you in the morning," Vince says, with the distinct tone of a man who has his face shoved into a pillow.

"Do you need to go?" Gene asks.

"No," Luis says.

"Yes," Vince says.

"Go sit in the bathroom," Gene says.

He watches Luis get up, can hear the rustling of sheets and then a short silence before a door latches and Luis slides to sit on the ground.

"Okay, hi," Luis says, his voice quieter, just for Gene.

"Perfect, now we can have phone sex," Gene says.

There's a long pause, long enough that Gene almost jumps in to backtrack, and then Luis says, "Seriously?"

Gene laughs and pulls his knees against his chest. He still hasn't gotten his heartbeat down to a reasonable speed, still feels like he could run all the way to Luis's hotel room in Albuquerque and get back to Oregon in time for tomorrow's evening game. He channels all that energy into the tips of his fingers, dancing along the side of his leg.

"I was kidding," he says. "But you seemed pretty eager, so I'm making a mental note."

"You're an ass."

"Maybe."

There's a pause just long enough for Luis to take a breath, and then, his voice far softer, he says, "I'm really proud of you, you know."

And that's much better than phone sex. Gene is grateful, as he tips his forehead onto his knees and grins so hard it hurts, that no one is here to point out how gone he is on this man.

"Yeah?" he asks.

"Always, yes. But especially today."

Gene has to swallow around the way that makes him feel—like he could cry, like he'd go through every bit of today's anxiety a dozen times over just to hear those words again—so he can say, "Thank you."

"Don't thank me, Nes. You should get some sleep. It was a big day."

"*You* should get some sleep."

But neither of them hangs up, and for the first time in his life, Gene feels that feeling. The *No, you hang up first* one that teenagers are supposed to get, but that he never did, because, as a teenager, years before he knew he was trans, years before he knew he was gay, he was never comfortable enough in his skin to fall for someone, or to consider that they might fall for him, too. But he doesn't want to hang up, and he doesn't want Luis to, either.

"Do you want to lay down with me?" he asks.

"Right now?"

"Yeah. If you want."

So Luis takes Gene back out into the main hotel room. He drags his weighted blanket, the one he lugs on every roadie, over his shoulders, and he nestles his phone up against the pillows, so it catches half his face and the crest of his shoulder and Dodger's head on the pillow behind his.

Gene settles into his own pillows, nestling under his quilt and watching Luis for all of two minutes before he drifts off with the lamp on and Luis sleeping on his screen.

# 19

## AUGUST

**Current record: 66–45**

The thing about auspicious starts is this: sometimes that's all they are. A start. Sometimes they don't last. Sometimes the second baseman comes off the injured list, and suddenly there's no room on the roster for someone who's gone near-hitless for a week.

So, sometimes you get sent back down three weeks after you got your call-up.

Gene stands on Beaverton's field, the day he gets the news, a few hours before the rest of the Beavers return from their roadie. Before the stadium comes alive again for tomorrow's game, he takes in the quiet. He doesn't cry. Not for the things he wants and can't have, and not for the disappointment that crashes into him, again and again, while he tries desperately to find the good.

The good: the familiarity of this field, the way its size feels uncrushing, the way its creaks and cracks are home; Vince, who texted him this morning to say he was sorry to hear the news; Joey, who called and let Gene talk about anything else; Gene's dad, who left a voice mail so Gene could have it on record that he's proud; the Beavers' season, promising even as they enter this final stretch; Luis, who will be home soon, who Gene will get at least another month of playing next to.

Four months ago, all of these things would have felt impossibly lucky to Gene. So he chooses to feel lucky.

He chooses to feel lucky when he picks Luis up from the airport in Jack's SUV, when Vince and Dodger pile into the backseat and Gene gets to listen to them rehash the entirety of the road trip—near-flawless, only a few losses to go with a streak of wins. He chooses to feel lucky that they have started to get along, that they can all laugh when Dodger sticks his head out the window and sneezes, loud and full-bodied.

He chooses to feel lucky for the laughter, for the things he still has—more than he ever thought he'd get.

By the time they show up for their home game, Gene would be lying if he said a part of him isn't glad, deep down, just to be in the same locker room with Luis again. Disappointed as he might be about the way the last weeks went, Gene can't pretend that he didn't miss playing with these people. When he and Luis walk in, post-warm-up workout, to the beat of Kyle, Kyle, and Kyle's playlist and the distinct sound of Vince grunting and groaning from the trainer's room, it's less like a letdown and more like a homecoming.

Then Baker calls him into her office.

She has her feet up on her desk and the sound turned off on whatever video she has playing on her phone. She gestures for him to close the door behind him. When he sits in one of the two chairs in front of her desk, she sighs, and flops the phone onto her desk, screen up.

Gene recognizes the video and briefly considers whether he might make his escape before she can start talking.

Alas.

"What the hell happened to you?" she asks.

"I don't know," Gene says.

"Get cold feet?"

Gene shrugs while video-Gene attempts to steal second base and gets caught by a full, painfully noticeable step. He'd misjudged the catcher's arm and had paid the price, and Portland lost by six runs anyway, so Gene hadn't beaten himself up too much about this particular fumble. They happen, that's baseball, and he tried again the next time.

Now, with Baker staring at him with no amusement on her face, he regrets the play more.

"That is one of the worst defensive catchers in the league," she says.

"I know."

"And you couldn't get a single bag off of him?"

Gene slides his jaw out and attempts to make eye contact with anything vaguely un-Baker-shaped in the office, but something about her disappointment acts like a gravity. It pulls his glance back in, and once he's looked at her, it's hard to look away. That would be like admitting to something.

"Don't pull that shit on my team," she says. "Got it?"

"Okay."

"Good. You're batting ninth today."

Gene blinks at her, like she'd flipped him off to his face, and then he schools his features. Baker has never been swayed by ego, and certainly not by begging. So he says, "Okay, Coach."

Sure enough, when he checks the lineup card taped to the side of a cupboard, his name has been moved from first to ninth, with Luis in Gene's usual leadoff spot.

"What happened?"

Luis has materialized at his shoulder, practically leaning his chin on it. He reaches around to run his finger along the lineup, as if he's trying to underline what his eyes don't want to believe. "That's not right. Is this what she wanted to talk to you about?"

"Yeah."

"What did she say?"

"That she's trying new things out."

Luis looks unconvinced.

"Oh well," Gene says.

"You sure?"

"As long as we win, who cares?"

But he has always liked batting leadoff. He takes some pride in it, and, this year, has turned to that fact whenever he catches himself sinking into doubt. Now, while that doubt tries to nudge in at his softest spots, he has no convenient achievement to point at and say, *Look—I have to be at least decent if they let me go out there and do* that *every night.*

Where that comfort used to be, Gene can feel a widening anxiety, and he does everything in his power to ignore it, to focus on the game ahead. On Luis's name and his, right there in a lineup together again.

They get a Gatorade bath following the game—both of them, shoulder to shoulder and speaking to Jen from the *Oregonian*, assigned to report on a Beaverton game for the second time in less than a week. The field has cleared out in the half hour or so since the game ended, and, once the reporter is gone, Gene lets himself grab Luis's hand for a second, a brief celebratory squeeze.

"Showers?" Luis asks.

Before Gene can say yes, Baker, walking up from behind them, interrupts.

"I'd like to keep Ionescu out here a minute," she says.

Luis gives him a look that says, *Listen, I care about you, but*

*Godspeed*, then retreats back into the dugout, grabbing his shit from the bench.

Baker waits until Luis is out of earshot. Gene holds out hope that she's pulled him aside to apologize for snapping at him earlier, to tell him he played well in spite of the shit week he's had. That kind of kindness—when it's warranted and earned—is not unheard of from Baker.

Instead, she says, "He's looking better. What do you think?"

"Nada?" Gene asks.

"Yeah."

"He played good," Gene says. "He always plays good."

"You don't think he's having a hard time?"

"No."

"So explain to me why he isn't in the majors right now," she says. "Explain to me why I had to bench one of my best players for a week."

"Why don't you ask him? He told me he only asked for the one day off."

She folds her arms. "You know your boyfriend asked to spend the rest of the season in Beaverton? Literally asked. Told the suits in Portland that he's not ready yet."

Gene blinks. He did not know that.

"You have anything to do with that?" Baker asks.

"You know I didn't."

"I know you tanked your chance in Portland."

"I didn't do that on purpose," Gene protests.

"Could've fooled me. I have never seen you play half that badly."

Gene bites the inside of his cheek, as hard as he can without breaking through the soft skin. "I'm sorry."

Plenty of people play like shit the first time they get to the majors—the pitching is better, the pressure greater, the expectations higher. But no one wants excuses. They want results.

"Maybe if you weren't fucking your teammate, it'd be easier to pull your head out of your ass."

Gene has long since passed the point of denying it. "That's not why I played badly."

"You sure about that?" she asks, unconvinced. "Because it sure doesn't seem to be helping."

"Is there a rule that says we can't?"

She adjusts her baseball cap and crosses her arms, which makes her look both more irritated and more imposing, something that few manage as well as she does. "There doesn't have to be a rule. I scouted you. *I* coached you. I know exactly what you're up against. I'm the reason you're here, and I'm trying to tell you how to *stay* here."

Gene hates conflict. He hates standing up for himself. In an ideal world, Gene would like his optimism and his kindness, his slightly teasing brand of friendship, to speak for itself. But Baker knows all the places to poke at, all the pressure points where he's barely hanging on.

As if to prove it, she says, "But if you piss away every opportunity that gets handed to you, I'm not going to waste my time anymore."

Gene folds his hat and stuffs it into the back pocket of his pants. He is tired, sticky from Gatorade. The field smells freshly mowed, the faint smell of broken bats and glove leather lingering around the edges of Gene's consciousness. The ground under his feet, however much it has rocked this season, still feels solid somehow. Like he belongs there.

"So you're saying I should break up with him?" Gene asks.

"I'm saying," Baker says. She pinches the bridge of her nose. "That if you want another shot, and you want him to have one, too, then yes. You should dump him now, before you fuck up both of your careers."

She sounds painfully genuine then—not angry but stern. Not pissed but asking him to listen.

"I'm not doing anything to his career," Gene says. He wants for it to be true. "We just play better together."

"The shit on the field is only half the battle," she says. Gene opens his mouth to answer, but she barrels on. "You can play well together all you want. Hell, you can fuck your teammate all you want, if that's all that it was. But if you're so attached that you can't play apart, if you both fall to pieces the second you get separated, then you are fucking yourself *and* Estrada *and* the team over." She pokes a finger against Gene's sternum. "If you still haven't figured out how to deal with people leaving, you're going to keep falling flat on your ass. This business is all about leaving, Gene."

He stares at her finger, and he wills even one thing she said to be wrong. When he comes up blank, he settles for, "You never call me Gene."

"What are you going to do if one of you gets traded?"

Gene shoves his hands into his pockets, digs his nails into his palms in the hopes that it will keep him from crying.

"Are you just gonna—what? Quit, and sit at his games with the rest of the WAGS?"

And that, *that*, being told to either follow her advice or relegate himself to sitting with the wives and girlfriends—that finally breaks him.

He sets his jaw, and the words spit out of him.

"Just because things didn't work out for you and you decided to be miserable about it doesn't mean I have to do the same thing. Hate your job and your life and your decisions all you want. I like mine."

He turns and walks off the field, ignoring Baker's voice calling him back. He'll be batting ninth until he retires, at best. Benched tomorrow, almost certainly. The thing is, fighting back did nothing to quell the insistent nagging in Gene's head that she's right. It doesn't help that she more or less said all the things Gene thinks to himself—that he's not good enough to afford a single fuckup, not worth the risk of letting himself love, and be loved.

As he makes his way down the dugout steps, he plays her words over and over again, his brain latching onto every syllable, the blow of them sharpening each time.

*Are you just gonna—what? Quit, and sit at his games with the rest of the* WAGS?

Even if she didn't mean it the way it sounds, even if she didn't think through the distinctly misgendering implications before she said it, it stings. To hear it laid out like that—that Gene is never going to be good enough to do anything but watch? He has never felt smaller.

Gene has built a whole career, a whole life out of finding the good in what he has. What he wants—well. What he *wanted*, before Luis showed back up and Gene fell for him, was to play his game, make just enough money to get by, and have a simple, quiet life that very few people paid any attention to. He wanted to put his uniform on and play.

He didn't want to start wanting bigger things, dream-sized things, but here he is. Wanting to start every game, to feel like a key piece of his team, to get Beaverton to the playoffs. Wanting to maybe, *maybe* get called up. Wanting to stay. Wanting to play with Luis. Wanting *Luis*. Wanting this life that people told him he couldn't have and that he tried so hard not to even imagine.

At the end of the hall, he runs bodily into Luis, freshly showered and eyebrows furrowed.

"Nes, what's going on?" he asks.

Gene shakes his head, not at all willing to have this conversation in the hallway, in the stadium, or, ideally, at all.

But then Luis wipes Gene's cheek, and Dodger presses his nose into Gene's hand, and oh—Gene is crying.

"Do you want to go?" Luis asks.

"Yes."

So Luis walks Gene out to his truck, reaches over the bench seat to unlock Gene's door, but doesn't start the engine when Gene climbs in.

"Nes."

Luis may have been fine with Baker knowing about them, but that was before their respective call-ups, before Luis's panic attack and Gene's very public failure. Gene doesn't want to know if Luis has changed his mind. He's had enough disappointments for one night. "I don't want to talk about it," he says.

"Okay, well, I do," Luis says. Firmer than Gene expects him to be. Luis has never pushed an issue Gene didn't want to talk about before. "What's going on with you and Baker?"

"She's pissed at me."

"Why?"

Gene shrugs, an embarrassingly helpless thing. "Because I'm a fucking disappointment."

It sounds too pathetic, hearing his insecurity and hurt out loud. He can't bring himself to look at Luis, so he turns his head away, presses his lips tight, the pink turning a brilliant, lifeless white. He looks ridiculous in the truck's side mirror, the exact opposite of the person Gene tries to be: sad, and small, over a bit of advice from someone who knows better than him. Heartbroken because he will never get the big, shiny dream.

Gene wants to be the bright spot in people's lives. He wants to make people laugh, not crease their foreheads with worry the way he has Luis's tonight.

He takes a deep breath, then asks, "Did you ask them to send you back to the minors because of me?"

"No." It's too automatic.

Gene stares at him, his face a challenge.

"A little bit," Luis admits, and Gene's last bit of hope drops straight out of his heart.

"Why would you do that?" he asks.

"Because things make sense here. Playing with you."

"What about college?" Gene asks. It's off topic, but then, also, it isn't. It's the thing that always nags at him, always makes him wonder.

Luis looks confused. "I got drafted."

"No, I mean, why didn't you tell me? I had to find out from the fucking Stanford baseball account."

That, Luis thinks about a little longer. "Because things made too *much* sense there. Playing with you. In a way I didn't understand, and it scared me."

"So it was my fault?"

"Nes, come on."

Gene tips his head back against the headrest. "And now you're just going to stagnate in the minors with me forever? Because it's easier? And that'll be my fault, too?"

"No. And you're not going to be in the minors forever," Luis says, and the sureness in his voice cracks Gene wide open—the exact kind of misplaced confidence Gene has waited his whole life for someone to have in him.

Because the thing is, he knows now: he just wasn't good enough.

He got his chance—that golden chance, the one he told himself again and again he would never get—and, like Baker said, he fell flat on his ass. He just, plain and simple, couldn't pass muster. Maybe he really did fall in love with Luis, with the way they played together, so deeply and so quickly that he forgot how to be good by himself.

"Remember how I told you my boyfriend broke up with me last season?" he asks.

"Yes."

"It wasn't because of the schedule. It was because he thought I was setting myself up for disappointment," Gene admits. He doesn't like to talk about this, didn't even tell Vince when it happened, but if nothing else, he feels like he owes Luis this honesty. "He told me that I was wasting my time, trying to get cis people to give me a shot, and it made him too sad to watch."

Luis's face morphs into something dangerously close to pity when he says, "Jesus, Nes—"

"I don't want you to feel bad for me."

"I don't," Luis says. "I love that you always try. That's one of my favorite things about you."

Gene closes his eyes against the earnestness of Luis's voice. "You are the only person who thinks I have a chance. And I'm not willing to let you bet your whole career on that—"

"Nes—" Luis starts.

"—because you're wrong," Gene finishes. And when he says it, he doesn't cry, because it would be unfair.

It's funny, in the worst possible way—because when Luis came to Beaverton, he thought Luis would fuck up his career, and he has. It's just that, he's ruined it in the opposite way from what Gene expected. He has shown Gene how good things can be, how much he misses out on when he lets himself settle.

But that doesn't change the fact that Gene doesn't have what it takes to play in the major leagues—that he had only the tiniest chance of ever making it there, and when he did, he wasn't good enough.

Maybe, also, Gene can't stomach the thought of Luis finally realizing that Gene isn't anything special. He won't say that part out loud, though.

When Luis does speak, it's even-keeled, painfully quiet, and he sounds more hurt than Gene has ever heard him. He didn't know Luis could sound like that.

"You can't just stop wanting something because you're disappointed. That's not like you."

It is absolutely like Gene to force himself not to want something just because the possibility of not getting it, the grief of losing something he never had, hurts too much. It's one of his best skills.

"You'll make it back," Luis says. It comes out far too hopeful, and Gene can't remember when Luis became the optimist between them.

"I won't," Gene says, and he knows it to be true, the way he sometimes knows Beaverton is going to win from the moment the first pitch is thrown. He has known since he signed with Portland.

"Well, you're not stupid for trying," Luis insists. "You're allowed to want things."

A month ago, Gene would have liked to hear this, before disappointment came bearing down on him. Now he wants to go back to the quiet ease of a game well-played, his little minor league team who can count on him. The way that Luis hopes for him, the way that Luis makes the dumbest, biggest things feel possible—it's too much.

So when Luis asks, "What do you want, Nes?"

And when he looks at Gene like he really wants the answer, like he believes Gene can give it—

Gene tells him, "I want you to take me out of the equation. Do you want to play in the majors?"

"Yes," Luis says, emphatic. Then, more honest, "I'm not sure. Maybe."

"Then I want you to figure that out," Gene says.

"Gene," Luis says, and Gene's name—which he loves and

which he picked and which he usually wants to hear but has heard too much today, in all the places it doesn't belong—doesn't sound right in Luis's mouth anymore. Not nearly familiar enough.

"And until you figure it out," Gene says, "I want some space. I'm not going to be the asshole who holds you back. I can't be."

Nothing has ever hurt worse to say. Nothing has ever felt even a fraction this impossible. Luis looks like he wants to say something else, but, mostly, he looks heartbroken. Gene hates that, but not half as much as he hates the thought of ruining something Luis has wanted for decades.

Luis drives him home. He drops Gene off in silence and waits for Gene to get inside safely before he reverses out of the long driveway. Gene pretends he can't see Luis crying through the windshield. He manages not to do the same until he turns a lamp on in his living room and finds it filled with all the things Luis helped him build.

That second bookshelf that Gene thought he could do without but filled with ease when Luis insisted they put it together. The coffee table where Gene set all the things he needed to pierce Luis's ear, the first night they kissed. The bed frame that Gene bought well before Luis got traded to Beaverton but which has since started to feel almost, somehow, like *their* bed—real and permanent and *home*—which is ridiculous, and the exact opposite of what Gene should have let himself feel.

Gene cries for that, back pressed against the apartment door, and he hates himself most for messing up the one chance he had to get them that dream, whole and real, together.

# 20

## SEPTEMBER

Current record: 89–54

NANCY: Entering the final game of the regular season, our Beaverton Beavers are tied with the Tacoma Rainiers for the division lead. Who would have thought at the beginning of this season that we'd be saying this?

DAN: Not me!

NANCY: Not me. We've watched that lead ping-pong between the two clubs pretty steadily since July.

DAN: Playoffs are still up in the air.

NANCY: That's right. All depends on the outcomes today. If Tacoma wins *their* game against Salt Lake today, Beaverton's out. Doesn't matter whether Beaverton wins their own game.

DAN: And if Tacoma loses?

NANCY: If both teams lose, Tacoma's still in. But if Tacoma loses and Beaverton *wins*—

DAN: Ah.

NANCY: —then Beaverton's in.

DAN: For the first time since the aughts.

NANCY: That's correct.

DAN: So how are you feeling about those odds?

NANCY: Let's hope Beaverton just focuses on putting together a good game of their own. Some of them have been struggling through this last leg.

DAN: You think it's fatigue that's slowed Ionescu down at the plate?

NANCY: I'm not sure—he seems fine, if a bit more subdued than usual, on the field. I'm still inclined to believe it's just a slump.

DAN: No better time to break out of a slump than right now.

NANCY: Agreed.

---

By the time they reach their final game of the regular season—the last of a four-game matchup against the Sacramento River Cats—Gene and Luis have picked their pre-game practices up again, have settled back into something like being teammates. Gene has managed not to think too hard about the things he's missing, because if he thinks about those things, he won't enjoy a minute of this last playoff push.

Not that he's enjoying it now. But he can pretend.

He sits in the dugout, suited up in Beaverton green for what could be the last time this year, sandwiched between Vince and Luis, waiting that breathless last few minutes until the lineups get called. He and Luis have the printed game notes tucked between their thighs, that careful space between them reinforced, a reminder Gene doesn't need of a heartbreak he can't forget, because he has thought of little else for the last month. They don't touch unless they have to.

On Gene's other side is Vince, who has turned out to be unsurprisingly excellent at leading a playoff-caliber team. *That*, at least, along with the ways he and Gene have gotten back to their old routines, feels completely natural. He'll pitch today.

Gene tries to remind himself that he may only have this one last game with either of these men. He should get used to the idea of them leaving, of himself staying behind and holding down the fort.

It hits him in his hollowed-out chest every time he remembers.

For now, though, they're here. Warm and present on either side of Gene, the two best friends he's ever had.

"You gonna decide this one for us, Nes?" Vince asks.

Luis raises his eyebrows, waiting.

Gene's never called a game wrong, once he decides. It's that stubborn will of his. But today, he doesn't know what's going to happen. Today, his stubborn will stays silent, replaced only by a desperate hope that things will work out, that, someday, they'll feel easier than they do right now.

"No way," Gene says. "Don't need to. Pitch us home, Altzy."

And pitch them home he does.

Vince cruises through the first eight innings, allowing zero hits and zero walks, zero hit batters, no errors, no base runners, the first time any Beaverton pitcher has managed the accomplishment. Some might call this a perfect game, but baseball players are a superstitious people. They call it a *Don't touch him, don't talk to him, don't even breathe near him* game.

They give him plenty of run support, and they give it to him early. Baker hesitates to use her ace for a full game, but with his pitch count sitting at eighty-nine, well below his limit, it wouldn't make sense to risk throwing a new guy in. That—combined with the real threat that Vince will burn the whole place down if he gets pulled—means he's jogging out to the mound for the bottom of the ninth.

Baker—who still isn't talking to Gene much, but whose steady presence has felt steadier over the past four games—shows him her phone as he leaves the dugout. The display reads:

SALT LAKE 5–TACOMA 4.

FINAL.

She doesn't need to say what it means. She nods, Gene nods, and she says, "So get out there, Nes."

The first two batters go down in three pitches apiece, simple strikeouts, and it almost looks like Vince will finish this pièce de résistance with an immaculate inning, because he's Vince fucking Altman, and this is nearly the postseason, and he can. He couldn't have picked a better day for it—rain-scented and seventy-two degrees.

They are all willing Vince to get this last out—however it comes, doesn't matter. Immaculate inning or no, this is history for their team, if Vince can throw that final strike across the plate.

Gene barely even prepares himself for the first pitch. Absolutely no part of him thinks that it might actually make contact with the bat. And it doesn't. It sails into Ernie's glove, no slower than the first pitch Vince threw today.

The two that come after are formalities, really.

When they crowd Vince—newly crowned perfecto king and forever captain of the team he didn't want—at the mound, Gene joins in, jostling him and tackling him into the dirt. Luis's arm against his, the soft look he gives Gene at the bottom of that pile, define the moment for Gene just as much as Baker hefting the Gatorade over their heads, as much as Vince's eyes streaming in relief and laughter and outright, unbridled joy.

The Beaverton Beavers are going to the playoffs for the first time since the aughts, and Vince has led them there, and Gene really does try to enjoy it.

"Let's get out of here."

Gene, leaning against the bar, raises his eyebrows at Vince. "I'm going to tell your husband that you're hitting on me."

"I'm not hitting on you. I'm old and tired," Vince says. He has a bar towel filled with ice applied to his shoulder, dripping down one of the playoff T-shirts the coaching staff handed out to every player.

"You can't leave your own celebration drinks," Gene says.

"They're not mine, they're for the team. And I can leave whenever I want."

This is a little bit bullshit, and they both know it. Vince quite literally put them on his back and hauled them across the finish line, and every ounce of this celebration—of any celebration for the rest of the year—belongs to him. Well, maybe a bit of it is for Baker, too, who has rocketed to the top of most people's Manager of the Year predictions. But most of it is for Vince.

Certainly it doesn't belong to Gene, who wrangled only one meager hit tonight and got stranded on first base.

"And," Vince adds, "you're moping."

"I am not moping."

Vince raises an eyebrow.

"I thought I was hiding it pretty well," Gene says.

"You are not. Let's go."

So he and Vince shove themselves into the back of a taxi.

They wait until they get to the hotel to talk, and on the way to their room, Gene tries very hard not to look at the closed door to Luis's. Gene doesn't know if Luis asked to be moved or Baker did it on her own, but after that conversation in Luis's truck, their room assignments reverted back to their April defaults: Luis with Ernie, Gene with Vince. Behind that door, Luis and Dodger are probably piled into bed, meditation podcast playing. He didn't come to team drinks. Gene did his best not to care, but he wishes he had a key card, wishes he could climb into bed with Luis and tell him he misses him, tell him he's had the worst month of his life, tell him how badly he sleeps without Luis wrapped around him.

Of course, it's his own fault he can't.

"So am I still not allowed to talk about that?" Vince asks, nodding his head toward the door Gene has spent the last ten seconds staring at. He punctuates the question by unlocking their own hotel room door and holding it open for Gene.

"There's nothing to talk about."

"Bullshit."

"We," Gene starts, and he doesn't know where to go with that sentence, because "broke up" certainly isn't right. He shrugs. "I don't know. You seem weirdly calm, by the way. Shouldn't you be, like, drunk off your ass and bragging that you threw a fucking perfecto?"

"I'm old. I get too hungover to drink off anyone's ass anymore."

Gene flops onto his bed, on his back, glad to have made the playoffs but already exhausted at the thought of needing to play postseason games on the road. He would pay good money not to sleep in another hotel again.

"But you're going to the playoffs. It's what you wanted," he says, because he feels bad that Vince is hanging out in their sad double room at Sacramento's La Quinta Inn.

"Can I show you something?" Vince asks.

"Sure," Gene says.

Vince lies down close to Gene.

"Okay," Gene says, "I may not have a quasi-boyfriend anymore, but Jack might be upset if we spend the night cuddling."

Vince rolls his eyes. "Shut up, I'm trying to show you—"

He scrolls through his email for a minute, then hands the phone to Gene. Gene looks for a few seconds, surprised at how it makes his chest swell.

"This is an adoption application," Gene says.

"Yes it is."

"Holy shit, Altzy."

Vince grins. "Yeah. We sent it in last night, so we'd have something good to look forward to no matter how today's game turned out. And it turns out—I care more about that than the perfecto."

"The perfecto is still pretty cool, though."

"The perfecto is still pretty cool, yeah." Vince grins at the ceiling, and Gene can almost hear it, broad and well-deserved.

"That's really great. I'm happy for you, man. I'm gonna have to hug you."

And Gene does, face buried in Vince's offensively well-muscled shoulder, resisting the urge to give Vince's back the very distinct pats that define a man hug. This is not a man hug, this is just a hug, and he will hang on as long as Vince will let him.

Then, he hears, "Can I give you some advice?"

To Vince's shoulder, Gene says, "I'd really rather you didn't."

"Too bad. I want you to know that it isn't worth it."

"What isn't?" Gene asks.

"Staying closeted so you can reach some arbitrary goalpost. I wanted to make the playoffs. I'm going to. But I don't care a third as much about that as I do about Jack."

"Okay."

"I'm thirty-eight. I have at least forty years to spend with him."

Gene gives a noncommittal sound. "Thirty, if you don't quit your secret cigarettes."

"Shut up. I'm trying to help you." Vince lets go of him then and looks him in the eye.

"Okay," Gene says, because until someone tells him a better way around the issue at hand, Vince's advice is all he has.

"What I'm trying to say is: if the choice came down to Jack or my awards, I'd have an empty mantel."

But it's not about being closeted, not for Gene. He isn't—hasn't been, not since college, not one day in his professional career. "That's really nice," he says. "But it's more, like—I can't make that decision for someone else, you know?"

"I know."

"Like, not just about being closeted. Maybe he wants the trophies. Maybe he doesn't want to be weighed down by some loser who can't even help his minor league team make the playoffs."

Because, the truth is, Gene understands it now—what Vince said all those months ago. The worst feeling is your team doing well without you, in spite of you. Because you want to be happy, and you want to celebrate, but you feel useless. There is a medium-to-large chance that useless feeling isn't only about the team's success but about the success he knows Luis will find—hard-won, and Gene will play no part in it.

"I told him to think about it," Gene continues. "And I assume he has, but he hasn't said anything." He begs himself not to sound as pitiful about it as he feels.

"What are *you* thinking?" Vince asks.

Gene shrugs. "That I miss him. But also that it doesn't change literally anything."

Vince hands him a tissue, and Gene realizes that he needs it.

"Are you done?" Vince asks.

"With what?"

"Throwing your pity party?"

Gene hems. "Maybe."

"Because if not, that's fine. Throw your pity party, I'd be a hypocrite to tell you not to." Vince pats himself on the chest. "Fuck knows I need one every once in a while. But when you're done, tell me, so I can tell you that you're an idiot, and there is no way this shitty team would have come together this year without you in the middle of that field."

"You played pretty well without me there," Gene says. And it's true—that road trip they took while he was in the majors was their best of the season.

"Because we watched all your games in the dugout, and told each other that we had to win for you. You're the glue, dude. Even when you're playing like total shit. And I'm pretty damn sure Nada would tell you the same thing."

Gene isn't ready to believe that yet. But he listens, and he tries.

# 21

## SEPTEMBER

Postseason record:

Pacific Coast League West Champions

PCL Championship record: 0–0

In spite of his occasional injuries and the limits his shoulder puts on him even when healthy, no one questions Vince's status as the team's de facto ace. He pitched the game that got them into the playoffs, and it stands to reason that, four days later, he will pitch the first game of round one. He has more than earned the long-overdue distinction.

The morning of that first game, Gene thunders down the Altmans' stairs with his duffel bag, long since packed. He rounds the corner into the kitchen. Jack is already pouring finely ground coffee into the small metal bowl of an espresso maker, preparing to pull a shot on the at-home machine he got Vince for his birthday last year. Gene waves to get his attention and signs, "Morning," when Jack looks up at him.

"Morning, Gene!" Jack signs back, his extended fingers curling into Gene's sign name. Lately, Gene hasn't felt much like the smile that name evokes, but coming downstairs, surrounding himself in the Altmans' happiness, helps. "Excited for today?"

Gene nods, cracking open the oven door to get a peek at the good-luck quiche Jack will have made. Jack snaps his towel against Gene's back with no venom at all, more like a gentle nudge than any real threat.

"Just looking!" Gene signs.

"Do you want to eat down here?" Jack asks.

Gene says, "I thought you'd never ask." He remembers the signs only for "think" and "ask," but he says it aloud, too, and Jack grabs a third plate. Then, when Jack is facing him again, Gene adds, "You coming to the game today?" This question he knows well—he asks it before almost every home game, as if Jack doesn't have a go-to seat just above the dugout. Gene can't remember the last time he saw someone else in that seat. Never, if he had to guess.

"Wouldn't miss it," Jack signs, each movement of his hands emphatic and purposeful, but easy.

An hour later, Vince pulls into his usual parking spot in the staff lot of Beaverton's stadium, turns the engine off, and does not move. It's the first time Gene has ever seen him nervous before a game. Sore, yes; cranky, frequently. But nervous? Vince doesn't get nervous. Vince has played for good teams and disappointing teams and historically terrible teams, and he has been a bright spot on every single one. It leaves little for a person to be nervous about.

Yet here he is, staring out the windshield at the welcoming embrace of their old-ass stadium, and the nerves are unmistakable in the set of his shoulders and mouth.

If they lose this game—if they lose, say, three games in a row and get knocked out of the playoffs in the first of two rounds—it could be Vince's last ever game as a pro. Gene is painfully aware of this fact, and if he had to guess, he'd say Vince is, too.

He reaches over and claps a hand on Vince's chest.

"Come on, old man," he says.

"Don't call me old. I'm not old today."

Gene yanks on the door handle and gets out of the car. "Sure, Altzy."

As if to punctuate his point, Gene slings both of their duffels over one shoulder and raises his eyebrows at Vince, who gives his shoulder a single prod before yanking his door open and facing the game ahead.

Luis waits in the locker room, head leaned against the locker stall divider, shoulders slumped. Gene can tell, with one glance, that Luis got even less sleep than usual last night, and he wishes more than anything that Luis would have called him. They could have stayed up together.

Of course, Gene told Luis not to do pretty much exactly that. It doesn't soften the blow of missing him.

They do their laps around the stadium, then drop into their familiar push-ups at the top of each section, and today, Gene does not try to impress him with one-armed push-ups or by shoving himself off the ground hard enough to clap before he falls back down. He lowers himself until the tip of his nose barely grazes the cement of the step, and then straightens his arms again until the pleasant discomfort cuts through the morning cold.

When they practice grounders, they don't do trick shots; the movements are tired but reliable, and Gene can't help but think of Luis in his truck, telling Gene that things make sense here, playing with him.

Ever since he and Luis started to practice together, since they started to play well and, more important, since he and Luis started to let each other into their lives off the field, too, Gene has marveled at how fun baseball can still be, years into his career, even when things don't go his way.

It isn't fun today. But they do their jobs, and they do them well, and if Gene can't produce at the plate, he can at least help Luis hold down the fort at the keystone. However much he has fallen apart over the last month, that has remained consistent.

It's better than losing him altogether, at least.

---

NANCY: We're seeing history today, as Vince Altman wraps up his warm-up pitches and takes the mound for the first time ever in a postseason game.

DAN: Almost twenty years into his career, he has finally made it, Nancy.

NANCY: Not exactly how he planned, I'm sure. He spoke pretty openly about wanting to get a ring with Portland.

DAN: Right, you have to imagine this is an exciting day for him.

NANCY: That's a clean strikeout to start the top of the first. It's been an incredible season for him. Pretty emblematic of the Beavers season as a whole—they had a fine roster, but very few of us expected anything approaching this kind of season. Vince Altman has been one of the biggest examples of that.

DAN: And we should get at least one more stellar performance out of him yet. He'll be on a limited pitch count today, working on slightly shortened rest after throwing a perfect game to close out the season.

NANCY: The first perfect game in Beaverton Beavers history, Dan.

DAN: It was a special thing to see.

NANCY: You just can't want anything but the best for this guy.

DAN: He pitches well wide for ball one.

NANCY: That did not look good.

DAN: The delivery was a bit off there—

NANCY: It almost looks like he's struggling with his windup.

DAN: That's ball two.

NANCY: Even wider than the first.

DAN: Ernie Gonzales is calling a mound visit. He's done a hell of a job getting this pitching staff in order this year, don't you think?

NANCY: Especially with most of them skewing so young. He has more than earned a long look in Portland next season.

DAN: Agreed. It looks like Steph Baker is calling out the trainer.

NANCY: Oh, that's never a good sign, Dan.

DAN: No it is not.

NANCY: His teammates are surrounding him at the mound, but the way he's holding that shoulder—

DAN: I don't think this is going to be the game he planned on pitching.

---

Gene really does try not to cry when they take Vince off the field, and he really does succeed, until Vince takes his hat off and puts it in front of his face to hide his own tears. The worst part of it is that Gene can't run off the field to find him, because Vince would never forgive him if he didn't see this thing through for both of them.

He takes his spot, the same as he has all season. He wipes his eyes, adjusts his hat.

Vince may not want to watch the team succeed without him, but Gene knows for a fact that he'd rather that than watch the team lose.

But the fact of the matter is, they find themselves in a six-run hole by the end of the first, it's turned into eight runs by the end of the second, and long relief quickly turns into bullpen damage control.

All teams make clumsy, avoidable mistakes sometimes, but today's whole game consists entirely of these mistakes, one after another, until Baker essentially just throws up her hands. A 12–1 deficit in the bottom of the seventh doesn't inspire considerable hope, even for the Genes of the world.

"Waste of fucking arms," Baker mutters, looking over her roster cards.

Gene hasn't helped matters. In his four at-bats, he has struck out all four times, by far his worst showing this season. It's saying something, too, considering the uninspiring numbers he's put up in the last month. If they had any chance of catching up, Baker would have replaced him with a pinch hitter a couple innings ago.

And then, as they enter the top of the ninth, down a whopping 15–1, courtesy of two singles and a homer in the eighth, Baker points at their backup infielder.

"Grab your glove, you're playing second."

Gene turns to her, ready to argue his case. If you play a shit game, you finish the shit game. You take responsibility for it. He shouldn't get to ride the bench while his teammates grind those last three outs.

But instead of pulling him, Baker looks him directly in the eye, something she hasn't really done since their blowup, and says, "You're pitching."

This garners a hearty laugh from Kyle Clark, the first emotion he's displayed all night that can't be classified in the "disappointed older brother" collection. Luis, too, looks like he's trying to hold back his amusement and failing terribly. Ernie just claps Gene's shoulder with his oversized catcher's mitt and nods toward the field.

"You know my signs?" he asks.

"I mean, yeah. That's not going to help, but, yeah."

As they walk onto the field, Gene ignores the announcers and grounds himself in each of his teammates' grunts of encouragement as they pass him by, and in Ernie's voice behind his raised glove.

"What's the plan?" Gene asks him.

"How good's your fastball?"

"Sixty? Sixty-five?"

"Oh, Christ," Ernie says, but his accent and his smile make it sound like a good thing, somehow. "Any curves?"

"Only my ass."

Ernie tips his head back and laughs, a short, loud bark of a thing. "You and me both. Well, this should be fun at least!"

Baseball has given Gene precious little fun lately. He has served up shit sandwich after shit sandwich of a game, playing just well enough to not screw over his team during their final playoff push. It keeps him up at night—more than any of the rest of it. More than Baker saying Gene will ruin Luis's career and his own. More than the looming threat of Vince's retirement and departure from Gene's everyday life. More than Gene's crushed hopes of ever playing well in the bigs. Not more than Luis's broken voice in his truck, the empty space in Gene's life where Luis should be—but close.

The opposing team's batter looks amused, seeing Gene up there on the pitcher's mound, and Gene can't really blame him.

Ernie flashes the sign for what Gene thinks might be a fastball on the upper-right corner. Those pitch signs are honestly a lot harder to read when he's sweating this badly. His contact lens prescription must need updating, too, because he's pretty sure Baker is flashing him a thumbs-up from the dugout, and *that* can't be right. But when he nods to Ernie and tosses the pitch Ernie might have asked for, and it lands in its intended spot—albeit at a comically slow speed—Baker gives a yell of approval from the dugout and claps her hand against the back of her clipboard.

It's one strike, sure. Gene isn't a pitcher, sure. They're going to lose this game—*badly*. Sure.

But that vote of support from Baker, and the way his whole team stands at his back, in spite of the jack shit he's done to help them over the past month? Gene raises his glove to catch the ball when Ernie throws it back to him, and suddenly the idea of throwing it again doesn't seem so onerous.

It seems, almost, well . . . *fun*.

They're going to lose anyway. He might as well make it as enjoyable as he can. If they lose laughing, well, that's better than losing with their heads hung.

Gene gets his first out of the game on a line drive caught with impressive ease by Luis, because of course it's Luis. He checks the dugout and finds Vince there, leaning his legs against the fence, his good arm hanging over its railing, clapping one-handed against the wood for that out like Gene is about to secure them an important win.

When Gene gives up a home run and Ernie calls a mound visit, Luis jogs in and stands at Gene's back, his elbow resting on Gene's shoulder and his glove covering his mouth. For all that has happened between them, that elbow still steadies Gene, reminds him how well his lungs and heart can work.

"He's got this," Luis says.

Ernie brushes him off. "Oh, I know. I just wanted to say, we're going to get this next guy to strike out. I'm calling it."

Gene covers his mouth and says, "Like fuck we are."

Ernie grins. "Decide it."

And, okay.

He can do that. He's not ready to decide a whole game, to feel that kind of confidence and surety, but one strikeout? He can manage that.

"Okay," he says. "We're gonna strike this next guy out."

Ernie jogs back to the dish, Luis bops his glove against Gene's shoulder, and Ross and Cooper give him quick, encouraging looks. The whole infield came in to stand at his back for that mound visit, like he was a real pitcher. Even playing his inarguably worst position in their worst loss of the season, at the most important moment, on the sixth mound visit of the game, they dragged themselves in to support him.

He throws absolute garbage to the next guy, not even trying to get the ball into the strike zone. And the guy swings at every one of them, striking out on an easy three pitches.

Ernie, not even bothering with a mound visit, yells, "What did I say!" loud enough for Gene to hear. Baker and Vince and almost every guy on their bench stand at the dugout railing, the rest of them reliable at Gene's back.

And maybe this is what it feels like—to let yourself be unremarkable, and to try your best anyway. Maybe, Gene thinks, while he shrugs at Ernie for calling a pitch Gene doesn't even know the grip for, this is what it feels like to let other people help you across the finish line. Maybe this is what Vince meant about the goalposts being arbitrary.

Maybe—*maybe*—this is what it feels like to let people love you even when you fail. Luis's elbow on his shoulder, *he's got this*—and he does. He has this team, and this game, and, he hopes someday, Luis.

He drives Vince and Jack home after the game, after Vince has been checked out by every trainer they have and scheduled for another MRI tomorrow morning. Jack sits in the backseat with Vince, and they don't talk about it, because Vince has asked them not to yet.

So, at a red light, Gene reaches his right hand into the backseat, the universal gesture of a dad requesting a bite of his kid's snack. What he gets is Vince's hand in his, long enough to give him a squeeze and meet his eye in the rearview mirror.

"Can I say something earnest, or are you not in the mood?" Gene asks.

"You have a green light," Vince says.

"Literally or figuratively?"

Vince sighs, put-upon in the most Vince way Gene can imagine. "Both."

And while Gene gets honked at by the guy in the obnoxiously large SUV behind him, he keeps his hand in Vince's and eases into the intersection.

"I love you, and I'm still going to love you when you leave, and you're going to be stuck with me no matter how far away you move. Can you sign that for Jack, too?"

Vince smiles and rolls his eyes, but he does as Gene asks. Gene keeps his eyebrows raised in expectation until Vince says it back.

"I love you, too," Vince says, his signing just as exasperated as his voice. "Now can you try not to get us in a car wreck? I already had to watch you pitch today, it's criminal that I also have to watch you drive."

When they get home, and Gene settles, disappointed but not in any way that matters or will last, he types at least a dozen different texts to Luis, every last one of them a variation on the same thing. That he misses Luis, that nothing has changed, but that he would rather figure out every bit of that complicated mess *with* Luis than spend any more time at all without him.

That things make more sense to Gene when Luis is there, too.

That he loves him, and will love him even when he leaves.

He deletes every text before he sends it, but he tastes those thoughts all night, rolls them around in his mouth until he might know how to say them aloud.

# 22

## SEPTEMBER

**Postseason record:**
**Pacific Coast League Champions**

**Triple-A Championship record: 0–2**

By some miracle, fueled by the need to make Vince proud, they win their first series. A week later, they are two games deep in the Triple-A Championship Series—they, the Beaverton Beavers, of low expectations and staunch playoff droughts, have stumbled their way to this precipice, have lost both of the first two games of this series, and will be eliminated if they lose another.

The morning of their first home game of the championship, Gene's anticipation has him two inches from death and more alive than he's ever felt.

He spends it in Baker's office, waiting for news on Vince's MRI results.

"I shouldn't have let him pitch on short fucking rest," Baker says.

"He looked fine in his bullpen. How were you supposed to know?" Gene asks. They have still barely been speaking to each other, but when he got to the stadium early and found her hovering over her cell phone, he popped in, sat down, and hasn't moved since.

"He's almost forty, and he's been throwing with a bum shoulder all season," she says.

"He threw a perfecto less than two weeks ago."

She rubs her hand across her mouth, then picks up her phone and chucks it at the wall, where it lands with a harmless, rubber-cased *thud* on the ugly taupe carpet.

"Sorry," she says.

"It's fine," Gene says. He's seen plenty of people throw plenty of things in plenty of clubhouses, even if it is, decidedly, his least favorite thing about sports. "Not my phone."

"Not that. I'm sorry I've been a dick," she says.

"Oh."

The shock of it, an apology from perhaps the world's most stubborn person, hits Gene with all the force of the phone Baker just threw.

"It's okay," he says.

"I didn't mean what I said. I mean, I did. I don't say shit I don't mean. And someone needed to tell you to pull your head out of your ass," she says. Once a coach, always a coach. "But I didn't mean it—the way it sounded."

"I know."

"You're a better player than Estrada anyway. If anyone's going to sit with the WAGS, it should be him."

Gene laughs. "He'd have to get a denim jacket. And learn how to, like, competently use Instagram."

"And get some highlights," Baker says.

"I like his hair."

"His hair is all right. I'll give him that."

"Wow. Even the lesbians are impressed with his product game," Gene says. "High praise."

"And you can tell him I said so."

Gene doesn't really tell Luis much of anything these days. He asks, "Do you really think I'm a better player?"

"Depends on the day, but I was trying to be nice," Baker says.

"That seems more accurate."

Baker gestures to him. "But I'll always root for the little guy first."

It means something to Gene, hearing her say this. Their careers look like two forks in the same road, sometimes by choice and sometimes by circumstance, but no one who has played or currently plays baseball gets what Gene has gone through better than she does. In some ways, being a man has made his career easier, and in some ways, being cis has made hers easier. There are things about her that he will never understand, and that sentiment goes both ways.

Still, when she looks across her desk at him, he knows she means that apology. She's hard on him because they have so much in common—the same reason she came to scout him in the first place. He'll always want her approval, and she will always be stingy with it, and Gene will never feel better than when he really, truly earns it.

"Nada would be so happy to hear that you don't think he's a little guy," Gene says, because it's easier than trying to sum all of that up. He knows she knows.

"He's a toothpick with shoulders and a pretty face."

Gene leans his forehead in his palm. He draws out the *o* when he says, "*Stop*, he's sensitive."

"And he isn't here to hear me." Baker leans back and eyes him. "Are we good?"

"I'm sorry I called you miserable."

"I am miserable," she says.

"Yeah, but I didn't have to say it."

She actually cracks a smile at that. "No. But it made me think about things."

"Uh-oh."

"I took that job at U of O."

Gene sits back up, his spine rigid. "*Seriously?*"

"Last week. I asked them not to announce it until our season ended. Date contingent on our playoff run."

"Holy shit, Baker."

She slings her feet up on the desk that Gene has only ever considered hers and which, come November, will apparently belong to someone else. "Had to move up the ladder at some point, and I couldn't do it here. Decided to switch ladders."

"Seriously? What changed your mind?"

"There was an opening for a pitching coach. In Portland. I got a call from the front office about it after we made the playoffs."

Gene raises his eyebrows. "Yeah?"

"Said it was mine if I wanted it." She crosses her legs at the ankles, puts her hands behind her head, the most laid-back Gene has ever seen her. "Worse pay, more travel, and less control than the Oregon job. Plus, I don't want to be a pitching coach. I want to manage a team. I'm fucking *good* at it," she says.

"You are. Fuck, I'm happy for you." He leans his elbows on her desk, and for once, she doesn't tell him not to. "You're not any less loyal for taking the job you deserve. You know that, right?"

"Yeah, well." She shrugs, nonchalant, but Gene can tell it means something to her. "I spent all season telling you to get used to people leaving, but I started thinking maybe we were the ones who deserved to get out of here."

Gene shrugs. "I can think of worse places to have spent the season."

"I'll come back to Portland someday. Maybe when their manager finally retires in a hundred years. But you better make me look good today, or Oregon's going to question that fat paycheck they're sending me."

"How fat?"

When she smiles, it looks devious, and she deserves an amount of money that makes her feel that way. "Embarrassingly."

"Good."

"Slightly less fat because I asked them to put some of it in the scholarship fund instead," she says.

"Wow. She's a philanthropist."

"Mostly I want to coach a good fucking team. Scholarships make that easier."

"I'm going to tell myself you're doing it out of the goodness of your heart."

"You go ahead and do that." She picks up the baseball on her desk and starts tossing it from one hand to the other. "And if I can give it to someone other than some meathead cis man every year, well, all the better."

It's so good, so distinctly Baker, Gene can't even bear to be upset that she's leaving. "I'm glad you're doing this, but we are categorically fucked without you next year," he says. "At least you're making it sting less."

"No, *Beaverton's* fucked without me," she corrects. "*You* will be long gone by then."

Gene squints at her.

"Because you're going to be in Portland, dumbass."

"Oh. Yeah, well." Gene wrinkles his nose. "We'll see."

She takes her feet down, so she can lean closer to him and use the scariest version of her coach voice. "No. You will. Because someone's gotta do it, and there's no reason it shouldn't be you. You're going to get your gay ass onto that diamond, and you're going to win me a championship, and then you're going to win one for Portland, too."

"They've lost almost a hundred games this season."

"You didn't let me finish. In about three years, you're going to win a World Series for Portland, after they spend some money on some decent pitching and"—she gestures to herself—"some championship coaches. Got it?"

Gene has about one percent of the confidence she appears to be attempting to instill in him. But he has never cared for letting Baker down, so he nods, and she nods, too.

"Good. And your little boyfriend can come, too, if he wants."

"He's not my boyfriend," Gene says, because he hasn't figured out how to talk to Luis yet, and he needs Baker to stop bringing him up.

"Sure he is," she says. "You can get your names hyphenated. It'll take up your whole back."

Gene laughs, but the idea makes him a little dizzy. It sticks somewhere in him, beats along with his heart. "Yeah, maybe by the time Portland wins that championship."

"It's a plan."

Even Baker's friend chats always feel like her coaching—hard, no punches pulled—but Gene loves that about her. She's a little awkward, and not known for her warmth, but she cares. She tries, when she wants to, and she's trying now. Awkward is all right in Gene's book anyway.

As they get deep into crafting their dream lineup for the eventual World Series–winning Portland Lumberjacks—Gene and Luis at the keystone, Ernie behind the dish—Baker's phone rings from the floor, muffled by the carpet but impossible to miss. She must have turned it up all the way, along with the vibration effect, in case she somehow managed to miss the air raid sounds of her ringtone.

"Shit, shit, shit." She fumbles to get up from her desk, tossing aside the clipboard holding her fantasy baseball notes.

Gene beats her to it, scooping the phone off the ground and tossing it at her. In the brief glance he gets at her screen, Gene reads the caller name—DOCTOR, DO NOT IGNORE in all capital letters.

Baker catches the phone with ease but fumbles to get the call to pick up, finally succeeding on her third try. "What are we working with?" she asks, followed by a five-second pause, and then her palm smacking the table. She punctuates it with a distinct, echoing "*Fuck!*"

Because it could be their last practice of the season, Gene brings Luis a bagel, wrapped in foil and baked fresh that morning, love shown the best way he knows how.

When he hands it to Luis, he says, "Can we talk tonight? After the game?"

Luis peels the foil back and peeks inside, gets a good look before saying, "Yes."

"Had to make sure I made it worth your while?"

Luis gives him a smile—a little tight, but there—and takes a bite. "No. I'm hungry."

They eat there, in silence, until all they have in their hands is crumpled-up foil. They make a silent agreement to skip their stadiums today, tired of running in circles to get to the same place. They'll cut straight to the parts they like best—the grounders, the teamwork, just them and the field and the plays they make best together.

While they grab the buckets, Luis asks, "Did you hear the news about Altzy?"

"Yeah," Gene says.

"How do you feel about that?"

Gene could hug him, here in the middle of the field, but he just says, "Sometimes people have to leave. I'm trying to get better about that."

"Oh, yeah?"

Gene drops his bucket by first, pulls his glove onto his hand. "Yeah. It's a work in progress," he says.

The way Luis smiles at that, soft and a little sad, Gene thinks maybe he could have sent those texts he typed and deleted last week. He also thinks about what Baker said, about names on backs and about getting his gay ass out onto that diamond.

Gene scoops up the first ball Luis bats in his direction and throws it sidearm into the bucket; the next, he makes a clean pick off the infield dirt, in the crown of his hat instead of his glove. He showboats, finding increasingly impractical ways to make each play, until Luis is laughing, until Gene has convinced himself that the idea forming in the back of his head could work, that Luis just might listen long enough to hear him out.

In the locker room, Baker has posted the day's lineup.

For the first time since he came back from the majors, she has Gene batting first. She catches his eye from her office, points at him. Gene can almost feel the pressure of that point, laser-like, in the center of his chest.

"You gonna prove me right today, Ionescu?" she yells through her open door.

Before Gene can answer, Luis says, "Yeah," at the same time Ernie calls, "Hell yes he is, Coach!" from his locker stall.

That morning, when Gene woke up, he told himself that if their season were to end today, at least they would finish out at home, the same way they started. Now, with two hours to go until first pitch, Gene thinks—what if they win? What if, until the season ends, they forget how to lose? What if he lets himself be honest, and he risks the disappointment?

What if he lets himself, for the first time in a month, be a fucking optimist?

He doubts it, but he hopes, and today the hope is stronger.

At the end of the Altmans' driveway, after a hard-fought win, Luis parks under the maple, old and creaking, the one whose leaves will be compost for the garden in a couple months' time. He turns the engine off, the action so familiar that Gene wants to pluck Luis's hand from where it rests on the bench seat and kiss the inside of his wrist, as slow as he can manage so the moment will last longer.

"Can I say something?" Luis asks, mostly to the windshield.

"You can say whatever you want," Gene says.

"I just mean—before you tell me whatever you're going to tell me."

"Yes."

"Okay." Luis takes a deep breath. "I really miss you."

Dodger nudges Gene's leg, as if agreeing with Luis.

The thing is, losing baseball used to be Gene's worst fear. But now, nearly at the end of the best and hardest season he's ever played, he isn't half as scared as he used to be. Maybe they'll win tomorrow, and they'll stay alive, and maybe they won't. Vince will retire and Baker will move on to a better job, and Luis will more likely than not get called up to the majors.

Six months ago, if you'd told him the position he'd find himself in today, Gene would have been afraid that he'd lose his connection to baseball entirely—what used to be the best, most thrilling part of his life, before Luis had crashed back into it.

But Baker will keep helping players like him, and Vince will be his friend long after he stops being Gene's teammate, and Luis—

Luis Estrada misses him, enough that he drove Gene home tonight to sit in his driveway together, no matter what it was Gene wanted to talk to him about.

It makes what he has planned significantly less scary.

"I miss you, too," Gene says. "Like, fuck, a lot."

Luis looks at him the same way he looked at Gene in that picture, from the Futures Game. Like Gene might be some kind of a miracle.

It makes Gene's breath dip and come slamming back into him, and it takes every bit of self-control he has not to lean across the bench seat and kiss Luis. He hasn't earned it yet. He might never earn it, but he'd like to try.

"Will you meet me upstairs in five minutes?" he asks.

"Yes," Luis says. "Why?"

"Because I planned a whole thing."

"Are you going to break up with me again?"

Luis says it with a wary smile. Gene mostly just wants to kiss his lips where they stretch, where they're still. He wants to kiss every inch of Luis.

"No," Gene says. "I don't think I could survive that again."

"Me neither."

"Really?"

He knows the answer. But a part of him wants to hear, out loud and impossible to refute, that he wasn't the only one feeling the way he's felt for the last month. He wants to know, when he goes upstairs and he steps out on a limb, there's a chance it will hold strong under him.

"You can ask Gonzo," Luis says. "He had to watch me mope for weeks."

"You told Gonzo?"

"No. But, y'know. I was gone all the time and then suddenly I was home every night watching *Legally Blonde* on repeat. I think he probably made some assumptions."

"*Legally Blonde*?"

"Specifically the part where she gets dumped and has a breakdown, yeah," Luis says. "It was very relatable, believe it or not."

Gene bites his lip. "Well, for the record, I didn't consider it a dumping. I wasn't totally sure we were dating, honestly."

Luis lowers his eyebrows, the good-natured laughter gone all at once. "Oh."

"No, like—I wanted to be. But I kept doing all these mental

gymnastics so I wouldn't have to admit that. I was scared you were going to leave, and then I was scared that you'd stay because you felt bad for me." Gene braces himself for whatever Luis is going to say. He promises himself he'll feel what he's going to feel about it, that he will resist the urge to spiral over it.

So Gene says, "Which was useless, because I was already in love with you, so what was I protecting myself from? I was already fucked."

Luis unbuckles his seat belt and leans across the seat, across a very curious Dodger, and kisses Gene so well, so slowly that Gene can think of nothing but getting his hands in Luis's hair, and about how much he missed the uneven slide of Luis's lips, the way he throws every bit of himself into a kiss even when he hasn't started to touch Gene at all.

It is a herculean effort for Gene to pry himself away from that kiss and hold Luis's face a careful six inches from his.

"Sorry," Luis says, biting his own lip exactly where Gene would like to bite it.

"No, but—I had a whole plan, and you're kind of ruining it."

"*Me?* You're the one who just said you love me."

"That was supposed to happen upstairs. And there was actually a bunch of stuff that was supposed to come before that." When Luis opens his mouth, Gene puts his hand over it. "If you tell me you love me, too, I'll kill you."

"Excuse me!" When Luis says it, it comes out undignified, perfect. "Who says I do?"

"I was trying to be confident." The funny thing is, he's not really faking it.

Luis grins under Gene's palm, and this is almost more distracting than seeing it, so Gene takes his hand back and yanks open the truck door. "Are you coming upstairs or not?"

"You said you wanted five minutes," Luis says, but he's already twisting the manual crank of the driver's-side window to keep the early fall drizzle from getting in.

"Whatever. Plan's out the window," Gene says. "Come up with me now."

Luis fits well in Gene's apartment. Months ago, Gene worried about having him here, about Luis seeing even the simplest of things, because Gene simultaneously wants to overshare every detail of his life and can't stand the idea of someone misunderstanding him. Most of the time, it means he shares only the brightest parts of himself, the parts that will make other people's days or lives better.

With Luis, he wants to be known, in his entirety. And it doesn't feel so scary, letting him in—it feels like coming home, in every sense of the word.

"Okay," Luis says. "Show me what your plan was."

Gene tugs Luis by the wrist, into the bedroom, which gets him a solid, interested eyebrow raise until Gene says, "Not that kind of a plan. You're so gay. Close your eyes."

The bed creaks under Luis when Gene sits him down. His eyelashes tickle the pads of Gene's fingers when he coaxes Luis's eyes closed, and he takes the opportunity to trace a finger along the ridge of Luis's nose, too, because he has always wanted to.

"Oh, *I'm* gay?" Luis asks.

"Shut up."

Gene rummages through his dresser, for the thing he knows is there but which he has not actually seen in over a month, since he shoved it to the back corner. He pushes aside underwear, socks, the stash of boxers and oversized T-shirts and cropped tank tops he likes to sleep in, until his fingers find the material he's looking for. In the back corner, amidst the things Gene keeps closest to his skin, he finds a jersey.

The perfect shade of home green, forest with a hint of teal.

Left here by accident one night, after Luis slept over and they got carried away in the morning. ESTRADA across the back in a perfect embroidered arc over his number, 19.

Gene shucks his T-shirt, his back to Luis. "You better not be looking."

"I'm not."

Gene checks over his shoulder in the mirror to confirm that this isn't a lie.

He starts to do the buttons up, then decides against it, prying them back out of the fabric until the shirt hangs loose on his shoulders. They wear almost the same size, Luis's a little longer, narrower at the hips and broader in the shoulders. It still looks exactly right on Gene.

"Shit, Nes."

Gene shoves his discarded T-shirt into the top drawer of his dresser and turns around, an accusatory finger pointed at Luis. Dodger lies next to him, tail going and mouth a broad smile.

"I told you not to look," Gene says.

"Why are you wearing my jersey?"

And here is the part where Gene had a plan. Where he mapped out each minute thing he would say to Luis. Like a postgame highlight reel, where the highlights are just Gene sticking his foot in his mouth again and again. Now that he's here, he finds himself a little lost as to where to start. So he opens his mouth and hopes it comes out right.

"You said in California that you didn't think you'd ever get to date and have a career."

"Yes," Luis says. "But—"

"Shh. No. I have to finish." Gene clears his throat. "And I told you that I'm shit at wanting things."

"You did."

"And that was true, and I am, and the idea of, like, wanting something and being disappointed is sort of paralyzing to me.

And I really, really fucking wanted to make it in the majors. I told myself for years that I didn't want that at all, and that I didn't care, and then you came here, and you gave me this impossible idea that I could do it."

"You can," Luis says, and he looks so earnest Gene could die.

"Still talking," Gene says. This time, he puts his fingers on Luis's lips, and Luis deposits a kiss there. "You are *the* most distracting man alive."

"Thank you."

"What I'm trying to say," Gene says, "is that I'm absolutely terrified, all the time, of everything, and I think that you get that feeling."

Luis jokingly considers this, giving a brief *hmm* and squinting one eye closed. "Yeah, a little," he says.

"But I would really like to be scared with you," Gene says. "If that's something you'd want."

Luis smiles, his mouth going a little silly. "And what would that entail?" he asks.

"I'm not saying you have to be out or something. Obviously I'm out, and I'm not intending to, like, downplay that."

"I'd never ask you to," Luis says.

"I know. So you don't have to be out, not to anyone you don't want to be out to. But I want you. And you asked me in California if I'd ever want to be your boyfriend, and I do. Want that." Gene's speech was supposed to end here, but he adds, "Like, so much that I invited this guy I sort of dumped to come over to my apartment and watch me put on his jersey. So I could tell him I want to be his."

Luis scoots forward, until he's barely on the bed. He slides his hands onto Gene's sides, and his thumbs do distracting things along Gene's ribs. "Even if I quit baseball?" he asks.

"You're not going to quit baseball. You love baseball."

"No, *you* love baseball," Luis says. "You were literally made to be on a baseball diamond. Which is kind of incredible, because you were also not at all made to be on a baseball diamond."

It's a fair assessment.

Luis goes on, so close Gene can feel his breath when he talks. "I love baseball when you're there. But before I got traded, I wanted to quit. And then that night when you found me in the bathtub?" He waits for Gene's nod of confirmation. "I had literally texted my agent asking how I could get out of my contract. I *hated* baseball for a while."

Gene holds his face, and he tries to wrap his head around the idea that someone so good—so talented, so emblematic of all the things Gene is most in love with about this sport—could hate it.

"I don't want to go back to playing without you, Nes," Luis says. "And I want to do something more stable, that I can love even when I'm the only one in the room. So I reached out to Stanford last month to see if I could finish my degree, and I'm going to start classes in January."

Gene takes as steadying of a breath as he can manage and reminds himself: he is trying to learn how to let people leave. "So you really are quitting?"

"Well," Luis says. Gene watches his chest expand, a deep breath, and all that air rushes out when he adds, "Yeah."

Before Gene can panic, before he can jump to the worst conclusion, he asks the only thing he really needs to know. "And that's what you want?"

Luis smiles. He turns his head and kisses Gene's palm, a lingering thing. "Yes," he says. "I love playing with you. I haven't been half this happy in years. But it's not the baseball that's made me happy, you know?"

The thing is, Gene has always loved baseball, every part of it, at every position he's ever played, on every team he's ever played with. For him, Luis was part of that joy, but never all of it. He had his baseball joy, and his Luis joy, and that absurd euphoria where they overlapped. He doesn't understand what Luis is feeling, but he doesn't have to. Luis deserves something that makes him feel that euphoria.

He nods. "Then I'm really proud of you for figuring that out. For doing what's right for you."

Luis's eyes shine, a little, when he smiles. "Thank you. Does that change things, though? For you?"

"Not at all," Gene says, no hesitation, and he means it. "I mean, I'll miss you. But—"

"You'll still have me. If you want me. I'll just be sitting somewhere else during your games. I've heard the Portland WAGS are pretty cool."

Gene runs a thumb along Luis's jaw, tries to memorize the way his beard feels—barely long enough not to scratch. "What if they never call me up again? What if I don't get the big fancy career?"

"Then I'll come to every Beavers game. But that is not gonna happen, Nes."

"What if I'm no good without you?"

Luis tugs the sides of the jersey, so the fabric pulls at Gene's shoulders. "Am I still not allowed to say that I love you?"

Gene tries to be chill about it. He really does. "I can't stop you," he says, like he didn't try to do exactly that less than twenty minutes ago.

"Okay. Well, I love you. And you're being stupid." Before Gene can even get his mouth open to protest, Luis says, "*Stop*. I have never seen another fucking player like you, and I'm never going to. I swear, it's like your feet never hit the dirt. You fucking float out there."

Resisting the urge to kiss Luis is perhaps the hardest thing he's ever done, but he manages to get out, "And you won't resent me if I get stuck in the minors? You won't think I'm stupid for wanting the whole dream?"

"I think it's stupid you spent so long *not* wanting the big things, Nes. I get it. But you're special. Let yourself be special."

"And what are you gonna do?"

"Finish school," he says. He smiles.

"No plans after that?"

"I think I want to *not* have a plan for the first time in my life."

He'll have a plan by the end of next week, but Gene loves him for it. So Gene kisses him. He has gone too long without kissing him.

"That's very mature of you," Gene says when he finally pulls back.

"Besides, I could always just be your trophy husband."

Gene grins. "We're talking husbands now? You haven't even agreed to be my boyfriend."

"Oh, I agree. Did I not agree earlier? Yes."

Gene is too big for the room, too big for the house, so tall and so full that he could take up the whole city block. "Really?"

When Luis nods, Gene goes to kiss him again, but before he can, Luis lets go of the jersey and pats Gene's side, standing up and pushing past him toward Gene's bathroom. There's the sound of Gene's dryer opening.

"That's it?" Gene calls. "All that and we're not even going to kiss about it?"

Luis's voice from down the hall answers, "So *impatient*, Nes."

"Less impatient, more insulted."

When Luis comes back in, he has a wad of green in his hand. He closes the door behind him, leaving Dodger in the living room.

"I figured it's only fair," he says, holding up the bundle of fabric. "If we're really committing to the bit."

He tugs off his own shirt and shrugs Gene's jersey on. There's the ghost of a grass stain in the armpit, because Gene can never get them out the way Beaverton's laundry team can. It looks perfect on

Luis. Somehow more different than it really should look, considering the sheer number of times Gene has seen him in this exact color, this exact jersey, just with a different name on the back.

"Turn around?" Gene asks.

And there it is. That name he never imagined he'd get to see on a jersey of his own, spelled out across the back of the boyfriend he never thought he'd get to have. As he did in California, with Luis's blue bedroom and still-sleeping profile lit gold by that perfect post-storm sunrise, Gene takes the most detailed mental picture he can manage, but this time, he does so with no urgency at all. Somewhere in the last hour, he has stopped worrying that everything is his last chance.

"Come here," Gene says.

Luis kisses him back slow and purposeful, unhurried but without any ounce of teasing to it. He holds Gene's waist under the open jersey, and Gene holds him exactly the same.

They wind up shucking each other of their jeans, peeling them off and letting their socks bunch up in the ankles, discarded on the ground. Gene nudges him back until his back meets the mattress, and then Gene follows.

Luis's hand fumbles above his head until he finds the nightstand drawer, but when he does, he grins against Gene's lips. After a few more moments of fumbling, he deposits Gene's strap-on next to them on the bed, then the bottle of lube Gene keeps next to it.

"Is that okay?" he asks.

Gene nods, his face hot and his heart hammering. He cannot say yes fast enough, or enthusiastically enough.

"Thank God," Luis says.

Gene scoots him back onto the pillows. When Luis's kiss stutters, Gene moves to his neck, to feel his breath hitch. He is normally so steady when they have sex—it's a special challenge for Gene to get him like this.

Luis pulls Gene in, legs tangled in Gene's and hands everywhere, his kisses unhurried and his chest warm. They stay like that for a good long while, until their lips go half-numb, until Luis reaches out for the strap of Gene's harness.

"In a rush?" Gene teases.

"I don't know what you're talking about," Luis says, placing the strap-on pointedly in Gene's hand.

"Wow. Needy." Gene moves down the bed, until he can kiss the inside of Luis's thigh.

Luis makes a protesting sound. "I have never been called needy."

"Good, because you can't get used to me topping. This is a sometimes occasion." Not that Gene is complaining—God, he isn't complaining.

"That's fine by me," Luis says. He looks unsurprised but amused, eyebrows high. Most of all, he looks beautiful, laid out with Gene's jersey open and pooling around him. He is steady for a moment, until Gene leans down to kiss the front of his briefs, mostly tongue.

"*Fuck.*"

And for as long as Gene can, he draws the rest of the night out. He moves his fingers, and then eventually his hips, slowly, until Luis nearly begs, and then moves slower still.

In the end, Gene kisses him until neither of them can focus enough to really kiss, their mouths just tipped open and bumping against each other. He lifts Luis's leg over his shoulder, and Luis's jersey falls most of the way off Gene's shoulders, held on only by his bent elbows. Luis holds his palm out for Gene to lick, and gasps when Gene does, before he wraps that hand around himself and moves his wrist to the same rhythm as Gene's hips.

After he finishes, he wastes no time at all grabbing at Gene's hips, pulling him closer. He undoes the straps of Gene's harness with shaky hands, laughing at himself until he manages to get it loose enough to toss to the side almost as desperately as he grabbed it in the first place.

Noodle-limbed and a little blissed out, Luis tips his chin back until Gene catches the hint and sits on his face, the same as and a thousand times better than the first time.

They lie there after, slumped and holding each other, Gene letting his hands wander across Luis's chest, looking for anywhere he hasn't touched yet, the spots he touches every time, and the places Luis likes to be touched best.

"You should wear my jersey more often," Luis says, his voice muffled and edging toward sleepy against the top of Gene's head.

"I was going to say the same thing," Gene agrees.

"Maybe it's a good-luck charm or something."

"Or we're just horny."

"Or both."

Gene taps a finger against Luis's sternum. "Can I say one more thing?"

"Shoot."

"I'm kind of in love with you." He said it earlier, yes, but when he says it now, there's no worry to it. It's a fact, known and adored and comforting, that they share.

Luis grins. "Kind of?"

"A little."

"Well, it's kind of a little mutual."

When Gene rolls his eyes—the only appropriate response to this bursting in his chest—Luis holds him tighter. He slides Gene onto his back, then runs his teeth against the skin of Gene's collarbone. Gene shivers, and he knows exactly how satisfied Luis would look if he glanced down. But he lets Luis carry on. He kisses Gene's neck, his scar, the tips of his fingers, the soft spot between his thumb and index finger, where Gene has always been a bit ticklish. Luis kisses these spots and chases each kiss with his tongue and a giddy, ridiculous, stunning smile.

# 23

## SEPTEMBER

**Postseason record:**

**Pacific Coast League Champions**

**Triple-A Championship record: 2–2**

They win two in a row, stretching the series to its fifth and final game. A bank of eight seats is reserved for Gene's dads, Joey, Mattie, Luis's mom and abuela, Dani, and Mia, all surrounding Jack's usual spot. When Gene wakes up that morning, he considers texting the woman who runs the ticket counter again, just to quadruple-check.

Instead, he buries his face in Luis's armpit. He doesn't need to wonder whether Luis has woken up. He probably never fell asleep in the first place.

"Vibe check," Gene says. The words come out 90 percent cracks.

Luis lets out a long, pursed puff of air, and Gene can imagine his eyes wide and staring up at the ceiling.

"That good?" he asks.

"Yep." Luis's voice is deeper in the mornings, based farther down in his chest than it ever is during the day. Gene likes how it rumbles under his hand, his head, his chest.

"Anxious?"

"Out of my mind. Yes."

Gene props his head up to look at Luis. He has impressive bedhead for a person who didn't actually sleep, and he looks offensively pretty about it. "Want a distraction?" Gene asks.

Luis scrunches his nose. "Can I be honest?"

"Please do."

"Yes, but I couldn't get it up for literally anything right now."

Gene laughs. He understands—anxiety does have a way of doing that to a person. But still he gives the spot under Luis's ear a kiss, noting the almost violent beat of his pulse, then kisses Luis's lips.

"That's okay," he says. "Want to take a shower together?"

Luis rolls out of bed so fast—his feet barely hitting the floor before the rest of him—that Gene can hardly adjust for Luis's sudden absence before he drops into the warm outline of where Luis was. Before he can get comfortable, Luis tugs him by the arm toward the edge of the bed.

"You're going to have to carry me if you want me to get up," Gene says. Luis's arms slide under him and lift, Gene's foot nearly knocking over the bedside lamp when Luis turns them in the direction of the bathroom. Luis's heartbeat goes and goes and refuses to slow, but this, at least, has made him smile.

"I'm putting you down before one of us slips and dies in there," Luis says, depositing Gene on the tile floor of the bathroom.

"If one of us died trying to take a shower together, do you think Baker would kill the survivor?"

"She'd wait until after the game. But yes."

Gene's bathtub is not made for two people, but neither Gene nor Luis has an imposing frame, exactly. They make it work just fine, even with the narrow width of the tub. The shower curtain won't stop brushing against them, but it's a trade-off Gene is willing to make.

Today, he gives Luis a kiss under the water, brushing Luis's hair back from his forehead. He tips Luis's head back, into the water, and instructs him to stay there while Gene leans around the curtain to grab the full-sized bottle of Luis's expensive shampoo that has migrated its way to Gene's apartment. He squeezes a dollop into his palm, and when he turns around, Luis squints through the water at him.

"What are you doing?"

"Lean down," Gene instructs.

Luis does as he's told.

Gene lets some of the shampoo fall into his other palm, then slides both hands into Luis's hair, fingers spread. Luis's head falls forward onto Gene's chest immediately, his shoulders losing nearly all of their tension in one rush, like a too-starched shirt getting rewashed. He wraps heavy arms around Gene's waist, lazy and loose, and lets Gene scrub at his scalp until the suds have taken over every bit of his head not currently smothered in Gene's chest.

"Lean back?"

Luis doesn't do so immediately, instead giving Gene's skin a quick peck and taking a deep breath. When he stands upright, his cheeks are red-tinted and his eyes a little wet.

"Sorry," Luis says. His voice comes out thick.

"For what?"

"That was just nice."

Gene tugs on one of Luis's ears. "Don't apologize. Rinse your hair, Dumbo."

He gets Luis's hair with the equally expensive conditioner, holding Luis's face in slick hands to kiss him.

"Okay?" he asks.

Luis nods, and by the time they get around to rinsing, the water has gone cold on their backs, their hands clingier on each other while they rush through the last few minutes of the shower.

When they meet Vince downstairs, in front of the house, he squints at them. "Are you the reason I didn't have any hot water this morning?" he asks Luis, who immediately passes the buck to Gene with a blaming finger.

"Let's not fight, boys. We have a game to win," Gene says. And it's true, they do, so Vince slaps the roof of his car with an open palm and gives a *whoop* more enthusiastic than Gene ever would have expected from him six months ago, considering everything he's gone through this season. There it is, though. Triumphant.

Vince, injured arm still in a sling, tosses Luis his keys. They stop for coffee on the way to the stadium, their hair not yet dried—Luis's black when it's wet, Gene's a deep brown and already starting to frizz in the heat, both of them looking soft and scrubbed and clean, smelling like the same soap. Vince sits in the backseat, singing along to the radio, sunglasses down and mouth full of his second breakfast.

When they arrive, hours early per their usual schedule, it still hasn't quite hit Gene that this might be his last game with this team, and these people. They are his family, as much as the people in the stands are his family. They love him as much as he loves them, and it's not a bad thing to want that, to know he'll miss it when this moment ends.

Gene will bat first, Luis second. They will form a wall at the keystone. The Kyles will patrol the outfield, Ernie will post up behind home plate. Cooper and Ross will fill out the rest of the infield, and their bench will wait at the ready in case someone needs to come out. Baker and Vince will man the dugout, where they have prepared options for every contingency. They've all read the scouting reports and the team-devised game plan a dozen times each: hasty annotations on the sides of well-worn packets of information, the printouts tossed into their locker stalls haphazardly when they're not in use. Gene's has so many margin notes it has devolved halfway into illegibility, but a sneaking part of him insists that the game plan doesn't really matter.

Baseball is a weird game. Strange, illogical things happen all the time. If they didn't, Gene wouldn't have gotten this far. If they didn't, Beaverton would have finished the year with a losing record and low hopes for next year's season, too. The game plan is all well and good, but there's something to be said for just showing up and doing your job as well as you know how.

So Gene will do that. Because in the end, it will be a game like any other. Twenty-seven outs, nine innings, a few hours.

The lead-up to the game passes in what feels like ten minutes, and suddenly they're gearing up for the real show. The energy in the locker room lingers in the realm of side-stitching anxiety, a far cry from post-loss moroseness or post-win exuberance, but still palpable.

When they're getting into their uniforms, Luis comes over to Gene for the eye black Gene has taken to painting on for him.

"Put your jersey on first," Gene says. "That's the order. Eye black last."

"Superstitious," Luis accuses.

"Yeah," Gene admits, "but I'm right."

Luis, rather than putting his jersey on, holds it out.

Gene stares at it.

"What?" he asks.

Luis raises his eyebrows, then smiles when Gene does the same. A silent agreement.

"Maybe they're good-luck charms," Luis says. "Worked pretty well for us last week."

Out of the corner of his eye, Gene can see Ernie's eyebrows inching toward his hairline.

"Can't argue with that," Gene says. Ernie whistles, not bothering to hide his eavesdropping.

Luis holds the jersey out again. Gene grabs his own out of his locker, and they trade.

They don't really have to explain beyond that. They stand there in each other's jerseys, tucking them in before Gene applies eye black to Luis's cheeks and a quick kiss to Luis's lips, and Kyle Rivera gives a distinct cheer of delight at that.

"I knew it," Ernie says. "You are always looking at his ass."

"What can I say?" Gene asks. "I like 'em clenched."

Ernie points at Luis. "No, I was talking to him. He is always looking at your ass."

Luis's face grows a little pink, but he doesn't deny it. No one in that room, to their everlasting credit, gives them a hard time. Some don't acknowledge it, and some look a little too intently at the floor about it, but the ones who matter jump immediately into teasing mode, and they are exactly the kind of family Gene can imagine himself winning a goddamn championship with.

Gene has walked onto the field unsure many times this year. He has started games confident, frustrated, nervous, excited, filled with dread. Today, he walks onto the field in love—with the game, with the team, with their shitty stadium, with Luis, with these people and the season they've made.

The game that follows is the hardest, best one they've played all season.

What starts off a straight pitchers' duel—strikeout after strikeout, groundouts and pop-ups, broken only by the occasional walk and even more occasional single—falls apart in the ninth inning, when Syracuse pushes four runs across in less than fifteen minutes. What had been a tie game going into the inning now sits at 5–1, and Beaverton has only three more outs before their season ends.

A few months ago, it might have sucked the energy out of their dugout. But today, it sends a jolt down the line, and Baker can sense it immediately.

With the heart of Beaverton's order coming up, having gone a combined oh-for-nine on the day so far, she elects not to send in a pinch hitter. Instead, she lets Ernie, Kyle Clark, and Cooper load the bases. When he goes out to wait for his at-bat, Baker looks Kyle Nguyen in the eye and tells him, "You get that ball over the fucking fence, and I will clean *your* fucking car. You hear me?"

"I'm holding you to that," he says.

"Go ahead."

He needs exactly one pitch to tie the game.

The high fly ball, loud and confident off the bat, has just enough mustard on it to carry over the wall, and even from the dugout, Gene can hear Syracuse's closer curse into his glove.

Just like that, it's 5–5 and a whole new ballgame.

"You did this to us," Baker says as Gene gets his batting gloves on.

"How so?"

"You love this extra-inning bullshit," Vince says.

"Gives me acid reflux," Baker says. She fixes her hat, the same five-count adjustment that Gene does. It's possible he picked it up when he used to watch her play.

When Gene walks onto the field, he wills it to feel like any other at-bat. He wills his nerves to calm and his knees to stay steady under him. Luis settles into the on-deck circle behind him. Gene only needs to get on base, then trust Luis to bring him home. They don't need to do anything they haven't done dozens upon dozens of times this year, and as thin as the air in his lungs might feel, there is a certain calmness it brings: knowing that they only need to do what they always do, and it will be enough.

With Luis's name on his jersey and Luis at his back, Gene stands at home plate, and he readies his bat.

# 24

## MARCH

**Five months later**

**@JenWertherPDX:** Gene Ionescu, who helped lead the Beaverton Beavers to the Triple-A championship last season, has made the major league roster out of Spring Training. For the first time in his career, he breaks camp with the Lumberjacks, & looks to be their starting 2B next year. (1/2)

**@JenWertherPDX:** It promises to be an exciting season for Ionescu, who had a rough start in the majors last summer but went on to win the MVP Award with Beaverton. He hit .402 for Portland in Spring Training, with two home runs—quite literally played his way into the lineup. (2/2)

**@JenWertherPDX:** (And, just for fun: here's a picture of recently retired former teammate Luis Estrada in the stands behind home plate. Note the number zero jersey.)

. . .

"How attached are you to these mugs?"

"Why?"

Gene holds one in front of Luis's face. "Because you have eight of them and they are all identical."

"They're nice mugs."

"Exactly. You should have two nice mugs and ten shitty mugs."

"Why?"

"You only use the nice ones for guests who won't find your shitty mugs funny." Gene pulls one out of his kitchen box and holds it up. "Like, see, I wouldn't want to give this chipped one to my tata. But he could use the *Star Trek* mug. And I'd want a nice one to give to your mom when she visits"—he holds up an example—"because I'm trying to impress her."

"My mom likes *Star Trek*."

"See? So we don't need yours."

"I'm not getting rid of them, Nes."

"Then I guess we have twenty mugs."

"It's a good thing we have all this cabinet space, then, isn't it?"

From Gene's perch on the countertop, he surveys their new apartment. Bright, with plenty of room for bookshelves and picture frames. Luis is right about the cabinets, too—abundant, many of them too high for Gene to reach—and the whole place feels this way: spacious, but not cavernous. Comfortable, but nowhere near boring. They stand in the kitchen, barefoot and comfortable and only halfway unpacked. Luis wears a soft T-shirt and tight jeans, hair tucked behind his ears. Since the season ended, he has let it grow just a little shaggy, closer to how he used to wear it.

Luis got started on the unpacking over his spring break, while Gene was playing the final few games of Spring Training. Gene's

Triple-A Championship MVP Award and Luis's second consecutive Gold Glove sit on the mantel, bracketing a printed and framed copy of the Futures Game picture. They kept Gene's bed—not particularly fancy but eminently theirs—and the coffee table. On the wall next to Luis's desk, they've picked a spot where his diploma will hang above Gene's when, in three months, he finally gets to walk across that stage.

When the time came, they opted for a one-bedroom, more expensive than Gene could have afforded or even considered on his own a year ago. They could have looked for a two-bedroom, for plausible deniability, but everyone on Gene's new team already knows about them anyway.

Relatedly, although Gene never checks Twitter anymore, Ernie has made a habit of texting him and Luis the best comments he sees, ever since the championship game. Gene's favorite is a picture of him and Luis after their win, crashed into each other in a hug, the outer letters of each other's names barely visible on their backs. A Beavers fan—a bisexual flag spelled out in hearts in their display name—has scribbled big red circles over their jerseys and captioned it with a particularly enthusiastic keysmash, then three question marks, then the rainbow flag emoji, followed by a longer set of question marks.

Ernie, the only other Beaverton player to make Portland's Opening Day roster, asked their permission before liking that one.

And for the first time since signing his contract, Gene didn't have to spend his offseason working a second job. He has instead taken daily trips to the Lumberjacks training facilities and started learning the names and faces around the stadium the way he got to know Beaverton's. He has gotten rained on in the nature park a half-mile away and almost convinced his Californian boyfriend to stop carrying an umbrella everywhere. More than anything, he has taken the time to live.

Today, that includes: a slow morning with Luis, a shared jog through Northwest Portland, an equally shared shower, a bit of unpacking, and, finally, a baby shower, for which Gene still needs to fill out the card.

"Just write 'Congrats' and that you're happy for them," Luis says. He leans over to look at what Gene has scribbled. "Or that works, too."

*Altzy & Jack—Glad you're staying in Portland so I can be the first one to sniff the baby's head, xoxo Nes (& Nada)*

After the season ended and they got ready to start their house hunt in earnest, Vince received an offer: pitching coach for the University of Oregon, working under the reigning Triple-A Manager of the Year, living in a smaller town and a quieter area nine months out of the year, just like they wanted, with school breaks off to spend with his new family in whatever city they pleased.

So, instead of buying a place in Bend, he and Jack kept the Portland house, less than fifteen minutes away from Gene and Luis's new place, and, as soon as their adoption application went through, started renovating the extra bedroom in pale green and soft lavender.

The chances of any of them winding up back in Beaverton next year are slim. Teams, and places—they're transient. The Beavers won't look how they did when they were Gene's family, but they will be there, different but resolute, ready to play some Oregon baseball. Gene will do the same, with Portland, fifteen miles and thirty minutes down the highway.

Gene slips the card into the envelope. He knit a blanket, too, in a nice array of greens. Never a master of the deadline, Gene stayed up late last night to finish it in time, but he managed to get it washed and blocked before lying down, and Luis wrapped a thick ribbon around it this morning.

"Do you think they'll name the baby after me?" Gene asks.

"I thought they picked a name," Luis says.

"Yeah, but I think that's a decoy."

"A decoy baby name?"

"So they can surprise me."

Luis nudges Gene's legs apart to stand between them and drops a brief kiss on Gene's lips. "I'm sure that's it, Nes."

Gene crosses his fingers while he pops the card into the gift bag.

"Do we have time to unpack another box before we head out?" Luis asks, already turning to survey the boxes still waiting to be opened.

"I'm not getting in another fight about the dishware."

"It wasn't a fight."

"Fine, I'm not getting in another spat," Gene says.

Nevertheless, Luis has started picking his way through the remaining cardboard towers, inspecting box after box and not opening any of them.

"You've walked past three perfectly unpackable boxes," Gene points out. If he lived alone, they would all remain half-packed for six months minimum. He appreciates that Luis kept the ball rolling, but also, *fuck* if it isn't a pain in the ass.

"I'm looking for a specific one," Luis says.

Gene tips his head back against the cabinets. "Great. He's looking for a specific one," he says to Dodger.

Luis lifts the box labeled KITCHENAID, ETC. onto the counter next to Gene.

"You have some important mixing to get done?"

"You're being—"

"—impatient. Yes."

Luis rips the tape off the box and hefts the aforementioned appliance out and into the spot they chose for it. The deep red looks nice against the tiled backsplash, and Gene has to take a moment to awe at the fact that he lives somewhere with a *backsplash*.

"Are you satisfied?" Gene asks when Luis has plugged the thing in and made sure it works.

"Just about."

"If you want to finish the kitchen, we're going to be late."

Luis holds up one finger as he ducks his head to look through the dish towels he used like packing peanuts. They'll need to be washed, but they don't exactly have time to throw a load in if they want to be on time.

"Nada."

"Found it. Close your eyes."

Gene does as he's told, but not without making an exasperated face. Between the two of them, he is usually the one to make them late to social gatherings.

"Okay, open them," Luis instructs after a brief interlude of rustling.

"Nada, if you're trying to propose to me, I'm going to kill you."

Not that he doesn't want Luis to, eventually—just not yet. He hasn't even gotten halfway sick of calling Luis his boyfriend. He wants to enjoy every moment of that before they move on to other words.

"No, I'd give you a heads-up," Luis says.

"Then I'm safe to look?"

"Nes."

When Gene does, Luis is standing there with a stack of shirts in his hand. No—jerseys. The number zero sits in the middle, with Gene's last name curved over the top, each patch embroidered in deep green on a background of pale mint over a mountain range intended to fall right above a waistband. Someone, probably Luis, folded the jerseys lovingly, so the back shows in full prideful glory, and when Gene lifts one, the fabric unfurls. The same sweat-wicking stuff he wears every day, but fresh and slightly chemical-scented, as if it just came out of a box in a warehouse, rather than having hung in the closet or a locker stall and gotten laundered after each game.

It's bigger than the one Gene usually wears—an extra-large to his small, the sleeves long enough to reach past Gene's elbows. It wouldn't fit him, and it wouldn't fit Luis.

"Okay, I'm definitely missing something," Gene says.

"Guess where I got those," Luis says.

"Where?"

"Guess."

Gene leans in and, his lips against Luis's, says, "Just tell me."

"The team store," he says.

"No you didn't." Gene backs up to stare at him, wide-eyed.

"I did."

Gene holds them to his face and inhales the smell, and he recognizes it now. The smell of a store-ironed shirt, hung up and crammed together with other fabric, never allowed to breathe until someone buys it and wears it and uses their favorite laundry detergent on it.

"When did they start selling these?" Gene asks. "No one told me."

"Me neither. I walked by when I came to pick you up the other day, and they were just . . . there."

"Hanging up?"

"Right in the window," Luis confirms. He leans his elbows on Gene's knees, face expectant.

"Why?"

"Because people are going to want them."

Gene tries not to cry at that. He really does. And still his voice shakes when he asks, "And these are for—?"

"Your dads, Joey, and Mattie." He tips his head down to where Dodger has leaned his chin on Gene's leg and adds, "I asked if they'd make one for a dog, but no luck yet."

Gene sets them aside and holds Luis by the face. "You are an idiot for paying for these. Thank you."

"Don't thank me. I got one for myself, too. Before they sold out."

Gene rolls his eyes and kisses him, a solid, purposeful thing. "How much did this trip run you?"

"Oh"—he wrinkles his nose—"I'd rather not say."

"I love you."

"Even though I'm an idiot?"

"Yeah. You're *my* idiot."

Luis holds him by the waist, his hands familiar and warm over the thin fabric of Gene's shirt. "I love you, too." He gives Gene a kiss, his teeth light against Gene's lip, and then, their noses still touching, he says, "You can pay me back in installments."

Gene pulls him in closer and gives his lip a bite in return. "That could be arranged."

They kiss, slow and deliberate, in their kitchen until the alarm on Gene's phone alerts him that it really, actually is time for them to go, and then they kiss for a few minutes longer. When the backup alarm goes off and Luis starts to pull away, Gene wraps his legs around Luis's waist and holds him a little tighter.

"Ten more minutes," Gene insists.

He tugs Luis back in with his heels against the small of Luis's back, and if Luis slides a hand between Gene's legs for those ten extra minutes, no one has to know. If Luis has a hickey under the collar of his T-shirt, no one but Gene will see it anyway.

When they finally do peel themselves apart, Gene sends a quick text to Baker, *Sorry sorry, running late*, and receives a quick response.

*No worries. See you soon.*

"She said no worries," Gene says.

"Yes."

"So what I'm hearing is, we can keep kissing."

Luis grabs Gene's shoes, setting them into Gene's waiting, upturned palms.

"Later," Luis says.

And, really, they have all week to kiss. The season starts tomorrow, and Luis will go back to California in a week to finish his final term at Stanford. But until then, they have a full seven days of home games left to fool around in their kitchen, their living room, their bedroom. They have all summer, and the offseason after that. A whole life ahead of them, if they want it.

Watching Luis slip his boots on, a curl falling onto his forehead and the early-afternoon sun bright through the windows, Gene knows—he will always want this lanky, anxious, beautiful dumbass. It will never get old, kissing him in this kitchen or the next. Waking up next to him, talking to him each day before anyone else.

So Gene lets himself want Luis, and this unlikely little life they have. No caveats, no asterisks, no gimmicks—he wants, and he wants, and he lets himself have it.

## Acknowledgments

Gene's story isn't likely, but it has never felt impossible to me—I hope stories of real-life queer and trans people in sports become mundane someday. An immense thank-you to everyone whose lives, love, and work bring us closer to that day. Thank you especially to Glenn Burke, widely considered the first openly gay man to play major league baseball, and to Lou Sullivan, widely considered the first openly gay transgender man. My life, and Gene's, would be far less possible without everything these men accomplished and fought for. "Grateful" does not begin to suffice.

To my editor, Katy Nishimoto, whose enthusiasm, generosity, and intelligence are unmatched. Thank you for always encouraging me to say what I truly mean, for allowing your authors space to be vulnerable, and for appreciating all the baseball details we had to cut. I don't think I realized, before I met you, what it would feel like to have someone truly get what I was trying to say—to see straight to the heart of the thing, and to treat it with such care. You are exceptional, it's true, but it's your sincerity and your kindness that amaze me most. I'm selfishly very glad you decided to edit books instead of becoming Pedro Martínez.

To my agent, Allison Hunter, for going to the mat for me, Gene, and Luis in ways I never could have dreamed of. Thank you for encouraging me to want big things for these boys and for myself, for seeing that, like Gene, I needed to hear that I was allowed and there was space enough for the stories I wanted to tell. Thank you to Nat Edwards for legitimately showing up in your softball jersey, and for bringing that level of dedication to everything you do. Thank you to Allison Malecha and Khalid McCalla for advocating for this book in places I never imagined it'd go. Thank you to Mads Cavaciuti and Cal Kenny for bringing Gene and Luis to the UK.

To the entire team at Dial, the publishing home of my dreams: Whitney Frick, Rose Fox, Andy Ward, Avideh Bashirrad, Debbie Aroff, Raaga Rajagopala, Jordan Forney, Tiffani Ren, Rachel Parker, Maria Braeckel, Donna Cheng, Jo Anne Metsch, Rebecca Berlant, Leah Sims, Jennifer Rodriguez, Meghan O'Leary, and everyone else who made it possible for this book to exist. You have all made me immensely proud and endlessly thankful to be a Dial author. Thank you to Alex Mendoza for bringing Gene and Luis to full and joyous life on the cover, and to Cassie Gonzales for your stunning design work and art direction.

To Jesse Leon for your time, your invaluable insight, and your care.

I cannot begin to express the degree to which Ruby Barrett and Rosie Danan altered the course of my life. Thank you for being the first people to ever make it to the last sentence of this story, for teaching me how to write romance, and for embodying all the very best things about this genre. I am of course grateful to Pitch Wars for bringing us together, but worlds more grateful for you two. I owe you a Kyles novella.

Pitch Wars also introduced me to a group of writers without whom this would have been far scarier. Thank you to Anita Kelly for writing books that made trans romance feel possible in a moment when I really needed it; thank you even more for being a friend, and for being there to discuss all things trans joy and cis nonsense. Thank you to Alicia Thompson for your friendship and award-worthy emails, for loving your team as much as I love mine, and for agreeing to still like me if we ever have to watch our teams face off in the ALCS. Thank you to the Pitch Wars Class of 2021.

To the Stanford Creative Writing and English departments and the Honors in the Arts program. Particular thanks to the following professors: Paula Moya for your immense expertise and always-wise critique; KJ Cerankowski and Nina Schloesser Tárano for leading me in independent studies that shaped everything I've written since; and Scott Hutchins, whose advice (of both the writing and life varieties), patience, and steadying presence kept me going while I tried to cobble together my first major novel project in the midst of a yearlong anxiety spiral. Thank you to the Undergraduate Research program, for the grant which allowed me to prioritize writing for the first time in my life.

To Alex Felix. You remain the best freshman-year roommate I could have possibly been assigned when we were eighteen and awkward and clueless. I can't imagine how different my life would have looked had someone else been waiting on the other side of that door in Roble, and I don't care to.

To the health care providers who have helped me with my own transition, which made it possible for me to write this book with the joy Gene deserved.

To Kate Preusser, and the team and community at Lookout Landing, for exemplifying the best of baseball, and showing how interesting, absurd, welcoming, and worthwhile this sport can be. To Kathy Diekroeger for compiling stories of life in the minor leagues. To KD Casey for recommending Kathy's work and being kind enough to ignore any baseball-related errors I made in this book.

To the Mariners, and to baseball in the Pacific Northwest. To Ichiro! To Julio(ooooo)! To the abundance of Kyles! And to Mitch Haniger, for deciding this team was going to make the damn playoffs. To Brent Masenhimer, for being both an exemplary educator and the first Mariners fan I ever knew. To anyone who knows what it is to completely love a team.

To the minor league players' union that was formed while I edited this book. To the players and advocates who worked for years to make that union a reality. The good insurance, reliable income, and stable hours made possible by my own union's contract allowed me the time and space I needed to write this book—to labor movements and workers' rights everywhere.

Thank you to my family, particularly: my sister, Alexa, for being my first teacher; my mom for organizing a writing journal at my elementary school so I could see my first-grade poetry printed in Comic Sans; and my dad for taking me to Powell's every time I come home, and for learning to love soccer so you could coach your kids' teams. I'm sorry I wrote about baseball instead.

And to Sarah. If I tried to list all the reasons, this book would never end—which is appropriate, seeing as there's essentially no chance it or I would currently exist at all without you. You're my soulmate, and I am so glad we broke up. I love you, bitch.

# The Prospects

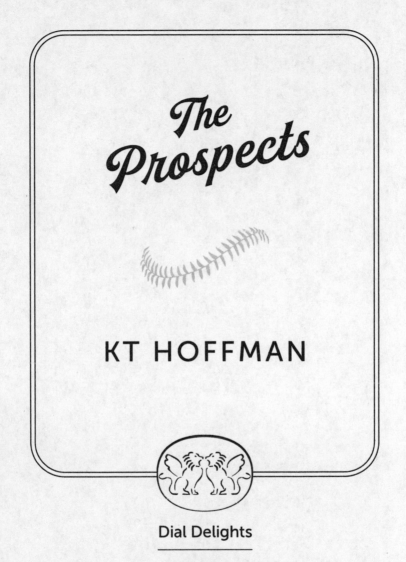

KT HOFFMAN

Dial Delights

*Love Stories*
*for the*
*Open-Hearted*

## A Note from the Author

I grew up playing soccer. Indoor or outdoor barely mattered, as long as I could play goalie. I loved the immediacy of it, I loved diving to make a save, the mud caking my uniform in the Oregon rain. Most of all, I loved being useful, important, *needed.*

Baseball, on the other hand, didn't work its way into my life until the summer of 2018. I had just graduated college with a five-hundred-page mess of an honors thesis in the form of a historical fiction novel, as well as the burgeoning realization that I was, possibly, a bit transgender.

Of the two options, I chose to focus on the novel. It was at least the kind of mess that felt fixable.

That novel was not *The Prospects*. But it, too, was about home, and community, and the aching want and quiet hurt that build up when you try to make yourself small. It, too, was about a baseball-playing gay man, though the baseball was more incidental.

In my research, I'd spent hours reading up on the invention of sugar packets. Weeks doing deep dives on mid-century queer bars. But even after three full rewrites, I knew nothing about the sport my protagonist loved. So I decided to follow the Seattle Mariners—the closest thing I had to a hometown team—for a few months. For a handful of hours each day, in the most aimless and confusing summer of my life, that team kept me company.

I learned quickly that baseball is a sport that demands optimism in the face of steep odds—a demand with which I, a queer trans person, was exceedingly familiar. As I fell in love with baseball and the hope it inspires, I realized I wanted to write a book where that optimism paid off. A story that felt triumphant and giddy and freeing, the same way a hard-fought, walk-off win in the middle of a playoff chase does.

Then Gene crashed into my life. Loud and laughing. Improbable and inconvenient. He played second base. He was gay. He loved his boyfriend, he loved his team—he *loved*. And he was unquestionably, delightedly trans.

He was always meant to be the protagonist of a hard-fought, walk-off win sort of a book. In 2018, I wasn't ready to write that book yet. I was still mostly closeted, and Gene's transness and gayness scared me. I loved him, but he made sense to me in a way I wasn't ready to face. Early drafts came out stilted, a little sad. But for all the changes that book would go through on its way to becoming *The Prospects*, Gene himself remained largely the same: an optimistic man, desperate to be needed and scared to be wanted, with a big heart and a quiet determination to prove himself.

There was also the fact that I'd never read a romance novel about people like Gene or Luis. But as genre expectations slowly shifted and I grew into my transness, this book became one. Neither Gene nor Luis looked anything like romantic heroes I'd seen on shelves, but they were the sorts of men I *wanted* to see there, just as Luis is the sort of man Gene wants to see on a baseball card. Loving, soft, kind. A little blunt, frequently oblivious. Willing to apologize, willing to cry. Short and wide-hipped. Skinny and life-alteringly anxious. Gay. Trans. *Beautiful*.

*The Prospects* is unequivocally a romance. But it's also a sports story, and, to me, sports—especially baseball, *especially* the minor leagues—are entirely about the story. They're about the dreams we have and abandon and find our way back to; they're about who we are when we walk off the field and have to keep living. And they are, of course, about who wins, who loses, and who gets left behind.

*The Prospects* is about the people who often get left behind—how we find each other and work to build something incredible in spite of the circumstances. It's about letting ourselves want those unimaginable dreams that we may never have seen someone like us achieve—the dreams we've been told we aren't allowed to have at all.

I hope, when you read this book, you feel allowed. I hope you stop feeling like you need permission at all.

*With love & hope & baseball,*
*KT*

## Discussion Questions

1. "Gene has no expectations of breaking into the majors. The career that he *has*—even if it pays like shit, runs him ragged, isn't the career of anyone's dreams—is still a fucking miracle for a guy like Gene" (p. 10). What does it look like for Gene to reconcile the life he wants with the life he has at the beginning of the book? If you've ever been in a similar place, feel free to share and talk about how those experiences deepened your read on Gene's journey.
2. "Ernie pulls [Gene] into a hug, the kind perfected by men in locker rooms" (p. 19). Talk about the intimacy of men in locker rooms. How is this intimacy unique?
3. At the end of Chapter Two, after Gene shows Luis around the Beaverton stadium, Luis continues to be unkind, while Gene is unrelentingly nice. Why is Luis being dismissive? And why does Gene continue to be outwardly kind in response?
4. As a professional baseball player, Gene finds himself around mostly straight and always-cis men. He has one firm rule with no exception: "He does not find his teammates attractive" (p. 33). This way, he never has to feel self-conscious about seeing his teammates naked, or with being naked himself around them. Eliminating the possibility of being perceived sexually feels easier for Gene. Why do you think that is for him?
5. Whether you are queer/trans or not, you can imagine having to

weigh the pros and cons of coming out. How do you think Gene, Vince, and Baker—and later Luis—came to this place with regard to coming out to the team? In what ways do their experiences differ? Consider what coming out changed and what it didn't.

6. Throughout the book, Gene describes the qualities that make a good baseball player, and whether he has them or not. What are these qualities? What makes for a bad baseball player?
7. Nancy and Dan are local celebrities, as Gene establishes early on. How does their commentary add to the reading experience of this book, and to the depth of Gene's universe?
8. Gene is very sensitive to other people experiencing discomfort or showing signs of pain: consider his reactions to Vince's increased drinking, Baker's annoyance about getting photographed, and Luis's panic attacks. Why do you think that is? How might Gene's own experiences be a factor here?
9. At the end of Chapter Four, Gene explains why he can't trust Luis: he's been closed off, he's ambivalent to the team's success, and he abandoned Gene once before when they were in college. Which of these reasons carries the most weight?
10. In Chapter Five, Gene realizes he's had a bad attitude toward Luis and is ashamed for having let this version of himself out. Why do you think he feels that way?
11. Gene can understand how lonely it can be to look different than the person you'd expect to find on a baseball card (p. 64). How does this speak to the increased scrutiny that marginalized people face, and the unrealistic standards of perfection that they are held to? How do you think this has an impact on Gene's and Luis's lives and careers? What about you and/or the people you love?
12. How do you think Gene's and Luis's respective relationships to baseball are affected by having fathers who were professional players?

13. Gene talks about the part of himself that knew he was trans before he consciously acknowledged it to himself. How it ached every time he tried to shove it down. He also explains how the same part of him resurfaces in the presence of his attraction toward Luis, now that they're on the same team again. Why do you think that is?
14. In Chapter Eight, we see that Gene's former coach is complicit in the transphobia Gene experiences from the scout. How can the trauma from something like this affect someone in Gene's position, in this moment and later? How could Gene's coach have been a better ally in that moment?
15. Luis experiences intense anxiety, and Gene finds pride and comfort in giving Luis moments where he can feel secure. What does Gene do right? Has this book made you think differently about supporting someone with severe anxiety? How so?
16. "It's hard, sometimes, to find the people you don't have to rehearse for" (p. 115). When Gene mentions he's gay to Luis for the first time and says that the information is available online, Luis responds, "I wanted you to tell me if you wanted me to know" (p. 94). Then when Luis reveals to Gene that Dodger is his emotional support dog, they both discuss the pressure as public athletes to be the versions of themselves who have "all the rules memorized, all the right moves rehearsed" (p. 115). How are Gene and Luis different when they step onto the diamond, as opposed to in their personal lives off the field?
17. "'Baseball or softball?' [Gene] is possibly the only person who can get away with asking Baker this question" (p. 122). Why? Think about how the layers of womanhood, transness, and queerness add nuance to the intent and impact of this otherwise misogynistic question. How do Baker's experiences as a lesbian and Gene's experiences as a gay trans man overlap and differ as they both try to carve out a space for themselves in a sport dominated by cis straight men?

18. The first night Luis sleeps over, Gene lets him stay on the couch while Gene sleeps in his own bed, not making a move. He "wishes he were a little braver" (p. 137). Do you think Gene's decision showed a lack of bravery? Why or why not?
19. Although Vince, Gene, and Luis are all gay men, they have very different views of and experiences with masculinity and manhood. For example, Vince struggles to ask for help carrying his bag or driving to dinner, while Gene sees vulnerability as a strength. In what other ways do Gene's feelings differ from Vince's? What about Luis's? Why might this be?
20. In Chapter Ten, Vince implies Gene can't understand how it feels to face assumed physical limitations because, as Vince says, "you're twenty-six, and you have your whole career ahead of you"(p. 251); in Chapter Nineteen, Baker tells Gene that he'll wind up sitting with the "WAGS" if he isn't careful (p. 279). How do these moments show the ways in which cis people in the LGBTQ+ community can engage in transphobia and harm, even if they are "well-meaning"? Do you think Vince and/or Baker understood the impact of their words?
21. Why is Gene specifically tested for his testosterone levels, and so much more frequently than his cis peers are tested for performance-enhancing drugs? In what ways does this show how our society is uniquely invasive toward trans people?
22. When does Gene officially let himself go from hoping to wanting?
23. In Chapter Fourteen, Gene mentions the challenge of navigating air travel and having an ID with his deadname. What kinds of relationships do trans people have with their deadnames? Use information readily available to you to research this and discuss.
24. Gene tells Baker he is happy to be an openly trans baseball player, but that he also never quite asked to be the first. What are the good and bad parts of being the first openly trans base-

ball player? Or the first person of any underrepresented group to do something monumental?

25. When Gene visits Luis's family, he reflects on "the act of a parent changing the shape of their home so it can fit you" (p. 212). How do you think one can be a good parent to a queer/trans child and change the shape of one's home to fit them?
26. The book mentions how a lot of queer and trans people don't experience the traditional milestones of love when they're young, such as this one between Gene and Luis during a phone conversation: "But neither of them hangs up first, and for the first time in his life, Gene feels that feeling" (p. 271). Why do you think that is?
27. How does Gene's ADHD manifest in ways that may challenge him, but also benefit him? What are some symptoms of ADHD? Do you or someone you love have ADHD? How does Luis find ways to support Gene as he navigates being a professional athlete and person with ADHD?
28. Vince pushes himself beyond a limit that is deemed healthy for him to continue playing baseball. How does ageism feature in the ways other characters talk about Vince, his career, and his retirement, or the pressure Vince puts on himself?

## Beaverton Beavers Starting Lineup
## & their walk-up songs

| 1 | **IONESCU, Gene** | **Second Base** | **#0** |
|---|---|---|---|
| | *"Rebel Rebel," David Bowie / "We Run This," Missy Elliott* | | |

| 2 | **ESTRADA, Luis** | **Shortstop** | **#19** |
|---|---|---|---|
| | *"Drumming Song," Florence + the Machine / "La Bamba," Selena* | | |

| 3 | **ROSS, Trevor** | **Third Base** | **#27** |
|---|---|---|---|
| | *"Calamity Song," The Decemberists* | | |

| 4 | **GONZALES, Ernie** | **Catcher** | **#3** |
|---|---|---|---|
| | *"Dancing Queen," ABBA* | | |

| 5 | **CLARK, Kyle** | **Left Field** | **#11** |
|---|---|---|---|
| | *"Tightrope (feat. Big Boi)," Janelle Monáe* | | |

| 6 | **COOPER, Charlie** | **First Base** | **#5** |
|---|---|---|---|
| | *"Fins," Jimmy Buffett* | | |

| 7 | **NGUYEN, Kyle** | **Right Field** | **#24** |
|---|---|---|---|
| | *"Seven Nation Army," The White Stripes* | | |

| 8 | **RIVERA, Kyle** | **Center Field** | **#38** |
|---|---|---|---|
| | *"Después de la Playa," Bad Bunny* | | |

| 9 | **ALTMAN, Vince** | **Starting Pitcher** | **#34** |
|---|---|---|---|
| | *"Barracuda," Heart* | | |

## Luis's Running Playlist

I have a lot more free time now that I'm not playing, so I'm training to run a 10k. I like how easy it is to see myself improving. And it makes things feel quieter for a while. Plus, Dodger loves it. Anyways, some combination of these songs usually gets me through a daily run. The best runs are when Nes tags along and we just talk, though. —LUIS

Listen, if I'd seen this playlist or that note I would have known that Nada's gay a lot sooner. —GENE

**Warm-up:**

—"Something To Say," Michaela Jaé
—"Boy Problems," Carly Rae Jepsen
—"Why'd You Come in Here Lookin' Like That," Dolly Parton
—"Jumpin', Jumpin'," Destiny's Child

**Minutes 2–10, when you feel like you might actually drop dead:**

—"Body," Megan Thee Stallion
—"I Can See You (Taylor's Version) (From The Vault)," Taylor Swift
—"Tití Me Preguntó," Bad Bunny
—"Toxic," Britney Spears

**The anxiety's catching up to you & you need some nostalgia:**

—"Lip Gloss," Lil Mama

—"Space Cowboy (Yippie-Yi-Yay) (feat. Lisa "Left Eye" Lopes)," *NSYNC

—"If You Want It To Be Good Girl (Get Yourself a Bad Boy)," Backstreet Boys

—"El Chico Del Apartamento 512," Selena

**You're starting to think that if you got this far, you might as well keep going:**

—"This Year," The Mountain Goats

—"THAT'S WHAT I WANT," Lil Nas X

—"I Wanna Dance with Somebody (Who Loves Me)," Whitney Houston

—"Screwed (feat. Zoë Kravitz)," Janelle Monáe

**The runner's high is a lie but at least you can't think a coherent thought anymore:**

—"WAP (feat. Megan Thee Stallion)," Cardi B

—"Dinner & Diatribes," Hozier

—"Digital Witness," St. Vincent

—"Fat Bottomed Girls," Queen

**The "I'm almost done" high is real, though:**

—"The Bitch Is Back," Elton John

—"2 Be Loved (Am I Ready)," Lizzo

—"Sweet Transvestite," Tim Curry

—"Run the World (Girls)," Beyoncé

**Cool-down:**

—"Free," Florence + the Machine

—"Malibu," Trixie Mattel

—"Lafayette," Orville Peck

—"Rainbow Connection—from *The Muppet Movie*," Kermit

## Gene's Bagel Recipe

*Yield: Makes 6 or 8, depending on how giant you want your bagels to be*

People feel strongly about their bagel recipes. I mostly feel strongly that even people who live in Oregon deserve good bagels. Some tweaks to a traditional recipe: first, some purists say a bagel can't be a bagel without barley malt syrup, but it can be hard to find in stores. I listed some alternatives—I think any of these makes a great bagel! Second, I don't have a lot of time or especially good planning skills, so I don't let my dough rise in the fridge overnight. The only rule you absolutely cannot break, in my humble opinion, when making bagels: you have to (have to!!!) boil them before baking.

These are best if you eat them the day you make them, but they can be frozen or stored for a few days in a sealed container. You'll just probably want to toast them after day one. — GENE

These are extremely fucking good. — LUIS

*Ingredients*

—7g / 2 ¼ teaspoons / 1 packet active dry yeast
—4 teaspoons (plus 2 tablespoons extra for boiling) of one of the

following yeast foods[*] (in order of my preference): barley malt syrup, molasses, or brown sugar
—1 ¼ cups warm water[†]
—480g / 4 cups[‡] bread flour
—10g / 1 ¾ teaspoons kosher salt

OPTIONAL TOPPINGS:
—Everything seasoning
—Sea salt (Nada buys the fancy flaky kind & I like to steal it for bagels)
—Poppy seeds
—Cinnamon sugar
—Cheese
—Etcetera—the world is your bagel shop, baby!

*Instructions*

1. Combine the water, yeast, and four teaspoons of your yeast food of choice. Whisk with a fork and let rest for 5–10 minutes. A weird-looking sort of foam will form along the top when the yeast activates.
2. Measure out your flour and salt in the bowl of a stand mixer or a large mixing bowl. I highly recommend a stand mixer if you have it, but if you are really buff, and/or want to be really buff, and/or just don't have a stand mixer, it can be done by hand.
3. Attach the bread hook to your mixer and start mixing on the

* Yeast eats sugar, so any of these options work. I don't really get the science beyond that because I am a baseball player. (Nada is telling me baseball players should try reading a book every once in a while.)
† About 95–105° Fahrenheit. It should feel like when you're running a hot bath or a shower—you should be able to keep a hand in the water for at least a couple seconds. If you can't, it's probably too hot.
‡ A kitchen scale is the easiest way to measure this, but no worries if you don't have access to one! Just be sure you spoon and level the flour, rather than packing it into the cup.

lowest speed as you drizzle in the wet ingredients. If you're going the mixer-less route, mix with a wooden spoon. It will look like there isn't enough water, but there is—it shouldn't be an especially wet dough. If you *gotta* add extra water, do it a teaspoon at a time.

4. Let your mixer keep kneading for 7–8 minutes on low speed (or knead by hand on the counter). The dough should be stiff and easily pull away from the sides of the bowl. It's ready when it feels elastic and smooth.
5. Form the dough into a ball. Lightly grease the bowl with cooking spray or another neutral oil, place the dough back into the bowl, cover with a lid or damp towel, and let rise on the counter for 1–2 hours, or until more or less doubled.[*]
6. When the dough has risen, gently punch it down and let it rest for 10 more minutes.
7. During those 10 minutes, line a baking sheet with parchment paper. Preheat your oven to 425° Fahrenheit and set a large pot with approximately 2–3 quarts[†] of water and two tablespoons barley malt/molasses/brown sugar to boil on the stove.
8. Divide dough into six or eight[‡] roughly equal portions. I personally like to weigh my dough out, but no worries if you need/prefer to eyeball it.
9. Shape your bagels. I personally roll each piece of the dough into a ball, then stretch a hole in the center. I'd recommend watching a video if this is your first time making bagels! Set your shaped bagels two-ish inches apart on the baking sheet and cover with a towel.

* This will generally take closer to one hour in warm weather, and closer to two hours in cold weather.

† I have never measured this in my life. I just fill a big spaghetti-cooking pot like . . . one-third to one-half full.

‡ If you want them to be the size you'd get in a bagel shop, do six. If you want to see your perpetually hungry boyfriend eat a whole bagel in thirty seconds flat, do eight.

10. When the water is boiling, carefully transfer 2–3 bagels at a time into the water bath. Don't crowd them. Boil for ninety seconds, then flip with a slotted spoon or spatula and boil for ninety more seconds. Remove from the water and place on the baking sheet.
11. If you're adding toppings, do so immediately after boiling—this helps them stick better. I personally don't like egg washes on bagels but do whatever floats your boat.
12. Repeat with remaining bagels.
13. Bake for 20–25 minutes, or until golden. They should sound hollow when tapped.
14. When they're cool enough to handle, you can slice them open and add whatever you'd like. I'm partial to grilled Halloumi and tomatoes, egg and cheese, or a classic schmear. Follow your heart.
15. Share with a friend/teammate/colleague you sleep in the same room as sometimes/boyfriend/whoever.

KT HOFFMAN is originally from Beaverton, Oregon, and currently lives in Brooklyn. He received his bachelor's degree in English and Creative Writing from Stanford University. If he isn't writing about trans hope and gay kissing, he's probably white-knuckling his way through the ninth inning of a Seattle Mariners game. *The Prospects* is his debut novel.

kthoffmanwrites.com
Instagram: @squashgoblin

## About the Type

This book was set in Electra, a typeface designed for Linotype by W. A. Dwiggins, the renowned type designer (1880–1956). Electra is a fluid typeface, avoiding the contrasts of thick and thin strokes that are prevalent in most modern typefaces.